PRAISE FOR SECRET OF THE SANDS

2009 READERS FAVORITE SILVER MEDALIST FOR FICTION-MYSTERY

"This is my kind of book. Please, please make a continuing series and a movie! The authors are extremely talented. I cannot praise this book enough. Fast paced, page turner, character development, fascinating plot…what more could I ask for."

– ReadersFavorite.com

"Their detailed storytelling paints a picture of ancient Egypt in all its glory. The reader feels they are a part of the book, living amongst the Kierani people. The end of the novel leaves the reader curious and wanting more. This reader can hardly wait for the sequel, Destiny of the Sands."

– Authors on the Rise Book Reviews

"This is a WOW of a book!!…For those of us who are lovers of the ancient worlds, Egypt, present and past, archaeology, the metaphysical, and mystical happenings, this is a great choice for you."

– Ellen in Atlanta, Amazon Vine Voice, Top 1000 Reviewer

"This is a beautifully written book and I enjoyed reading it very much, and I would readily recommend it to anyone looking for a good story to read."

– Jym Cherry, reviewer, Sonar4 Science Fiction & Horror eZine

"This novel is innovative, concise and enthralling. Fluctuating between present day and ancient Egypt, the pace never decelerates. The reader is treated to plausible theories regarding many riddles of this mysterious civilization. This time-honored culture is so clearly portrayed with characters which are so skillfully brought to life that one can easily imagine they are actually present as events are unfolding. The story comes to a clear conclusion yet leaves the reader desperately hoping there will be a sequel…. or a trilogy…. or even better yet, a whole series of these phenomenal books!"

– www.allthesebooks.com

"The authors have successfully woven a story based on archeological events mixed with their own ideas of what happened to the Sphinx and the mysteries surrounding it."

– www.sabrinareviews.com

"Rai Aren & Tavius E. write a spellbinding mix of mystery, history, fantasy, and adventure in this tale of two histories - one told in the present, the other told from the past - telling a story of misused power, learning how to trust, and the fate of civilization."

– www.TeensReadToo.com

"A deep probing mystery riddled with prophecy and danger, Secret of the Sands uses Egypt and her mythology as a backdrop to delve into the meanings of life and religion."

– McNally Robinson

"Rai Aren and Tavius E. have crafted a fast-paced, exciting novel overflowing with mystery and intrigue. The tension is constant. The characters fully developed. And the plot gripping. Ancient history and present day relevance are so expertly intertwined, that you might forget you are reading a work of fiction."

– Thomas Phillips, author of The Molech Prophecy

"Secret of the Sands has BLOCKBUSTER written all over it! ...Fans of what might be called the "Indiana Jones" genre of fiction will be thrilled with Secret of the Sands. Like a race horse on steroids it blasts out of the gate in the opening prologue and doesn't stop running until it reaches the finish line. This remarkably well conceived and well executed first-time novel by Rai Aren and her co-author, Tavius E. is loaded with adventure, prophecy, mystery, secrets, deception, epic-scale battles, romance, good guys, bad guys, liars, cheaters, scoundrels, and, of course, heroes...Secret of the Sands is a thrill-ride..."

– Gary Val Tenuta, author of The Ezekiel Code

"The description that initially comes to mind is Indiana Jones, with a bit of Stargate, Mummy, and 5th Element, yet remaining completely unique. Secret of the Sands is an excitingly vivid, page-turning adventure infused with history, humor, and excitement. Rai Aren and Tavius E. have created a spectacular story with characters that I just love or simply love to hate. Like National Treasure, there is just enough historical and scientific fact mixed in to make the fictional story plausible and fun. And what a wonderful way to spotlight archaeological theories that have lost the public eye. I kept wanting to read and, by half-way through, I didn't want to put it down. Secret of the Sands was a thrill ride until the very end and I loved every minute of it!"

– Marauder, Deputy Headmistress of the
Official Potterholics Annonymous

"Secrets, deceit and lies can make almost any novel exciting. But, add to that, two stories simultaneously told then throw in some romance, science fiction and a power struggle and what do you get? A true page turner that takes you on one heck of a journey."

– Michael Balkind, author of Sudden Death & Dead Ball

"I'd recommend this to anyone who is enchanted by ancient civilizations and the mysteries of how things might have come to be, such as why and how the Sphinx was constructed."

– Ruth Ann Nordin, Historical Romance Author

"The pacing is flawless, the characters well-defined, the history thoroughly researched. The authors have done their homework, and I can't wait for the sequel. I would enthusiastically recommend this novel to anyone who wants a real page-turner!"

– Norma Beishir, author of Chasing the Wind & the bestselling
novels Angels at Midnight & A Time for Legends

"This book bounces back and forth in a fascinating balance between modern day archeologists and a theoretical civilization from 12,000 years ago…The story is told in a deft, yet casual style that makes it accessible and fun for any reader."

– Donald Gorman, author of Paradox & The Red Veil

"The authors take us on a wild rollercoaster ride full of secrets, romance, lust, seduction, loyalty, royalty and deception that takes place 12,000 years ago where all is not as it seems. Two modern day Indiana Jones type archaeologists discover the secret of the sands and unravel the mysteries and dangers the secret holds."

– Mike Monahan, author of Barracuda

"Secret of the Sands is far from your typical archaeologist-finally-finds-ancient-archetype scenario. It is much, much more. Definitely a book that one can say 'satisfies your thirst, yet leaves you quenching for more...'"

– J.R. Reardon, author of Confidential
Communications & Dishonored

"While I've certainly enjoyed my share of novels, few of them have left me wanting to rush out and by the sequel as much as this one does."

– Debra Purdy Kong, author of Fatal Encryption &
Taxed to Death

"It is my belief that Rai Aren & Tavius E. fit as Master Storytellers and Great Authors."

– Lance Oren, author of Chances R & Huracán

"Have you ever wondered how old the Sphinx really is? Have you been intrigued by the mysteries swirling like the desert sands around this awesome ancient monument? Rai Aren and Tavius E. have written a mesmerizing story in which two young archaeologists discover an artifact that could provide all of the answers. But they are not the only ones who are interested in this relic, for it holds a power unlike anything seen on Earth before... This novel is packed with adventure and suspense, and the style is fast-paced and filled with vivid description."

– Susan Jane McLeod, author of Soul and Shadow &
Fire and Shadow

"A wonderful, exciting story!"

– Lila Pinord, author of Min's Monster, Skye Dancer
& Evil Lives in Blue Rock

"The mark of a truly good story is one that transcends the ages. Although the writers may base some of their novel in the past, a good yarn echoes into the present and future, as well. Secret of the Sands cherishes love, family and honor, condemns evil and treachery and presents us with a tantalizing theory of what lies beneath the great sphinx."

– Ann B. Keller, author of The Devil's Crescent & Crenellations

"Secret of the Sands is a very entertaining and exciting tale of ancient Egypt and modern archeology. The authors succeed in painting the ancient world and its characters in realistic and memorable fashion. Secret of the Sands is a story of adventure, wonder, betrayal, forgiveness, suspense, and action – all the elements that so often can be weaved together into a blockbuster movie. I hope this tale gets the opportunity to reach the big screen – I'll be amongst the first in line to see it! Fans of adventure tales like Indiana Jones will love this book."

– P.Martucci, New York, USA

"Secret of the Sands mixes mystery, ancient Egypt, romance, and as well as paranormal elements to make a fascinating novel."

– Cheryl Koch, Amazon Vine Voice

PRAISE FOR DESTINY OF THE SANDS

"High adventure, past and present, merge into a multi-leveled tale of epic proportions in this triumphant sequel to the best-selling novel, Secret Of The Sands!"

– Gary Val Tenuta, author of Ash: Return Of The Beast and The Ezekiel Code

Books by Rai Aren & Tavius E.

Secret of the Sands
Destiny of the Sands

Books by Rai Aren

Lost City of Gold
Revelation of the Sands

For news on upcoming releases and exclusive bonuses, signup for
Rai's newsletter and get a **FREE** copy of Lost City of Gold:
raiaren.com/Subscribe

RAI AREN
& TAVIUS E.

SECRET
OF THE
SANDS

RFS  PUBLICATIONS

THIRD EDITION – Published by RFS Publications, December 2016

ISBN-10: 1482575124
ISBN-13: 978-1482575125

Visit Rai Aren & Tavius E. on the World Wide Web at:
www.secretofthesands.com

Visit Rai Aren on the World Wide Web at: www.raiaren.com

Cover design by Gary Val Tenuta, GVTgrafix:
www.bookcoversandvideos.webs.com

Book formatting and design by:
Maureen Cutajar, www.gopublished.com

To the myriad of life on earth and all its mysteries and magic that inspire us and fire our imaginations every day…
~Rai & Tavius

SECRET
OF THE
SANDS

"History is the version of past events that people have decided to agree upon."
~Napoleon Bonaparte

Circa 10,000 B.C.

Strangled shouts echoed throughout the temple as torchlight flickered outside the entrance. Several battle-hardened soldiers pounded on the door, trying to force their way in.

Inside the temple, breathless and frightened, two young priests desperately tried to bar the door. Three other priests raced to the back of the temple to an inner sanctuary. Their long black hair was in tight braids, and they wore long, flowing, white robes and dark brown leather sandals. Their skin had a beautiful golden sheen to it. Around each of their necks hung an amulet in the shape of an ankh, with a glittering stone in the center of it.

One of the priests was carrying a book of scrolls, held tightly to his chest. Inside the small room stood a wooden altar with low benches in front of it. The chamber walls were decorated with paintings of sacred scenes, ceremonies and images of worship. The priests moved the benches aside, frantically working to uncover a well-hidden trap door.

One of the priests whispered, "There is no way out from here, we must do something!" The language they spoke was an ancient one.

"We have no chance to escape," another said, "but I must hide the book in the chest below. It must be protected. You have to keep them out long enough!"

The three of them finally managed to open the trap door, which revealed a steep set of stairs leading down a dank, dark passageway carved from the earth.

"I will be right back!" he said.

With scrolls in hand, he raced down the crude earthen stairway. At the foot of the stairway was a stone chest with a beautiful, large, intricately detailed ankh carved into its lid.

The priest opened the chest and withdrew one of two protective jeweled cylinders in which he placed the book of scrolls and sealed it tightly. He ran his finger reverently over the smooth carven ankh on its lid, invoking a silent prayer that the secret and powerful knowledge contained within would somehow remain safe.

Time was running out. The intruders were breaking through the door. In desperation, the priests above the secret passageway slammed the trap door closed, shutting their companion in below. Quickly, the priests concealed the trap door and placed the benches back over it.

They heard the clanking of steel and menacing voices shouting. They knew their enemies were coming through. Bravely they stood to face the onslaught of soldiers who were now merely seconds behind them.

As the first soldier burst into the temple, one of the priests hit him on the back of the head with a staff, knocking him unconscious. A second soldier was struck in the face with a torch and fell screaming in agony to the ground.

One of the priests reached into a pocket of his robe and grabbed a small pouch. From it he took some powder and tossed it into the face of the next soldier who came through the door.

The man grasped his throat, his eyes burning, struggling for breath. The fine powder, working quickly, seared his vocal cords, his lungs. His death would be a silent one. The powder, lethal when inhaled, choked the last remaining breaths out of him. He fell to the ground at their feet, his eyes frozen wide in disbelief.

Still more soldiers rushed into the room. The priests fought valiantly but they were no match for the merciless and vicious soldiers, in number or sheer brutality. The two priests who had initially tried to hold the doors were savagely stabbed in the stomach, dark red blood staining their once-pristine white robes. They collapsed to the ground, succumbing to the fatal wounds.

One of the younger priests, witnessing his companions brutally slain before his eyes, screamed with anguish and raced forward to avenge their deaths. From the lifeless hands of one of the soldiers he grabbed a sword and lunged at the attackers, striking a blow on one of the soldier's hands.

The man cried out in pain. Injured and filled with rage, the soldier struck back, driving his blade into the young priest's chest. The soldier smiled malevolently as the young man dropped to his knees and looked down to see the hilt of the sword protruding from his chest.

Struggling for breath, his eyes disbelieving what his body could not deny, he fell to the ground. As he lay dying at the soldier's feet, a single tear fell glistening down his cheek.

Suddenly, a blinding blue light shone through into the temple from somewhere outside, disintegrating nearly everything in its path. A low rumble followed then grew in intensity. A massive explosion shook the very ground. Deafening sounds, thunderous, ensued as wood and stone were blasted into pieces. Fire and intense heat tore through the temple collapsing the ceiling, trapping and crushing everyone inside. All was left in ruins.

Back in the cellar, the lone priest, in fear and confusion, heard the terrifying explosion. Then a deadly silence…

1

The Discovery

Present-Day Egypt

"I don't know if I will ever get used to working in the heat of the Egyptian desert. I honestly think I am about to pass out," Alex moaned. Her full name was Alexandra, but she preferred the simple, boyish name Alex.

"I told you to get a better hat, the holes in that one are going to sear your brain," Mitch said.

"But it's my favorite hat! Besides, I think it makes me look a little like Indiana Jones," she said smiling and cracking an imaginary whip, as her long blond ponytail bounced and her bright blue eyes flashed with playfulness.

Mitch laughed at his partner, his darker eyes and complexion providing him more defense against the burning rays. "Back to reality, Alex! We have serious work to do and if we don't speed things up, we're toast. Dustimaine wants those ancient tools that were found yesterday to be cleaned and categorized by the end of the week."

Mitch and Alex were members of an excavation team working near the Great Sphinx at Giza. They reported to Professor Abner Dustimaine, who assigned them to finish up a site he had moved on from. The site was a large cellar, with an earthen stairway leading down into it. It was not far from a much larger site where he had found numerous ancient tombs, and where he was now focusing his own efforts. Very little had been found in the ancient cellar he left Mitch and Alex to work on, a few tools, broken pieces of pottery, but nothing of major consequence.

"I think Old Dusty really has it out for us," Alex said as she brushed a few wayward hairs out of her eyes.

"Really? I never would have guessed that," Mitch deadpanned. He then looked up at the massive monument that had fascinated them their entire young careers. "But at least we are working relatively close to the Sphinx."

"Yeah, that is true," Alex said, gazing up at it. "I guess I shouldn't complain so much. It is extraordinary," she sighed. After a few moments she looked back to her partner, "But we're not actually doing our own work yet, are we? All we're doing is making sure the boundaries of Old Dusty's site are clearly identified and to search for any additional items he was too busy to look for. I'd bet if we both fell over dead right now, he wouldn't even notice!"

"Sure he would, it would create more work for him having to cart out our corpses, and then he'd have no one else to do his grunt work for him. He'd be seriously choked with us if we kicked the bucket," Mitch laughed. He then turned a bit more serious. "It is still an honor and a privilege to work in Egypt, Alex. It was our dream, remember?"

Alex nodded, thinking back to her father, Dr. Devlan Logan, who she had always idolized. A celebrated Egyptologist himself, he was responsible for igniting his daughter's interest in Egyptology, opening her eyes to all the magic and wonder of one of earth's longest-lived and most accomplished civilizations. His death had hit her hard. Alex wiped away a tear, "I know you're right, Mitch. I shouldn't complain so much. This is what we always dreamed about. It's just so hard sometimes. I wish someone out there would give us a chance to do something bigger, you know, recognize our potential, like my dad did."

Mitch smiled at her warmly. He knew how much her father meant to her and how much she missed him. "They will, Alex, they will some day," Mitch said encouragingly, but inside, he felt exactly as she did.

"Logan! Carver!" a middle-aged man shouted at them.

"Oh no," Alex whispered as the Professor stomped towards them.

Following closely behind the tall skinny frame of Professor Dustimaine, was his ever-present shadow Fessel C. Blothers. Fessel's father was a wealthy philanthropist, who over the years had given millions to the university. As a result, Fessel was given a position that other more-deserving students were not given the chance for, in spite of his poor marks. Fessel was widely resented, but money could buy many things, even a spot in the highly competitive Egyptology program.

"Professor Dustimaine, we weren't expecting you…" Mitch started to say.

"You two are falling further behind every day. What the devil are you doing out here?" the Professor demanded. He looked around, "Why did you let the workers leave so early?"

"Professor," Alex said, "they had put in a full day already and Mitch and I need to catch up on our cataloguing."

"Oh for crying out loud," he said, shaking his head. "Those workers are here to be used, and you two don't work them hard enough. The University's paying for them and we expect full value for our money! You two are the only candidates falling behind, if that means keeping the workers here for longer hours to get ahead so be it. The rest of us have no problem making them work overtime."

"But Professor," Mitch tried to explain, "we don't actually need them right now…"

"I don't care what your excuses are, you are pampering those workers." He leaned closer to them, "If you don't get your act together and start producing better results, I am going to have you both kicked out of the program!" With that, he stormed off.

Fessel, still trailing behind his boss, looked back at Mitch and Alex, sneering.

"Little rat…" Alex whispered under her breath, glaring back at Fessel.

Even though they were still upset from being reprimanded and were growing very tired, Mitch and Alex soldiered on. They were clearing away some dirt and sand to allow them to get a good start in the morning and move on to the finer, more detailed work.

"Ugh, I am so sweaty!" Alex groaned. "My clothes are filled with sand and my back is aching." She sat up and tried to stretch a little. "This has been one crappy day."

"Didn't you mention something earlier about not complaining so much?" Mitch grinned at her.

"You're heartless! May millions of grains of sand find their way into your underclothes," she retorted.

"Already done," he said as he sat down. "Have I mentioned how much I hate Dustimaine?"

She laughed.

Pushing themselves even harder and ignoring their own weariness, thanks to Dustimaine's harsh words, Mitch and Alex continued to work in the hot Egyptian climate for another couple of hours. Dehydration kept threatening them as their water supplies dwindled. They had not meant to stay out so long.

Finally, Alex sat down, exhausted. Her mood had darkened and she had grown quiet. It had been a long day, very long, with little to show for their efforts. She wondered if they ever would. She sighed and took a long drink of water, leaving only a few drops left. She felt unusually tired, defeated. A sense of hopelessness welled up. She kept these feelings to herself; she didn't want Mitch to know. Alex closed her eyes. A heaviness overtook her as she fell fast asleep.

She awoke. She was alone. She panicked, how long have I been asleep? she wondered. Where was Mitch? She called out, but her voice sounded distant, strange. Why was it so dark? Surely there should be some light this close to Cairo.

Her heart started to beat fast. This was wrong, very wrong. She tried to yell out, but her voice was drowned out by a sudden, ferocious windstorm. Sand pelted her. She covered her face. She stumbled around, trying to feel for shelter. She couldn't see. She couldn't hear.

She tripped over something and fell hard. She looked down, her pant leg was torn. Whatever she had tripped on glinted in the moonlight. She looked closer – it was a smooth stone chest engraved with an ankh.

She reached out to touch the chest, laying her hand on it, but it was searingly hot. She cried out, her hand now badly blistered and burnt. She tried to get up, but she stumbled and fell. The air thickened, the wind stopped.

The chest started to glow like steel in a forge. She heard a massive explosion behind her. It came from the direction of the Sphinx.

She turned to see a wall of flame shooting towards her. The heat was intense, her lungs burned in pain. She screamed, turned and ran.

"Alex!" Mitch yelled out. His partner had suddenly screamed and taken off like a shot from where she had been resting. She had scared the living daylights out of him. He watched as she blindly ran from their site. "Alex, stop! What are you doing?" He got up to go after her.

Not hearing her partner, she ran blindly away from the flames she still saw and felt. Her footing was uncertain, unsteady. She didn't see the slight depression in the sand. Her right foot landed in it full flight, stopping her dead in her tracks. She fell hard.

Mitch came racing up beside her. "Alex! What the hell has gotten into you? Are you hurt?"

She heard him this time. She was disoriented, confused. "Where were you?"

"What do you mean where was I? I've been near you the whole time, working while you catnapped." He noticed her leg, "Geez Alex, you scraped your leg pretty good, it's bleeding."

She looked down at her torn pant leg, stunned, but she had already torn it, hadn't she?

"Come, I'll help you up." He lifted her to feet, but she winced in pain.

"I-I think I sprained my ankle," she said.

"Man, you took a bad fall," Mitch said. "You are quite the klutz you know," he grinned.

She laughed a little. Mitch always made her feel better. "I think I sprained my big toe, too."

He just looked at her shaking his head.

"What? I'm serious, I'm hurt!" she pouted, her head clearing. "Why are you looking at me like that?"

"Why did you go running off all of sudden like a mad woman? One minute you're sleeping quietly, the next you freak out and run away? Something crawl up your pant leg?"

She playfully swatted him.

"You scared the crap out of me, you lunatic," he said. "Seriously, what was that all about?"

She thought for a moment, remembering the images of the flames. She suddenly remembered her hand. She gasped, holding it out, expecting to see burned flesh. But there were no burns. She felt slightly disoriented. Slowly more details came back to her, "I must have fallen asleep and started dreaming. It seemed so real."

Mitch listened as she recalled the strange and frightening reverie. "Whew," he said. "I think you must have got some serious sunstroke today." He felt her forehead; it was burning hot. "Come on, let's get going." He helped her as she limped along beside him.

"Wait," she said, "what did I trip over?"

"Probably your own feet."

She elbowed him, "I did not."

He feigned injury, then laughed, "Alex, you ran off like your hair was on fire."

She looked around at the spot where she fell. She tried to kneel down to take a closer look, but winced again. "Could you help me down?" she asked.

Mitch helped lower her gently. "Maybe we should get you bandaged up first."

"No," she replied distractedly, ignoring the growing bloodstain on her pants. "Later."

"Stubborn as ever…" he sighed.

"My foot hit something solid."

"Like a rock?" he asked facetiously.

"Here," she pointed as she leaned over to brush some sand away. "This is no rock."

He knelt down beside her. She was right. It was definitely not a rock. "Help me dig this out."

"Hang on a minute," Mitch said, "I'll go get our tools."

Excited, they quickly established a small work area and set to clearing away the sand and rocks.

A smooth, stone surface was revealed. Their eyes grew wide as they saw what appeared to be a large, carved ankh, the Egyptian symbol of immortality, of life.

"I don't believe it," Alex said. "My dream…in my dream, I tripped over this."

Mitch couldn't believe it either. It was just as Alex had described. "Either this is a helluva a coincidence or you're developing psychic powers."

"Whatever it is, I think we were meant to find this," she said.

"Fate, my dear Ms.Logan?"

"Why not?" she replied, shrugging her shoulders. "We're due for a break if you ask me."

They resumed digging. Finally, the mysterious chest was freed from its long-hidden, desert-resting place. They fell back and sat in the sand, both staring dumbfounded at what they had unearthed.

For a few moments, they were speechless, not taking their eyes off the chest. It was about one foot tall, by two feet long and one foot wide. It appeared to be carved from solid granite and was covered by strange-looking hieroglyphs. However, the most prominent symbol was the first one they had seen on the top of the chest. It was the only one on the lid, an intricately carved ankh, about twenty inches long.

"The ankh is figured so prominently, it's very unusual," she said.

Mitch nodded, "It's usually accompanied by a series of hieroglyphs. And look at it, it has detailing in it like nothing I've seen before."

"These symbols look an awful lot like ancient Egyptian hieroglyphs," Alex started, "but they're kind of different. I can't read them." She looked to Mitch and realized he was having the same problem. "Maybe this is an early form we haven't come across before?"

"Maybe…" he replied, as his fingers gently, but shakily, traced the symbols. "These carvings are so smooth, as if they've never been weathered, like they were carved by a laser beam just yesterday, yet they're not sharp."

"Want to open it?" Alex asked.

"Let's examine it more closely first and see if we can decipher anything else about it," Mitch said.

They continued to study the strange hieroglyphs.

"I don't get it. I can't make any of these out," Mitch said in frustration.

"Do you have the most up-to-date list of known hieroglyphs?" Alex asked. "Maybe it's a collection of obscure, little known glyphs."

"Yeah," he replied, "it's here somewhere." He rifled through the many pockets on his vest for a small book of hieroglyphs. He put on his reading glasses and began flipping pages in the well-worn book. After a few moments, he said, "Seriously, Alex, I can't find them."

"Well, maybe your eyes are going," she quipped.

"You take a look then, smarty-pants," he said handing her the book.

She looked through it, but also to no avail. "Very strange, looks like we have some research to do, or…"

"Or what?" Mitch asked.

"Or maybe we can find some answers by looking inside," she said.

"Maybe," Mitch replied, looking at it. "I just don't want to break anything."

They examined the chest further, but it seemed to be just a simple lid on top, no latches, nothing to undo.

"Well, I don't see any harm in opening it," Mitch said, "unless you think because of your dream that it's booby-trapped and going to blow up on us."

"Don't be silly," she said, her unease over her dream quickly being replaced by excitement and curiosity at the very real artifact before them.

They painstakingly cleaned the caked-in sand out of the groove between the base and the lid and pried the lid off. They carefully laid it down on the sand beside them. Inside the chest were two metal cylinders, silver in color. Alex and Mitch each picked one up to examine.

"Mitch, they're…they're metal," Alex whispered incredulously.

"Amazing…" he said.

"But this isn't, I mean, no one has ever, there's no record of such things…" she started to say.

"I know, I can't explain them either." Mitch looked at Alex for a moment. "What have we found? I mean, as strange as finding metal objects like these is the fact that they are as intricately carved as the chest."

Alex was silent for a moment, trying to make sense of what they had discovered.

As they examined the finds, they saw that this time the ankh was carved on the top and bottom of each of the cylinders. Inlaid in each of the four ankhs were gems that seemed iridescent. Glowing as if from within, the sapphire, emerald, topaz, and ruby-colored gems shined and sparkled with untold depths. They were far more beautiful than any gem Mitch or Alex had ever seen.

"These are incredible," Alex exclaimed. "Alone they would be priceless." She paused. "Mitch, nothing like this has ever been found before in Egypt."

"I know," he responded, "they're going to be invaluable additions to the Cairo Museum. I think people are going to start taking us seriously now."

"What type of metal do you think these cylinders are made of?" she asked.

"I have no idea. They feel strong, like iron, but the metal is so silvery and perfectly smooth."

"Do you want to open them?" Alex asked as she continued to gaze at the cylinders, fascinated. "Maybe they contain documents of some sort."

She reflected on how the one thing that has been missing from Egypt's ancient history were written records of how and why its' magnificent monuments were built.

Mitch shook his head, "No, not here. It's getting dark. I think we should go talk to Professor Dustimaine first, let him know what we've found. This could affect the direction this entire excavation is taking."

"That's exactly why we shouldn't tell him, Mitch!" Alex protested. "You said it yourself, you've heard rumors about him taking credit for his candidates' work. How hard have we worked just to gain enough status to participate in this dig? If we take this to Old Dusty, he's just going to grab it away from us and take all the credit. I bet he wouldn't let us near any of this again once we handed it over. Just think about what we'd be giving up. This could be the discovery of a lifetime!"

Mitch considered her comments. "You're right, but eventually we're going to have to tell someone. If Professor Dust Bucket found out that we've kept finds from him, he'd kill us first, strip us of our meager credentials second, and then send us home. We are already in hot water with him. You heard him earlier. He'd make sure we'd never work in the field of archaeology again. Besides, where do you think we're going to get the time to do any additional research?"

"Tell you what, why don't we just do a little homework on our own first, get a little less sleep for the time being. We'll quickly analyze this ourselves, and then, when we have something more solid put together, which is unmistakably our work, we'll bring it to him."

"I suppose it wouldn't hurt to find a few answers on our own. It would show we have initiative and that we're resourceful," Mitch conceded. "Maybe then, he'll start respecting us a bit more."

"He'll have to!" she exclaimed. "Here, let's pack them up."

They carefully placed the cylinders back inside the chest, and hid it in a duffel bag, which they carried back with them along with the rest of their equipment.

"Do you think we can keep this out of sight from Dustimaine?" Mitch asked. "We have to watch out. He sometimes has that skinny little weasel, Fessel, check up on us."

"We'll be cautious," Alex assured him.

"Let's go find Jack and Bob," Mitch said, "I'm sure they'll be pretty interested in what we have to show them."

"Hang on," Alex stopped him, "let's keep my dream to ourselves, alright. I don't need anyone thinking I've lost my marbles or anything."

"Too late!" Mitch gleefully replied.

She smacked him, "Seriously, Mitch. Not a word!"

More Questions Arise

Mitch and Alex brought the duffel bag containing the chest to the lab where they knew Jack and Bob would still be working. As usual, they were the only two left. Mitch and Alex found them surrounded by numerous empty chip bags, chocolate bar wrappers and cans of Coke, for Jack, and Diet Coke, for Bob.

"Hey guys," Alex greeted them, "how was work today?"

"Ahh, now there's a sight for sore eyes," Jack said, smiling widely. "We thought we were the last two people on earth."

"I see you've already had dinner," Mitch added, looking around amusedly at the junk food bone yard.

"Well, had we known we were having company, we would have saved some," Bob replied sarcastically, as he wiped his hands on his old, worn Star Wars t-shirt. Bob was a rather messy, rotund sort, with thick, scraggly black hair.

"Yeah, thanks anyways, looks like it was very appetizing," Alex said with a hint of disgust.

"Don't knock it Alex, desperate times call for desperate measures," Jack said with mock seriousness. He was a short, skinny fellow, with light brown hair and a long pointed nose.

Jack and Bob were the best of friends as well as co-workers. They were lab technicians, who help analyze and date the finds that the archaeologists bring in. Together, they refer to themselves as 'Rogue Squadron', in reference to their favorite films.

"So, to what do we owe the honor of this visit?" Bob asked.

"Well, we have some things we need to open in a controlled environment," Mitch replied. "Which is why we came to the lab."

"These things will need to be dated as well," Alex added.

Mitch placed the duffel bag on the table, pushing some piles of papers out of the way in the process. "This is just between us, we need you both to swear an oath of secrecy."

"Done," Jack answered for both of them. "What's in the bag?"

Mitch unzipped the bag, pulled the chest out and set it on the table.

"Wowza! Where did you get that?" Bob asked.

"We found it at the end of our dig today after the workers left," Alex said. "Actually, it was kind of by accident." She looked at Mitch, a silent communication passing between them, and continued, "I ran to get some tools when I tripped over it, buried in the sands."

Mitch said nothing.

Bob laughed a big, booming laugh, "You tripped over it? Wow, impressive!"

"Hey, stuff it big boy, that's how they found the entrance to Tut's tomb. Besides, the important thing is we found it, no matter how glamorous the technique." Alex crossed her arms and gave him a challenging look.

Jack added, "Didn't a donkey find the Valley of the Golden Mummies by stepping in a hole?"

"Jack…" Alex warned.

"Ok, ok, so what's in it? Have you opened it yet?" Jack asked.

"We did," Mitch replied. "Remember your oath!" He lifted the lid. Jack and Bob pulled in close to look at the two shining cylinders lying inside.

"Cool," Jack said.

"Whoa…what do we have here?" Bob exclaimed furrowing his brow.

"We don't know exactly what they are," Alex said.

"Have you opened them?" Bob asked.

"No, not yet," Alex answered. "That's why we came to see you two. If there are documents of some sort in there, we want them handled very carefully."

"Understood," Bob replied. "Bring them over here," he said as he motioned them to the environmentally controlled unit they used in the handling of delicate artifacts. The enclosed unit had misters in it, which provided humidity to protect fragile or brittle objects. On either side were built in gloves, used to reach inside the specially designed plastic housing, without damaging the artifact.

"Thanks Bob, we were hoping you guys could help...you see, we haven't exactly shown this to anyone else yet," she said.

"Not even to boss-man Dusti-lame?" Jack said, grinning mischievously.

Mitch and Alex just shook their heads.

"Sneaky smugglers, aren't you?"

"They have good reason to be, Jack," Bob replied in their defense.

"I know. I'm just impressed. Personally, I fully support these actions!"

Mitch brought the chest over to Bob and carefully removed one of the cylinders. He handed it to Bob, who had a look of amazement on his face as he felt the smooth metal in his hands. "I've never seen or felt anything like this. You say you found this on the site you were working on?"

"That's right," Alex answered.

"What are they made of?" he asked.

"We have no idea," Mitch answered. "Metallurgy isn't our strong suit."

"I see," said Bob as he looked at the mysterious cylinders. "Guess you'll need our help on that too."

"Yup," Alex answered.

Bob smiled. He liked feeling needed by his two highly educated pals. "Well...this might be an obvious observation, but we've seen a lot of items from that site, and, well...this doesn't exactly fit the profile, you know. I mean, the ankh is obviously Egyptian, but..."

"Bob, we know. We know exactly what you're saying, please just open them," Mitch interrupted.

Bob looked at them then looked over at Jack, who raised his eyebrows and shrugged. "Fine," he said, placing both cylinders inside the casing. He looked closer at them, his attention riveted. "These are extraordinary! They must be priceless."

"That's kind of what we were thinking," Alex agreed.

"You guys are going to be famous! Hey Jack, we should get their autographs now, while they're still not worth anything! We could make a fortune selling them on eBay!"

"Focus Bob," Alex playfully admonished him. "Can you see a way to open the cylinders without damaging them?"

"Hey, that's why they pay me the big bucks," he laughed.

"You'd better not be getting big bucks if all I get is little bucks!" Jack piped in.

"None of us get big bucks, Jack, we're lucky to get anything more than food and shelter," Mitch said. "Now quit distracting him!"

They all watched as Bob closely examined the ends of one of the cylinders. He reached for a small tool and began to trace the edge of one of its ends. Slowly, he began to pry at the tiny groove, pausing every few seconds to re-examine it. Finally, it gave way, the lid popping up slightly.

He looked up at Mitch and Alex whose noses were nearly pressed against the case. Alex gave him a nod, indicating for him to proceed. Bob carefully pried the top off and after taking a deep breath, angled the cylinder a little to let whatever was inside, fall gently into his waiting gloved hand.

They all gasped at what slid out. It was a book, bound with a soft cover, about ten inches by fourteen inches in dimension. Inside it had several pages made from papyrus.

Alex grabbed Mitch's shoulder. She could feel he was as tense as she was.

In the top right hand corner of the dark brown cover were some symbols embossed with a form of gold leaf.

"Those are similar to the symbols that are on the chest," Alex whispered to Mitch. "Bob, flip through a few of the pages, gently."

They watched as he painstakingly turned the first few pages, which were quite bent having been rolled up for so long. The pages were filled with the same strange type of symbols as on the cover, none of which Mitch or Alex could read.

"Wow!" Bob exclaimed. "Look at this, the papyrus is still in excellent condition, the writing doesn't appear to be faded at all. Those cylinders must have been airtight to keep the papyrus from drying out and becoming brittle. What time period would you guys say this belongs to?"

Mitch and Alex looked at each with wide eyes. Both were silent for a moment.

"We're not sure Bob," Mitch replied, his heart pounding.

"You can't read these?" Bob asked, pointing to what he thought were ordinary hieroglyphs. He couldn't read them himself, but he knew that Mitch and Alex were experts at translating ancient Egyptian writing.

"No," Alex answered, her mind racing. "Let's open the second cylinder."

Again, Bob carefully pried open the ornate top, and out slid two individual papyri. Slowly and carefully, he unrolled them, as everyone held their breath.

The first papyrus had a painting of what seemed to be some kind of strange funeral scene. The other papyrus had a painting depicting an outdoor ceremony or celebration with what seemed to be a royal couple standing with their hands outstretched, as if in blessing. The figures in the painting were wearing long flowing robes. The man was tall and clothed in emerald green, the woman in a golden gown. Both had large amulets around their necks. Their skin appeared tanned and painted with a lovely golden sheen. Their hair was jet-black and each wore golden circlets atop their heads. The plates of food and bushels of crops beside the royal couple would indicate they either had a good harvest or were hoping for one.

"Who are they?" Bob asked. Without answering Alex glanced over at Mitch and instantly recognized he was having the same problem as she was. "Guys, this couple – who are they?" he repeated. Mitch shook his head.

"We don't know," Alex responded.

Bob raised his eyebrows, surprised at her answer. "It's a pharaoh and his queen though isn't it?"

Neither Mitch nor Alex answered him. They just continued to scrutinize the painting for clues as to who these people were.

Jack was now leaning over both Mitch and Alex, his bony fingers digging into their shoulders.

"Ow, Jack, you're puncturing my skin," Alex complained. Mitch laughed.

"Sorry," he said. "Then move over, I can't see!" He then realized that they still weren't answering Bob's last question. "What is it? You guys have funny looks on your faces."

"We're just having trouble placing this, that's all," Alex answered, not making eye contact with him. "We don't recognize the figures. I think we have some homework to do."

Jack kept looking at them. He knew them well enough to know something was up, "Really?" he asked. "This has you stumped? Well, this is a momentous day. You two usually know everything!"

Alex swatted him. "Stuff it!"

Jack laughed. He loved to get a rise out of people.

"We may not be able to place it right now, but that doesn't mean we won't be able to at all," Mitch replied. "Bob, can you close the book again, I'd like to copy down the glyphs from the front of it." He took a seat and jotted them down as best he could into the small leather-bound notebook he always carried with him.

"All right guys, we now need to find out how old these things are and what the story is with those cylinders," Mitch stated as he got up. "This may be one of the most important discoveries in our lifetimes or it may be an elaborate hoax, either way we need to put it into some kind of context for starters. Jack, Bob, you two start working on determining the age of the scrolls, the chest, and the cylinders. Alex and I will work on putting these things into context as best we can and searching for any other references to this royal couple. And let us know if we can safely take the scrolls out to analyze them more closely."

"Gee, is that all? We can have that for you by morning," Jack said with as much sarcasm as he could possibly muster. "Anything else?"

"Jack, we're sorry to do this to you, but we don't have much time. We can't keep this hidden for too long," Alex said. She put her hand on his shoulder, "We're going to be pulling some late nights too. We'll owe you huge."

"Yes, you will," he said smiling at her.

Alex shook her finger at him.

"Hey," Jack quickly replied, "if you and Mitch want to keep this hidden, we'll have to wait until no one is around in the evenings, or else get up extra early before anyone shows up. We can't very well have this stuff laying around for prying eyes to see, now can we? And you know Bob and I are not morning people. We're vampires, thank-you very much!"

Mitch and Alex laughed, shaking their heads.

"But vampires who drink Coke!" he added.

"Diet Coke!" Bob interjected.

"Speak for yourself," Jack replied.

"I just did!" Bob protested, taking a playful swipe at Jack's head.

Jack ducked in the nick of time.

Mitch and Alex laughed again at the comical display. If there was one thing Jack and Bob loved, it was mystery and intrigue.

"Hey, before you go, can you guys tell us anything else?" Bob asked. "These are the most unusual items I've ever seen. I mean, from first glance the scrolls look incredibly old, but these cylinders they were in…this doesn't make sense to me."

"Believe me, Bob, we are as surprised and confused as you are," Alex said. "We just don't have any other answers for you right now. Without speculating, it would be helpful to determine even a ballpark age of any of this. That's going to tell us a lot of what we need to know and point us in the right direction at least. We wish we had more information, that's why we're counting on you two. Huge!" she said smiling.

"Alex, I'm also going to make a sketch of this chest so we have some things to study while we leave the rest with them," Mitch said as he sat down again and made as accurate a copy as possible of the chest and its intricate markings.

"Ok, done," Mitch said, closing up his notebook. "We'll touch base with you guys in the morning. If you need anything else, if there's anything we can do to help, please let us know."

"Oh, we will," Jack replied emphatically.

"Call us the minute you find anything out," Mitch said. "And thank-you both!"

"Yeah, yeah, just make sure to keep the Cokes coming!" Jack replied.

"And remember, diet for me!" Bob called out as Mitch and Alex prepared to leave.

"We won't forget!" Alex said, waving.

They walked to the door, and looked at one another. "I don't know what to say, Alex."

"I know," she replied.

"What the hell do you think we've found?"

"Something big."

3

Spring Ceremony

Circa 10,000 B.C.

The region was lush, tropical grassland, filled with a myriad of living things, each extraordinary and vital in its own way. The large river that flowed there gave life to this fertile land. Presently, this land is known as Egypt and the river it is blessed with is called the Nile, but in this time, those names were not yet known. The desert sands that now blow in Egypt conceal, in their untold depths, many things. In this ancient time however, the river was twice the width it is today, and all along its shores, people had settled not far from the main city, established on the plains to the west of the river. Wild animals abounded, crops were plenty, and the people were well cared for by their Royal Family.

"Traeus, are you ready for the ceremony?" asked his wife, the beautiful Queen Axiana. "I do not think it would look good for the King to be late," she teased him.

Traeus, twenty-seven, and Axiana, twenty-three, were the young King and Queen of these people and have been married for three years. This was a special day, the annual Spring Ceremony to celebrate the harvest season. It was a time of community and to give thanks for the blessings the land has brought them.

"I am, my love, but Alaj has chosen not to attend," Traeus replied, deeply disappointed that his brother, Prince Alaj and his wife, Princess Zazmaria, would not be participating.

Axiana looked down, "I know, I spoke with Zazmaria." She looked back to her husband, "What did Alaj say his reasons are this time?"

"He said that since I, the elder brother and King, will be there, his presence is not required. Our father would have been utterly anguished to see this. People are beginning to whisper about his and Zazmaria's increasingly frequent absences from official functions. I worry that I cannot even keep my own family together. What if the people lose confidence in me? I have only been King for two short years."

She walked over to her husband and caressed his face, "My husband, the people love you and they trust in their King. Your father would have been very proud of you and all that you have done since his passing. The people know with whom these problems lie and it is not with you."

Traeus embraced her, "I could not imagine a life without you, my wife."

Axiana smiled. "Then do not, for I am here for you," she said as she kissed him. "Traeus, I tried to talk to Zazmaria about this, but she is hostile towards me. I do not understand her, I have always tried to reach out to her, to make her feel a part of this family."

"It is not your fault, I know your efforts have been sincere," her husband said and kissed the top of her head. "But, ever since Father's death two years ago, I have noticed that the two of them have become increasingly closed and withdrawn from the rest of the family. I can only think his death must have hit them hard, but I cannot help but worry that there is something more to their words and actions. When our mother died, I did not notice such an immediate difference in Alaj. Maybe still having our father eased his pain at the time. I know it did mine."

"I think losing both your mother and father within such a short timeframe may have taken an even bigger toll on Alaj than we realized."

Traeus thought for a moment. "Perhaps…" He took a deep breath. He seemed so worn. "Our family has achieved so much in the twenty-eight years our people have been in this land. To see it fall apart, to begin to disintegrate…"

Axiana knew this issue would not be solved easily. "Come my love, the people are waiting for us and our troubles will still be here when we get back. Let us turn our attentions to more happy thoughts. It is a beautiful day," she said as she took her husband's hand.

Traeus knew that this was a very important event for his people, but his heart was still heavy with worry and doubt. His greatest fear had always been that he would fail as King, fail his people and not be able to live up to his father's example.

Prince Amoni met Traeus and Axiana as they headed down the long courtyard, through the extensive Palace grounds to where the ceremony would take place at the large outdoor temple adjacent to the main priests' temple. The prince, who was just about to turn fourteen years old, was the youngest of the three brothers in the Royal Family. "Where is Alaj?" Amoni asked. "Is he joining us at the ceremony?"

"He and Zazmaria chose not to come, Amoni," Axiana replied, putting her arm around the young man's shoulder. She noticed how his face fell when he heard the news.

"Come, we do not want to be late," Traeus said as he took the hands of both his wife and brother. He worried about how all this affected Amoni, but today they had duties to perform and they must focus on that.

Together, the three of them walked to the front gates of the Palace grounds where the Royal guard, dressed in ceremonial uniforms, would accompany them to the ceremony.

The people were already gathered at the outdoor temple, waiting with anticipation for the Royals to arrive. They were a proud, hardworking people, who had faced much hardship and upheaval in their lives. They call themselves the Kierani.

The guards bowed as the Royals approached.

King Traeus, Queen Axiana and Prince Amoni were dressed in their finest garments. Traeus, a tall, well-built man, wore a long tunic over loose linen pants. His tunic was made of emerald green silk and exquisitely embroidered. His shiny jet-black hair, a shared trait among the Kierani, was adorned with a beautifully crafted circlet of gold. It was intricately carved with their family name, Selaren, and interwoven with symbols: the ankh, representing the life force, which the Kierani people worshipped, along with images of the sun.

Axiana wore a beautifully fitted, burnished gold, full-length silk dress, which was striking with her long black hair that had been swept up for the ceremony. Loose curls hung delicately at the side of her face, and she too wore a circlet of gold atop her head. She was widely regarded as the most beautiful woman in Kierani society. She was small-boned with delicate features and had warm eyes of a deep brown, flecked with gold. She wore long dangling gold earrings encrusted with topaz. Her skin tone was slightly lighter than that of her husband, but all Kieranis had a stunning natural golden sheen to their skin.

Prince Amoni was dressed in a tunic and matching pants of deep red. Around each of the Royals' necks were heavy gold necklaces, long and also embossed with symbols of the sun and the ankh. Precious gems were inlaid: rubies, sapphires, emeralds, but the main feature of these Royal adornments was the image of a lion, seated with a long thick mane.

The lion was revered and worshipped in Kierani culture. To them, it symbolized strength, grace, and protection. There were stories amongst their folklore of a magical lion, named Amsara who had once saved a legendary King. Forever after, a male lion had been kept by the priesthood as a symbol of this protector, and cared for its entire life. It was invariably named after the first, Amsara.

The ceremony was to begin at high noon. All along the wide walkway and the surrounding grounds and gardens were throngs of people, cheering as the splendidly clad Royals passed by, smiling and waving to their people.

Lining the walkway of the temple were the members of the priesthood, each of whom bowed as the Royals passed. The priests wore long, flowing white robes, and their long, black hair was tied back in the traditional braids worn by members of the priesthood. Around their necks they wore the ceremonial ankh, each priest's name was engraved on the back. Topaz glittered in the center of the ankhs, sparkling with golden depths in the bright sun.

The priests held high positions in Kierani society. They were the spiritual leaders of the people and among their ranks were educators, architects, scientists, healers and community leaders, and trusted advisors to the King. The priesthood was as ancient as the Royal Family itself.

At the end of the walkway stood Assan, the widely respected Head Priest, along with two high-ranking members of the priesthood, Odai and Senarra. Odai was the primary keeper of the lion Amsara. The Head Priest himself was mentoring Odai to one day succeed him as head of their order. The role of Head Priest had many important responsibilities and was a noble and greatly respected position, one that was held for life.

Seated in the crowd was one of the priests who possessed a wonderful, natural artistic ability. He was sketching images from the ceremony on papyrus. He was planning on painting it in later as a memento of this special day and later presenting it to the Royal Family as an official gift from the priesthood.

The ceremony would take place on a small platform, which had been erected beside the fountain. Behind the platform, tapestries were draped with the Royal Family crest, a standing lion, with a sun image over its head encased within a large golden ankh.

Soft breezes blew on this warm, sunny day. As King Traeus, Queen Axiana and Prince Amoni took their places on the platform, the crowd erupted in loud cheers. Leading members of the military, in dress uniforms, also joined the Royal Family.

At this moment, Traeus felt the absence of his brother and the Princess keenly, but he tried not to let his disappointment show. The King stepped forward, "My people, it is a great honor to be standing before you today, for the annual celebration to mark the start of our harvest season."

Musicians who were seated on either side of the platform began to play stringed instruments with melodious bells. Additional musicians were weaving through the crowd, playing a cheerful song. People began to sway along to the music. Children laughed, playfully following the musicians around.

King Traeus motioned, and the music became very soft, then stopped. "Today, we come together to share our prayers and wishes for a plentiful harvest. It is tradition to mark the season with food and song surrounded by our friends, families and neighbors." He stretched out his hands and dancers appeared, dancing in time to the music, which had started up again.

Scantily dressed young men and women carried baskets of flower petals, which were tossed into the air. They danced throughout the crowd, much to the delight of the onlookers. Queen Axiana and Prince Amoni clapped along-side King Traeus.

Head Priest Assan now stepped forward for his turn to address the crowd. "We now present Amsara, the living embodiment of the legendary Royal guardian."

Odai had disappeared behind the platform for a moment then re-appeared in front of the stage with the lion Amsara, who had been waiting behind the draped tapestries with another keeper to make his appearance.

The crowd erupted with cheers of delight seeing their beloved lion. It was only during official ceremonies that most people saw him. Otherwise he was kept in his lair with his three lionesses in the habitat behind the main temple.

As the crowd clapped and cheered, Odai ran down the long walkway with the lion running beside him. The priests stood up and bowed to Odai and the lion as they ran past.

Assan continued, "It is our honor as members of the priesthood to take part in this blessed event. May the coming year bring health, both spiritual and physical, to each and every one of you. We ask this in honor of the living force which flows through us all. We give thanks for our blessings and for those who govern us, House Selaren, your Royal Family!" Assan bowed.

The King, Queen and young Prince stepped forth to accept the exuberant applause from their people.

King Traeus lifted his hand, "And we give thanks to you, our people, for your hard work and worthy efforts, and for your loyalty to us…"

"Not everyone is loyal to you, King!" an angry man yelled.

"We want action!" another man shouted. "When are you going to get us out of here? We have been trapped too long already."

A small mob formed, pushing their way through the crowd to the King and Queen. The crowd panicked. The Royal guards quickly surrounded the group of protesters, trying to restrain them, but their shouts could still be heard.

"It is his family's fault we are living in misery!"

"King Traeus has done nothing for us. You are but a pale shadow of a greater king!"

"It is time for House Draxen!"

The Royal guards subdued the mob and escorted them out of the area.

Traeus called for calm. "Please accept the baskets which have been provided for each family present today," he said, clearly flustered. He was trying not to let on that the protest bothered him, but it only preyed on his growing sense of self-doubt.

At the far end of the courtyard several ox-driven wagons had pulled up and the coverings were taken off. Each household would receive a basket of bread and fruit, which had been prepared from the Royal bakery and orchards. The people were grateful and eagerly accepted the gifts from their beloved Royal Family.

Traeus tried to smile as the dancers and musicians resumed their performances and the priests and priestesses began to mingle through the crowd. Many families chose to stay and make a picnic on the lawns with their baskets, enjoying the music and dancing. However, in spite of so many happy countenances, he could not shake his uneasiness. The protest had been a bold one, and the mention of the Draxen name had been particularly brazen…and alarming.

CHAPTER

4

Ambition

Prince Alaj and Princess Zazmaria had cloistered themselves in their private chambers for the duration of the ceremony and the events that followed. As the day was nearing its end, Alaj was gazing at the setting sun through a window. It was a beautiful sunset that seemed to bathe the landscape in a warm glow and reflect across the water of the garden pools a myriad of colors from gold to amber to the deepest red.

"My brother will be pleased, even the heavens seem to be participating in the Spring Celebrations," Alaj said with a hint of resentment in his voice.

"Axiana came to me today to see why you chose not to attend with the rest of the family," Zazmaria replied. "I told her not to go behind your back or to use me to convince you to bow to their wishes."

"I am just tired of being told what to do all the time," Alaj said as he turned to his wife, looking at her wearily with the same emerald green eyes as his older brother.

Alaj was also a tall man, though not as tall as the King, and had a slightly more slender build. "Traeus thinks we should pretend that we are a solid and happy family. I am not happy, so why should I? I have told him time and again I would like to take on a bigger role in our family, be more involved in making the important decisions. Why should I not have more of a say in how things are run?" he fumed.

"I agree, my husband," Zazmaria answered. "I feel as though I too am little more than a figurehead. I grow tired of our subservience to him and that disingenuous little wife of his." Zazmaria, a year older than the Queen, was greatly envious of her, and deeply resented her own secondary place in the Royal Family. "We should share power more equally with them. Is it not our right?"

Prince Alaj nodded, "It should be. I see every day how Amoni watches us. I see how he looks up to Traeus. I know he is young still, but I could start training him to look after some of the farmers and villages, but Traeus will not even consider it. He keeps saying that Amoni needs to focus on his education, that it is too soon to introduce him into the day-to-day responsibilities of our family and so everyday, in so many ways, I am diminished in the eyes of our people, of Amoni…of you."

Zazmaria walked over and looked at her husband, "Then you should do something about it. It is not right the way Traeus treats you. When your father died, I thought that you and Traeus would share power. He is only two years older than you are." She wrapped her arms around her husband's waist, and a new glint emerged in her eyes. "We need new ideas in our leadership, new ways of doing things. Our people need you Alaj."

Prince Alaj looked directly at her, concern etched across his handsome face. His wife was a very beautiful woman. She had thick, long black hair, wide-set topaz eyes that seemed to sparkle in candle or firelight, and full lips. Alaj loved her very much and wanted to make her happy, but right now he was unsure of how to do that.

"What would you have me do, my wife? Traeus would never relinquish any power to me, not if he could help it."

"Listen to yourself," she snapped suddenly and pulled away from him. "He has you brainwashed into submission. You have to stand up to him and be strong. Take what you want! He walks all over you because you let him," her gaze was challenging, the tone in her voice serious, and now utterly cold.

For a moment Alaj did not know what to say. He was seeing a side to his wife he had not recognized before, though they had been married for two years. "Zazmaria, it is not such an easy thing to influence a King or to wrest any power from his grasp. It is much more complicated than that…"

"It does not have to be," she said, cutting him off.

Alaj looked at her curiously, "What do you mean by that?"

She paused for a brief moment, thinking, then smiled and came up close to him again, her icy tone now melting away. As her finger traced a line down his smooth cheek, she looked deep into his eyes then ran her fingers through his silky black hair. "All I want, dear husband, is what is best for this family, for you and I." She leaned over to kiss his neck, "Is that so wrong?"

The Creation of Amsara

This was a day the King had long been looking forward to. It had been six months since the Spring Ceremony and he, Prince Amoni, and leading members of the priesthood, would be touring the construction site of the most ambitious project of his reign, a gigantic limestone monument of a seated lion. When completed, it would stand an incredible sixty-five feet tall, be a sweeping two hundred feet in length, and its face would be an imposing twenty feet wide.

The monument would be both a larger-than-life representation of the mythical lion Amsara, as well as its namesake. This tour had been put together by the man heading up the project, Victarius, Traeus' Chief Engineer, as an official update on the progress of the King's project.

Although construction had been visible around the massive body for quite a distance, King Traeus wanted to see the work up close for himself and have the opportunity to discuss specifics with the head of the important project.

"Victarius, I am very impressed with the progress that has been made so far," the King said as he shook the seasoned engineer's hand. "You and your team have accomplished much since beginning this project. Your leadership is to be commended." Traeus hoped that this monument would restore his people's confidence in his own abilities as king.

Victarius had long been considered the best in his field and as such, was awarded the position of project leader. The tall, thin, kindly old man had worked for the Royal Family his entire career.

"Thank-you your Highness, it means a great deal to me to know that you are satisfied with our progress. I will certainly pass along your comments to my team. It will mean much to them to know you are pleased with their work. They have worked tirelessly, laboring long hours of their own accord, and have never wavered in their enthusiasm for seeing it completed."

"Good, good. I know it will be glorious when complete. I can see even now how beautiful it will be," Traeus said, smiling up at the creation coming to life.

It was an enormous feat to quarry the rock, then to add on to it to give the body strength. Traeus gazed at it in wonder, it was colossal and yet he could already see the artistry inherent in it. The graceful, flowing lines of the body already appeared quite lifelike.

Traeus was excited to see the finished project. In his mind, he pictured what it would look like once the head and mane were sculpted and the monument painted and covered in brilliant hues. He imagined his people being thrilled at the sight of their silent and regal protector, watching over them for all eternity. Traeus knew it would be an important symbol for his people, and give them something to focus on, to unify them…something they could all believe in.

Traeus thought back to his father, the celebrated King Mesah, who had originally conceived of the idea many years ago. Traeus recalled how after his mother, Queen Elenia, died, his father had devoted himself to developing the concept for this large-scale project. Sadly, he had not lived long enough to see his dream become a reality.

"Victarius, did you ever think the day would finally come when my father's vision would begin to take on life?"

"Well, your Highness, we had many other important things to focus our energy on through the long years. It is actually a relief to get back to work on something that is not purely focused on survival. But to answer your question, yes, I knew this day would come eventually. King Mesah was a man with a strong vision for his people and he combined his remarkable will and ability to motivate others in achieving great things, just as his son is doing now."

Traeus was moved by his kind words and smiled appreciatively. "Thank-you Victarius, your confidence inspires me," he said.

Just then, the Head Priest Assan, along with Odai and Senarra joined them.

Prince Amoni, who had been off talking to one of the engineers, ran over to rejoin his brother when he saw the priests and priestess arrive. The young Prince was the first to greet them.

Odai was closer in age to Amoni than most people in the Prince's life and was Amoni's favorite companion. The young Prince did not have occasion to spend much time with many people his own age due to his position, and since the Royal Family and the priesthood worked so closely together, he and Odai had many opportunities over the years to spend time together. Amoni looked up to Odai.

"Odai, what do you think of the Amsara monument so far?" Amoni asked as the two younger men lagged behind the rest of the group. "It is really starting to look like a lion now, would you agree?"

"Yes, the artistry is truly astounding. It sends shivers up my spine just looking at it."

"I know! Me too! They say they are only three months away from starting work on its head. I can hardly wait to see what it will look like!"

"Amoni, please come join the rest of the group," Traeus called out. "We should all listen to what Victarius has to share with us about the project."

"Yes, brother!" Amoni ran to catch up to the rest of the group.

Assan and Senarra were already talking to Victarius. Odai also joined them and extended his arm to Senarra.

Victarius continued, "I was just saying that the work has proceeded ahead of schedule. King Traeus' idea to create the stone figure from the existing limestone formation was pure genius. If we had tried to create it in the original location that had been chosen and transported the necessary rock, it would have taken far, far longer and used up considerably more resources. This allowed us to double the original size of the design."

"Thank-you Victarius, but remember it was originally my father's idea to create it. I merely found a way to do it faster and larger, with less work. My own impatience was likely my true inspiration," Traeus laughed.

The rest of the group laughed along. Their laughter was cut short as they saw Prince Alaj, visibly upset, hastily approaching them.

Traeus silently groaned.

"Thank-you for including me on your private little tour," Alaj fumed.

Traeus' cheeks flushed with embarrassment at his brother's rude comments. He felt himself getting angry, but he did not want to make a further scene. Traeus would have to swallow his pride for now and disregard Alaj's insults.

Taking a deep breath, he said to his brother, "We were just discussing the incredible work Victarius' team has done. It is quite an accomplishment, would you not agree?"

Alaj glared at him. "Tell me something, how much do you think that same amount of effort could have accomplished if say…they were working on something useful, such as improving our farming technology or building better and safer water craft for travel along the river?"

Alaj did not wait for an answer. Zazmaria's continuing influence had emboldened him. "Perhaps you should have listened to me when I said this was not a practical project for our people right now. I am not the only one who feels this way. There are many people who are disgruntled with the direction things are taking. If I were you, King, I would take the protests seriously."

No one said a word as they waited for their King to respond to the accusations.

Traeus tried to measure his words carefully. "Alaj, perhaps you and I can continue our debate on this matter at a later time in private. For now, you are more than welcome to join us as Victarius completes the tour of the project." Traeus, not waiting for Alaj to answer, nodded at Victarius to continue.

Victarius had just begun to speak again, when Alaj interrupted him, still on the attack. "Traeus, could you please explain to me why it was more important to you to have members of the priesthood here rather than your own brother? I see that Amoni was quite obviously invited."

Amoni turned a crimson shade of red, he felt guilty and embarrassed at having been singled out this way. He resented both his brothers at this moment for letting things come to this.

Traeus looked at Assan briefly, conveying an apology with his eyes. He then turned to his accuser, "Alaj…"

"Why did you look at Assan just now? I am the one speaking to you!" Alaj was in no mood to be made the villain. "I am tired of these insults! I am always taking a backseat to the priesthood. You dishonor me with your actions, King. I am a Prince and by rights should be included in these matters." Alaj had long felt envious of the place the priests, especially the Head Priest, Assan, held with his brother. It seemed to Alaj that they had more power than he, having frequent audience with the King.

"Alaj, please, not now," Traeus whispered as he pulled him aside. "I apologize for not inviting you. That was my decision and mine alone. But you have never supported this project since I took it over, in fact you have become an outspoken opponent of it."

Alaj did not respond. He only glared at his older brother.

"Tell me then Alaj, why would I ask you to suffer through something which you have such disdain for?" Traeus asked, trying to stay calm and keep his composure.

Alaj felt himself getting even angrier now. He would not allow his brother to pacify and silence him so easily. "What I think about it is irrelevant! You have put together an official tour and I should have been invited! Amoni is here. Members of the priesthood are here. How do you think this looks to everyone?"

Traeus wanted to say something about his absence at the Spring Ceremony to which he had been invited and expected to attend, but decided against it. The argument, which he had been trying to avoid, would only become full-blown if he did. "You are right, and I have already apologized for it, Alaj. I should have included you. Now, please, shall we let Victarius continue?"

The tour continued amid such ongoing tension. Alaj kept his distance from Traeus and asked no questions during the remainder of the tour. He looked at the giant shape being sculpted, and though he could not help but admire it aesthetically, inside he deeply resented it.

That evening, after touring the construction site and staying around to discuss the project with Victarius and the others, Traeus and Amoni retired to the Palace library. They had walked together in silence, passing the two large granite statues that Traeus had commissioned of King Mesah and Queen Elenia. Alaj had left the site early, not speaking to either of them as he departed.

"Brother, may I ask you a question?" Amoni started off tentatively.

"Of course, Amoni, you may ask me anything," Traeus replied.

"Why do you and Alaj fight all the time?"

Traeus inhaled deeply, he should have expected this question. How could he explain a complex and troubled relationship to his younger brother, when he was at a loss to understand it fully himself?

"Amoni, it is difficult to explain. I regret that you have to bear witness to such displays. It is not how I would have our family be. Alaj and I do not agree on many things. Ever since our father died, he has become increasingly resistant and hostile towards me. He questions my decisions, continually disagreeing with me on how we should use our resources."

"I know, but does he not see how wonderful and inspirational the Amsara monument will be for our people? It symbolizes something we revere greatly. I think it will be amazing!"

Traeus smiled at Amoni's passion. "Thank-you Amoni, I am very happy to hear that. I only wish Alaj felt the same way."

"Things seemed so much simpler when father was still alive," Amoni said sadly. "I miss him."

"I do as well. He was a great man, a great King, and a great father," Traeus replied, as his own fears and doubts began to surface again.

Amoni nodded in agreement. "There is one other thing that bothers me," he said.

"What is that?" Traeus asked, looking at his youngest brother.

"Well, I think Alaj does have a point on one thing. You seem to regard the priests so highly. They are involved in everything you do. You constantly consult with them on all kinds of matters and yet Alaj, a Prince, is not granted the same privilege. It seems to me as if their opinions and ideas are more important to you than his."

"Oh Amoni, that is not the case at all. I depend on their advice and experience in many matters, especially Assan's. Being King is an enormous responsibility. There is much I still have to learn and much I am uncertain about. I wish Alaj could be more supportive of me, but he refuses."

"But Alaj does not seem to view the priests the way you do."

Traeus nodded his head sadly, "He used to though. He was raised the same way you and I were, but since I became King it is as though he wants nothing to do with them or me. He fights me on almost everything now."

"Do you think he wanted to be King instead of you?" Amoni asked.

"No, I do not believe so, he has never coveted power. I still believe he holds our family's best interests at heart. He just has different ideas on how to achieve that. But he has to realize that I am King now. These decisions are ultimately my responsibility, and that is a difficult job. I could use his help, rather than his animosity."

"Do you not wish to be King?"

"No, no Amoni, that is not it at all. Being King is a great privilege and honor. I will not deny there are times, when I wish that not all this responsibility had been placed solely on me. But that is exactly why I depend on Assan and the rest of the priesthood. I cannot manage it all alone, no one could, not even our father. But Alaj has somehow forgotten that. I only hope I can be as good a King as our father was."

Amoni smiled at his brother, "You already are, brother. I am very proud of you."

Traeus was deeply moved. He had not realized how much he needed to hear those words.

6

A Startling Find

Present-Day Egypt

Neither Mitch nor Alex got much sleep that night. They had handed over the mysterious chest and its even more mysterious contents to Jack and Bob. Their heads were spinning with possibilities, with hope. Perhaps this would be their shot at the big leagues: important excavations, recognition, funding, and most importantly, respect. They envisioned themselves meeting with prominent Egyptologists to discuss their fascinating find.

The next morning they met a little earlier than usual. Alex was downing her first cup of black coffee in record time. "Couldn't sleep?" Mitch asked.

"Not a chance, you?"

"Not a wink," he answered, then paused for a moment. "So…no funny dreams?"

"No," Alex frowned, "now just please drop it. It was probably just the effects of sunstroke cooking my brain." She saw Mitch start to grin. "Don't even go there." She headed back to the coffee pot, and quickly changed the subject. "You should try this, Mitch. It's the elixir of the gods…mmm, just the aroma is heavenly."

"No thanks, give me good old-fashioned orange juice any day."

"Boring! How you wake up in the morning without a good kick-start is beyond me. I'd be comatose without my coffee," she said as she got up to pour herself another cup. "Mitch, are you thinking what I'm thinking?"

"About the coffee? I doubt it," he replied.

"Very funny, I mean about our theory. What if this was something that could prove we're right?"

"Don't get your hopes up, Alex," Mitch said.

"Too late!" she said as she sat down again. "We found that chest close enough to the Sphinx. Maybe it's exactly what we've been looking for, what we've been hoping for. Maybe the writing in the scrolls details construction plans that could tell us who built it and how…and when. Dating these materials could be our proof."

"Alex, I don't know what we found and neither do you. I mean metal cylinders, from Ancient Egypt? It's crazy! The metal was…well I'm no engineer, but refined you know? This isn't polished bronze or copper we're talking about. It looked…"

"Advanced," Alex finished the sentence.

"Exactly! They couldn't be more out of place. There is no way Ancient Egyptians had the technology to create such things. Something doesn't add up."

"I know, but you saw that papyrus painting, the book of scrolls, they looked old. And the people in the painting weren't people we've been able to identify or place. There has to be some kind of explanation. So maybe they lived here prior to the known historical record. There are gaps in the record, time periods we're not sure about. We may have found an earlier pharaonic line!"

"I know what you want, Alex, I want the same thing. All I'm saying is that we shouldn't jump to conclusions here. That we believe the Sphinx predates the pyramids by at least 5000 years is one thing, finding proof is quite another. We've ruffled enough feathers already with this idea and now we're hoping people from thousands of years ago could manufacture sophisticated metals? We'd be laughed out of Egypt…or worse."

Alex smiled sadly, "I remember playing out in the dirt in our back-yard when I was a little girl. I'd play archaeologist, burying my toys and then going on a pretend excavation with my little plastic shovels, pails and some of mom's Tupperware and dig them up again. Then I'd go running inside the house to show my dad what I'd found, imagining the most incredible finds in the history of archaeology, things the whole world would talk about. He would always play along and together we'd make up some fantastical ancient history for my 'relics'." She paused, lost in the memory.

Mitch listened patiently, thinking also of his own warm memories. Dr.Logan had always been like a second father to him, something Mitch had desperately needed growing up.

Alex's father named her Alexandra after the Egyptian city of Alexandria, as well as Alexander the Great. He had been a big admirer of the young military leader and genius who had such an enormous influence on the history of Ancient Egypt.

All Alex ever wanted to do was follow in her father's footsteps and make him proud of her. Since she was a little girl she had dreamt of her father seeing her get her PhD, of one day working together, here in Egypt, the land that held his heart for thirty years. She wiped a tear from her eye at the pain of the memory. Her dream had been shattered one terrible day, the day her father was taken from her and her mom in a devastating car accident, the result of a drunk driver who stupidly chose to get behind the wheel late one night, while her father drove home from working late at the university. He never made it.

She shook her head, pushing the thoughts out of her mind, and looked backed to Mitch, trying to manage a small smile. "And now here we are…for real."

"For real…" he repeated. "If only people could see this, what we've found, we could actually be taken seriously." He lowered his eyes, " And maybe my family would finally believe in me."

"They do, Mitch," Alex said sympathetically. "They just didn't understand your choices. That doesn't change how they feel about you, though."

"Doesn't it?" he said bitterly.

He hadn't spoken to his parents in almost two years. They hadn't made the effort and neither had he. Mitch came from a family of medical doctors who had expected him to follow in their family's proud tradition. After all, it had brought them all status, wealth, important ties to the community, and influence.

Mitch's own choice to pursue a career in archaeology had been met with shock, subtly scorned, and never, ever respected, even though he had talked about nothing else his entire young life. They thought he would grow out of it, and eventually come to his senses and choose their path. When he didn't, his mother and father had tried to talk him out of it, for months. Then, they just grew distant. Even his older brother and two sisters had withdrawn from him.

Mitch was left feeling like an outsider and a disappointment, maybe even an embarrassment, though they were far too refined to ever say so, at least to his face. He knew by the little things they would say to others, or, more importantly...not say. They would often leave the topic of him out of conversations with their friends and peers about the family's various activities and accomplishments.

Thankfully he had Alex's family to help him overcome some of those hurts. The two had grown up together being the same age and living on the same upscale street, just a couple of houses down from one another. He spent more time over the years at their place, on weekends and for family dinners than he did at home. Amongst the Logan's, he fit in, he belonged. He would be grateful forever for that.

Both Mitch and Alex had grown quiet. There was no need to say all this out loud. They had talked about it all at great length over the years. They knew each so well, better than anyone else in their lives. They could immediately tell what was on the other's mind.

Alex polished off her coffee and got up for another. "Well, since we can't take out an ad in tomorrow's paper about our find for fear of being labeled crackpots and frauds, shall we go check on the boys before we start the day?"

"Oh yeah, definitely," Mitch answered, grateful to be changing the subject. "I'm kind of surprised though that they didn't call last night with any preliminary finds."

"Yeah, me too, I was hoping they would. Do you think they'd be up this early? As Jack reminded us, they're not morning people." Alex looked at her watch. It was five forty-five am.

"It wouldn't hurt to check."

Alex nodded and proceeded to chug down her third cup of coffee. Mitch shook his head at her.

As they headed over to the lab, they could see at a distance there were lights on.

"Let's hope that's them," Alex said. They got there and opened the door. Sure enough there were Jack and Bob.

"Morning guys," Alex greeted them as she and Mitch came over to where they were working. She looked at them curiously.

"You two are up early," Mitch said. "A little unusual for you guys, isn't it?"

There was no response at first.

"Guys?" Alex ventured, "Why are you wearing the same clothes you were wearing last night? I mean, I know fashion isn't exactly your strong suit, but…"

"You didn't!" Mitch said. Now that he had a close look at them he saw that their eyes were glazed and red and they definitely weren't acting like their usual selves.

"What time is it?" Jack finally asked wearily.

"Almost six bells," Mitch answered. Jack and Bob both groaned.

"You stayed up all night?" he asked.

"Yeah, we did," Bob answered.

"Why?" Mitch asked.

"Why do you think?" Bob shot back. He was a little edgy from lack of sleep. "Tell me the story again. You guys found the chest within the perimeter of Dustimaine's site? In the large cellar?"

"Yes," Alex answered.

"Was there any evidence it was planted?" Bob asked.

"No, we found it fairly deep down, in a previously undisturbed setting," Alex answered.

"And you're not pulling an elaborate prank on us?" Jack asked.

"No, why do you ask that?" Mitch asked, looking from one to the other.

"Now, why would we ask that, hey Bob?" Jack mimicked. "Do you think we like staying up all night locked up in labs? Do you have any idea how much Coke and Diet Coke the two of us have ingested since last night? We are not well Carver, and if this is some kind of joke or you didn't tell us everything you know…"

"Jack!" Alex stopped him. "We're not playing tricks on you! I can see you two aren't quite in your right minds, but would you mind doing your best to fill us in on what you've found out so far?" She looked around. She saw the scrolls, the cylinders and the chest. Everything looked intact.

"Well, the scrolls are old, we know that for sure," Bob said.

"How old?" Mitch asked.

"You'd both better sit down," he said. Mitch and Alex complied. "Nearly 12,000 years old."

"What?" they both asked simultaneously.

"Preliminary radio-carbon dating tests indicate the scrolls are authentic," Bob replied, both excited and perplexed. "The tests say they are almost 12,000 years old!"

"12,000 years…?" Mitch said, stunned.

"I don't believe this," Alex exclaimed, her mind racing. "Mitch, do you know what this means? The symbols we couldn't read, this is why! They weren't derived from hieroglyphics, they preceded them!"

Mitch was shaking his head in disbelief, "Bob, are you sure about this?"

"Yes, at this point anyways. I've checked the experiments over several times. The results weren't too hard to determine because the book was in such excellent condition. Having been kept sealed in those airtight cylinders and protected inside that chest has preserved its condition perfectly. But keep in mind I have limited test equipment here in the field to do Carbon 14 tests. All of my preliminary tests have to be verified with the lab at the university. They can do thorough Carbon 14 tests using Liquid Scintillation Counting and Accelerator Mass Spectrometry methods," Bob said as he pointed to the ancient items.

"You two probably remember from your archaeology classes," Bob looked at Mitch and Alex, "radiocarbon dating tests are only viable on organic matter. These tests should work on the two paintings and the book of scrolls as they were made from papyrus. However, the Carbon 14 tests won't work on the cylinders or the chest."

No one was speaking, they were all just listening, fascinated.

"That leads us to another story," Bob continued, "if these items are roughly 12,000 years old, then we could assume the cylinders and chest could be the same age as well, ignoring the fact that it's an absurd notion considering how advanced the cylinders look." He rubbed his eyes. "Jack and I can try to do preliminary Potassium-Argon Dating tests and then send the samples to the lab for Electron Spin Resonance Dating tests, which will hopefully confirm how old the chest is. The cylinders are going to be a little more tricky, but I can call in some favors to get this done quickly and quietly." Bob leaned back and wiped his forehead with his handkerchief.

Mitch and Alex considered the results in silence as the magnitude of this discovery hit them.

"Regarding the chest," Jack started, "there's something interesting we found out about it."

"What about it?" Alex asked.

"Looks like a plain and simple chest doesn't it? Except for all the weird symbols, of course," he added.

"What are you saying Jack?" Mitch prodded him.

"Well, you see, I thought I would take a closer look at it…"

"And?" Alex said impatiently. She knew Jack was trying to drag this out for effect, but her curiosity was getting the best of her.

"Jack, get to the point, quickly, if you don't mind. We haven't slept and I don't have the stamina for this right now," Bob said wearily.

"You know, you can be very rude sometimes," Jack replied, feigning hurt feelings.

"And you can be very irritating. Get on with it!"

"Fine!" Jack huffed. "I examined the chest carefully, thinking that was as good a place as any to start," he said, "and I found something odd…the chest has a false bottom. It was very well designed, mind you. I think I've just watched too many spy movies. Anyways, I spotted it. Come here and I'll show you."

Mitch and Alex felt like they were in a dream.

He pointed to a slab of stone he had removed, about half an inch thick, "It's cut from the same stone, fit to the exact dimensions."

"How did you…?" Mitch started to say.

"I was just examining it with a magnifying glass under bright lights. The chest is carved from a solid piece of stone, but I thought I noticed a thin line around the bottom, no wider than a hair, like it wasn't cut from the same piece of stone. At first I thought it was just shadows, but they were constant shadows. So I carefully felt around with a fine tool. Once I was certain I was on to something, I got Bob to help me and we tipped it. I carefully worked at it, until it came loose. We didn't want to break it. I tell ya, I had major hand and arm cramps, it took some doing, but we managed worked it free and intact, I might add!" Jack smiled proudly.

"And…" Alex asked nervously.

"And, my dear Miss Logan, we found this," Jack handed her a Ziploc bag with another small piece of papyrus in it. "I figured it would be best to keep it in a plastic bag for now, we didn't want to handle it too much."

"Good thinking," Alex said. She took it, her mouth dropping. Mitch came over to look at it as well. "These are hieroglyphs, Egyptian hiero-glyphs, and these…"

"Are the same style of symbols from the chest and the book of scrolls," Mitch said. "This is…"

"Another Rosetta Stone?" Jack offered, raising an eyebrow, referring to the discovery of the stone tablet that enabled Egyptologists to finally decipher hieroglyphs. Mitch and Alex just looked at him for a moment. He was absolutely right. Speechless, they returned their gaze to the precious piece of papyrus. "You're welcome, we were happy to find it for you," he added.

Both Mitch and Alex looked up and smiled at their pals, "You guys are the best, most amazing, most talented, clever…" she started.

"All right, all right," Bob said.

"No, no, what were you going to say after clever? Handsome? Charming? Brilliant?"

"Yes, Jack, that's exactly it, see now you can add telepathic to that list," she said, laughing.

Jack was grinning from ear to ear.

"Wait a minute…" Mitch said suddenly as a thought occurred to him. "I mean this is great and everything, but…"

"But what Mitch, is something wrong?" Alex asked.

"Well not wrong exactly," he started to say, "but if this is authentic, then it means there were people who had knowledge of this before-unknown ancient people or were from their time, and those people were also around for the periods of Egyptian history we are already familiar with."

"But there has previously been no record of such knowledge being passed down or such people living in ancient Egypt, let alone this form of written language," Alex added.

"This is unbelievable!" Mitch said. "Either someone had already found this and inexplicably said nothing, somehow translated it and then left it hidden, or whoever the people were who created these things, existed across both time periods. But there is no record of such people. I don't understand how this is possible."

Alex also realized the implications, "Bob, do you think it's safe for us to take the scrolls with us for analysis or are they too fragile?"

"Well, ordinarily, such incredibly old, written material would be too fragile to expose to the air, requiring special handling, but I had a careful look at them. They're still in amazingly good shape. They must have had some kind of protective treatment applied to them in ancient times. It looks like the term 'ordinary' doesn't apply here. I'd say you could safely begin examining them."

"We can start deciphering them, see what they say, find out who these people were," she said to Mitch.

He nodded, "Right," his eyes were wide with excitement and antici-pation.

Alex looked at the papyrus in the Ziploc bag then to the scrolls, "There isn't a huge number of symbols on it, considering the size of those scrolls, I wouldn't expect we have everything, but it's certainly a start. A fantastic start!"

"Incredible," Mitch exclaimed. "I can't even begin to say what this could mean." He paused for a moment, "And you're right Alex, we have to start somewhere. What we don't have we can perhaps interpolate, take educated guesses from context. Oh man, we have a lot of work to do," Mitch said as he ran his fingers through his hair. This is what he and Alex had lived for, hoped for all their lives, a part of history to discover that no one else knew anything about.

"We do, but it will have to be done in our off-hours, we can't get too far behind in our other work remember," Alex said, "and we can't keep this too long. We'll have to tell someone, Dustimaine, soon…but not until we have some answers."

"Guess you guys may finally have something to back up your crazy theories," Jack said smiling.

"You mean about the age of the Sphinx?" Bob asked.

Jack nodded, "That's exactly what I mean."

"It's not so crazy," Alex protested. "There are indications of rainwater run-off on the Sphinx itself and the walls around it that in all likelihood happened in a time where there was a lot more rainfall than there is today. In fact, some people have already theorized that those times could be as far back as 7000 to 9000 years ago. So, we're not the only ones barking up this particular tree."

"This could be the first solid evidence ever found to support such a time frame, and now it looks like it could be thousands of years older than even the boldest estimates had ever pegged it," Mitch stated.

"You know what Dustimaine is going to say if he hears you two bringing that up again," Jack said.

"We're not telling anyone anything yet, not until we have a few more answers," Alex replied.

"She's right," Mitch said. "We may have a start on things, but we have way more questions right now than answers. We'll analyze the scrolls and see what we can learn first."

"Agreed," Alex said, clapping her hands together. "So Bob, you'll look into having the cylinders analyzed?"

"Will do, and don't worry, I'll be discreet," Bob assured them.

"Thanks Bob," Mitch said.

"This is extraordinary, you've both done so much. I don't know what to say, we certainly didn't expect you two to stay up and do so much in one night," Alex said.

"Do you honestly think we could have left this once we started to realize what we had?" Jack piped in.

"No, I guess not," she agreed, laughing. "Mitch and I are going to have to get going and start getting ready for the day. You two should go get a couple of hours of shut-eye, then a nice long shower."

"Yeah, I could sure use a break, my eyes are so blurry I can barely see," Bob said as he rubbed them. "And I've got one mean headache."

"Alex and I will start looking at the scrolls tonight to see what we can find," Mitch said. "We need to keep this stuff locked up obviously. We can't be seen carting it around. Here," Mitch said as he pulled out a set of keys from his pocket. "Alex and I have a couple of lockers for our own use. This is the only spare key we have, so don't lose it," he said as he took a key off a key ring and handed it to Bob. "It's for this locker here," he said as he walked over to a series of lockers at the back of the lab. "It should be big enough. Let's lock everything up for now, before people start showing up for the day. You and Jack can come get the cylinders and scrolls when you have time and when no one is around."

They put the scrolls back in the cylinders and placed them inside the chest. They wrapped it up in the cloth, placed it back in the duffel bag and secured the locker.

"We'll touch base with you two after the day's excavations are done," Alex said. "Thank-you guys so much, we knew we could count on you. Just don't let anyone see or hear anything. We don't want Dr. Dust Bucket taking this away from us."

"Will do," Bob replied, mock-saluting them. "C'mon Jack, let's get out of here, we'll come back in a couple of hours."

"I'm all over that!" Jack said, now desperate for some sleep.

"Well, this is going to be the longest day ever," Alex said, wishing they could continue on this find right now.

"You know it," Mitch concurred.

The warm Egyptian Sun was setting down into the western horizon, shining a reddish-golden light over the land. The days were getting hotter as summer approached. It was getting late. Mitch and Alex had a particularly busy day and they were finishing up work later than they had hoped.

"Mitch! Alex!" Bob shouted, as he ran towards them. "I've been waiting for you, I have…" Bob said, trying to catch his breath. "I have to talk to you!" He motioned them over to where they could speak in private. "We have your results from the university," he said in a hushed voice, though he could not contain his excitement.

"Wow, we didn't expect them so fast," Alex whispered. "And?"

"It's confirmed. The scrolls are for sure almost 12,000 years old."

"Mitch, this is it!" Alex said excitedly as she grabbed his shoulder.

"So they're for real…" Mitch said, keeping his voice low. Bob nodded his head. "What do we do now?" Mitch asked, sounding worried. "Now that we know what we have here, should we inform Dustimaine?"

Alex shook her head, "Not yet. Let's take this one step at a time. Besides, we haven't had a chance to study the scrolls. I don't want to show our hand…yet."

Mitch smiled, "You realize, don't you, that we are getting deeper and deeper into trouble. We may not be able to pull ourselves out so easily."

"Why is that? That it's so easy to get into trouble, but not so easy to get out?" Alex remarked.

"Guys, guys, we need to go see Jack right away, there's more…we had the cylinders analyzed," Bob said. "We have the results and there's something else we need to tell you right away, but not here." He was looking around for anyone who might be within earshot. Mitch and Alex suddenly became a lot more serious.

"Then let's go right now," Mitch said. They followed Bob to the lab where Jack was waiting for them.

"Finally! Where have you two been? Have better things to do?" Jack asked sarcastically.

"Of course not, we were just bogged down with stuff and couldn't get away any earlier," Alex said.

"You'd better believe nothing else would be better than what we have to share with you," Jack replied.

"What have you found out?" Mitch asked.

Bob looked nervously over at Jack, neither one of them knew how to start.

"Guys, what is it, is something wrong with the cylinders?" Alex asked, concerned.

"Well, wrong is a subjective term…" Bob said.

"Yeah, exactly," Jack agreed, shaking his head.

Mitch looked at Alex. She shook her head that she didn't understand either. "Would either of you mind just being direct with us?" she asked.

"Well," Jack started, "you know about the age of the scrolls, the age was confirmed."

"Yes," Alex said, "continue."

Bob was too uncomfortable to talk about this, so Jack continued, "Well, Bob had the analysis done on the cylinders and they are uh…unusual."

"What do you mean unusual? You mean they're the same age as the scrolls?" Mitch asked.

"Yes, that's part of it, it seems quite likely that they're the same age, but…" Jack stalled.

"Jack! For heaven's sake, spit it out or I'll strangle you!" Alex was never one to be patient in matters of mystery. Jack feigned an expression of shock.

Bob finally worked up the courage to speak. "The metal alloy in them is not a known material. The elements are not part of the periodic table," he said just as quickly as he could get the words out.

Mitch and Alex just looked at him for a moment, blankly. Being scientists they understood intellectually what he was saying, but they were having trouble processing the information.

"Not…part…of the…periodic table?" Mitch repeated.

"Right," Jack said, "this metal has a completely unknown origin. It does not match anything known to modern science."

"This is a previously undiscovered metal? You mean something science has not yet identified?" Alex asked. "How is that possible?"

"How do you think?" Jack replied, raising his eyebrow.

"Jack, are you crazy? Maybe you should recheck the data," Mitch said.

"Already done, my man, twelve times," Jack answered.

Bob nodded in agreement, "We had to pull in some huge favors for this. We may not have any favors left. We didn't believe it ourselves at first. How could we?"

Alex sat down, "Are you saying this is extra-terrestrial in origin?"

Bob went crimson and couldn't answer.

"Hey, hey, hey, slow down!" Jack said. "All *we're* saying is it's not anywhere in the scientific record. We'll leave it to you two to draw your own conclusions."

CHAPTER

7

Into the Fire

Mitch and Alex told Jack and Bob to take the rest of the night off. The two had worked non-stop for two days and they knew they had to be exhausted. Plus, now that they had done their analyses it was time for Mitch and Alex to take the contents of the cylinders and begin their own. In light of what they had learned, they were almost afraid to. It looked like it was their turn to forego sleep this night. They made sure everyone else had left the lab for the night so they could work alone.

Their heads were swirling with ideas and possibilities. The metal of the cylinders troubled them greatly. There had to be some kind of reasonable explanation, something they had missed.

They had decided to focus on the task at hand and not let their imaginations run away with them. They began by conducting an overview of everything they had found so far, before proceeding to actually decipher the text. They hadn't gotten too far when they had come across a few interesting and startling finds.

At first glance, the text in the book of scrolls looked similar throughout, written in essentially the same language, but the writing style in the first half of the book was different. It was a more complex and ornate form than in the latter sections. The writing style of the title on the book's soft cover more closely matched that of the latter sections.

Unfortunately Bob had not been able to pinpoint the ages of the book or the papyrus paintings any further, but they postulated that the earlier sections of the book were likely a fair bit older than the later ones. The glyphs in the first part of the book were not as close a match to their 'Rosetta stone' papyrus, which they had dubbed the 'crib notes', as the pages nearer the end. In fact, they couldn't find any positive matches in the older sections right away. That would take further study, as the text was more intricate and stylized, much like old English compared to modern vernacular.

Mitch decided to take a closer look at the papyrus they had quickly glanced at earlier, while Alex continued to scan through the book of scrolls. Mitch found the painting quite intriguing. At first glance it appeared to be a depiction of some kind of funeral scene.

"Mitch! Look at this!" Alex exclaimed as she pointed to a drawing on one of the pages.

Mitch dropped what he was doing to see what she was pointing out. He could not believe his eyes, "It can't be..." he whispered.

"I know! I know! I swear my heart has never beaten so fast," she said. "What do you think?"

Mitch could only stare at the depiction before him.

It was eerie, yet something they had long pictured in their own minds. It was of a monument carved in the form of a seated lion. It was extraordinary in the detail, the curvatures of the body, the paws – the head crowned with a thick mane. The lion's gaze was serene, beautiful – powerful – the features were exquisitely carved and painted. The mane was painted red, brown, tan and bright gold, the golden eyes were rimmed with black, and the body seemed to have a coppery-bronze sheen to it.

"Mitch, say something, this has to be it – it, it's exact. The shape, the relative size to its surroundings, the pose. Everything except..."

"The head," he said, finishing her sentence.

She nodded, "This can't be a coincidence Mitch. This has to be it!" She stared off for a moment, "This is the proof that we've hoped for. The

Sphinx is nearly 12,000 years old and it originally had a lion's head, which at some later date it was altered to be the head of the pharaoh. We were right all along! Though it's even a lot older than we thought…"

"Alex, hold on a minute. I think there's an awful lot here we don't know."

"But Mitch, it's right here! Besides, if you'll recall, archaeologists have speculated that the Sphinx may have originally had some kind of covering over it. This shows that to be the case. And you know that in Ancient Egypt, showing an animal, particularly a lion, in this fashion indicated it represented a protective deity. It fits. This could be our proof!"

"Alex, are you forgetting the cylinders these things were found in? I don't recall us discussing those kinds of possibilities before."

"Well, we'll get to the bottom of that…somehow. There has to be an explanation, some kind of mix-up in the results…"

"And if there wasn't a mix-up, if the results are accurate? Then what?" Alex didn't know what to say to that. "Exactly my point," Mitch emphasized. "We are getting ourselves into trouble here, we've already kept this stuff too long without telling anyone."

"Mitch, are you nuts? We can't show this to anyone now! Look, if what the results are telling us is accurate, and that's a big if I might add, we cannot just hand this over – we don't know what would happen if we did."

Mitch looked away.

"Look, let's just stay the course for now. We'll start deciphering the actual texts. That has to give us some answers at least. We'll work as fast as we can and once we know more, we'll decide what to do then."

Mitch shook his head. He knew they were getting deeper and deeper into hot water and he was getting very nervous about what they had possession of. If they were caught with these items and hadn't reported it, they could be jailed. "You realize we are risking our careers doing this, don't you?"

"I'm hoping this is going to make our careers," Alex replied. "Please Mitch, let's just keep working on this a bit more. We have to do this, it's the opportunity of a lifetime."

"All right, but we have to keep in mind that we can't do everything on our own. There are people we have to answer to eventually," he said.

"I know, I know," she said. "I'll go make some coffee, I'll grab an orange juice for you, and we can get back to it. What the heck, it's been awhile since we stayed up all night, it'll be fun," Alex smiled as she got up and headed over to the coffee pot and fridge.

"Or perhaps if you could fall on your face again and stumble onto a relic with the answer, that would save us a lot of time and work," Mitch said with a straight face, trying hard to suppress a grin.

Alex gave him a withering look, muttering something about the intelligence of non-coffee drinkers under her breath.

8

Trouble in the Royal Family

Circa 10,000 B.C.

"Good day, your Majesty, are you ready for our morning walk?" Queen Axiana's handmaiden, Mindara, asked. She was a kind person with a warm smile, and light green eyes, which gave her face a youthful quality. She always kept her long black hair tightly braided down her back, so it would be out of the way and out of her eyes.

"I was thinking about going out alone today," the Queen responded.

The two women had been friends since they were children, they were the same age and although Mindara worked for the Royal Family, she was also Axiana's closest confidante.

"Oh," Mindara replied, disappointed, "is anything wrong?"

"I have just had a lot on my mind since Traeus and I visited the priests almost five months ago. I have not been feeling well or sleeping well in the last while, but it may only be stress over wanting a baby. I am also taking the new remedies Senarra had prescribed to help Traeus and I conceive."

"I understand, if you need to talk to me, about anything at all, I am here for you," Mindara replied, smiling reassuringly.

"Thank-you, Mindara," Axiana said as she embraced her friend.

Axiana walked to the gardens, which were located behind the Palace, in the southern part of the Royal compound.

The eighty-room stone Palace building was located in the center of a forty-acre compound. The multi-storied, curvilinear structure was made up of several interlinking sections. The servants' quarters were located in a separate wing attached to the Palace. Within the compound were the barracks where the Royal guards lived. Numerous tropical trees and plants decorated the courtyard and provided pleasant shade. Orchards were also kept providing fresh fruit year round. Colorful banners, gleaming from the tops of towers and spires, proudly displayed the Royal Family's crest.

A three-foot high hedge enclosed most of the compound with an immense gate barring entrance to the Palace from the north. Affixed to the gate was a set of massive walls and battlements, on top of which, Royal soldiers regularly patrolled. Directly south of the gardens was a dense tropical forested-area, affording security and protection, with its wildlife and thick foliage.

The gardens were meticulously cared for by the groundskeepers and were lush and alive with beauty – all kinds of fragrant, colorful flowers, birds, fruit trees, small ponds with fish and turtles. Little stone pathways wound their way through.

The Queen had been walking with no particular path in mind for about twenty minutes, when she thought she heard some rustling off in the distance. She followed the sound to the one of the outer edges of the gardens, but still did not see anything. She listened for another moment and realized the sounds were coming from behind a row of bushes that lined the outer walls.

Curiosity getting the best of her, she decided to press through the bushes to see what the noise was. As she walked through, branches getting entangled in her hair, she called out, "Hello? Is someone back here?" She paused for a moment, hearing further rustling.

Then a voice answered back, "Who is there?"

"It is Axiana. Zazmaria is that you?" she asked as she made it through to the other side of the bushes.

Zazmaria stood up quickly, brushing off her skirts, a basket by her side. "I was not expecting anyone. You startled me." Zazmaria's voice was crisp.

"I was just going for a walk. I needed some air. I have not felt too well lately." Axiana looked away, momentarily lost in thought. "When I heard you through the bushes I thought I would come see who it was tucked away in this far corner."

"I see," Zazmaria replied. "Well, is there something I can do for you, your Highness?"

"Oh no, not at all. Please Zazmaria, I have asked you so many times, just call me Axiana. We are family. We have no need of such formalities between us." Axiana looked over at the basket and decided to try and change the subject, "What are you picking?"

"I, uh I, keep my own herbs back here, out of the way, so that the cooks do not find them and use them all for their own creations. Just some of my favorites, no one knows they are here."

"Well, I will not tell anyone," Axiana smiled. "May I give you a hand with anything?"

"No, I am almost finished," Zazmaria answered abruptly. "You mentioned you had not felt too well lately. May I ask what is the matter?" Zazmaria's tone had changed all of a sudden. She seemed interested and caring now rather than just bothered.

Axiana hesitated. She was unsure of what to say, how to answer. She found it difficult to talk to Zazmaria, let alone confide in her. Axiana smiled, she had for so long wished to bond with her sister-in-law. Perhaps this was a chance to do just that. "Well, actually, I needed some help, I mean Traeus and I needed help." Axiana felt a little awkward, but continued, "We have been trying for an heir for quite some time…"

"And you have been unable to conceive?"

Axiana nodded. "We finally decided to seek some guidance. Priestess Senarra provided me with some remedies. We understand she is very skilled in these matters. I am certain her remedies will help. I may be simply adjusting to them. I have had some difficulty sleeping, but I think may be just putting a lot of pressure on myself."

"I understand, this is an important part of life, especially for a Queen," Zazmaria responded.

"Exactly! It is one thing to desperately want to be a mother, which I have always longed to be, but being Queen and knowing everyone is watching you, waiting, eagerly anticipating the birth of an heir...it is overwhelming," Axiana conceded.

"I can imagine," Zazmaria replied, her expression darkening for a moment. "Axiana, I think I can help you with this. My great-grandmother developed a recipe for a special tea for this problem. It cannot guarantee you will have a child, but it was designed to help a woman relax, and allow nature to take its course more freely. I could prepare some for you if you like."

"That would be wonderful, Zazmaria! I would appreciate any help you could give me."

"I will stop by your rooms tonight."

"Thank-you so much," Axiana beamed. "I will see you this evening, then."

Zazmaria watched the Queen walk away then resumed her work, deep in thought.

9

☥

Potions and Herbs

Two more weeks had passed, and now giving in to frustration, the King and Queen had gone to consult with the priesthood again. The Priestess Senarra was particularly gifted in the areas of healing and alchemy and she often taught those disciplines to the younger members of the order. She was the foremost healer in Kierani society despite her young age, and was the primary healer attending the Royal Family.

Senarra performed some tests, including checking the Queen's blood pressure and heart rate, she said nothing, but had a look of concern in her face. Finally, she performed a detailed examination of Axiana's eyes to complete the series of tests.

"Your eyes are showing signs that something is wrong. May I ask about your diet and exercise routine if there have been any changes, or if you are stressed about anything, or have been feeling ill recently?"

"I-I just thought it was all the worry about having a baby. I have felt somewhat nauseous the last while and I have not slept well. I take walks almost daily and try to take proper care of myself," the Queen assured her. "In fact, I have not even gone sailing in quite some time, and I cannot tell you how much I miss that!" she laughed, then continued, "Though, feeling ill the last while, I do not think I would have been able to."

Axiana was an experienced sailor and navigator. It was something she had grown up with. A love of sailing ran in her family, they would often go sailing for family outings, packing picnics, exploring nature. Those were some of her fondest childhood memories. Her husband, however, was never keen on her sailing alone.

"I understand," Senarra smiled. "You have shown remarkable resolve if you have voluntarily banished yourself solely to land!" They both laughed. "Have you been eating or drinking anything different lately? Something you started having after our last meeting?"

Axiana thought back. "The only thing new is an herbal tea that Zazmaria gave me, but that was a couple of weeks ago. She said that it might help to relax me, to help me conceive. I have been having some nightly."

"What is in it?" Senarra asked.

"Flowers, some spice I think. I usually take it with a bit of honey."

"It sounds innocent enough," Senarra said, "but perhaps you could bring me the recipe from Zazmaria. I would like to be thorough in my analysis."

"Certainly, I will speak with her tomorrow."

The next day, Axiana brought the recipe from Zazmaria to Senarra and exchanged it for the potion Senarra had created for her, which she was to take morning and night for one week. Senarra studied the tea recipe. It was a normal tea blend except for one ingredient Senarra was unfamiliar with, but it seemed harmless enough, just an herb Zazmaria grew in the garden. Senarra decided however to at least mention it to Assan.

The Queen left with her new potion, buoyed with hope.

That night, after Axiana had taken her dose of Senarra's new potion, she decided to retire early. She fell asleep and started dreaming almost immediately.

She saw herself taking the potion Senarra had given her. She poured some into a jeweled goblet, and drank it down. It seemed to react within her instantly. She felt a warm, white light passing quickly throughout her body as the potion worked its magic. She felt herself float above the bed, lighter than air, and saw the light all around her. She felt she was being renewed, healed.

She looked around the room and saw she was no longer floating above the bed, but she was walking along the banks of the great river. Ahead she saw a full moon, which seemed to cast a white light for miles.

Suddenly she was standing on the water, still feeling a beautiful warm light all around her. She felt her stomach tingle and surge with a strange, but pleasant sensation. She held her belly and felt it grow beneath her hands.

She heard a sound and turned around quickly. Zazmaria was standing on the riverbank staring intently at her. Zazmaria raised her hands as if in offering, but Axiana could not see what she held.

Immediately, Axiana felt a change in the water and she fell through the water's surface into the icy, dark depths of the river. She struggled to reach the surface, but felt herself sinking ever lower, darkness now completely surrounding her. She felt her system going into shock.

Axiana awoke with a start, and sat straight up. She was covered in a cold sweat and was shaking. She wondered how a dream, which had started out so comforting and peaceful, could end up so terrifying.

10

⚱

The Draxens

The guards stood at attention as Zhek, grandson of Lord Draxen, entered his grandfather's private chamber, which overlooked the courtyard of their large, expansive residence.

The home was called the Draxen Stronghold. It was situated on the edge of town, but due to its immense size and imposing appearance, it dominated the district, dwarfing the other homes nearby.

The Draxens were a powerful, wealthy family, second in status and influence only to the Royal Family itself. For generations, the Draxens had exerted strong political influence over Kierani affairs and had been involved in all matters and decisions of importance.

Lord Draxen, the patriarch of this family, was personally involved in every aspect of their business and other affairs and ran things with ruthless efficiency. Discipline and obedience were paramount in his world, and it was very much, his world. He was a strong man, both in word and deed, and in spite of his eighty years, was still a very intimidating person and greatly feared.

However, since the new King had come to power, things had changed and not to the Draxens' benefit. Lord Draxen, although not liked by

King Mesah, had nevertheless been tolerated by him and given a voice in most matters due to the family's long-standing social position.

Now that Mesah's son Traeus had become King that relationship had diminished. Traeus was keeping matters more within the Royal Family and less and less did he involve those outside his tight inner circle. Upon King Mesah's death, Lord Draxen had anticipated having even greater influence over the decisions of the Royal Family who would now have a young and inexperienced, and he hoped, malleable, King leading it, but he had been sorely disappointed.

"Grandfather, I have just come from taking a look at the construction site. It seems work on it is progressing rather quickly."

"Yes, Zhek, so I have noticed," Lord Draxen replied rather coldly. "It is inconceivable that Mesah's eldest son thinks he can get away with keeping us out of that project altogether. Never before has our family been excluded from participating in, and profiting from such an undertaking."

"I know Grandfather, but perhaps we should not be so...disappointed," he offered. "After all, it is only a stone monument."

"Only a monument!" Lord Draxen nearly exploded. "Is that what you think?"

Zhek was taken aback at the sudden and unexpected outburst. He had been treated harshly most of his life by his ruthless grandfather, but in spite of that, he still had a strong sense of loyalty to the man who had basically raised him from the age of six, when Zhek's parents were killed in an accident. Zhek, though only twenty-seven years old, was the foremost ranking member of the Draxen clan, next to his grandfather. He even outranked Lord Draxen's own surviving sons.

Zhek was an only child. He had tried many times to ask his grandfather about the cause of the mysterious accident, which took his parents' lives, but Lord Draxen would never talk about it. He would only say that it was too painful for him to talk about the death of his eldest son. Still, Zhek tried hard to live up to his father's example.

"That giant lump of rock you saw out there is much more than a simple monument, and do you know why?" Lord Draxen asked.

"It is going to be symbolic, be..." Zhek stammered.

"It is going to be the largest scale project ever undertaken here, and due to its 'unique' design, will pack an emotional and spiritual punch like nothing the people have seen since coming here!" Lord Draxen said impatiently.

The King had informed the Draxens about what was being undertaken, but had declined their offer of assistance in both the planning and construction phases of the project, in spite of Lord Draxen's earnest protestations.

"As a result, that monument will resonate with the people, draw them together and focus all their attentions and sense of loyalty and gratitude, and on whom do you think?" Lord Draxen asked. He moved to within mere inches of Zhek's face, "Not to us."

"I understand," Zhek said, backing away.

"Do you? I am not certain that you do," he said as he stepped forward again. "Now that Traeus is King, this also sets precedence, a dangerous precedence for us. For you see, Zhek, what is to prevent him from blocking our participation in the future, on even more important projects or decisions? If he achieves this on his own, he has proven himself, that he does not need or want our help, and in effect he will have severed certain political ties with us. Then, the next thing we know, the Draxen family will have no part in deciding the future of our people!" he shouted. "This is no oversight on his part, this is deliberate. He will regret this – mark my words, Zhek."

Zhek did not know what to say to that, he knew his grandfather did not make idle threats. But whatever else Lord Draxen was, he was an extremely intelligent and ambitious man who fought hard for his family's interests and would do anything to protect them. Zhek knew just how dangerous his grandfather could be when he felt an injustice had been done to him or his family.

Lord Draxen took a deep breath and composed himself. He would bide his time. He looked at Zhek standing there and thought how of all his children and grandchildren, Zhek was the only one who had shown the level of ambition and potential he required for his second-in-command. He needed Zhek now more than ever – everything was at stake. He knew he had been hard on Zhek throughout his life, but it had been to push him to be a strong, tough leader, capable of taking care of the family once the torch was passed.

"How are the training exercises coming, Zhek?"

"Very well, Grandfather," Zhek replied as he walked over to the large window overlooking the courtyard, relieved the topic had changed to something Zhek felt confident in. "Our soldiers are adapting to the new weapons and tactics. Our military leaders are adopting new strategies for the weapons that are available. Other Houses, including the Royal Family, have adopted strategies similar to ours. However, it would seem we are still holding our military superiority over all of them, even the Royal Family."

"But the Royal Family has its allies," Lord Draxen remarked, "and the support of the people. They would fight for their King. It is rather strange. The people still cling to the old ways of governing. They do not demand a new leader, when by rights they should, but old alliances are still maintained, still mired in the past," Lord Draxen said with contempt. He reflected on matters he had not yet shared with anyone, "We must maintain our military preparedness."

"We have been able to recruit and train new soldiers," Zhek said optimistically, "and we have tried to do it as secretly as possible."

Lord Draxen smiled, pleased, and watched the Draxen soldiers drilling and training in the main courtyard. "Excellent. You have done well."

He paused for a moment, his thoughts going back to their earlier discussion, "Zhek, I want to keep a closer eye on the activities at the construction site. King Traeus must have a compelling reason for keeping us away from it, to break with the old traditions…perhaps there is something there he does not want us to see. And if that is the case, it is within our best interests to find out precisely what it is."

"A wise precaution, Grandfather. I would agree, the Royal Family cannot be trusted or taken at face value," Zhek replied.

"Exactly. See you are beginning to understand," he smiled, patting Zhek on the shoulder. "Have our top spy, Jace look into this matter – quietly. I want to know anything and everything I can about what our young reticent King is up to."

"Yes, Grandfather, I will take care of it at once," Zhek said and bowed as he left.

Lord Draxen continued to watch his soldiers instructing new recruits on tactics and how to use their new, crude weapons. The Draxens had built a large wall, which now surrounded the grounds behind the main house, to hide such activity.

Traeus' father, King Mesah had tried time and again to dissuade Lord Draxen from building such a wall, but without success. He had greatly disliked what it represented – one family closed off from the rest of their society.

The Draxen Stronghold was not built for luxury but for strength. The main building was located in the center of the grounds, stood several stories high and was currently the tallest structure in the city, but that would change once the Amsara monument was complete, another insult from the Royal Family. Multiple balconies, located high above ground surrounded all sides of the building, allowed the Draxens to monitor all who came to their building and provided them with a high ground strategic advantage.

A spacious courtyard in front of the building permitted large numbers of troops to train or defend the manor. A thick wall of roughly hewn stone encircled the complex. The wall interconnected with several towers containing un-paned windows, where Draxen soldiers stood on guard day and night.

Many people secretly spoke of their intense dislike for the unattractive and militaristic compound. Its design was at odds with the beauty of the rest of the city and cast an imposing shadow over all who passed by.

11

Unveiling Amsara Ceremony

I t had now been three and a half years since Traeus became King and the day had finally come to unveil the completed Amsara monument. As the first large-scale project in his reign, he had been anxious to see it finished. Now that day was here, he could not be more excited and hopeful about the impact it would have on his people.

Traeus had gathered his subjects in front of the massive limestone creature for the official Unveiling Ceremony. Everyone had come. Victarius and his team had been assigned a special seating area at the side of the stage, which had been erected for the ceremony, as places of honor for their hard work and dedication.

Also seated near the front of the crowd were Commander Koronius and his captains. The Commander was impressed with the young King. He wished very much that Traeus' father, the Commander's good friend and life-long leader, King Mesah, could have been there to witness this proud moment.

The Royal Family, including the reluctant Prince Alaj and Princess Zazmaria, who had both initially declined to attend until Traeus made it clear that they would not get away with that behavior again, were all dressed in their finest garments, bejeweled and attractively groomed. They were protected from the midday sun by a multi-layered canopy.

King Traeus stepped forward to make his speech, with his Queen standing proudly by his side, "For so long now Chief Engineer Victarius has overseen the project that my father envisioned many long years ago. Victarius and his talented team have been working tirelessly to craft a magnificent stone figure. You all know it. It is a symbol of the mythical lion, Amsara, who long ago saved a King."

Everyone was familiar with the legend of the ancient King Narmethon, whose life was saved by a magical lion, and who then went on to lead his people into an age of peace that lasted a thousand years.

Head Priest Assan, Priest Odai and Priestess Senarra also stood next to the Royal Family as was customary for official functions.

Odai had the male lion, Amsara, with him. The lion was on a leash, and sat calmly by observing the crowd while his friend and caregiver Odai stroked his thick mane. Odai had found the lion cub nine years ago in the bushes several leagues south down the river. Its mother had abandoned it and the cub was barely alive.

Odai and Senarra were new to the priesthood at the time. They had joined that very same year. They had been sent to gather herbs for one of their lessons in herb lore. Odai heard a soft whimper in the distance and went to investigate. He found the small, dying cub and immediately took it in. Odai had begged Assan to allow him to take care of the cub and keep it at the temple. Assan agreed, recalling the legend of King Narmethon. This cub's life had been spared by providence so Assan decided to name the cub Amsara and designated it the living embodiment of the legendary creature.

Amsara shook his massive head and nuzzled Odai's hand. Senarra smiled at the heartwarming sight.

Traeus held his hands out to the crowd, "This gift that your Royal Family presents to you – to all of you, will be a symbol of our combined strength and endurance. Sadly, my father, the great King Mesah, died before he could see his dream come to life, but our family pledged to see his vision through to completion."

Alaj bristled at that comment. Traeus knew damn well that not everyone in the family pledged themselves to this.

Zazmaria looked up at her husband whose steely gaze was fixed on the crowd. "They certainly do buy into his blatant propaganda," she said in a hushed tone.

Alaj did not answer, but continued to stare straight ahead.

Ignoring the whispers he detected behind him, Traeus went on with his speech, "Today, we are blessed to have with us both the living embodiment of Amsara and now an eternal representation of your protector that has risen from mere stone, which will watch over you with immortal eyes. In memory of my beloved father, King Mesah, it is with great honor and pride that I present to you, Amsara, the eternal lion!" Traeus now stood with his arms outstretched, his garments blowing in the soft breeze.

As if on cue, Amsara, the living, breathing version stood up.

The crowd cheered as the series of tarps made from fine Kierani linen were pulled from the front of the colossal monument and the breezes made the covering seem to float away, revealing, at long last, the grand achievement.

The people gasped when they saw the magnificent countenance of Amsara, regally sitting facing due east, so that each day it would welcome the dawn. The face had been painted to make it look at once life-like and yet otherworldly. Its face seemed to be imbued with wisdom and grace as it stared out over the horizon, as though it knew it would one day guard hidden things, deeper mysteries. The golden eyes were strikingly rimmed in black and whiskers were sculpted into its face. Its mane was carved to be thick and full and was painted in shades of brown, red and tan, with bright golden streaks throughout it. The curve of the body was realistic, one could well imagine the beast standing up at any moment and letting out a deafening roar.

The entire body had been overlaid with a protective outer covering, which had a beautiful coppery-bronze sheen to it. The effect was dazzling as the sun hit its surface. Each morning, the rays of the rising sun would make a dramatic spectacle, as though each new day would now begin with a miracle in which they could all share.

Traeus read aloud the inscription that had been elegantly carved into the outer covering of the monument's chest, between its massive paws, "

'May Amsara protect and watch over you through eternity as the stars watch over him.'"

Thunderous applause broke out.

Traeus felt a great sense of satisfaction, knowing the words had a deeper meaning, a deeper purpose than would be made known for now. He glanced over at Alaj, he too seemed momentarily awed by what he saw, but then a shadow swept across his face and he became angry. Traeus caught Zazmaria staring at him with a look of barely concealed contempt. She quickly looked away when their eyes met.

Members of the Draxen family had also watched the ceremony. Lord Draxen was still incensed that his family had not participated in this project. To make matters worse, Jace had still not been able to find out anything more about it, which infuriated him.

The King had kept an unprecedented level of control over the project. No one, except those working at the site, had been allowed near it.

Lord Draxen stood up. "We are leaving!" he ordered.

Zhek took note of Prince Alaj and Princess Zazmaria's demeanor. He watched them both closely throughout the whole ceremony. He got up at his grandfather's request, but as they left, he looked back at the Prince and Princess.

The King and Queen retired to the Royal couple's bedroom after an exhausting day of ceremonies and pageantry.

"Today was a very tiring day," Axiana said, as she removed her jewelry and ceremonial attire. "But a momentous one."

"The Amsara monument will give our people a sense of hope and purpose," said Traeus. "One day, it will reunite all our people."

"Yes dear husband, but I was not referring to that."

Traeus looked puzzled.

She reached across for his hand, "My husband, I have something to share with you," she said as she placed his hand on her belly. "I met with Senarra early this morning and she explained to me why I have been feeling ill lately."

Traeus, speechless, looked into her eyes, his own tearing up. "You are saying…"

She pulled him close and kissed him passionately. She looked deep into his eyes and beamed, "You are going to make a wonderful father."

CHAPTER

12

♀

The Beginning of the Legend

T he city was abuzz with news of the pregnancy. People talked of nothing else. It was widely believed that the new Amsara monument had brought good fortune. Many small offerings of flowers and handmade objects were left, both at the Amsara site as well as at the Palace gates. The elated King and Queen reveled in the out-pouring of love and well wishes that flowed into the Palace.

Axiana's pregnancy was going remarkably well, she felt in great health. Incredibly, Senarra informed her that there were two heartbeats. The Queen was having twins. Traeus happily received the news and saw it as a special blessing bestowed upon them, but Axiana was concerned. Senarra had cautioned her that there was a chance that one twin may not survive. Twins were not common among the Kierani people, nor were there a history of them in Axiana's family.

Finally, the day came when Axiana went into labor, attended by Senarra and Assan. The twins, one girl and one boy, were born healthy. Both had thick shocks of black hair, the same as their parents.

"Your Majesties, have you chosen names for them?" Senarra asked the elated new parents.

Traeus stood by Axiana's side, beaming. Axiana looked up at her husband, who nodded and replied, "Yes, we have, but we wanted to wait until after they were born to announce them. Axiana had a dream one night that we were having a boy and girl."

Axiana spoke up, "Their names will be Tramen and Anjia."

"Wonderful, strong names," Assan smiled. "The name, Tramen, it means, 'Warrior of Light', does it not?" he asked.

"Yes," Axiana replied kissing her newborn son's head. "And Anjia means 'Carrier of Light'".

Assan smiled and placed his hands on each of the twin's heads, "Tramen, Warrior of Light and Anjia, Carrier of Light, you are given to your parents King Traeus and Queen Axiana as blessings beyond measure, to uphold and embody the values of your people. May those of us who are here to teach you be endowed with wisdom and understanding so that we may guide you well along your journey through life. Know always, the power you have within and may you use that power for good and for the benefit of your people and for each other."

He then placed a small pure gold ankh over each of the baby's hearts, bowed his head, placed a hand on each of the baby's heads, and closed his eyes reciting a prayer in the ancient tongue.

Both twins seemed alert and attentive and had not uttered a single cry since he had placed his large hands on their tiny heads. Assan finished, looking at each of them and smiled. He gave the amulets to Traeus, "Please take these sacred amulets, which have been infused with the life of your children, and they in turn, with the power of the ankh – our symbol of everlasting life."

13

☥

Secrets

Victarius made his way into the King's office carrying an armload of papers. Both Traeus and Assan were waiting for him inside. Victarius greeted them.

"Good day," Traeus greeted the Chief Engineer.

"I brought what you asked for. These are the blueprints for the device along with the tunnel and chambers, which has been designed to house it underneath the Amsara monument. My team and I just finished the plans late last night," Victarius said as he unrolled the documents and set them on the table. "Your Majesty, do you have a name for this device you have commissioned?"

"Actually, Assan has come up with a name that has an historic origin. This device will be called the Pharom," said Traeus.

"Pharom?" Victarius asked. "I have never heard of such a name, but then again I studied the sciences, not history."

"But Master Victarius, history is a science," Assan interjected. "If we do not know our past, especially the mistakes, we are destined to repeat them, would you not agree?" Victarius smiled and then nodded his agreement. Assan continued, "Do you recall the ancient legend of the lost travelers and how their misfortunes could have been avoided?"

"Ah yes, I do remember that tale, interesting illustration," Victarius remarked. "I would have to say then, that your choice of names is perfect, Assan."

"What is the status of the design for the Pharom?" Traeus asked.

"Well, out of necessity it will be a highly complex design. We will begin work on the specifications once the chamber is completed. As discussed, it will all take a long time to complete. It really is ingenious to adapt your father's design of the monument to incorporate this device. However, I do believe we have all the resources we require to construct the device... I mean Pharom."

"Thank-you Victarius," Traeus said.

"I feel compelled to add though," Victarius continued, "we must proceed with every precaution. What we are creating is powerful, and as such must be treated with the utmost care and protection. The Pharom in the wrong hands would be disastrous."

Traeus nodded, "I understand the gravity of the situation."

Assan thought for a moment. "This reminds me though of another legend, the one that told the story of how a young boy was able to harness a similar energy without any sort of technological device. It was said he used the energy to communicate with others in mysterious ways, over great distances with only the power of his thought."

"Assan," Victarius laughed, "you put too much faith in children's stories. It will be an incredibly daunting task to create this technological device as you call it, which will attempt to achieve our King's aims. I hardly think it would be possible to achieve such things without it."

"With all due respect, Chief Engineer," Assan said, "I believe many things are possible that we do not yet know how to achieve, and many things that will be understood one day, remain as yet a mystery, hidden from us, though we seek this knowledge in earnest."

Suddenly Alaj barged into Traeus' office and slammed the door behind him. His sudden entrance caught Traeus, Victarius and Assan off guard. They had no time to conceal the blueprints on the table.

"I heard you were in 'private meetings' today and were not to be disturbed. Tell me brother, what are you doing here? Anything I should be informed about, but somehow was not?"

Traeus ignored the cynicism in his voice, "Good day, Alaj."

Assan and Victarius also politely greeted the angry Prince.

"What are these?" Alaj inquired abruptly, as he pointed to the blueprints and walked right over to them, ignoring the greetings. Luckily for Traeus, the blueprints for the design of the Pharom were underneath those of the chamber and tunnel.

"It is just part of the full design of the Amsara site. They are blueprints for a tunnel and chamber underneath the site, which I have directed Victarius to complete," Traeus said as matter-of-factly as he could. He decided that since it was too late to hide the blueprints, he would just try to downplay the matter altogether.

"Why have you not mentioned this before?" Without waiting for an answer, he asked, "What is this chamber supposed to be for anyways? I do not remember seeing this in our father's plans," Alaj asked as he hastily looked over the blueprints.

Victarius was visibly nervous. Assan's face bore no expression.

"Alaj, calm down, it is nothing to be concerned about. Just something I decided to add on…" Traeus had started to say.

Alaj rudely interrupted him, "You never change, do you? Hiding things from me, making secret plans!" He was fuming now.

"Alaj, it is merely a chamber for the priests to keep their most sacred items and a place for their private meditations. It was my idea to add it on to our father's designs. I thought it would be a valuable, functional addition to the Amsara monument to give it even greater meaning and purpose," Traeus replied coolly, trying to maintain his composure.

"The priests? They already have several temples!" Alaj shouted. "This is a pretty elaborate design. How did they talk you into this?"

"Nobody talked me into anything, Alaj. I told you, it was my idea and mine alone! They are going to use it for special meditative practices," Traeus responded hotly.

"Well, how generous of you. They really have the King at their disposal. If only the rest of the people were so fortunate," Alaj replied with heavy sarcasm. "Special meditative practices? What does that mean anyways?"

Assan quickly realized Traeus was digging himself into a very deep hole, so he decided to try to salvage the situation. "Prince Alaj, if I may offer – they are ancient customs within our order, and there are also things we, in cooperation with the King, would like to achieve for the people. The Amsara site is especially significant to us. Having this area below it to use for these practices will aid us in being of better service to the people. The advantages, though not immediately apparent from these plans, will be great, I assure you and will be for the benefit for all."

The only thing that made Traeus feel not entirely horrible about this exchange was that there was also a measure of truth in Assan's statements. "Helping the priesthood helps all of us, Alaj. I wish you could see that," Traeus added.

Alaj looked from Traeus to Assan and back again, his eyes narrowing. "No one else knows about this do they? Just your little group here?" No reply came. "Ah, I thought so. Tell me brother, how do you think our people would react to the priests having such special – not to mention – secretive, privileges?" He shot a disparaging glance at Assan.

"Alaj, the people will be informed of everything we are doing here…in due time," Traeus said emphasizing his last words.

"Why is it necessary to have this secrecy at all? Especially from me!" Alaj shouted.

"You are making more out of this than there is," Traeus said.

Alaj laughed bitterly, "I do not think so! You insult me. You are the one who has now created all the suspicion through your secret plans and secret meetings. Maybe I should just start informing people of this!"

"Alaj, please, I do not wish to argue with you all the time." He was afraid this conversation was getting out of control. "I need you elsewhere, you know how much I depend on your help to run this society. Do not overreact to this!"

"Me? I am not the one conspiring in private meetings!" His tone was now becoming quite hostile. "I do not agree with or support having elaborate and costly private underground chambers for priests! It is absurd!"

"Enough, Alaj!" Traeus shouted, matching his brother's tone. "I understand you do not approve of these plans, but we are not doing anything to harm you or anyone else, nor are our aims selfish. However you must learn to afford me the respect that is due a King. I have the right to make decisions I think are in the best interest of our people. When the time is right I will tell our people of this project, but that is my responsibility, not yours. Do I make myself clear?"

"Have it your way, for now brother. But I will not forget this," Alaj warned.

14

Zazmaria's Impatience Grows

"Alaj? What is wrong?" Zazmaria asked as she heard her husband slam the door to their chambers.

Alaj sighed heavily, he was in a foul mood and really wanted to be alone, but he knew his wife would not let it go. "My brother has been keeping a rather large secret from me it seems."

Zazmaria saw how angry he was. "What secret?"

"I just happened to walk in on a private meeting. He is finalizing plans for a tunnel and chamber below the Amsara monument. Supposedly, it is for the priests and their 'special meditative practices'. Apparently they collectively decided I did not need to be informed."

"What? I have never heard of these 'special meditative practices'. What does that mean?" Zazmaria asked.

"Good question, I asked the very same thing myself without getting much of an answer."

"Well, why have they not told anyone about this?"

"Interesting, is it not?" Alaj commented, raising an eyebrow.

"And this is just for the priests?" she asked.

"Apparently so."

"That is quite the preferential treatment. Is that not a bit excessive, even for them?" She continued, "Not to mention suspicious since there have been no announcements about it, even within the family?"

"Exactly my point," Alaj stated.

"Why does this chamber have to be located beneath the monument? Are their temples not good enough for them anymore? Now they must hide below the ground?"

"The explanation I was given for the exorbitant expense of effort and resources is apparently because the image of the lion Amsara has such special significance for them, and will help them to fulfill their roles in our society better. It is ridiculous!"

"Whose idea was this?" she asked, suspecting the answer.

"My dear brother Traeus."

"I thought so. How long has this been going on?"

"Oh I would guess since they began constructing that damn monument! And now, even now that I know, he does not want me involved. He said I am needed elsewhere and that I should not make too much of it."

"I have told you for a long time, Alaj that you were not being treated as you deserve to be. I do not trust him and neither should you!"

"Zazmaria, I do not wish to get into that old argument right now."

"You are right, Alaj, what we need to discuss right now is how we can begin to change things. We cannot allow this to continue any longer."

"What do you suggest I do? Force him to tell me things? He is the way he is."

"He is that way because you allow it. You have to stand up to him! You have to be stronger than that, Alaj. And yes, I do think you have to be forceful about it. You are a Royal Prince. You deserve to be involved in all these decisions. Do you think it is right that those arrogant priests practically outrank you? It is a disgrace!"

"Enough! I do not need this from you right now!"

"You know what you need right now, husband?" she shot back. "Courage and the strength of your convictions! You are not included in these matters because you allow Traeus and Assan to walk all over you! They are making a fool of you!"

"Stop it!" he shouted at her. "I am leaving! Thank-you wife, for your kind shoulder of support." Alaj went to leave the room.

"You yourself have allowed this to happen and it will keep happening as long as you let it!"

With that Alaj slammed the door behind him.

15

A Dream Points the Way

Present-Day Egypt

Afterr a long and exhausting day in the field, Mitch and Alex headed back to their rooms for a quick shower and dinner. Neither of them had spoken much throughout the day, they were trying very hard to catch up on their excavation work to avoid the wrath of Dustimaine and had been focusing on the task at hand.

However, their thoughts were becoming more and more consumed with the mysteries they had unearthed. They continually worried about keeping the chest and its contents a secret. Even more than that, they worried about just what it was they had found, what it might represent. They were in possession of the first real evidence in history that the Sphinx predates the pyramids by several thousand years. That alone was incredible. What the cylinders represented and the possibilities they raised haunted them, in their waking hours and in their dreams.

That night, sleeping fitfully, the two archaeologists dreamed a strange dream…

Walking along the perimeter of the Sphinx complex late in the evening, Mitch and Alex were searching for something.

"Mitch, watch out, you nearly stepped on that crystal. What is it doing here anyway?" Alex asked as she bent down to pick up the small shiny object which had suddenly been illuminated by the dazzling moonlight shining down from the night sky, casting an ethereal glow around the great Sphinx.

All of a sudden, they heard a deafening roar along with another incredibly loud sound, like that of a giant rockslide. They looked up and saw that the eyes of the Sphinx had begun to glow, green and gold. The light from its eyes became more intense and then they saw movement. The roar had come from the Sphinx itself, and without warning the great limestone creature raised up on it on its haunches, the moonlight even brighter now, shining down on the massive body, which appeared to be breathing.

Falling backwards, the two startled archaeologists found they could no longer move. They lay helplessly in the sand, watching with unblinking eyes the inconceivable sight before them.

Slowly the creature stood up on all fours, raised its head, which was no longer the image of a pharaoh, but that of a majestic lion with a living mane blowing gently in the soft night breeze. It let out another roar, but this time it was not deafening, but seemed to cry out in great sadness. Then it looked down at the two tiny beings lying at its massive paws and seemed to be communicating silently with them. Words, if you could call them that, came so fast that Mitch and Alex could only stare, frozen in mind as well as in body.

The creature bent its enormous head down towards them and seemed to peer right down into their souls. Then as suddenly as it came alive, it was motionless yet again, seated in its eternal resting place, the head restored to that of the Pharaoh Khafre. At that moment a bolt of lightening came crashing down from the sky.

Mitch and Alex each woke up with a start.

16

☥

The Papyrus

Mitch and Alex returned to their rooms after the day's work. Neither one had mentioned the strange dream from the previous night. Alex was especially reluctant to do so. They settled in for a night of analyzing scrolls. They were looking at the papyrus they had put aside earlier, considering what it might represent.

"I still think it looks like it could be a funeral scene," Mitch said.

"Yeah, possibly, but we should try to see what it's telling us about these people. Funerary rituals are an important part of a culture, saying many things about a people's beliefs and values, and this looks sufficiently different from Egyptian death rituals to be a bit of a mystery."

Mitch nodded, "There are a number differences, for example the lack of the usual gods present, mummification scenes, and canopic jars for starters. All right, let's break it down and see what we can learn."

"What I find intriguing is the loose style, it's almost abstract in a way," Alex commented.

The background of the papyrus was painted a deep, azure blue, with an interesting pattern of stars present in the sky. The Sphinx, once again with the lion's head was also clearly evident in the top left hand corner, with some kind of beam emanating from its body. On their first cursory glance of the papyrus the other day, they had seen the lion there, but, in light of what they had learned since, they realized what it actually represented.

Alex was examining the star pattern on the papyrus, "Mitch, do you think it's possible that those star formations are not just mere designs drawn for artistic effect?"

"What do you mean?"

"Well, with what we've learned so far, I don't want to leave any stone unturned, you know," Alex said. "I want to scrutinize every aspect of these things and I'm just wondering if the stars on this papyrus could be actual constellations." She looked at the intricate depiction of stars that had been painted.

"Possibly. You know we could get Jack and Bob to run that computer program that can turn back time, so to speak, and show how the constellations we see today appeared at different points in history," Mitch added. "Then we could get them to compare it to this papyrus, see if they get a match."

"Great idea! But let's run this over to them later, I'd like to keep examining it for a bit longer."

Down the right hand side of the papyrus were three of the now-familiar symbols that they were going to translate. However, it was what was front and center in the picture that perplexed them.

There was an object, shaped like an obelisk, and to the upper right of it, was a bright star. The obelisk seemed to have some kind of rays coming from it. Below the object, was a person, lying on a bed, they could not tell if the person was meant to be dead or was simply asleep. The person appeared to be wearing some kind of ceremonial robe. There were depictions of other figures as well. Below the bed, as though it was floating above water, were three wavy lines.

"Do you think the person lying on the bed is dead?" Mitch ventured. "Perhaps the person is journeying into the afterlife, represented by the rising sun? This might be his family standing below him, one mourning, one looking towards the future and one receiving the everlasting life of the sun."

"Could be, but they all look the same. Maybe it's all one person," Alex replied, scanning the ancient image closely.

"Well, yeah, but they might not have bothered with differentiating appearances. Or it could be showing the person moving into the afterlife. But what are these rays coming from two of the figures, the Sphinx-lion and whatever that obelisk-like thing is?"

"I don't know, some kind of life energy maybe? Why don't we translate the symbols on the papyrus, see what that could tell us."

They searched the 'crib notes' for the strange glyphs. "Mitch, here's one, ok, let's see what the corresponding hieroglyph represents. Here, this one is the hieroglyph representing heaven."

"That can also just mean the sky, or simply the area above someone or something," Mitch clarified.

"Right," Alex agreed. "Ok, this one means 'to go' – such as in moving or perhaps traveling from one place to another." They looked at each for a moment, "Let's come back to that, shall we?" Alex said. They were still avoiding a certain topic of conversation.

"This one," Mitch pointed out, "it corresponds to the hieroglyph of the lion's head and paw, which means a beginning, either of an event or some kind of object."

"So, what do we have, a beginning, to travel, and heaven or sky…" Alex put her head in her hands. "I can see what that could be saying, but the person or persons represented – what does it mean in the context of what it's showing?" Alex sat thoughtfully for a moment, thinking back to the previous night. "Mitch, this might sound crazy, but what if it's all the same person, and what if that person is dreaming?"

"Dreaming?" Mitch replied, his eyes going wide.

"Yeah, dreaming. Here he's asleep, in his dream he's waking up. Maybe he's dreaming of the Sphinx-lion, and of the obelisk," Alex speculated.

"Did you say dreaming of the Sphinx?" Mitch asked, in an almost whispered tone.

"Sure, maybe that's what these three wavy lines and these rays are, to show that it's all seen from a dream state." Alex looked at Mitch, who had grown pale. "Are you ok?"

"It's just, I-uh, well, I just remembered something. Maybe it's nothing," he shook his head.

Alex leaned forward, "Mitch, what is it?"

"Well, I didn't mention anything before, but this just reminded me of something."

"Go on," she answered.

"Last night," he said, "I had a dream, it was the strangest thing. I dreamt we were out by the Sphinx and it came alive."

Alex stared at him, speechless. She had tried to put the bizarre dream out her mind, her second one, but now…

Mitch noticed his partner had turned ghostly white. "What?" The way she looked at him told him what he needed to know. "No way!"

She nodded.

"The same one?" he asked.

"Uh-huh," she replied.

"I don't believe this!" Mitch said. "How can this be happening?"

Alex felt a cold chill run down her spine.

For a time, they just sat there silently, their minds racing, trying to make some sense out of this.

"At least it wasn't just me this time," she said, relieved.

Mitch frowned, "You know, the first time, it was just you that fell asleep."

"That's right!" she said. "I can't tell you how much better that makes me feel."

"Thanks," he deadpanned. Then a thought occurred to him, "Alex, remember the dream that Tuthmosis had? He dreamt of the Sphinx when he was still a Prince, it told him he would become the next Pharaoh. His dream came true."

Alex just looked at him.

"This means," he continued, "that the Sphinx has a long history of conversing with people through their dreams. So you see, maybe we're not crazy!"

"You want these dreams to come true?" she asked.

She had a point. "No," he answered, "definitely not."

"Right," she said, "these dreams are scaring the hell out of me."

"Well, what do we do now?" Mitch asked.

"Something external has to be affecting us," she said.

"The chest and the cylinders," Mitch said.

"Exactly. Remember what Jack and Bob learned about the metal, 'not part of the periodic table' I believe is how they so cleverly put it. We have no idea what other properties it could have."

Mitch nodded, a light going on. "Like drawing you to its location through a vision it planted somehow."

"Precisely," she answered. "Well, Tuthmosis, not-with-standing, perhaps we should keep this to ourselves?" Alex ventured. "Maybe Tuthmosis understood what the Sphinx was asking or saying, but I sure as heck didn't."

Mitch smiled, "Agreed." He thought for a moment. He took another look at the dream papyrus. "Alex, look at this, this obelisk is featured prominently, so that would tell me it has significance for whatever this is showing – death, a dream, whatever. But we haven't come across anything like it in this excavation."

"We need to find it," she said.

"Absolutely, but where do we start looking?"

First thing the next morning, Mitch and Alex had brought the dream papyrus to Jack and Bob and asked them to perform the star position analysis to see if the depiction of the stars were random or not. Once again, they decided not to bring up the subject of dreams.

At the end of the day, Mitch and Alex had once again settled in to continue deciphering the book of scrolls and search for something that would help them explain what was going on, when they heard a furious knocking on the door.

"Guys! Open up, it's us!" It was Jack and Bob. They continued to pound on the door.

"All right, all right, we're coming, don't bang the door down!" Mitch answered.

"Hi," Jack said breathlessly as he pushed his way past Mitch.

Bob just shook his head, "He's rather anxious. He was running like his hair was on fire to get here, I could barely keep up."

"Damn straight I'm anxious," Jack said as he took a seat at the table beside Alex, where Mitch had been sitting. Mitch didn't say anything about having his seat stolen. "Sit, guys, sit, we have something to show you."

"Coffee?" Alex offered.

"No thanks, I take my caffeine from a can," Jack replied. "We have the results from the computer program on star position analysis," he said as he laid some papers and the papyrus out on the table.

"Wow, you guys are fast," Alex said.

"We know," Jack replied. "We did the comparison of what is shown on the papyrus and just kept backdating the timeline until we found this," he said as he pointed to the results. "The depiction of the stars is not random, nor just for artistic touch – that is how the stars looked over Egypt around 12,000 years ago. And here, within it…that's the belt of Orion."

"Now you see why he's in such a state," Bob said.

"Do we ever," Mitch acknowledged. "I'd say our body of evidence is coming together rather irrefutably."

"These people, they had incredibly advanced knowledge and so long ago," Alex said. "Written language, construction of the Sphinx-lion, astronomy, metallurgy and yet…we have known nothing of their existence before now. How could they have vanished so completely from the historical record?"

"Good question, maybe we'll find some answers in the scrolls once we have them translated," Mitch said.

"Can we help?" Bob asked.

"Thanks, but why don't you two take a break – take the rest of the evening off, you've been working pretty hard," Alex said.

"Are you sure? We don't mind," Bob offered.

"Alex is right, go rest, relax a bit, you can be sure we'll be calling on you again soon," Mitch smiled.

Alex beamed at them, "Thank you guys so much. You are THE BEST!"

"Yes we are," Jack grinned, "Well, alrighty then, Rogue Squadron is just a call away!" he said as he jumped up. "C'mon Bob, let's go play some of the computer games we brought along that have been gathering dust. We've got a fridge full of Cokes and Diet Cokes and many bags of chips waiting for us!"

"Sounds good to me! Bye guys, call if you need us!" Bob said as they headed out the door.

Mitch and Alex turned back to the task at hand. They knew they would not even begin to get close to deciphering everything as they had so few symbols on their 'crib notes', they just hoped to be able to glean some of the larger concepts.

Alex flipped through some of the pages in the later half of the scrolls, when she came across another interesting drawing. "Mitch, look at this," she said.

"Looks like some kind of chamber," he commented.

"It does, it has a long entranceway and a double-chamber. There's a large obelisk in the first chamber – the second chamber is showing some kind of platform with a smaller obelisk on top of it. What if…?"

"What if what Alex?"

"The obelisks, does one of them look like the same one as on the dream papyrus?" she asked.

"This one, the smaller one looks most like it. The other one has an opening or marking on the top of it. But obelisks are very commonly found. They're probably just ceremonial."

"Maybe, but what if they're not?" she asked, looking closer at the page. "What is this – on top of the chamber?"

"I'm not sure. Maybe it was part of a larger drawing they didn't complete, " he said also taking a closer look at it. "Wait a minute…."

"What is it?" Alex asked looking at the drawing, trying to see what he was seeing.

"This outline, it looks like…it is!" Mitch quickly grabbed for the papyrus that depicted the dream or death picture. "Look, look at the bottom of the lion monument – it's drawn exactly like what's on top of this chamber. These chambers are underneath the Sphinx!"

"And then, maybe so are our mysterious obelisks!" Alex exclaimed. "This is incredible!"

"I know," Mitch said. "There have been speculations about secret tunnels underneath the Sphinx before," Mitch said. "People have searched and searched and found nothing."

"But remember, those people hadn't found anything further about its age either or who built it, let alone strange metallic objects."

"Good point," he acknowledged. "So now what? We can't just grab our shovels and go digging around the Sphinx for hidden entrances to secret tunnels and chambers."

"That is a problem," Alex concurred. "The answers must be in the scrolls. We'll keep looking, start deciphering what we can of the text and go from there."

"Even if we do find answers, we won't be able to do anything about it," Mitch pointed out.

"Well, we'll take it one step at a time and cross that bridge if and when we come to it." She thought for a moment, "We need to figure out who these people were."

17

The Twins

Circa 10,000 B.C.

Four years have past and the twins were now nearly five years old. Princess Anjia was blessed with her father's striking emerald green eyes, while Prince Tramen had his mother's eyes, a remarkable deep brown flecked throughout with gold.

Though still young, they regularly demonstrated maturity beyond their years. They loved to play and chase each other around as any five-year olds would, but there was something a little unusual about them.

Traeus and Axiana did their best to raise their children in a positive and supportive environment filled with learning and various challenges suited to their age. Though they did not have any prior experience as parents to compare to, they intuitively sensed that the twins had been born with abilities they were at a loss to fully explain.

Anjia especially seemed different from the start. She seemed to have a strong intuitive ability, the results of which most people dismissed as simple coincidences.

Zazmaria had always felt bothered by the young Princess and, to an extent, by her brother. Neither twin had ever warmed up to their Aunt.

Zazmaria also noticed Princess Anjia's seeming abilities. She had been intrigued by stories she had heard throughout her life about people who possessed the ability to somehow see future events, to 'hear' the thoughts of others, to sense things about people, places or events. Zazmaria was deeply envious and suspicious of such people, As such, Anjia's rejection of her, in particular, greatly disturbed Zazmaria. Her resentment and growing hatred deepened day by day, she herself descending ever further into darkness and despair.

Assan too, watched Princess Anjia with growing curiosity. He noticed how the Princess especially, seemed mature far beyond her years, almost as if she was able to understand effortlessly the complex world around her. In fact, they seemed to perfectly complement one another. They would often whisper things in each other's ears, or just look at something, then look at each other and grin and nod knowingly.

The twins, though young had already begun being tutored, and learned quickly from the priests. They loved being taught new things and absorbed it all with great enthusiasm.

18

Mysteries Arise

The time had finally come for the King to oversee the installation of the Pharom. Four long years had passed since the day when Victarius brought the finished plans to him and here they were about to make the dream a reality. So much had happened since then.

Traeus was filled with nervous anticipation. He knew the power they would be unleashing. He, Assan and Victarius had discussed every detail at great length. Every precaution had been taken to ensure safety, but it was still a remarkable and dangerous object they had created.

Victarius had warned Traeus about it ever being mishandled. The Pharom was incredibly sophisticated and had to be handled with the utmost care and only by trained people. Security would be tight and access to it would be restricted.

In spite of their precautions, Traeus was still worried. In fact, the Pharom could have been ready for installation weeks earlier, but Traeus had insisted on further tests of the Pharom as well as the specially designed double-chamber. Engineered with the hidden features that Traeus had requested, the inner chamber housed the platform that would ultimately hold and power the device.

Assan had wisely suggested they wait until late at night to begin their work so they could ensure the utmost secrecy. Traeus had his top guards led by Commander Koronius assist with the movement and installation of the Pharom.

All involved knew the danger inherent in their task. The Pharom, once activated, would be surging with incredible power – power, which must be carefully contained and constantly monitored.

Slowly and quietly the Pharom was transported to the site. Even the entrance to the tunnel and chambers beyond had been disguised as an extra security precaution. Traeus' guards had ensured that no one was around to witness anything before the signal was given to begin to move it.

Assan had assigned Odai and Senarra to wait outside the entrance-way for them. Four of the top Royal guards were charged with the responsibility of transporting the device. The Pharom had been housed in a specially designed container and it needed to be carried very gently, ensuring no banging or jostling of the precious cargo.

Assan, nodding to Odai and Senarra, motioned the guards transporting it to follow him inside. Once inside, they lit torches and through the long, narrow, sloping tunnel they walked.

They reached the entrance to the first chamber – a set of metallic doors carved with ancient Kierani inscriptions. The doors, which included a sophisticated locking mechanism, had been costly and difficult to create, but Traeus had wanted the utmost security for the Pharom.

Odai and Senarra waited until the King and his party had passed. Traeus had ordered two of his guards to take Odai and Senarra's place guarding the entrance to the tunnel.

The group walked through the first chamber, which was stunningly designed with large columns and painted walls. The torchlight flickered on the walls, seeming to give life to the paintings. A large limestone obelisk stood in the center of the room.

"Please follow me," Assan said as he walked to the back of the room. He opened the second entrance.

This time it was a single door, which had a similar locking mechanism as the first. They entered the rear chamber, which was much smaller and unadorned, except for a platform in the center of the room.

Assan walked around the platform, motioning for the guards carrying the Pharom to halt and wait. All eyes were upon him.

Traeus' heart was pounding. This was a moment he knew he would remember for the rest of his life.

Holding a torch, Assan read the inscription on the platform and spoke some ancient incantations designed to offer protection as he waved the large ankh he wore around his neck over the platform. No one else said a word. Finally he asked the soldiers to set the container down. They did and Assan, still speaking in the ancient language, said further incantations over it.

"We are ready, your Highness," he said finally.

Traeus nodded then turned to his Chief Engineer, "Victarius, will you do the honor of placing the Pharom on the platform?"

"Of course, your Majesty," he replied as he bowed and stepped forward. "Once it is installed, it will become active immediately. I must warn you all – the effect of the power surge may make anyone inside the chamber nauseous and dizzy. The effect will be temporary as long as exposure is limited. Even those who will be assigned to monitor and maintain it will need to be kept on strict shifts of limited duration."

"I understand, Victarius, but I wish to remain here for a short while. Assan will also stay. Commander Koronius, perhaps you would like to have your men wait outside?" King Traeus asked.

"Yes, your Highness, but with your permission, I would like to remain here with you during the installation."

"Of course," Traeus replied. The Commander spoke with his men, who exited the chamber then he resumed his place by Traeus' side.

Odai and Senarra waited at the entrance to the rear chamber, this was something they did not want to miss.

Before Victarius placed the Pharom on the platform, the King spoke to his most trusted people, "This is a momentous occasion for us all. From this moment on, we will be entrusted with a great responsibility in safeguarding that, which has been so faithfully and painstakingly created. I thank you all for helping to bring this dream to fruition. We are taking a bold step forward. Victarius, your team's achievement is without compare."

"Your Highness, without your support and vision, it could not have been accomplished. We are very grateful for your ceaseless faith in our abilities," he answered as he bowed respectfully.

"May the hands that have been entrusted with this most precious creation, be ever worthy of that trust," Assan added.

Traeus nodded. "Victarius, please proceed." A hush fell over the room.

Taking a deep breath, Victarius slowly reached inside the container and retrieved the heavy device. With a look of deep concentration on his face, Victarius held it over the platform with great care, ensuring correct placement. He lowered the metallic device until it latched into place. A low hum began.

Within moments of the Pharom's installation, everyone in the chamber began to feel nauseous.

"It seems to be working properly," Victarius said as the hum faded away, until it was barely audible. "It is done, your Majesty. With your permission, I will stay behind to ensure it is functioning correctly, but it would be best if the rest of you leave now, in case the effects intensify. We are still dealing somewhat with the unknown here."

"I agree, Victarius, but make sure you are not overcome by the effects yourself. You may be a brilliant engineer, but I doubt you are immune to its power," Traeus replied.

"I will join you shortly," Victarius assured him. The rest of the group left the room.

Once Victarius determined the Pharom was operating properly, both chambers were sealed and locked. The entrance leading into the tunnel was also sealed. When the doors were closed the entrance was practically invisible.

Traeus had not wanted to post guards at the entrance since that would only arouse curiosity and rumor. Instead, they had designed an entrance so sophisticated, a person could be standing right next to it and not know it was there. The King decided to keep four guards disguised as maintenance workers nearby.

Traeus and Assan walked back to the Palace accompanied by Royal guards. A short ways from the site, Traeus turned and looked back at the magnificent structure outlined in the starry night. "We have done it, Assan. All the years of work, planning, worrying, it was worth it. We have succeeded."

"Yes, your Majesty, it is a time of great significance for our people," Assan agreed.

Traeus thought for a moment, "I only wish we could share it with the people, tell them what we have done so they could share the joy and pride of accomplishment…and of hope," he said wistfully.

"We are sharing it with them in a way, your Highness. It is there for all of us, and everyone will benefit from it, they just will not be aware of what is happening for now. It is better this way, it would not be prudent to risk anything else," Assan answered.

"I know, of course, you are right. But, it has been hard keeping such a thing secret."

"We would do our people a great disservice by telling them, getting their hopes up, when who knows…"

"Yes, there are no guarantees this will work, at least not in our lifetimes. But it is such a remarkable device."

"It is indeed," Assan replied. "Someday…"

They looked at the Amsara monument, each with his own thoughts about what it meant to him.

Anjia's Vision

Axiana woke up with a start in the middle of the night feeling panicked. She sat up, looked over at Traeus, who was in a deep sleep. She got up and decided to check on the twins in the adjacent room. She slowly and quietly opened the door so as not to wake them. However, fear gripped her as she looked into the room, Tramen was sleeping soundly, but Anjia's bed was empty.

She looked around the room. Anjia was nowhere to be seen. Axiana ran over to Tramen and woke him up. "Tramen, Tramen, wake up, honey, wake up."

The sleepy little Prince half opened his eyes and said, "Mommy."

"Darling, where is your sister?" Axiana asked trying her best to stay calm and not frighten him.

"She is sleeping," he replied, barely awake.

"No, honey, she is not here. Did you hear her leave the room? Did you talk to her?"

"No Mommy, I was sleeping, I did not hear anything."

"Sweetheart, I am going to go find her, I am sure she is close by. Go back to sleep, Tramen." She glanced at the window in the children's room, which was still closed.

With that, she kissed her son's forehead and hurried out of the room to wake her husband. She shook him, "Traeus, please wake up, Anjia has left her room."

Traeus awoke with a start and bolted up, "What? Where is she?"

"I do not know. She is just gone. I asked Tramen if he heard her leave, but he heard nothing, he thought she was still asleep in the room."

"It is all right," Traeus assured his frightened wife, "we will find her." He hurried to summon the guard posted at the end of the hallway. The soldier ran over.

"Did you see Princess Anjia leave her room?" Traeus demanded.

"No, your Majesty," the guard shook his head, "I saw no one leave the rooms. I have been posted here all night, no one has come out."

"The window in the children's room is still closed, how did she get out if not this way?" Axiana asked.

"I am sorry your Majesty, but I saw no one leave," the guard replied nervously.

"Come, we will search the Palace, she must have snuck out some-how," Traeus said to his wife. "Guard, remain here."

"Yes, your Majesty," the soldier replied.

The rest of the Royal guards were alerted to begin the search. The staff also began looking for the missing Princess. Mindara had been woken up and asked to watch Tramen.

For nearly an hour, they frantically searched the Palace. The entire staff had been alerted and was participating in a room-by-room search of the Palace, fanning out to cover the grounds as well. The search, proving fruitless, was then expanded outward from the Palace.

After nearly forty-five minutes, a young guard came running back to the Palace in search of the King and Queen. "We found her! Please, your Majesties, you must come quickly!" he exclaimed.

"Where is she?" Traeus asked as he grabbed his wife's hand.

"We found her standing in front of the Amsara monument! She seems fine, but she is not acknowledging or answering anyone. She is just staring up at the monument."

Traeus and Axiana looked at one another in shock. How had she traveled so far in the night on her own, and why? Worried and confused, but relieved their daughter had been found, they ran quickly, following the guard.

When they arrived, they saw the tiny form of their daughter still standing in front of the great stone monument. As they got closer, the scene was eerie.

The night was bright and clear and the moonlight seemed exceptionally bright. It shone down over the colossal monument, casting a long shadow. Standing squarely in front of its paws was their daughter. Anjia's long black hair shone in the bright moonlight. She stood completely still in her long white nightgown, seemingly unaware of the excited party racing towards her.

When they got closer to her, the rest of the search party held back and Traeus and Axiana stepped forward. Axiana called out, "Anjia, are you all right? Mommy and Daddy are here."

No response came, no movement at all.

As the frightened parents walked up and knelt on either side of their daughter, they could see that she appeared calm, she was in no apparent distress, and had no obvious injuries. Not responding to her parents' questions, Axiana reached out to lightly touch her arm. At the touch, Anjia suddenly broke out of the trance and looked at her mother and a smile crossed her face. "Mommy!" the girl hugged her relieved mother.

"Anjia, I am so happy to find you," Axiana said.

"What are you doing out here? Why did you leave the Palace?" her father asked.

"Amsara called me. I came to talk to him," she answered, as though this was nothing out of the ordinary.

"How did he call you, Anjia?" Axiana asked.

"In my dreams, he told me to not be afraid, that he would protect me."

Axiana looked at Traeus. He too was at a loss for words.

"How did you walk so far on your own and without anyone seeing you?" Axiana asked, trying to conceal the fear in her voice.

Anjia shrugged, "I just did."

"You should not have left the Palace without us, Anjia. It is not safe," her father gently admonished her.

"But Amsara said it would be all right," she replied matter-of-factly.

Traeus looked his daughter straight in the eyes, "You must not do it again do you understand me?"

"Yes Daddy, but is he not beautiful?" she answered, once again looking up at the immense stone figure, still bathed in moonlight.

Traeus did not answer her, he did not want to encourage her where this monument was concerned, though he admitted to himself, the sight was quite spellbinding. Instead he turned back to the head guard, "Go find Assan and tell him to meet us in our chambers right away. We will carry her back to the Palace."

The guard nodded, "Yes, your Majesty, at once."

Traeus stood and picked his daughter up, "Let us go back home, it is still nighttime, we need to get you back to bed. Tramen is worried and misses you." As they headed back, Traeus gave his wife a serious look, "We will talk with Assan. Perhaps he can give us some answers."

Axiana nodded and they walked back to the Palace, accompanied by the remaining Royal guards. Anjia rested peacefully in her father's arms, humming a strange tune. A look of peaceful contentment was on her face. She then fell fast asleep.

The worried King and Queen brought their sleeping daughter back to the twins' room and left her in Mindara's care, along with Tramen. They then returned to their private chambers to wait for Assan's arrival.

As they related what had happened with Anjia, Assan's face was intent, yet controlled. After he was told of the events, he stood and went to the window, silently gazing out towards the great Amsara visible in the distance, still bathed in moonlight.

Traeus had a very specific concern about his daughter's behavior. "Assan, do you think it could be the Pharom that is causing this? She is only a young child, she knows nothing of the true purpose of the monument, nor the power of what lies hidden below it. Do you think somehow, she senses this power or is affected by it?" Traeus asked.

"What is contained below is very powerful, it may be having an effect we did not predict."

"Is she in any danger – could it be harming her in some way?" Axiana was deeply concerned by what she was hearing.

"I do not believe that to be the case. I think it is more a matter of her being more receptive to it, in a sense, but I do not think it poses any risk to her health."

Traeus paused for a moment, thinking on what Assan had said. "I realize this is a strange question to ask Assan, but she has always seemed…different somehow. I just do not understand what is going on with her, she is only five years old!"

Assan suspected there was something unusual about Anjia before, but had not wanted to worry her parents, but now that was out of his hands. "Your Majesties, the Princess does seem to possess an unusual gift of insight. In light of what has transpired tonight I believe it is her mind trying to interpret the energy it senses. This did happen shortly after the Pharom was activated."

"That is true," Traeus realized. "That must be part of what is happening to her. Should we shut it down?"

"No, I do not think that is necessary at this point. I think that whatever is happening is part of a latent ability she possesses."

Assan's comments reminded Axiana of another concern, "Assan, I have often wondered about something. Do you remember the potions Senarra gave me when I was having trouble conceiving?"

"Yes, of course," he replied.

"I know you did not create them yourself, but do you think it might be possible for the potions to have had anything to do with Anjia's behavior or abilities? She and Tramen also seem connected as well, on some deep level, more than just brother and sister."

Assan thought for a moment, measuring his reply, "I am aware of what Senarra prepared for you and I can assure you, your Highness, she would never have given you something that could have in any way harmed you or your children. The connection you observe between the Prince and Princess is not all that unusual, twins, though rare, are known to share a deep connection – being able to sense things about one another, seeming to communicate without words, sense when one is hurt. It must be the experience of sharing the womb, growing together, being linked to each other through the mother."

Assan paused then continued, "However, the potion that was created for you was very powerful and it was meant to counteract toxins in your system. The potion had never been made before or since."

Traeus and Axiana were watching him, nervously anticipating his next words.

Assan looked at them, "It is possible there is some correlation, that the combination of elements in your system somehow affected her in particular, perhaps due to something unique about her physiology but, and I stress this, any effect would only have enhanced abilities or characteristics that were already there. In no way could it have created those abilities in an unborn child."

"So, our daughter, do you think she is all right then? Should we be worried about her?" Traeus asked.

"I believe she is fine, but she should be watched closely. As her parents, you are in the best position to do that, but I would ask that you please let me know if you observe any other unusual behavior, even the smallest thing."

"We will," Axiana replied. "I will also think of ways for her and I to spend time alone together, to talk. Perhaps she can open up to me about things she is experiencing, even if she does not fully understand them herself."

"That is an excellent idea, your Highness," Assan agreed. "I think that is all we can do for now."

Rumors and Fear Grow

Zazmaria had not been sleeping well for the last few nights. Headaches, a sense of unease and nameless fear had plagued her and she could find no rest. The continuous arguments with her husband were wearing on her. He never listened to her anymore and she hated him for it.

The wine with the evening's meal, which she had eaten alone, had not calmed her frayed nerves, so she decided to walk over to the small temple on the Palace grounds and try to seek some kind of solace there. She wanted to be alone and knew the temple would be empty at this time of night.

The temple was only a short walk from the Palace itself, it was towards the back of the grounds, past the main garden area and near the burial chamber where King Mesah and Queen Elenia were entombed. Zazmaria rarely went there, or to any of the temples in the city for that matter, but tonight, for some reason she decided to go.

As she approached it, she could see a faint light coming from inside. The light drew her closer. Once inside, she could smell the familiar aroma of incense burning near the altar. She stood in the doorway for a few moments, uncertain as to whether or not she should proceed.

The temple consisted of some cushioned seating places, and long, deep red draperies covered the windows on either side of the temple. From the outside, the soft light through the thick drapes cast a warm, red glow. At the far end of the temple was an altar, with a large, golden ankh in the center and behind it hung a large bronze carving of a sun image. Candles were lit, their flames flickering in the draft of the open door.

'*What can it hurt?*' she thought to herself. '*I will not stay long.*' Down the narrow, stone aisle she walked, gazing toward the dimly lit altar. When she reached the front and knelt down in the front row, bowing her head, she felt the burden of her troubles bearing down on her as though they would press her into the floor and crush the very life out of her. She remained still for a short time, her eyes closed, breathing deeply, trying to relax and calm her troubled mind. After a while, she lifted her head and slowly sat down facing the altar. She watched the smoke from the incense wafting in the faint breeze. The smoke seemed to come alive and dance for her. She watched it, her eyes losing focus, the many nights of sleeplessness weighing her down.

Her mind drifted into the places in her heart she shared with no one. A dark feeling of wrath began to grow in the pit of her stomach, twisting its way first to her chest and then to her throat, until it seemed as though it would strangle the very breath out of her. At that moment, a vision began to appear in her mind's eye.

Anjia, now a young woman, was standing a thousand feet tall, holding a leash. Attached to the leash was the monument of Amsara, but it was not made of stone any longer – it was now alive. It stared at Zazmaria with a menacing gaze, a low growl emanated from its belly.

Terrified at the sight and sounds of the living monument, her eyes looked quickly up again at Anjia, who stood as though she was its master. Her gaze was penetrating, her long hair flowing behind her. The moonlight seemed to cast a white glow over where she stood, appearing to bathe her in a soft white luminescence.

Suddenly, Anjia's eyes also began to glow with the same white light and in that moment, beams of this light shot from her eyes towards Zazmaria. It seemed as though the light was searching and searing her very soul.

"I know what it is you seek, I know what it is you are willing to do," the figure of Anjia spoke.

Zazmaria, frightened beyond words, gasped and fell backwards. She felt the back of her head impact on something solid. As she looked up, she was no longer standing before Anjia and Amsara, but rather she was back in front of the altar, lying on the floor.

She got up, her head throbbing in pain. She felt the back of her head and realized she was bleeding.

Terrified, she turned and ran down the aisle, through the temple doorway and into the darkness back to the Palace. As she ran back, she cried convulsively. The memory of her vision remained with her as though it was something imprinted on her mind, never to leave.

"What does this mean?" she whispered. "Why is this happening to me?" She stopped, motionless, staring straight ahead. She thought to herself, '*The girl…she can peer into my heart. She sees things. She will try to destroy me one day!*'

She continued on to the Palace, her mind racing. She headed towards her chambers, meeting up with her handmaiden, Medetha, who helped take care of her wound. Though Medetha expressed concern at how the Princess was injured, Zazmaria did not want to talk about it.

Medetha offered instead to bring the Princess some tea along with an herbal remedy to ease the pain and help her sleep, which Zazmaria accepted. Medetha left the room and Zazmaria stared out the window for a few moments, looking out at the moonlit garden, shivering.

Medetha returned with the tea and remedy she promised. "My Lady, take only one teaspoon of the mixture with your tea. It is quite a strong remedy. There is enough here for tomorrow evening as well, if needed."

"Thank-you Medetha, I appreciate your help. That will be all for tonight," Zazmaria said.

Zazmaria slept fitfully that night, tossing and turning for hours. In a semi-conscious state her mind kept replaying the vision she had in the temple, over and over again. The remedy was not helping, so she got up and mixed the rest of it in a glass of water and drank it down. She sat down in a chair at the window for a while and then began to drift off. But no true rest would come to her this night. Her mind, still ill at ease from the events of the evening, now began to conjure up nightmares.

Zazmaria was back in the Palace temple, looking at the altar. She heard footsteps at the door. She turned but no one was there. When she turned back around to face the altar again, the lights in the temple had dimmed and the smoke from the incense had thickened, almost choking her. She could barely see. Coughing and nearly blinded from the smoke, she went to leave when she sensed a presence. She was certain someone was there. Not daring to move, she felt a soft breath at her ear.

"I know what it is you seek. I cannot allow this."

With those words, she felt a strange sensation in her heart – she felt a wetness and dizziness. She looked down, and there in her chest a beautifully jeweled dagger had been thrust through her heart. Losing strength, she fell to her knees. Before her stood Anjia, again as the young woman in her vision, this time of normal height, with a large, striking, gold pendant of Amsara around her neck. Anjia stood staring down at Zazmaria, a slight rueful smile on her face. 'It had to be,' she spoke.

Just as she felt herself dying, Zazmaria screamed, "No!"

She awoke with a start. Her mind was riddled with fear.

21

A Fateful Meeting

One week later, Princess Zazmaria was walking alone along the river, trying to collect her thoughts. She was still intensely disturbed by the images she had seen. She had taken to spending more and more time alone.

Medetha kept trying to accompany her, to talk with her, but as much as she liked Medetha's companionship, Zazmaria felt distant from her too. Zazmaria was becoming increasingly isolated, increasingly gripped by fear.

She heard the crush of leaves beneath a heavy footstep. She stopped in her tracks and turned, "Who is there?" No answer came. She called out again, "I heard you, now show yourself, that is an order from a member of the Royal Family!"

Still there was no response.

Now even the birds seemed to have silenced themselves. "Identify yourself immediately or I will call for the guards!"

"I think not, my Lady," a man said as he stepped out from the shadows of the brush, his head covered by a hood. "I have been watching you and I know you are alone."

"Do not come any closer, I am warning you."

"Princess Zazmaria, pray tell, what will you do if I do not obey your Royal command?" the man's tone was slightly mocking. He slowly stepped closer.

"I am perfectly capable of defending myself," she said as she slowly reached for the dagger she had begun carrying with her since the evening of her nightmares of Anjia's attack.

The man laughed a slow, menacing laugh. "Your Royal Highness, I am sure you are, but I too am a capable warrior," he bowed his head slightly, his arms outstretched. He was only a few feet from her now. He removed his hood.

"Zhek? What is a Draxen doing stalking members of the Royal Family?" She was visibly shaken.

"Not members, your Highness…only you." He had a twisted smile on his face as he continued to walk closer to her.

Zazmaria backed away slowly, trying to disguise the fear she felt at being alone and cornered by this man. "What do you mean by that? What is it that you want, Zhek?"

"I just want to talk to you, my Lady," he bowed an exaggerated bow. "We have mutual interests, I think, you and I." He was grinning at her in a knowing way.

"We have nothing in common Zhek, and do not look at me in that manner! You should show more respect to a member of the Royal Family than leering at her. And do not think we are not aware of how your family feels about us. Your family remains an unspoken enemy, in spite of its pretense. I am not fooled by it."

"I apologize if I am making you uncomfortable, and you are right in the sense of our families being at odds, but that is not what I am talking about, Princess," Zhek spoke her title with a condescending edge to his voice.

"Stop speaking in riddles and get to the point Zhek!" Zazmaria was feeling less frightened, but more agitated at the smugness of his tone and the way his stance was meant to intimidate her.

Zhek was a very tall, muscular man and he was using his imposing size to place her at a disadvantage. "Need I spell it out for you, your

Highness? Very well then." He stepped even closer. He was now standing directly in front of her, only inches away.

Zazmaria's hand remained on her dagger.

"You and I have much in common," Zhek stated. "I have observed you many a time at official functions and you have never appeared to be very close or friendly with anyone other than your husband. I suspect that you resent your place in line for the throne. As long as King Traeus is in power, you and your Prince husband will be bound to simply follow his lead. Quite meaningless and unimpressive roles, I dare say," his eyes glinted as he spoke the insulting words.

Zazmaria, enraged and insulted by his brash comment, went to strike him across the face. Zhek caught her wrist and held it firmly, a smug grin creeping across his face. "My, my, Princess, hit a nerve have I? Let me share another thing I have observed. You and your husband have yet to produce any children, while King Traeus and Queen Axiana have been blessed with two beautiful, healthy heirs. Rather diminishes you and your husband even further, does it not?" His eyes had a cold gleam in them.

Zazmaria struggled against the strength of his grip, reaching with her free hand for her dagger. Zhek caught that arm too and pinned both hands behind her back. "I know this infuriates you, but in spite of your indignation, you know I am right." His voice had softened somewhat and his gaze was penetrating.

"You are nothing but an ill-mannered thug, Zhek. You know nothing about me!" She continued to writhe within the iron-grip he held her in.

"Oh no, Princess? I think I know you better than you realize." With that he bent his head and brazenly kissed her, a lingering passionate kiss.

Zazmaria was stunned and to her dismay and confusion, she found she had stopped struggling. Zhek lifted his head and looked deep into her eyes, gently released his grip, took her hand, which still held the dagger and kissed it softly. "Such a weapon, my Lady…"

Zazmaria was too stunned to speak. She still held on to the dagger, more as a result of being too shocked to move than any further menace.

Zhek was staring at her intensely. "Perhaps you and I should give some thought to forming a friendship Zazmaria. I think we have a number of shared interests and I would very much like to explore them further. I will leave you to think on this awhile. We shall meet again soon. Until next time, Princess…" Zhek bowed his head ever so slightly to her.

With that he let her go and strode away, disappearing into the brush from which he had emerged moments ago. Zazmaria stood speechless staring after him.

Several minutes passed, her head spinning, her heart pounding. She did not know what to make of the effect both his words and actions had on her. She straightened herself up, turned and headed back to the Palace. Her mind was now in further turmoil.

A Plan Is Unveiled

"So, have you made contact?" Lord Draxen's voice was low and menacing, full of expectation that one did not dare disappoint.

"I have Grandfather," Zhek bowed his head towards him.

"And?" Lord Draxen asked.

"And, we have had a conversation. I think I raised some important questions in her mind. I believe she will be receptive to me. I have pointed out how we could be mutually beneficial to one another."

Lord Draxen smiled a wide, sickening smile, stood up and put his wrinkled hands on Zhek's shoulders. Zhek was much taller than him. "Well done! I am glad you can follow my directives so well. I knew she would be the right choice to get what we need. I want you to pursue this as far as you can. You must gain the Princess' confidence and trust, so we can begin to infiltrate the Royal Family."

He squeezed Zhek's shoulders and gave him a knowing look. "We have already observed that she does not have a good relationship with other members of the Royal Family and the rumors would indicate that her marriage is not as solid as it should be either. So you see how simple and perfect a plan this is?" he smiled.

"Yes Grandfather," Zhek replied. "However, I do not think we should underestimate the Royal Family. People can be unpredictable, especially people with that much power."

"Do not worry, Zhek. We will be the ones in control, which means they will be underestimating us."

"You are right of course," Zhek replied, though inside he felt a measure of trepidation as to where this could all lead. Seducing the Princess would be scandalous and potentially dangerous, and he did not share his grandfather's confidence that such a situation could be so easily manipulated to their advantage.

Zhek was considered by most people to be a very attractive man and a desirable potential husband due to his family's wealth and power. His wavy black hair was thick and shiny and he kept it long and pulled back, adding to his roguish allure.

He had piercing, sapphire blue eyes, full lips and high, sculpted cheekbones, one of which was marred from a still-visible scar he received when he was only seven years old. His grandfather had seen fit to discipline him severely for lying. He had struck him hard across his little face. Never again did Zhek cross his grandfather.

"I am glad you see things my way, Zhek," Lord Draxen said, "because the sooner we get some answers about what they are up to, the sooner we can begin making plans of our own. You do whatever you have to get information from her – specifically about the Amsara site for starters."

The old man gazed out the window, his mind twisting and turning. "Our spies have reported suspicious activity around it for quite some time now. At first I thought it was just work related to the completion of the construction around it, but such work would not have gone on this long."

He turned back to Zhek, "Something else has to account for the strange comings and goings there and we need to find out what that is as soon as possible. I do not trust King Traeus, or anyone in that family, even remotely. If they are up to something, we need to know what it is. A great deal depends on you right now, Zhek. Do not disappoint me."

"I understand and I will do my best to not disappoint you, Grandfather," Zhek said as he bowed his head slightly. "If you will excuse me then, I have much to do and to plan."

23

☥

Betrayal

"So, have you given any more thought to what I said?" a voice whispered in Zazmaria's ear.

It had been days since their last encounter. This time Zhek had snuck up behind her in the crowded outdoor market.

Startled she wheeled around to face him, then her face flushed and she turned away.

"Ah, I can see that I have had an effect on you at least. I daresay you have thought of little else since our last meeting," he whispered into her hair as people jostled around them in the noisy marketplace.

The Princess was wearing a headscarf and had managed thus far to go unrecognized.

"You are most arrogant and presumptuous," she shot back. "What makes you think I gave you another thought?"

"Because Princess, I can hear it in your voice and I saw it in your eyes when you looked at me a moment ago," he replied in a silky voice. He was pressing close to her, still no one around them taking notice of anything unusual.

She quickly elbowed him in the stomach.

Winded he coughed and retreated slightly.

"I bet you did not see that coming, did you?" she said as she wheeled away.

Zhek followed, holding his stomach, but laughing to himself. "Well as much fun as this is, shall we continue our exchange later, in private?" He had moved close behind her again, and this time, touched his lips lightly to her neck.

Shocked at his brazenness, she again tried to elbow him.

This time he was prepared and braced her arm. "There is a small house on the edge of town – it is secluded. I am sure you have seen it. It is painted red and has a long winding walkway leading up to it. It belongs to my family, but no one lives there. Meet me there tonight, we will talk further."

"How dare you…" she had started to say, but Zhek had disappeared into the crowd. She touched her neck where he had kissed her. She tingled all over, but she did her best to dismiss it. *'That despicable rogue,'* she thought angrily to herself, *'who does he think he is?'*

She returned to the Palace a short while later. She and Alaj had still not been getting along, anytime they saw each it was either an argument or silence. Alaj had not even shared her bed the last few nights. Her loneliness had grown with each passing day.

Later that evening, she tried to go to sleep, but she was wide-awake. Her mind raced with may thoughts. She tried everything to get comfortable, to relax, but nothing worked. As the hours passed, her restlessness became increasingly unbearable for her until, finally, she got up, dressed, and grabbed a cloak and left. She did not tell anyone where she was going. She simply walked out. She knew how to get out of the Palace unseen.

Soon enough she found herself outside the little red house on the edge of town. The night was cool and there were scattered raindrops, but she stood outside near a large tree for a long time staring at the house. It was dark inside, except for a single light placed in the front window.

"What am I doing here?" she whispered to herself, but with one step following the next she found herself at the door. She went to knock, but before she could, the door opened. There stood Zhek.

"Come in, my Lady, it is cold outside and it is starting to rain." His tone surprised her. He was very courteous, not in his previous self-important, condescending way. This time he sounded sincere. "I just started a fire," he said, politely motioning her inside. He was wearing a loose caramel-colored tunic, which accented his tanned skin, over fitted black pants.

Zazmaria, consumed with nerves, only managed to nod. She stepped inside and he closed the door quietly behind her.

"May I take your cloak? You look wet, I will fetch you a warm blanket."

She hesitated for a moment then allowed him to remove her dark brown cloak. Underneath, she wore a deep burgundy silk dress, which complemented her honey-colored skin and topaz eyes. The way her gown flattered her was not lost on Zhek and, smiling to himself, he retrieved a soft, woolen blanket for her, which she took and wrapped herself in.

"I do not know why I am here," she stated defiantly.

"I understand, but what matters to me is that you are here. The why of it? Well, that is something we can figure out later," Zhek smiled at her. "Would you care to sit down, your Highness," he said as he pulled out a chair for her.

The table had been lit with a single candle, which cast a soft glow around the room. The flame danced, enticing them to sit near it. Zhek admired the way her eyes sparkled in the candlelight.

She took the seat, all the while eyeing him suspiciously.

He laughed a soft laugh.

"What is so funny?" she snapped at him.

"Oh, just the way you are looking at me as though I am about to strangle you or something," he said as he took a seat across from her. "Tea?"

"Fine," she answered. "Is it so odd that I would be mistrustful of you?"

"No, not at all," he replied and handed her a cup of tea. She took it without saying anything.

"My pleasure," he said.

She looked at him. "It is not poisoned is it?"

"No, and I will demonstrate by taking the first drink." He poured himself a cup, and took a couple of sips. "See, nothing to worry about."

"I would not go that far," she shot back. She looked at him closely, the candlelight cast curious shadows across his face. "If you do not mind my asking," she ventured, "what is that scar on your cheek?"

"Ah that, yes, it is a little hard to miss," he smiled.

"It is not that," she replied, "it was just the light from the candle…"

"It is all right, I should not be so embarrassed by it. I have had it most of my life. My grandfather scolded me when I was a child. It never really healed properly."

"I see," she said, staring intently at him, waiting to see if he would say anything else about it, but he did not. She was intrigued by this story and by the flicker of emotion she saw on his face. She could almost see the little boy in him, vulnerable and sad. Something about it resonated within her.

"Princess…"

"Zazmaria," she corrected him. She disliked being called Princess, she felt as though it was an obvious admission of her place in line for the throne.

"All right, Zazmaria, I would like to apologize for some of the things I said to you before. Or rather, how I said them. I meant them, and I think you will admit to the truth in the statements, but how I approached the subject matter, well I behaved boorishly. You deserve better than that and I am sorry."

She did not reply. Zhek was approaching her in a far different matter this evening and it was catching her off-guard. She did not know quite what to make of it.

Zhek took her silence as an opportunity to continue, "I only wanted to approach you because I honestly believe we have mutual interests, you and I."

"Oh?" she asked.

"Yes," he replied. "It is no secret that you and your husband are not close to the rest of the family and my family has been greatly displeased with Traeus' reign."

"We know that, Zhek. It has hardly been a secret."

"I am sure. But recently there has been far more cause for concern…such as when there is so much secrecy…" he said.

"Secrecy? What are you saying?" she was clearly surprised by his comments.

"You tell me. Something has been going on around the illustrious Amsara site for quite some time now. My family is tired of all this mystery. Why should we not know what is going on? Perhaps it is nothing of consequence, but knowing the House Selaren, I highly doubt it."

"Has your family been spying on us?" she shot back.

"I am just a concerned citizen asking a responsible question," he countered genially. "So then, could you tell me what is truly going on at that site?"

Zazmaria did not reply.

Zhek regarded her carefully for a moment. "Your lack of response is interesting, my Lady. Either you are not willing to say, or…"

"Or what?" she snapped.

"Or," he said, his eyebrows rising, "you do not know either." He laughed out loud, reading her reaction. "That is it. Tell me then, does your husband keep you in the dark about everything?"

She slapped him hard across the face and jumped up in a fury, "You bastard! You have no idea what goes on between my husband and I."

Zhek flew out of his chair, grabbing her hand, "You have a nasty habit of hitting me."

"Yes, well you have a nasty habit of asking for it, you insufferable swine."

"Ouch," he replied feigning hurt feelings, then took her hand and placed it on his chest.

He was a large man, taller and more powerfully built than her husband. Zazmaria was angry with herself for taking notice of such details.

"Correct me then, your husband does keep you informed of such things?"

Zazmaria did not say a word, did not move. She was mad, insulted, confused, scared and it all combined to keep her motionless and silent.

Zhek's other hand slid down her back, just a wisp of a touch, resting on her low back. It sent shivers down her spine.

"We have observed Prince Alaj, and not to offend you, but he does not seem to be much of a leader." Zhek looked down at Zazmaria. His lips brushed her forehead, "Nothing to say? Not even in your husband's defense? He lightly kissed her forehead this time, "Silence can speak volumes, you know."

Zazmaria's heart was beating rapidly. Zhek's hand traced a line down her neck and shoulders, then down her arm. Keeping her one hand pressed against his chest, he stroked her other hand until she closed her eyes, lost in the moment. Slowly her hand moved to his arm and wound its way up from his forearm to his well-developed upper arm.

He pressed his cheek to the side of her hair, taking in the scent of her thick, lustrous tresses and whispered in her ear, "I hope your husband knows what a lucky man he is to have such an exquisite woman as his wife." He lightly nuzzled her hair and watched the firelight shine on the silk of her dress. "I have been in awe of your beauty from the first moment I laid eyes on you."

Zazmaria caught her breath as she took his words in. It had been a long time since anyone had said such things to her. She was drawn to this man. She had been unhappy for so long and she felt very alone…but not right now, here in this moment. She looked into his sapphire-blue eyes, then down to his full lips.

Zhek bent down and kissed her, a kiss filled with passion and hunger.

Zazmaria, taken aback at first, slowly let herself be drawn in. He was a desirable man, no matter the circumstances and he seemed to know just how to touch her. She undid the leather strap that held his hair back and let it fall in waves about his face and shoulders. She ran her fingers through it. It was thick, yet silky to the touch. Having his hair loose gave him a wild, almost primal quality.

Encouraged by her touch, he slowly began to undo her dress, kissing her shoulders by the firelight.

In turn, she opened his shirt, revealing a strong chest, muscled from years of physical exertion and toil. She ran her fingers over it. It was hard, pure masculinity. She saw a large, dark birthmark over his heart. It was in the shape of a star.

He watched her fingers exploring his body, settling on the mark. His lips pressed to her ear, "It is a Draxen family trait shared by the men. We all have it. Every generation."

She kissed it softly, letting her lips trace its shape. Zhek groaned with the sensual feel of her lips on his skin. His body responded to the subtle invitation.

Zazmaria felt herself falling, falling, afraid of where she was heading but too filled with desire to care at this moment. All that mattered to her now was the way Zhek made her feel. She had not felt this alive in a very long time, and she savored every kiss, every touch – every precious sensation. She tingled all over.

Zhek continued his assault on her senses. Encouraged by her responses he passionately made love to her in front of the fire.

She fell asleep afterwards with Zhek still holding her. She awoke and looked at him while he slept. She was puzzled by what had just happened and by how natural it felt. She did not know why exactly, but she was drawn to this man. He was physically very attractive to her, but that was not the only thing. Something about him made her feel…alive.

Zhek slowly opened his eyes. "Well hello, beautiful," he smiled, "are you a dream? Something as beautiful as you cannot possibly be real." He leaned up on one arm, pulling her close, "Let me find out for myself if you are just a dream," he pressed his lips to hers and kissed her, a long, slow, searching kiss. He pressed himself against her and she melted into him again. He caressed her hair, tangling his fingers in it, then releasing them and letting his fingers slip to her small shoulders, gripping her firmly.

Slowly he pulled her down on top of him. Zazmaria reveled in the sensations of their bodies pressed against one another. "You are exquisite Zazmaria, I have never felt so completely drawn to anyone in my life."

She became quiet, once again studying the scar across his otherwise flawless features. "This must have hurt," she said softly as her finger traced the rough line, barely touching him.

He winced slightly, turning his face away.

"I am sorry, I did not mean to hurt you…"

"It is probably more the memory of the pain that anything, though it has always felt a bit strange, a little numb I guess."

"How old were you when it happened?" she asked.

"Very young, very small. Some lessons one never forgets," he did not look at her, instead he shifted her gently to lie next to him.

"I see," she answered, turning once again to face him. "Your grandfather, he raised you?"

Zhek nodded, but said nothing.

"He was pretty cruel, I gather."

"He did what he felt he had to do, he always has," Zhek replied.

"But it still must have been humiliating to be hit like that, especially as a small child," she ventured, curious about this man and his history. "That kind of experience changes you somehow, heightens your sense of vulnerability, not knowing for certain how to be good enough to avoid such things."

"You learn pretty quickly to watch out for yourself, to protect yourself and read others."

Zazmaria looked at him sharply, making a connection in his statement. "And you are reading me now?"

"Just as you have been trying to read me. It is a natural response, would you not say, to an unfamiliar situation?"

Zazmaria did not answer right away, lost in her thoughts, "I guess one does develop certain…defenses."

Zhek nodded. "Especially when you do not feel like you quite measure up, am I correct?" he asked.

Zazmaria looked at him in shock, her eyes tearing up before she could stop it, or hide how his words made her feel.

"You do not have to say anything, I understand," he said as he kissed her forehead softly.

Zazmaria lay there, with the tears now falling down her cheeks. They did not speak on it any further. After awhile, she fell back asleep in his arms.

An hour later, she awoke with a start, clutching her chest. Another dream.

Startled, Zhek also woke up. Seeing her almost gasping for breath, he took her face in his hands and asked, "Zazmaria, what is it? Are you ill?"

She hesitated to answer, letting her head clear. She took deep breaths to calm herself, trying to put the disturbing image out of her mind. *'Why did I see her again? Why now?'*

She turned to look at the man lying next to her, his eyes searching her face for some kind of answer. She knew how fraught with danger this situation was, what his family was about, but still, she had never before felt so quickly and powerfully connected to anyone, not even her husband.

"Zhek, I, I…"

"Yes, what is it?" he asked.

She did not want to talk about the dream, or what she thought it meant, but she needed to confide in him. The dream had led her thoughts to something specific. "Before, when you asked me about Amsara…that has been a point of contention between my husband and I."

"I am not surprised, as I have said your husband seems weak, timid. Nothing at all like you, my little lioness," he said as he began to kiss her neck.

Zazmaria shivered as the feel of his soft, full lips sent electric shocks through her system. She had never felt this way before – emboldened, beautiful, desirable, worshipped. She loved every sensation he created in her.

"Zhek, what are we doing, you and I?" she asked suddenly.

He looked deep into her eyes. "I think we have much in common, Zazmaria. We have always lived in the shadows, waiting for our time to come and I do not think either one of us can accept that any longer. And if I may be so bold, I feel as if I have always known you in a way, as though we are meant to be here, together."

Zhek paused, looking down at her hand that he now held, "This must seem ridiculous to you."

"No…no, it does not."

He looked up at her, his eyes wide.

She continued, "I feel the same way, I cannot explain it, I barely know you…"

He kissed her, "You need not explain it. I think you know me very well. We are the same you and I and I think we want the same things. Zazmaria everything we have been denied in our lives, it can be ours. I believe there is nothing we could not accomplish together. Nothing...." He continued kissing her.

"Zhek," she said, he stopped and looked into her eyes. "I told you Alaj and I do not agree on some things. You are right about him – he is not a strong leader. He and I have been utterly kept in the dark about what is going on with the Amsara site. Traeus claims that there is nothing for Alaj to be concerned about."

"But you do not believe him?" Zhek asked.

"Would you?" she asked.

"No, but my perspective on the situation is a little different than yours."

"Not so different, really," she countered. "Alaj and I are no better informed than your family."

"But you are convinced there is more to the story?"

"Why else would Traeus hide it?" she said.

"Indeed. It must be infuriating to know he does not trust or value his own brother enough to keep him informed of projects his own family is working on."

"Exactly! But my husband does not seem to understand that. He is being made a fool of, and I along with him! Effectively, the priests are in a far greater position of power than my husband!"

"How can any man, let alone a Prince, stand for that?" Zhek stated, eager to encourage her anger. He knew he had hit a sore spot. "Tell me, what exactly did Alaj find out about the monument's purpose, its real purpose?"

"Just that there is a tunnel and chamber below it for the priests to meditate in and yet I have not seen them coming and going from the site. Traeus has never allowed anyone else to go inside."

"I see our King treats his own family no better than he does his people. Whatever he is up to could be dangerous to us all. I think he needs a lesson in respecting others, would you not agree?"

"I have had that very same thought...for a long time," she replied.

"Then we have a mutual understanding," Zhek smiled.

Zazmaria looked into his eyes for a long time. However it was getting late and she knew she had to leave. "I must be going, Zhek."

"Zazmaria, before you go, please remember the things I said tonight – I meant them. I think much has been missing from both our lives. I think we have a great deal to offer one another," he said. "You and I could be very good for one another. Your husband may not be the type of man who is willing to risk change, but I am."

And with that, she moved towards the door, looking back at him as she left. Her life within the Palace now felt like a prison.

CHAPTER

24

Pharom

Present-Day Egypt

"Why haven't you two finished this section?" Dustimaine demanded. "You're lagging further and further behind. I want an explanation!"

He wasn't even waiting for an answer. "I warned you last time to speed things up. Your slow progress is hampering the excavation. I have people I have to answer to, and if you start making me look bad, you are going to be very sorry. I promise you that!"

"We're sorry, we will speed things up…" Alex started to say.

Dustimaine cut her off, "I've heard that before and yet now your area is even further behind!"

Khamir, who overheard the exchange, felt very bad for them. Khamir was the workers' supervisor and the primary liaison for Mitch and Alex. They had liked him immediately when they met him, something about him exuded a quiet confidence. He was well respected by the workers and he seemed sincere and genuine. He had also shown a real interest in Mitch and Alex.

"The annual gala is tomorrow night. Everyone who's anyone in Egyptian archaeological circles will be there and I want to be able to say with confidence that we are going to finish on time and with some impressive results. I also expect you two to be there and be on your best behavior. And for goodness sake, dress appropriately! I don't want the two of you, or your two sidekicks, Jack and Bob, looking like you haven't seen the inside of a shower stall in weeks. Now get to work! I don't want any more delays!"

With that he stormed off, muttering something about the embarrassment they were causing him.

Khamir watched him leave.

Mitch and Alex hadn't even had a chance to say anything else. They looked at one another then noticed Khamir looking at them.

He quickly turned his head when they saw him.

"How embarrassing was that?" Alex whispered. "I feel like I'm in grade school being chastised by a teacher."

"Do you get the feeling he doesn't like us?" Mitch asked. That was now their running joke.

Alex laughed, before becoming serious again, "I just wish he wouldn't do that in front of the crew, they'll lose respect for us."

"He has a point though," Mitch whispered. "We are falling further and further behind. We're spending too much time on other things."

"Crap, what are we going to do?" Alex asked.

"We're going to have to re-deploy some of the workers to try and cover more area faster," he answered.

"They're going to wonder why we're doing that, they're pretty comfortable with the way we've assigned things up to now."

"We'll deal with one problem at a time," he replied.

They walked over to Khamir and explained the changes they wanted. He nodded, "Is there anything else I can do to help you right now?"

"No, we wish there were though," Alex replied. "But thank-you, Khamir. We're sorry to have to do this to you."

"I understand – it will be done, do not worry," he said as he bowed his head and turned to go and talk to the workers.

"What did we ever do to deserve him?" Alex said quietly to Mitch as they watched Khamir talking to his men.

"This is going to get even more tense, you know," Mitch said. "We're running out of time. The longer we wait…"

"I know, I know, you don't have to finish," she sighed.

"Alex, we've got to take this seriously, we've kept the chest and its contents for too long now. They might not understand even when we bring forth our findings. We could be in a lot more trouble than we've bargained for."

She took a deep breath, "Maybe, but it's not like we're planning on stealing it or selling it. Our intentions are good."

"Let's just hope that when the time comes, they take that into consideration."

Mitch and Alex headed over to the lab at the end of the day. They had previously told Jack and Bob about the possibility of secret chambers below the Sphinx that might contain the two mysterious obelisks. Jack and Bob would have bolted right out the door then and there to try and find the chambers if Mitch and Alex hadn't informed them of what the consequences would be for attempting an unauthorized excavation.

"You two look like zombies," Bob said as Alex went straight for the coffee. Mitch plopped himself down in the nearest chair.

"Dr. Dust Bucket has been giving us a pretty hard time, we've had to step things up a lot. He's blaming us for the excavation falling behind schedule," Alex moaned as she sat down beside Mitch.

"Well, it is sort of our fault," Mitch admitted. "If we weren't spending so much time trying to decipher the scrolls, looking for clues to the possible location of an entrance to the secret chambers underneath the Sphinx, we'd be a lot further ahead. I think we're just getting tired. The pressure's mounting, you know."

"What have you guys found so far?" Bob asked.

"For starters," Mitch said, "the title of the book. The writing style of it is more like the later, or newer parts of the book so we were able to translate it, '*The Book of the Old and New World*'. We suspect that the earlier parts of the book are actually far older. The writing is sufficiently different that we can't yet glean anything from the first half of the book."

"Is that like Old and New Kingdom labels when referring to Egyptian history, or like the Old and New Testament of the Bible?" Bob ventured.

"Probably exactly like that," Mitch replied, nodding his head. "Which is great, only we can't decipher anything from their earlier history yet, which would tell us so much."

"What else have you deciphered?" Jack asked.

"Well, the symbol for the word 'power' keeps showing up over and over again. But we don't know enough of the symbols to determine exactly what it's saying," Alex said.

"What is the hieroglyph for that again?" Jack asked.

"The 'was scepter,'" Mitch answered.

"Interesting," Jack said. "Any others?"

"Heaven or sky, travel or move, and the one for beginning. We also see the seated lion represented over and over again, and the symbol for light, which could also mean sun, or time for that matter," she said.

"Some of the symbols on our 'crib notes' were just a few letters," Mitch added, "so it's taking us awhile to spell words out and of course we don't have all the letters. We're looking for words that are repeated a number of times for starters. We've found a couple."

"Like what?" Bob asked.

"Kierani." Mitch answered.

"What does that mean? Is it someone's name?" Bob asked further.

"Kind of," Alex started, "we think it's the name of whoever these people are."

"You mean they don't call themselves Egyptians?" Jack asked.

"That's the way it seems," Alex replied. "We also translated a word which we think was the original name of the Sphinx – 'Amsara.'"

"Amsara," Bob repeated. "That's pretty. What does it mean?"

"We don't know yet. There's still a lot we haven't been able to translate," Mitch admitted. "We also don't see anywhere where they talk about mummification or the usual gods, from what we can tell. Whoever they were, they were definitely unlike the ancient Egyptians we're all familiar with."

"One of the most intriguing symbols we've translated though," Alex said, "is the symbol for power shown with the image of an obelisk. On the pages showing hidden chambers below the Sphinx-lion, there were two obelisks depicted. One larger obelisk and with a marking or opening at the top is shown in the first chamber, but it only appears once in the scrolls. The other, the smaller one without that marking or opening, that's the most commonly represented one and the one shown with the symbol for power. There's another word we have seen only a few times, but we don't know what it means. We pieced it together from the letters we had."

Mitch nodded, "It spells, 'Pharom'. It's always shown with the smaller, plain obelisk and the symbol for power."

"What do you think that is?" Jack asked.

"Well, it may be someone's name, perhaps a powerful king or pharaoh who was responsible for building the lion monument and the hidden chambers," Mitch said looking over to Alex.

Jack looked at Mitch and Alex shifting in their seats. "What? What is it guys?"

Alex took a deep breath, they hadn't been sure if they should say anything else, but she decided to go ahead. "What we really suspect is that it's the name for this obelisk we keep seeing, and that it may be much more than a simple relic."

"How much more?" Bob asked.

"Like we said, it's always shown with the symbol for 'power,'" Mitch said. "We're not really sure what to think. It's represented on one of the scrolls with some kind of 'rays' coming out of it."

"Rays coming out of it? What the heck does that mean?" Bob was becoming even more concerned.

Jack was giggling to himself.

"What are you laughing at?" Bob asked.

"Maybe it's a brain probing device, we can test it on you when we dig it up," Jack quipped.

"At least it would have something to probe, not like some people in this room," Bob fired back.

"Oh yeah? My brain would be far too sophisticated for it…"

"Fellas!" Alex stopped them. "Bob, to answer your question, we don't know at this point what it is. We can't even begin to speculate," Alex tried to reassure him, but she knew it wasn't helping much. "We'd need to see it for ourselves. And we need to keep piecing together more words."

"This chamber, the obelisk, it could give us a lot more answers…if only we could find it," Mitch said.

"Yeah, that would be a tremendous find. Who knows what else might be hidden down there?" Alex said.

"And you guys are sure the chamber is down there – beneath the Sphinx?" Bob asked. "I mean no one has been able to find any evidence whatsoever of that."

"Yeah, we know," Mitch said. "Even if it is there, it will be a cold day in hell before we ever get near it."

"Can you imagine Dustimaine's reaction to that kind of request?" Jack laughed. "He'd make sure you two were the next mummies added to the shifting sands of Egypt."

"Don't worry, Jack and I would dig you up," Bob offered sympathetically.

"Oh gee, thanks, and maybe he will have been kind enough to hide our canopic jars with our bodies. With our organs and corpses, you could put us back together," Alex replied.

"Hey cool, you guys would be Frankensteins! You'd have to obey our orders!" Jack said.

"You're all losing your minds, I swear!" Mitch laughed. "I think we all need more sleep."

The Assassination

Circa 10,000 B.C.

Axiana had been very worried about her daughter since the night she was found by the Amsara monument, having walked out there in her sleep. The little girl had not been disturbed at all by that night. It had been just over a week and Axiana had patiently observed her daughter, looking for signs of anything unusual, but saw nothing of the sort and much to her relief, there had not been a repeat of that frightening incident.

Axiana had however become convinced that the truth was locked away deep within her daughter and that perhaps if the two of them had some time alone, away from the daily distractions, she might be able to reach her.

"Sweetheart, how did you sleep last night?" Axiana asked.

"I slept good, but Tramen was noisy in his sleep."

"No more dreams of Amsara, darling?"

"No, no more, Mommy," Anjia replied.

"Maybe you and I could go sailing down the river tomorrow, just the two of us."

"That would be nice Mommy, but Tramen will be sad," she said.

"I will take him out another time. You and I can sail down the river and have a picnic lunch, and play along the riverside. What do you think, sweetheart?"

"It will be so much fun! I love you, Mommy."

"I love you too, my darling girl," Axiana kissed the top of her head.

Just then, they heard the crunch of leaves, not far away, "Hello, is anyone there?" Axiana called out.

"It is just me, Zazmaria," she replied as she emerged from a grove of trees behind the bench where they had been sitting. "I did not mean to startle you, I was just picking some berries out back. I was on my way back to the Palace to wash them." She smiled, "Good day, Anjia."

Anjia did not reply, instead she buried her face in her mother's dress.

"Anjia, there is no need to be shy," Axiana chided her gently.

Zazmaria smiled, "Well, if you will excuse me, I am going to head in."

"Can we give you a hand with that?" Axiana offered.

Zazmaria pulled the basket in tight to her, "No, thank-you, I can manage."

A few moments passed before Anjia peered out over her shoulder watching her aunt disappear into the Palace. Finally, she lifted her head.

"You do not have to be shy, honey," her mother reassured her.

"I am not shy," Anjia replied.

"Then why did you hide your face?" Axiana looked at her daughter for a moment, "What is it Anjia, why are you acting so strange?"

She shrugged her small shoulders. "It is just…"

"What is it sweetheart? You know you can tell me anything."

"I know. I just do not like her. Tramen does not like her either."

"Your Aunt Zazmaria? Why not?" Axiana asked surprised at the admission.

"I do not know. I feel cold when she is around. She is creepy. I think she is mean too."

"Anjia," her mother admonished her, "that is no way to talk about a member of your family. You are a Royal Princess and you must at least be polite to people. Do you understand me?"

"Yes," she replied sullenly, looking down into her lap.

"All right then. Let us go back inside to play with your brother. Later,

I will help you get ready for our sailing trip in the morning. We will have a wonderful day tomorrow."

Axiana made sure she packed all the necessary items for the day of sailing with her daughter. She was planning on exploring and strolling along the area east of the river for herbs and plants. Axiana had an argument with Traeus the previous night about this trip. He did not want her to go, but she insisted she needed to do this for Anjia.

Her husband felt that it was getting too close to the annual flood season and that the trip could be dangerous, but she had argued he was being overprotective. The flood season was not due to start for a few more weeks. She insisted she and Anjia would not be in any danger. They had some beautiful weather lately, warm sunshine and cool breezes and Axiana wanted to take advantage of that. She reminded him that she had been sailing all her life and not to worry so much.

Traeus asked her to at least wait until the whole family could go together, but she was insistent on having her mother-daughter time with Anjia, to connect with her one on one and see if she could get her to open up about anything she might be keeping inside. Traeus lost the argument.

He could see Axiana was determined and that there was no talking her out of it. He conceded to allow her to go, but only if a dozen guards escorted them. He assured her he would instruct the guards to allow the two of them some privacy to enjoy their trip. Axiana agreed to this one compromise.

Axiana had a tough time telling Tramen he could not come with them on this day. She had tried to explain that she and Anjia just needed some mother-daughter time, but she could tell how disappointed he was. He had never before been excluded from a family activity.

"But who will protect Anjia?" Tramen asked his mother with all seriousness. "I could bring my sword and protect both of you."

Ever since Traeus and Axiana asked their son to look after his sister after her sleepwalking incident, he had taken on the responsibility with the utmost seriousness, even to the point of asking Commander Koronius for a weapon. The Commander had the King's armorer make a wooden toy sword for the young Prince.

"Your father has ordered many guards to accompany us, dear," Axiana assured her son.

"Tramen, you and I can play when we get back," Anjia said.

"All right," Tramen replied, still looking a little sad.

"Your Uncle Amoni would like to teach you some swordplay today with your new wooden sword. That way you can learn to protect Anjia better. Mindara will make you both a picnic lunch, too. Would you like that, Tramen?" his mother asked.

Tramen's face changed from disappointment to excitement, "Yes Mommy, I will practice until I am really good!"

Tramen giggled as Axiana drew him to her and gave him a hug and kiss. "I love you, my son."

Then it was Anjia's turn, "I love you too, Tramen. Thank-you for wanting to protect me," Anjia said giving him a big hug.

Tramen thought to himself, *'Why are they being so mushy?'* He noticed that girls liked hugging, kissing and saying 'I love you' a lot. It was not that he did not like kissing his sister and mother, but he was five years old now and yesterday Commander Koronius called him a 'young man'. All this hugging and kissing in front of the Royal guards was quite embarrassing for him, but he replied, "I love you, Mommy. I love you, Anjia."

As Axiana and Anjia approached the docks with their escorts in tow, an additional two-dozen of the King's finest guards and sailors were also there waiting for them.

"How are we going to get some privacy with all of these soldiers?" Axiana commented to her daughter.

"I guess Daddy is very protective of us," Anjia said.

"Yes, he is," Axiana said, the irritation was evident in her voice. "Commander Koronius, what is the meaning of this? My husband said that there would only be twelve guards coming with us."

The Commander bowed politely to the Queen and Princess. "Why your Highness," the Commander replied with an exaggerated sense of unknowingness, "what do you ever mean? I am simply taking these soldiers for a training session on the river today, while the other guards accompany you and the Princess."

"So many of you just happen to be going today and with so many weapons?" Axiana asked.

"Of course, most of these lads are not used to the waters, like you are, your Highness. That is why I thought it would be a good idea to give them more experience on the river. It is a perfect day for it, would you not agree?"

"And the weapons?" Axiana asked, raising an eyebrow.

"We could not very well have a proper training exercise unarmed, could we?" he explained.

"No, of course not," Axiana said, not accepting any of it.

"Besides, you can never be too careful. It is best to be prepared for anything," the Commander said with as much sincerity as he could muster.

"That makes absolutely no sense to me," Axiana laughed. She could never be mad at this kind, old soldier.

"We will be sailing south down the river, in the same area you and your original complement of guards are heading. Quite a coincidence," Commander Koronius stated.

"Incredible," Axiana said. She would have to have a talk with her husband about this when she returned at the end of the day.

"Since some of your lads are going on a training exercise, you can take these other lads with you in the other three boats," Axiana pointed to the Royal escort surrounding her and Anjia. "My daughter and I will take my personal sailboat."

"But, your Majesty…" one of the escorts, who was being reassigned, protested.

"That is an order," Axiana said firmly. "We all know that I am the best navigator and sailor here. I can take care of myself and my daughter on a sailboat."

Commander Koronius was about to argue with her, but he saw her resolve. She was the Queen and he was compelled to obey her wishes. "Very well then, your Majesty, though I agree under protest," he said.

"Understood. Do not worry, I will inform my husband this was my idea and mine alone and that I did not give you a choice."

Axiana set her sails to head south. After a while, she landed her sailboat near a lush and uninhabited region. They spent the day walking, picking up various herbs and plants, and watching the wildlife. Commander Koronius and his men allowed the Queen and Princess their privacy.

Axiana saw no signs that her daughter was troubled, much to her relief. At the end of the day, they packed up to head back to the Palace. Axiana cast off the sail and headed north, with the rest of her entourage following behind.

Several leagues into the trip back, Axiana noticed the weather had unexpectedly taken a turn for the worse. "Your Highness!" Commander Koronius shouted as loud as he could from his boat. "There is a storm brewing up ahead! We need to move you and your daughter onto this larger boat for safety."

Axiana nodded her head in agreement. Off in the distance, she could see pitch black, threatening clouds approaching. By the looks of things, the storm was approaching quickly. Although Axiana had sailed through storms on the river before, she was the only adult in the boat. She now had her daughter to think about. She was not going to risk her safety.

At that moment, she heard a soldier on one of the larger boats shout, "Lookout!"

Axiana turned to see a waterspout spring out of nowhere.

"It is heading straight for us!" one of the soldiers shouted over the sudden and violent winds.

"There are more of them over there!" another soldier shouted as five more of the deadly waterspouts appeared around them. Three of them were heading towards the boats carrying the Royal soldiers. The captains of the boats had to take evasive actions to avoid the watery twisters. In doing so, two of the crafts collided.

Commander Koronius watched helplessly as his Royal soldiers fought against the powerful and sudden storm. He yelled at them to catch up to the Queen's boat. They struggled frantically against the now ferocious winds. They were falling further behind their Queen's boat.

Desperately Commander Koronius tried to force his own craft ahead, without any regard for his own safety.

Axiana realized she must get to her escort crafts before the full fury of the storm hit them. She would have to either wait for the other boats to catch up, or else she would have to turn her boat around, and sail towards them. It started to rain hard. The easterly wind, which she had used to sail up and down the river, was replaced by a stronger wind from the north. The northerly wind hit the Queen's craft straight on and the sailboat came to a dead stop.

"Mommy, why have we stopped?" Anjia asked, frightened.

"We just need to change our direction to get through, sweetheart," Axiana said as calmly as she could.

The increasingly strong current started to push her boat back. The rain poured down on them, drenching them. The skies were pitch black, only the numerous lightning bolts revealed the angry, dark clouds.

Axiana had only two choices; she could adjust the angle of the sails so that they could catch the wind correctly to move the boat forward, or try to steer the boat into the proper direction to catch the wind, but steering the boat might not get the boat to where she needed it to be in the current torrential conditions.

Axiana pulled the cord to adjust the sails, but the cord ripped apart and the rope holding the sail and center beam together on the starboard side flung loose. "Oh no!" Axiana cried out.

Anjia remained quiet and frozen, watching her mother work frantically in the merciless storm.

Without any support on the starboard side, the rope on the port side also flung loose. Without the ropes holding the sail and the beam in place, the force of the winds turned the sail, twisting the center beam, snapping it in two, almost capsizing the boat. The sudden and violent storm tossed the boat around like a toy amidst the angry waters.

Anjia screamed and clung to her mother. Axiana held Anjia tightly in one arm and tried to steer the rudder with her other arm. She noticed that she still had the piece of cord that had ripped apart. She looked at the cord and noticed that there were brown burnt marks and a white residue on the ends of it. It looked as if some sort of chemical had burned through the cords and the ropes holding the beam. The chemicals would have needed time to burn the ropes – time that she and Anjia had used to go wandering in the wilderness.

"Mommy, I am scared!" Anjia cried.

"Me, too, honey. I am doing the best I can. Do not worry, we will be all right!" Axiana yelled, looking out into the menacing darkness, praying her words would prove true.

The break in the beam also broke apart several parts of the boat. The sailboat was quickly taking on water and began to sink. Axiana seeing that they were about to go under, grabbed the barrel of drinking water she brought for their trip, and emptied it.

"Honey, I am going to do something to keep you safe, you have to try and be still for a moment!" she shouted through the lashing winds. She quickly tied Anjia to the barrel with the rope she was still holding – the same rope that had once held the sails together. *'The empty barrel should float,'* she thought, *'it should help keep her above water.'* The barrel was too small to support an adult.

With one big crash, the waves finally tore the sailboat into pieces.

Axiana and Anjia were thrown into the turbulent waters. At first, Axiana also held onto the barrel that Anjia was tied to, but she only ended up dragging both of them down into the water. Without thinking and acting purely on instinct, Axiana let go of her daughter.

"No! Mommy!" Anjia cried, as she resurfaced to the top of the water. Anjia only saw a glimpse of her mother before the waves swept them apart. Anjia held onto the barrel, crying for her mother who had disappeared under the waves, until eventually the little girl succumbed to darkness…

CHAPTER

26

☥

Chaos

I n the city, the effects of the sudden storm were also being felt. The storm had hit the Royal Palace and other buildings with gusting winds and sporadic flooding. Trees were whipping in the wind and reports of damage and injuries around the city came pouring in.

This was the worst storm they had ever experienced. Chaos and confusion were rampant as people desperately tried to hold their homes and loved ones against the punishing rains and terrible winds. This storm was different. It had come on without warning and had taken everyone by surprise with its sudden intensity.

The storm had also battered the main temple, but its sturdy walls of stone had withstood the beating. The priests had been scrambling to help those caught in the storm and had gathered people near the front of the temple. Provisions were brought in from the priests lodgings, kitchen and dining hall in the wings behind the main temple complex.

Back in the priests' private wings, a young priest named Essen, yelled out, "Odai! Odai! Come quickly!"

Odai, at the far end of the temple, heard Essen calling out and came running. Essen was wildly waving him down the hall, which led outside the temple complex.

"What is the matter?" Odai called after Essen, who had not stopped to explain, but kept on running ahead. Nearly out of breath, Odai finally caught up with him as he was entering the garden, which preceded the lion habitat.

"Hurry Odai! It is Amsara, something is wrong with him!"

"What do you mean? What has happened?" Odai asked, feeling a sudden sense of panic.

Finally, they had stopped at the entrance leading to the lion's den and Essen turned to explain, "Odai, I honestly do not know what happened. I had checked in on him and the lionesses to make sure they were safe from the storm and they were all fine, they had gone into their housing once the rains had started."

Essen's voice rose with panic, "I checked on the lions again not ten minutes ago and they were sitting quietly in the corner of the den watching the rains die down when Amsara's ears suddenly perked up and he started to growl, low at first, then he got up and he began to pace. I thought maybe the storm had upset him. But then he just went wild. He ran into the outdoor enclosure and began clawing at the fence, roaring. Then he started running back and forth along the fence at the back of the den. I have no idea what startled him."

Essen paused to catch his breath. "He will not stop. I did not know what to do, so I came looking for you."

Odai stepped forward carefully, he could hear Amsara going wild inside, roaring and shaking the mesh fence. He could not imagine what was wrong with the big cat. He had never heard him act this way. Odai's heart was pounding as he slowly and quietly opened the gate leading to the den.

As Odai approached, Amsara stopped his rampage momentarily, sensing his presence. Amsara came running over to where Odai stood, a mere foot from the fence.

"Amsara, what is wrong? The storm is over now. There is nothing more to worry about." Odai's eyes searched the big animal, looking for signs of injury or illness, but found none apparent.

Amsara looking intently at the man who had saved his life and cared for him ever since, began growling, obviously trying to communicate something to his life-long friend.

"What is it?" Odai looked around the enclosure, but still saw nothing out of the ordinary, save for some re-arrangement of the foliage and an overturned water dish and food container.

Suddenly Amsara ran to the back of the pen, and then stood up on his hind legs, clawing at the fence. The cat's focus was beyond the confines of the enclosure. Whatever it was that had his attention was far outside. Odai still could not detect what the lion was seeing or yearning after.

"What do you think is wrong with him?" Essen asked nervously.

Odai shook his head, "I have no idea, but one thing is clear, he wants to get out. Maybe he felt vulnerable being cooped up during the storm." Odai thought for a moment as he watched the majestic creature in obvious distress and made a decision.

He turned back to Essen, "Go get his harness and leash. I am going to take him out and see if that will calm him down."

"But Odai, is that safe? He does not look like he could be handled right now." Essen was visibly worried about the prospect of the 450-pound predator being taken out in his present state of agitation.

"I trust him and I believe I can handle him. Please, go now!" Odai ordered.

Essen nodded and ran back into the building adjacent to the lion's enclosure.

"Sshhh, Amsara, I will help you, please calm down," Odai said gently.

Essen came running back, leash in hand. "Here you go!"

Odai took the leash, and placed his hand on Essen's shoulder, "I am going in now. Go back and make sure the path is clear. I do not want anyone else nearby to further startle or upset him when I take him out. Run, quickly now!"

Essen gave a nod of his head and ran back out. Odai could hear him hollering for everyone to vacate the pathway.

"All right, I am coming in Amsara. It is going to be all right. I will take you outside and we will go for a walk."

Ordinarily, taking Amsara outside for a stroll was not an issue. The lion was fairly tame and was used to people. But Odai knew this could be a dangerous situation – unpredictable. However, the part of him that communed daily with this creature said to trust him. Amsara needed something, and Odai was determined to help him.

Taking a deep breath, he unlocked the gate, leash in hand. The ground was soaked from the heavy rains. Amsara turned his attentions towards Odai who was walking towards him, the edges of his long, white robes becoming muddied.

Surprisingly, the cat quieted down and sat down before Odai as he always did when having the harness and leash fastened.

Once that was done and Odai had a good handle on him the lion sprinted through the doorway. Odai, stumbling to keep up, ran behind him, still hanging onto the leash. Once outside the temple complex, the lion gave a huge, bellowing roar and bolted. The sudden movement caused the leash to snap free from Odai's hand and the giant cat took off running straight towards the river. Odai did not have a chance to stop him.

Running after him as fast as he could for a few minutes, desperately calling out the lion's name, Odai finally realized there was no hope of catching the swift animal. He could only stare helplessly after the quickly vanishing form of his longtime companion. He dropped to his knees and prayed fervently for the lion's safe return.

The lion raced determinedly towards the river, driven by instinct and a single purpose, instilled at birth. As he neared the river, he stopped and sniffed the air. His keen ears and eyes were also attuned to the slightest movement or scent. He ran towards the river's edge, and once he reached it, he pushed through the thick, wet brush. He spotted a body floating nearby. He swam out towards it, and with his teeth, he grabbed at a piece of rope that was tied around the small form. He pulled and pulled. The child was loosely tied to a barrel.

The rope, which still held the girl, was nearly frayed right through, but miraculously it had somehow held on. She was tangled with weeds from the river. Amsara carefully grabbed onto her clothing with his powerful jaws and swam back to the riverbank. Once there, he pulled her ashore.

The barrel got caught in the weeds and the last threads of the rope snapped free, with part of the rope still wrapped around her waist. She was not moving and was barely breathing.

Amsara licked at her face, but the little girl did not stir. He pushed at her side with his nose, but still no response. He kept nudging her shoulder and head until finally, the little girl coughed, spitting up some water, but quickly lost consciousness again. Again Amsara licked at her face, sniffing her for signs of life. Amsara's attention was then drawn to the sound of far-off voices. He let out a deafening roar in response.

Odai and three other priests from the temple, including Essen, had set out on a search party, calling out as they tracked Amsara's path as best they could through the muddy fields and grasses. Then, they heard Amsara's call.

The huge cat came running in their direction. Odai spotted him first, and took off towards him, his fellow priests following closely behind. Before Odai could reach him, however, Amsara turned and ran back towards the river.

Now Odai could make out a shape on the ground ahead of the running form of the great lion. He ran towards it and realized it was a child lying on the ground, Amsara now standing over the motionless figure.

Odai raced up and knelt on the ground beside the child. As he brushed the hair away from the child's face, he gasped. It was Princess Anjia. He attempted to resuscitate her. By this time, the other priests had caught up. They were stunned to see the Princess lying there.

Odai worked frantically to revive her. Over and over he blew breath into her tiny form, pressing on her chest to get her heart beating and to get her to breathe on her own.

Finally, the Princess gave a great cough and water came pouring out of her mouth.

Relieved, Odai then noticed the rope that was still around her waist and removed it. He examined it and though it was wet he could see that the ends had strange marks that looked like burns on them. He looked up and noticed the barrel tangled in the weeds by the riverbank.

He ran over to look at it and saw that the same rope was also tied around the barrel. He grabbed the end of the rope and noticed the very same burn marks on it. He looked back at the Princess and realized that she must have been fastened to the barrel during the storm. He decided to put the piece of rope that had been fastened around the Princess' waist in his pocket and take it with him. He would show it to Senarra.

He remembered Assan mentioning that the Queen and Princess had planned to go sailing today and that the King was not happy about them going alone so he had assigned a large contingent of guards to accompany them. *'But where was the Queen or her guards? Where was their boat?'* Odai, fearing the worst, wasted no time, picked the Princess up and ordered two of the priests to remain behind.

"I will take her back to the main temple. It is closer than the Palace and there will be healers there that can help her. Essen, take Amsara and bring the empty barrel and remaining rope with you. You two – see if you can locate the Queen. She and the Princess set sail this morning. If you find anyone else, say nothing of the Princess yet, until we know if she will survive."

27

Legend of a Prophecy

Carrying Anjia, Odai arrived at the main temple and set the little Princess on a bed. Amsara would not return to his den, he remained outside of Anjia's bedroom.

"Go get Senarra – quickly!" Odai ordered Essen, but it was unnecessary, she ran into the room at that moment. Odai looked up, his face grave, "It is the Princess – she nearly drowned, there was some kind of accident. We found her near the river. Can you help her?"

Senarra, shocked, knelt down beside the unconscious, soaked Princess, and placing her head on the Princess' chest, listened to her lungs. "She is breathing, though I think there may still be water in her lungs."

Senarra desperately worked to get the remaining water out of the little girl's lungs. Odai stood back watching. Essen and two other priests who had witnessed their arrival stood silently near the door.

Odai turned to Essen and whispered, "We must notify Assan. Where is he now?"

"He was helping with the relief efforts at the Palace."

"Summon him at once, but say nothing. I will explain to him what has happened. I will also watch Amsara."

"Understood," Essen said as he left.

Odai took Amsara's leash. Stroking the big cat's mane, his thoughts filled with fear and uncertainty.

Anjia coughed up some more water, then finally began to breathe normally again on her own.

Senarra grabbed a blanket and began drying her off. She closed the door and then got the Princess out of her soggy clothes and wrapped her in a clean, dry, soft blanket. She laid the Princess down, and the exhausted little girl fell asleep, her tiny body overcome from the harrowing ordeal.

Senarra opened the door to see Odai, who looked lost in thought, and whispered, "Odai, she is all right now. She will be fine. What happened?"

Odai, staring at the little Princess, shook his head in amazement and related the events leading up to this point. "It was unbelievable, Senarra, how Amsara did what he did. He hates to swim!"

Odai was trying to process everything that had happened. "How he could have possibly known she was in danger, to save her…"

Finally Brother Essen, with tears in his eyes, returned with Assan. "The Queen's body has been found. She is dead."

"This is the rope that was tied around the Princess' waist," Odai said, still shaking from the terrible news. He showed it to Senarra and Assan. They were alone with the unconscious Princess. "The ends of the rope have strange marks on them. It does not look like the ropes just snapped off. They look as if they were burned somehow. Senarra, you are a specialist with alchemy. What do you think?"

Senarra, trying to maintain her focus on the matter at hand, wiped away her tears and examined the rope closely, "This is very strange. These burn marks could have been caused by chemicals, but not by any I have ever handled before, this was thick, strong rope. Chemicals that could do this are certainly not readily available. Whoever did this, knew exactly what to get and where to find it. Mixing this kind of compound is not only dangerous but also quite sophisticated. A person would have to be extremely cautious handling it, it would burn badly it if came into contact with skin. Something like this is definitely not common knowledge."

"Do you think someone purposely tried to harm them?" Senarra asked, frightened at such an idea.

Assan, deep in thought, remained silent.

Odai panicked. "Someone else must have known the Queen and Princess were going sailing today. How long would it have taken for these chemicals to burn through?"

"It is hard to say without knowing the exact composition, but it would only have been a matter of hours, no more."

"I do not know what to think right now," Odai replied, his mind racing with all sorts of terrible thoughts.

"Do you both recall the legend of King Narmethon?" Assan asked. His expression grew darker and even more serious.

Senarra nodded, "Yes, of course, King Traeus dedicated the Amsara monument to his legend."

"And the prophecy that is tied to that legend?" Assan asked.

Senarra recalled the prophecy she had been taught as a child. She recited it from memory:

'Though times are troubled and hope may fade
Let not your hearts despair

For one day a child shall come to you
Bringing light and salvation in your darkest hour

You will recognize the chosen one
As she shall be brought forth by a magical creature

From the ashes the one who will save you
Will also be saved to one-day reign in peace and love

This child will see far and know much of your hearts
Beware those who fear her, for they shall also try to destroy her'

Assan nodded and continued, "You told me how Amsara raced to rescue the Princess. He saved her life. It was a miracle how it happened. There was no way he could have heard or seen anything near the river at this distance. He sensed her life was in danger somehow and was able to find her in time."

Odai paused, realizing the gravity of what he would say next. "This prophecy was written long after King Narmethon's reign. It refers to the next ruler who will bring light and salvation to our people at our darkest hour, just as King Narmethon did. It says we will know this child because he or she would also be saved by a magical creature, the same way King Narmethon was. That is Amsara! That is why he did what he did. He was destined to do so! Just as I was destined to find him as a cub so he would live and fulfill his purpose."

Assan nodded, "Precisely."

Senarra understood, "Someone suspected Princess Anjia's destiny as the Chosen one. 'Those who fear her…shall also try to destroy her.'"

28

A Difficult Decision
Must Be Made

Assan had made his decision. "Princess Anjia is in danger, grave danger. She cannot remain here. Someone out there has designs on destroying the Royal Family and our people's future. The assassin or assassins have a powerful knowledge of chemistry." He shook his head, realizing the terrible peril they were in. He set his shoulders, "She must be hidden away for her safety."

"Shall we inform the King of…" Odai started to say.

"He cannot know of this," Assan interrupted him.

Stunned silence filled the room.

"No one else can be told what has happened, not even her family."

"But, your Grace, we cannot…" Odai tried to protest.

"Odai, whoever killed the Queen knew the storm was coming," said Assan.

"How can that be possible?" Senarra asked, greatly troubled.

"There is a legend about an ancient witchcraft that allows a person to read the skies. Many did not believe in such powers, but there have been rumors through the ages that this witchcraft is still practiced. The assassin must have known a storm was approaching and sabotaged the Queen's boat before she set sail. This was all made to look like an accident. This assassin is very powerful and skilled, thus extremely dangerous."

Odai and Senarra stared at Assan in disbelief.

"The possibilities are too many and too varied. Under these circumstances, there is no way to protect the Princess if she stays here," Assan said. "We cannot allow her to be put in further danger. The only way to guarantee her safety is to pretend that she is already dead."

"But surely she would be safe within the Palace, under heavy guard," Senarra protested.

"No, she would not!" Assan shouted. "Whoever did this succeeded in assassinating a Queen, right under the watch of three dozen Royal guards, including Commander Koronius himself! The assassin had access to the Royal family. It could be someone within the Royal household working together with enemies of the family or on their own. We cannot be certain where this threat is coming from. The Princess barely survived, and only by the miracle of prophecy. A terrible sorcery and evil is at work and we have been utterly blind to it!"

Assan was deeply angry with himself for not foreseeing such danger. He paced the room. "We cannot tell the King of the suspicious circumstances of the accident either. He must believe the storm alone caused the accident."

Senarra looked to Odai. They could not believe what they were hearing.

Assan saw how anguished the two young priests were, "You are asking yourselves, how could I make such a decision, keep so much from our King and tear his only daughter away from him? What gives me that right?"

They just kept looking at him, so he continued, "We know the Princess' life is in immediate danger. King Traeus would never agree to being parted from his daughter and we cannot be sure we could protect her if she were to stay. A dangerous and lethal enemy has gained intimate knowledge and proximity to the Royal Family. Until we find out who is responsible for this treachery no one must know she survived. We will act as if we believe it was just the storm, a tragic accident."

Senarra could not hold back her tears.

Assan was placing a great burden on their shoulders, but he knew he had no choice. "I am sorry, I wish there was another way. I am prepared to take full responsibility for this. We must work quickly now. I will personally inform our King of the Queen's death. I will tell him that the Princess' body was most likely lost to the river, but that the search continues. It will buy us time."

"What can we do?" Odai asked, his voice hoarse.

Assan paused for a moment to think. "I know a family that lost their only child. I have only met them once. They are kind and caring people. They faced their loss with great strength of heart though they were obviously devastated. They live in the farthest village north of here. It is the first house you will come across as you reach the village. Their names are Uta and Ehrim."

Odai and Senarra's faces blanched.

Assan continued, "You must take the Princess to them. Tell them only that she was orphaned, her parents were killed in an accident and she had no other surviving relatives, that she needs a home and parents." As the twins were still so young, they had not yet traveled. No one outside the city had ever seen them.

"I understand, we will see this done," Odai replied. Senarra lowered her eyes.

Assan put his hand on their shoulders, "This is an enormous responsibility I know, but there is no one I have more faith in than the two of you."

He looked at Senarra who had stood still as a stone, "The Princess will need a gentle voice and kind heart to tell her what has happened, where she is going, to comfort her in this dark hour and prepare her for what is to come."

"I will do my best," Senarra replied.

"I know you both will," Assan said. "I will see that the evidence of Anjia's survival remains hidden, then I must go to await the arrival of the Queen's body and to make the... other arrangements."

"Your Grace, in time, when the King learns of what was done here this day, do you think he will ever be able forgive us?" Odai asked.

Assan looked grave. "As I said, I will take full responsibility for this decision. You must go now."

Lives Change Forever

Senarra looked at the sleeping Princess. "I helped her parents conceive her, I cannot believe I am helping to take her away." She wiped away her own tears, steeling herself to face this sad task.

"Come, we must act quickly, there is very little time," Odai said.

Amsara still stood guard at the door to the room.

Senarra walked over to a chest of drawers in the room. She searched through to find something suitable the small girl could wear. Anjia was still wrapped tightly in the blanket she had put her in. She found some clean linen undershirts and she chose the smallest one.

Odai turned away to allow the Princess her privacy.

Anjia began to stir. Senarra stroked the girl's long, shiny hair, looking at the innocent face.

"My chest hurts, my throat is sore," Anjia said as she touched her tiny hand to her chest.

"Yes, you swallowed a lot of water, but you will be fine now," Senarra said as she gently patted Anjia's hand.

"My Mommy, where is she?" the little girl asked.

"Do you remember the storm, Anjia?" Odai asked softly.

"Yes."

"It was very bad, you almost did not survive," he said. Odai looked to Senarra, she nodded for him to continue. "We think your Mommy saved you from drowning."

Anjia's gaze drifted, she recalled the harrowing storm, the water coming into the boat, her mother letting go of the barrel and disappearing into the waves…

"Princess, we are sorry to tell you this, but the Queen, your Mommy, she…"

"She is gone…" Anjia whispered, her lip trembling.

Odai and Senarra were speechless, she knew…

The little girl started to cry. Senarra held her tight. "I want to see my Daddy," Anjia spoke in her tiny, breaking voice. She looked up at Senarra with expectant eyes filled with tears.

Odai replied to her instead, "Princess, please listen, it is not safe for you to stay here. We are going to bring you to a different home for a while where some very kind people will take care of you."

Fear instantly took hold of her. "No! I want my Daddy, I want to see Tramen!" Anjia struggled in Senarra's arms.

Odai replied, trying to calm the panicked child, "Anjia, I know this seems scary and that you are hurting and frightened, but you must trust us. Your Daddy and your brother are not safe either and the only way we can keep them and you out of harm's way is to hide you away from here. What happened today was horrible, but if you are not taken away and protected, it could happen again. Your family is not safe." Odai paused letting his words sink in. "Someday, you will see them again, I promise."

Anjia was shaking. "But I will be all alone."

Odai, trying to keep his own emotions in check, replied, "No, Princess, you will never be alone. We are going to bring you to a loving family, they will look after you and care for you, until it is safe to come home."

"But I want to see my Daddy and my brother before I go," she pleaded.

Senarra answered, "Anjia, we must go quickly before someone sees you. Someone tried to kill you, we do not know who it was, but until we do, no one must be told where you are. You must also never speak of any of this. You must never tell anyone who you are or what happened today."

"But why would someone want to kill my Mommy and me?"

"It is complicated," Odai replied.

As Anjia looked from Senarra to Odai, a thought occurred to her. She calmed down and then said the most startling thing, "This is because I can share my thoughts with Amsara. People think it is strange, sometimes they do not believe me."

"Some people do believe you," Odai replied.

Senarra asked cautiously, "Anjia, you... understand that you are special?"

"Amsara told me one day my life would change and that I should not be afraid. He told me he would protect me and that I must trust him. He said he would speak through someone who would do what he asked."

Anjia looked directly at Odai, "Are you doing what he asked?"

Odai could barely keep his jaw from dropping, "Yes, Princess, I believe so. There is a prophecy that tells of a special child who would be saved by a magical lion. Did you know that our lion, Amsara, saved you today? It is because of him that you did not also die."

Odai had not considered telling her any of this, he did not want to overwhelm the young girl, but it was clear now that it must be said.

"I remember...fur on my face. Amsara licked my cheek and pulled me away...somewhere."

"Yes, yes," Odai said, bursting with pride over the heroic actions of his magical lion. "Amsara saved you and stood guard over you until we arrived. Somehow, from far away, he knew you were in trouble and went running to find you."

The Princess looked at Odai for a long time, considering what he was telling her. "Then I will go with you," she said, accepting her fate.

Senarra took her tiny face in her hand, "And you will keep the secret of this day until the time comes when you are to be brought back home? It may be a very long time."

"I will," the girl replied with wisdom far beyond her years. "But I will miss my family."

"They will miss you too," Senarra replied.

Odai stood up, "Then I will go and arrange our transportation. Wait here for my return, I will not be long."

As he exited the room, he nodded to the two priests, "Please remain here for now."

Then he looked down at the lion still waiting patiently at the door, and kneeled stroking the cat's mane, "She is safe now, Amsara. You have done well. We will take care of her now."

30

The Aftermath

Back at the main temple, Assan went about the painful and perilous business of orchestrating the cover-up. Someday, he prayed, the King would find it in his heart to forgive him for the deception and for separating his beloved daughter from him. Faith would have to carry the Head Priest through the difficult times ahead.

Assan knew he must act quickly. The storm had passed, the chaos would be subsiding and questions would be asked. Questions he must prepare himself to answer. He had little time before the Queen's body arrived, and keeping that information under control until he could speak with the King would be difficult.

Assan tracked down the priests involved and instructed them to never reveal what they knew and why. He emphasized that the very survival of the Royal Family depended on their faith in this decision.

Assan had learned that Commander Koronius had survived the storm, along with several of his men. He decided to have the Commander alone brought to the temple and informed of the Queen's death. He was to be told the Princess was missing and presumed dead.

At last, the Queen's body arrived and was taken to the inner sanctuary of the temple. Assan received her then left to return to the Palace to deliver the grim news.

King Traeus was seated at a table with a few of his administrators going over what they had learned so far about what needed to be done to help people recover from the storm and the progress of the relief efforts.

There was a knock on the door. It was Assan.

Traeus stood up.

"Your Highness," Assan bowed, "I must speak with you in private."

Sensing a serious tone and without needing a word from their King, the rest of the people in the room silently cleared out.

Traeus looked at Assan, searching his face. Finally the door closed.

"Your Majesty, may we sit down?" Assan asked.

"What is it Assan?" Traeus asked as he continued to stand.

Assan took a deep breath, and spoke in a low voice, "I deeply regret the sad news I am about to give you. The Queen…"

Traeus went ghostly white. His voice shook, "Assan, no, please just tell me she is all right."

"I am sorry your Highness, the storm overtook her craft…she did not survive."

"No! No!" Traeus cried out. "This cannot be!" he squeezed his eyes closed, shaking his head. He slumped into his chair and wept.

"Your Majesty, I know this is difficult, but we have brought her body to the temple sanctuary." Assan hesitated. "Your Highness, there is something else…"

The King looked up quickly. "Anjia," he whispered, his voice cracking, "where is Anjia?"

"She…she was lost in the storm. They have been searching the river for any sign of her, but it has been too long…I am sorry."

Traeus cried out, "No! My precious daughter, my wife…" He stood, shaking. "Why?" he yelled, grabbing a chair and hurling into a wall.

He fell forward onto the table, pounding it with his fists, "No, no no…"

Assan ran over to his King to try and calm him, but Traeus shrugged him off. Then, in a fury, Traeus took hold of the heavy wooden table and over turned it. He stood there panting.

"Your Highness," Assan spoke, "I am so sorry. This is a tragic loss, but you are not alone. You have many loyal people around you who will help you through this."

Traeus looked at Assan, the tears streaming down his face, his voice barely audible, "I want to see my wife."

"Of course, your Majesty," Assan bowed, "I will take you there at once."

A King's Good-Bye

Assan accompanied the devastated King to the main temple. Once inside, Traeus took a deep breath and tried to brace himself for what he was about to face.

At the far end of the temple stood Commander Koronius. He stepped forward to meet his King.

"Your Highness," Commander Koronius said. He bowed deeply, "Please accept my deepest sympathies over your loss. Words could never express my sorrow and regret…" Koronius struggled to maintain his composure. "I take full responsibility. I offer my life in their place."

Traeus shook his head, "Please, Commander, just tell me what you saw, tell me everything. I want to know about the last hours of my precious wife and daughter."

For nearly an hour they sat at the front of the temple as the Commander relayed the events: the trip down the river, the time on shore and the terrible journey back when out of nowhere the storm struck.

Traeus listened intently.

"Her Majesty was extremely brave, your Highness, she tried desperately to keep the sailboat intact. She fought so hard to save Princess Anjia and herself."

Commander Koronius paused as the painful memories replayed themselves in his mind. "Her sailboat just came apart in the force of the winds and waves. It happened so fast. One moment she was fighting to keep the boat together, the next they disappeared. The waterspouts had surrounded us… she was too far away for us to reach her in time. We tried, your Majesty, we tried so hard, but…"

"Commander, I am sorry for those among your men who also perished this day. If you have strength left, please go now to help in the recovery efforts."

The Commander swallowed hard. "At once Your Majesty." He got up and bowed, his eyes red with tears. He left the temple.

"It is time your Highness," Assan said gently. "We should proceed to the inner sanctuary. Much still needs to be prepared."

Traeus nodded sadly.

Assan led his King into the small, candlelight chamber.

As Traeus took in the sight before him, the finality of the moment seared onto his soul.

There, laid out in front of the altar was his wife. Her long dark hair, now dried, glistened in the candlelight. She looked as though she was sleeping, but there was no rise and fall of breath that would indicate life. Still, she looked beautiful, almost peaceful.

Assan remained by the door, turning away to allow his King privacy in his grief.

Tears once again streamed down Traeus' face. "My love…my precious Axiana. We should have been together until old age."

He gently touched his wife's shoulder, then her hair. He leaned over to look at her beautiful face. The long eyelashes, her perfect features…the full lips he had kissed so many times. Without thinking, he bent down and lightly kissed her, but her lips were now cold. One of Traeus' tears dropped onto her cheek. Traeus watched as it fell down her cheek, as though she too was crying at the separation.

☥

Tramen

O nce back at the Palace, the King sent for Mindara to meet him in his private study. She had been looking after Tramen while Axiana and Anjia had gone out for their sailing trip. Mindara knocked.

Traeus called for her to come in and to close the door behind her.

She immediately saw that something was wrong, terribly wrong. "Your Highness, you sent for me?"

"Please sit down, Mindara," Traeus motioned to a chair across from him. She had a very bad feeling.

"You know how much we have always depended on you…" the King started to say. "You are a very important part of this family." Traeus turned away as he struggled to keep his emotions in check.

"Is everything all right? I know the storm was…" Mindara's voice trailed off.

Traeus shook his head. "No, Mindara, everything is not all right and it never will be again." He paused searching for the words. "My wife, my daughter …" the tears welled up in his eyes again and he put his hand over his quivering lip. "The storm, there was an accident…"

Mindara inhaled sharply, "No, you cannot be saying…"

Traeus was too overcome with grief to answer.

She began to weep. Then a thought occurred to her, "Tramen…"

Traeus' voice was hoarse. "My son is now without a mother or a sister."
He took a deep breath, "I need to tell Tramen, but I do not know how."

Mindara's heart broke. "I will help you."

Traeus and Mindara walked to the room Tramen had shared with his sister. Traeus dismissed the guard who had been posted outside the room.

Inside Tramen was still playing with the toy sword Commander Koronius had fashioned for him, fighting imaginary armies.

"Daddy!" the young boy exclaimed. "You are back! Did you see the storm? It was so scary!"

Mindara stepped into the room behind the King.

"Hi Mindara!" Tramen said.

She smiled at him.

"Son, we need to talk you about something. Please come sit beside me," his father said, patting the bed beside where he had sat down.

"When are Mommy and Anjia coming back?" Tramen asked as he dashed over to sit beside his father. "They will be soaking wet from the rains!"

Traeus steeled himself. He knew these next moments would forever alter his son's life. "That is what we need to talk to you about Tramen." Traeus tried to find the courage to continue, "You see, the rains were very, very heavy out on the river during the storm and the winds were very strong too. It created twisters in the water."

"Sounds scary," the little boy replied, his eyes wide.

"It was very scary. This was the worst storm our people have ever seen." Traeus paused for a moment then continued, "Your Mommy and Anjia were caught right in the middle of it. There was no warning – they could not avoid the storm." Traeus looked closely at his son's face, "Son, I am so sorry to have to tell you this, but they did not survive. They are gone…"

"What do you mean?" Tramen asked, panicking.

Mindara knelt down in front of him, "Tramen, they died. We are very sorry."

Traeus looked at his son, he could tell he was in shock, trying to process what he was hearing. He decided to just get all the horrible news out at once, "Tramen, there is one other thing." He hesitated. He knew this would be the most difficult part for his son. "We found your mother's body, but your sister, she was lost to the river, we have not found her body yet."

"Then maybe she is alive!" Tramen exclaimed, tears filling his eyes.

"Tramen, listen to me," Traeus held his little shoulders gently and looked into his eyes, "too much time has passed. She could not have survived this long. We have to accept the fact that she is gone, too. Son, I am so sorry."

"No! I did not feel her die! It is not true!" Tramen broke free of his father's grasp and ran to the other side of the room. His small face was red with anger and pain. "We must look for her, I can help. I will run all along the river, I will run and run until I find her! I said I would protect her! They should have let me come today!" He was becoming hysterical.

"Tramen, please calm down," Mindara pleaded.

"Son, we do have people out searching for her body, but it is too late to save her, you must understand."

"No!" he cried, trembling.

Traeus held his son tight to ease his shaking. He stroked his hair, "I miss them too." He reached into his pocket. "Tramen, I want to give you something." Traeus had taken Axiana's favorite pendant, a beautifully fashioned gold ankh. "This belonged to your mother. I think she would have wanted you to have it." Traeus placed the chain around his son's neck.

Tramen took the pendant in his hands, staring at it. The golden ankh glistened. "It was Mommy's?" he asked, sniffling.

"Yes, my son, it is very special. There is an inscription on it." He turned it over, and read it to his son, "'May this symbol of life protect you, all of your days.'"

Tramen held onto the pendant tightly and cried.

☥

Confusion

"Zazmaria! There you are!" Alaj yelled. "I have been searching everywhere for you. Where have you been?" Alaj came running as he spotted his wife near one of the back entrances of the Palace.

She was soaking wet and shaking, mud splatters were all over her dress, her arms, and her face. Her hair was disheveled and there were tangled weeds in it. She seemed shocked to see her husband, who quickly grabbed her by the arms. She winced, but did not answer him.

"Zazmaria? Did you hear me? What happened to you?"

"Nothing, Alaj, I just got caught in the storm." She pulled away from his grasp.

He noticed what looked like a large burn mark on her in the inside of her lower left arm. He pulled her arm back gently to have a look at the injury, which appeared very red and blistered.

Zazmaria again winced from the pain.

"My wife, you are injured! What happened to your arm?"

She did not answer.

"It looks burned," Alaj said. "We must get you to a healer at once."

"That is not necessary," she replied, pulling away without making eye contact. "I can take care of it. A falling branch hit me. It must have scraped my skin. I have ointments that can heal it." She started to leave.

"Wait Zazmaria," Alaj persisted. "I was terribly worried about you. Where were you?"

"Just outside near the edge of the Palace gardens, collecting herbs. I-I took cover under a tree until the storm passed."

"Where is your basket with the herbs?" he asked looking around.

"Oh," she looked down at her empty hands, "I must have dropped it in the storm. It all happened so quickly." She turned to walk away again.

"Zazmaria, are you sure you are all right? We should take you to a healer."

"Alaj, please I will be fine," her voice now had a distinct edge to it. "I am simply a little dazed from being outside in the winds and rains. If I need anything I will call upon Medetha."

Her husband would not be put off so easily, "Do you not even want to know what else has happened here? Many of our people have been badly hurt, many are missing and several are confirmed dead."

She just stared at the floor, expressionless.

Alaj stepped closer to her. "Zazmaria, this has been one of the worst days in our people's history." His voice filled with emotion as he continued, "Zazmaria, Axiana and Anjia are missing. They have not been seen since they went out for a sail this morning."

Zazmaria's back stiffened, but still, she said nothing.

"Did you hear me? What is wrong with you?" Alaj was almost yelling now.

She looked up, her anger clearly surfacing, "What do you want from me?"

Just then they heard footsteps behind them. It was Assan.

Zazmaria was startled. Her face flushed red.

"Assan," Alaj acknowledged him.

Assan bowed low, "Your Highnesses, I have been sent to find you on behalf of King Traeus. You must come with me at once, it is urgent."

He turned to look directly at Zazmaria, "I am sorry your Highness, I realize this is an inopportune time for you, but it cannot wait."

"May I at least dry off and change my clothing?" Zazmaria asked indignantly.

"I apologize, but I must insist you both come with me now. I will have dry clothing brought to you," Assan waved over one of the servants who happened by. He instructed him to retrieve items for the Princess.

"Now, your Highnesses please follow me."

Zazmaria grew increasingly agitated, "Where exactly are we going?"

"King Traeus has requested to speak with you both in his private study. Prince Amoni is already there, waiting. The King will explain everything when we arrive."

Alaj was concerned, "What is this about Assan?"

"The King wishes to personally inform you," Assan replied, as he continued on.

Alaj and Zazmaria followed silently behind the tall figure of the Head Priest.

They reached the door to the study. A servant came running up from behind with a towel, a robe and dry slippers for Princess Zazmaria. He bowed as he handed her the items. She snatched them from his hands, dismissing him with a wave of her hand. She toweled off and put the robe and slippers on overtop her damp clothes.

Assan then opened the door and motioned for the Prince and Princess to enter. Traeus was seated with his back to the door. He did not rise to greet them. Assan closed the door behind them and led Prince Alaj and Princess Zazmaria to chairs across from the King. It was then they noticed Amoni sitting in a corner of the room. Mindara was also there with her arms around him. Amoni was shaking and had his hands pressed to his face, crying softly.

Alaj realized who was missing from the room. Alarmed, he asked, "Traeus, what is going on? What is wrong?"

Traeus lifted his head. Pain was etched all over his face. "I have just come from seeing my son. I have terrible news." He straightened up and looked at both Alaj and Zazmaria, tears filled his eyes. "There was an accident on the river today, Axiana and Anjia were caught in the storm. Their sailboat was severely battered by the storm. It broke apart…my wife was thrown overboard. Several guards perished in an attempt to save them. Anjia was no where to be found…"

Alaj interrupted, "What are you saying? Are they out searching for them?"

Traeus lowed his eyes, his voice shaking with grief, "They found Axiana…she drowned. My daughter is also presumed dead. They have been searching along the river, but there is no trace of her. She cannot have survived…"

"Oh, Traeus, no!" Alaj cried out.

Amoni again began to sob. Mindara tried to comfort him, as her own tears fell.

Assan stood silently near the door, unobtrusive, observing the proceedings. He noticed Zazmaria had not said a word. Her face bore no reaction or emotion. She held her left arm close to her body, and slowly started to rock back and forth, ever so slightly.

"Zazmaria, you were also caught in the storm today?" Assan asked suddenly.

Zazmaria jumped, not expecting anyone to ask questions of her at this time. "Yes…yes I was," she looked at him then quickly turned away.

"Your arm, is it injured?" Assan asked.

"It is nothing," she snapped. Everyone in the room was now looking at her, making her extremely uncomfortable.

"May I have a look at it? Perhaps I can help," Assan offered as he started to walk towards her.

"No, no, I am fine. We have other concerns right now, please," she answered as she pulled her arm in tighter to her body. Her whole posture was turned away from Assan, and she would not look at him.

Assan stepped back to where he had been standing, still watching her.

Alaj turned his attention back to more immediate concerns. "Traeus are you sure? Is it not at least possible Anjia is still alive? Even the smallest chance?"

"I wish that were so, Alaj. My wife and daughter had numerous guards accompany them on the trip, including Commander Koronius himself. They have searched extensively, but found nothing. Not a single trace of her."

"Axiana, where…" Alaj tried to ask, but he could not speak the words.

"She is in the temple, her body is being prepared…" Traeus' voice broke off.

Assan stepped in, "We are making funeral preparations. The funeral for both the Queen and the Princess will be in four days according to custom. May I suggest…"

Zazmaria suddenly jumped up from where she was sitting, "If you will all please excuse me, I am not feeling well. I am going to retire to my chambers."

She turned to Traeus and bowed slightly. "I am sorry for your loss. I apologize for having to leave, but I think the storm has taken quite a toll on me."

Not waiting for a reply, she swiftly turned and left the room, not making eye contact with anyone else, leaving her disbelieving husband staring after her.

Alaj, utterly shocked at his wife's behavior, turned to his brother, "Traeus, please forgive her…she is not herself."

Alaj looked back at the door she had left through. "I must attend to her, please excuse me." He stood up, "I am deeply sorry for your loss brother. We all grieve with you, it is our loss as well."

As Alaj left the room, he locked eyes with Assan who seemed to study him curiously for a moment.

Assan broke the gaze first then bowed, "Your Highness."

Alaj, feeling confused, bewildered, and overwhelmed by everything that was happening, simply nodded and left.

He ran down the hall after his wife, "Zazmaria!"

She was walking quickly and was about to turn the corner when he began running after her.

"Zazmaria, wait! I want to talk to you!"

She did not stop, did not look back, pretending not to hear him.

Alaj raced to catch up to his wife. He finally reached her just as she was about to close the door to their private chambers on him.

He blocked the door with his hand, "Zazmaria! What is the matter with you? Did you not hear me calling you?"

"Alaj," she whispered hoarsely, "I told you I am not feeling well, I wish to be alone right now. Just let me rest."

"What do you mean you wish to be alone right now?" he asked incredulously. "We have just been informed that Axiana and Anjia have both died today, the city is in ruins from this killer storm which also took the lives who knows how many others, you yourself were hurt, and yet you refuse to talk to anyone? You want to be alone? This is unacceptable!"

"Alaj," she said through gritted teeth, "I am dealing with this in my own way. Just let me be. We can talk later, if you still wish to." Again she tried to close the door on her husband, but he would not be pushed aside.

"That is not good enough Zazmaria!" he yelled at her. "Something is wrong and I want you to tell me what it is. Talk to me! Let me help you. Let me at least look at your arm."

She stepped back and hissed at him, "Leave me be. I told you I will take care of it. I do not want yours or anyone else's help right now. I want to be ALONE!" With that, she slammed the door shut in his face.

34

☥

Sadness and Loss

Queen Axiana's body had been prepared according to Kierani custom. She was interred in the burial chamber alongside King Mesah and Queen Elenia.

In light of not having his daughter's remains, Traeus had one of the artists from the priesthood create a painting of her to be hung in the burial chamber next to her mother's sarcophagus.

The painting had turned out beautifully. It was a scene depicted in the Palace gardens on a sunny day with the flowers were in full bloom. In the background was the Amsara monument, the sun glinting off its coppery bronze body and the golden streaks of its mane. Princess Anjia was playfully running away barefoot, clad in a simple white, loose-fitting dress. She looked back over her left shoulder, an enigmatic smile on her face, her emerald green eyes sparkling. Her long, black hair was blowing softly in the breeze, with a couple of strands blowing across her face. In her left hand, she carried an ankh.

Traeus loved the painting so much he had a second copy of it created so that it could be hung on a wall inside the Palace.

A Royal funeral always began an hour before sunrise. The Royal

Family would walk to the site where the official proceedings would take place. Leading the way would be the priests, who were the physical embodiment of the Kierani spiritual beliefs. The priests lit the torches they would carry during the journey from the Palace through the city streets to the river.

Once the sun came up the torches would be extinguished. The ceremony would take place at the edge of the river where prayers for the souls of Queen Axiana and Princess Anjia would be said.

The funeral was meant to symbolize the cycle of life in one day – being born with the rising of the sun, then the rest of the day is spent as life would be, sharing time with family, friends, and loved ones. Celebrations, spiritual moments, the sharing of meals, community banding together, giving offerings at the temple would occur throughout the day. Then three hours before sunset there would be a feast at the Palace followed by a formal reception.

At sunset, symbolic of life's end when the Kierani believed that the soul would be joined with the setting sun to rise again in eternal life, the torches would be relit, and another procession would make its way to the Palace temple and burial chamber for the conclusion of the funeral ceremonies.

It was now time for the Royals to host the formal reception at the Palace. Members of the priesthood, heads of leading families, along with members of the military came to offer their prayers and condolences.

King Traeus, Prince Tramen, and Head Priest Assan were seated on Royal chairs at the far end of the reception hall along with Prince Alaj, Princess Zazmaria and Prince Amoni.

The Draxen family also made an appearance. As Zhek approached, he eyed Zazmaria. She avoided eye contact with him, until he was standing directly in front of her.

"My deepest sympathies are with you," Zhek spoke, his comments directed to the Princess. "With you both, of course," he added when he noticed the look her husband gave him. "If there is anything I can do…"

Alaj cut him off, "Thank-you Zhek, but we will be fine. A family bands together in times of sorrow and tragedy."

"Of course," Zhek nodded curtly to Alaj and walked away, brazenly giving Zazmaria a long sidelong glance as he left.

Her cheeks flushed, but she said nothing at all.

Traeus felt drained from the day's proceedings. He looked at Tramen sitting beside him. He was so proud of his son, he had held up extremely well under difficult circumstances. However, Tramen had barely spoken all day.

Odai and Senarra were in line. They had been dreading facing their King and his family, feeling like traitors.

Odai and Senarra, who were trying to hide their nervousness, walked up and bowed before their King. "Your Majesty," they greeted him.

"I understand you are each to be commended for your efforts on the day of the storm. Assan has spoken very highly of how you both selflessly handled the pressure you were put under."

Odai spoke first, "Your Majesty, we are simply honored to serve your Family." Odai then looked to Assan who gave him a knowing glance and nodded his head ever so slightly.

"We wish to express our deepest sympathies to you and your Family, your Majesty," Senarra added, shaking slightly.

"Thank-you both," their King replied.

As Odai and Senarra passed Prince Tramen, their sense of guilt and shame grew. They merely bowed, avoiding eye contact, and mumbled something about their sorrow for his loss.

Tramen stared at Odai with a curious expression on his face.

Odai suddenly felt very anxious and uncomfortable.

Tramen spoke up suddenly, though he had spoken to no one else this day, and asked Odai point blank, "Did you see my sister?"

Odai was completely stunned and speechless at the question. Senarra went pale.

The King, overhearing his son's question, was instantly concerned as to where this was going. He leaned over to his son and in a hushed voice said to him, "Tramen, no one saw her that day after she disappeared into the water. Please do not bring this up now."

Tramen, undaunted, looked back up at Odai, "Did you see her?"

Odai struggled for a moment, lowered his eyes, and replied, "I am sorry, Prince Tramen, I wish I could tell you that I had." With that he bowed and he and Senarra walked away.

35

Lovers Reunite

Tthe night following the funeral, Zazmaria was edgy and unable to sleep. Alaj was working late again. He had taken over many of the King's duties, while Traeus looked after his son and tried to come to grips with the tragedy himself. Zazmaria decided to take advantage of his absence.

She slipped on her dark brown cloak, grabbed a black scarf to wrap around her head and snuck out of the Palace to the small red house she had met Zhek at before. She had no idea whether he would be there, but as she neared the house, her heart leapt. She could see a faint light coming from inside. The house appeared undamaged from the storm. Someone was there.

She crept up to the window and peered in. She could see a candle had been lit on a table, but could see no one inside.

"I have been waiting for you," a deep voice spoke from behind her.

She nearly jumped out of her skin. She looked into the darkness as the shape of a man came towards her. "Zhek," she whispered.

"Please come in, the house is warm," he said, looking longingly at her.

Once inside Zazmaria looked around nervously then removed her scarf.

"We are alone, you know," Zhek assured her.

"Yes, of course we are, I just – well, it is hard to get used to sneaking around like this. I think it is probably best one does not let one's guard down, would you not agree?"

"Yes, one can never be too careful," he smirked. He sat down and motioned for her to sit down next to him.

She continued to stand, still looking around the house.

"Zazmaria."

"What?" she turned to look back at him.

He was holding out his hand to her. The light from the candle cast mysterious shadows across his face. His lips were full as they spoke her name. "Zazmaria, come sit with me. I have missed you. It was difficult seeing you at the reception seated next to your husband. In spite of the somber day I longed for you in that moment. I do not know if you could sense it."

She took a deep breath, her heart beating faster. She was so attracted to this man, in spite of her misgivings about what he represented. She felt compelled to go to him, to be held by him. As she sat next to him, his strong arms encircled her, and she melted into his embrace. She had felt so alone, so estranged from everyone in the last few days. Feeling Zhek's warm body holding her was soothing, as if it could make all her fears fall away, at least for the moment.

Zhek reached under her chin and lifted it to him, bending down to kiss her passionately. Slowly he removed her cloak as he continued to kiss her. She moaned softly and pressed herself closer to him.

"I was so worried about you during the storm," he whispered in her ear, kissing her graceful neck.

"I was one of the fortunate ones that day," she replied as she began to undo the ties of the dark green tunic he wore. She also loosened his hair. As the full, dark waves fell around his shoulders, she fingered the gold pendant around his neck, his family crest. It sparkled in the candlelight. It seemed exquisitely bright resting against his tanned, muscular chest. She kissed the star-shaped birthmark over his heart, so unique, so sensual. A masculine brand, she mused, to set him apart from lesser men.

He breathed deeply now, his fingers caressing her thick black hair. Returning the favor, he loosened the pins that held it up and it cascaded down her shoulders. He began to unbutton her form-fitting emerald silk dress as he asked, "Where were you when the storm hit? Were you hurt at all?"

"I was caught outside on the Palace grounds. I took cover, it was only my arm that was hurt."

As he slipped her dress off her shoulders, he saw her arm. It was still quite red. The mark was long and angry looking. She had taken to wearing long-sleeved garments to cover it up. "This must be painful," he said as he lifted her arm to kiss it.

She quickly pulled it away before he got the chance. "It is fine, I am using healing ointments on it. It should be better in a day or two."

"A day or two? It looks much worse than that. Let me look at it. What happened?"

"Zhek, leave it be, it is merely a scratch, I scraped it on a tree branch in the winds." She started to pull her dress back up.

"Wait, wait, I did not mean to pressure you. I am only worried about you."

"Perhaps you can worry about how the rest of my health is doing," she challenged him with a raised eyebrow.

Zhek smiled, "Ah yes, my darling, I should be attending to all your needs, you are quite correct. Hmmm, I sense your shoulders need looking at," he again pulled her dress away from her delicate shoulders, and kissed them. "I think the small of your neck needs attention too," he continued to caress her with ardent kisses.

Slowly she relaxed and surrendered herself to the moment. Zhek picked her up, and carried her to the bedroom.

After making love and falling asleep in each other's arms, Zazmaria began to have the same nightmares again. She awoke with a start in a cold sweat. She was being haunted in her sleep and she began to fear why.

"What is it, what is the matter?" Zhek asked.

"Nothing," she replied uneasily, "it was just a dream. Go back to sleep."

"Do you want to talk about it? Maybe I can comfort you?" Zhek said as he snuggled up to her and kissed her back.

"No, I hardly remember it now," she said as she pushed him away. "I must go. It is late. Alaj will be back soon."

Zhek was more fully awake now. "Zazmaria, you have seemed distant all night. Is there anything you want to tell me? Anything you want to talk about?" He looked deep into her striking topaz eyes, "So much has happened in the last few days."

"No, Zhek. There is nothing," she said averting her eyes. "I have to leave." She got out of bed and started to put her dress back on.

Zhek got up and wrapped his arms around her. She leaned back into him, seduced by the feel of his skin against hers.

"Are you sure you have to go so soon?" he pleaded with her as he nuzzled her neck.

"Zhek, stop. I cannot stay. It is very late."

Disregarding her protests, he pulled her back into bed. "Zazmaria, before you go, tell me what actually happened in the accident. The circumstances seem so strange."

"What do you mean strange?" she asked, suddenly on the defensive. "Their sailboat capsized during the storm. It was an unfortunate tragedy. Nothing more."

"I know, but word is that the Queen's boat came completely apart. Does that not seem peculiar to you?"

"What is so 'peculiar' about a small sailboat being thrashed apart in a vicious storm?" she shot back angrily.

"I do not understand why you are getting so angry. People are just talking that is all. They are surprised it had not been built better to withstand such things."

"Who are they Zhek? Some wretched people with nothing better to do than speculate on matters they know nothing about?"

"Why are you getting so defensive?" he asked, then paused for a moment. "It has nothing to do with you…does it?"

Zazmaria, caught off guard by the question, glared at him, "How would it?"

"Well…if one were to look at the situation objectively, it does not exactly hurt your position in the family, does it? Or Alaj's for that matter? I know you never liked Axiana. I know how you had resented her, her position as Queen, and her children, the Royal heirs. How you also despised her because you have been unable to have children of your own," he said as he reached to caress her belly.

Zazmaria slapped Zhek hard, so hard that he fell back on the bed. "How dare you! How dare you say these things to me! You think you know me so well?"

Zhek let out a small laugh as he held his throbbing cheek. He could taste blood in his mouth. "My, my, quite a lot of anger you have pent up inside. Really, Princess, I think I know you better than you think."

Zazmaria seethed with rage.

"You have nothing to fear from me, Zazmaria, I am on your side, remember?"

She did not respond, but finished getting dressed.

"Your poor injured arm," he said as once again he noticed the injury. "Must be painful. By the way, do you know you talk in your sleep?"

She looked at him, panicked.

He grinned slowly, reading her expression. "Yes, you say some very interesting things sometimes. I guess you have a lot on your mind." His smile now turned threatening.

Zazmaria swallowed hard. She did not know what to say. She left without another word and ran all the way back to the Palace. Tears of frustration, deep fear, and anger spilled down her cheeks, blown by the cool night winds.

Zhek watched her go, her reaction told him much.

CHAPTER

36

☥

A Turn in the Road

O ver the next couple of weeks, Zazmaria felt too ill to go out.
She knew Zhek would be anxious and wondering what had
happened to her, but she was so tired, and deep down, she was
still angry with him. These days, it felt as if she was angry with everyone
and everything around her, and those feelings were beginning to take
their toll on her.

No matter how much sleep she tried to get, she was constantly fa-
tigued. Medetha had checked on her regularly, concerned about both
her arm, which, in her mind, was taking an unusually long time to heal,
and this sudden onset of ill health.

Alaj, who had been working non-stop, rarely shared meals with his
wife anymore or even saw her before she was asleep. He was not even
aware that she was experiencing this strange illness.

Finally, Medetha suggested she see a healer.

"Medetha, I am just tired, nothing more. I have not been sleeping
well. I am sure I will feel better in a few days."

"My Lady, you have been nauseous everyday for two weeks, I am
concerned about you. I really think you should let someone have a look

at you. Perhaps you have developed an infection from the wound on your arm?"

"It is not infected, my arm is healing fine," Zazmaria replied, irritated that people were still asking about it.

"Then it must be something else. This is not normal," Medetha stated as she placed a cool cloth on Zazmaria's forehead. "Perhaps you could consult with Assan or Senarra, they are very knowledgeable about many illnesses."

"No!" Zazmaria said with sudden anger. "I do not want to see any priests. Do not bring that up again!"

"I am sorry, my Lady, I did not mean to upset you," Medetha said, worriedly. She paused as she removed the cloth, dipped it in the cool basin of water again and placed it back on Zazmaria's forehead.

The Princess seemed to calm down after a few minutes, keeping her eyes closed.

"My Lady, there is one other thing I would like to ask you. It is a delicate topic, but I feel the question must be asked."

Zazmaria opened her eyes, curious. "What is it?"

"Well, your symptoms, they could mean something else." Medetha hesitated.

"What, Medetha? What could they mean?" Zazmaria asked as she sat up.

"Forgive me for being so forward, but could you be…with child?"

Zazmaria was speechless. The thought had not crossed her mind.

"Princess Zazmaria? Please say something."

Zazmaria was too stunned to speak.

"Is it not at least possible?" Medetha asked.

Zazmaria took the cloth from her forehead and dropped it on the floor. She stood up and walked over to the window of her chamber, her arms wrapped tightly around her. Slowly her hands moved to her belly.

She turned to look at Medetha. "I-I had not thought of that. Alaj and I had tried for so long, I had given up all hope."

"Perhaps hope has found you," Medetha replied, smiling warmly. Nothing would make her happier than to see the Princess with child. "This would be wonderful news, if it is true."

"Could it be?" Zazmaria whispered to herself. Her mind was racing with the possibility…with many possibilities.

"My Lady, I know methods that may tell us if you are with child."

Zazmaria looked at Medetha for a long moment. "Prepare them."

37

✟

A Plan Is Hatched

Present-Day Egypt

"Fessel, I want to talk with you, in private," the Professor announced as he burst into Fessel's small cramped office, interrupting an afternoon nap.

"Yes Professor, of course, I was just resting for a moment, it was a busy morning," Fessel said as he jumped up, smoothing his hair, unaware of the sleep creases evident across his cheek.

"I'm sure. Come to my office."

Closing the door behind them, Dustimaine told Fessel to take a seat.

"Fessel, you know that due to the nature of my position, I am not always able to do certain things myself, which is why I hired you as my assistant."

"Yes sir, of course," he replied, leaning forward with anticipation.

"Fessel, I need your help with an important task and I will require this matter to be kept in the strictest of confidence. Do you understand?"

"I do sir. What is it you would like me to do?" Fessel asked.

"I need you to find out exactly what Mitch and Alex are up to after dig hours. They are falling further and further behind in their work.

Something must be taking up their time. I need to know what that is. I want you to go through their rooms, their journals, whatever you can find and report back to me on anything that doesn't seem to relate to the site they are assigned to. Can you handle this?"

Fessel beamed, "Absolutely, sir!"

"Good. I want this done tonight. The party this evening is the perfect opportunity. Everyone will be there so no one will be around to witness your activities. Cocktails are at five and dinner starts at six pm sharp. Be ready by then. I will provide an excuse for your absence. As long as you are done by eight no one should be the wiser. Take a pair of the gloves we use in handling artifacts, cover your tracks well, we don't want anyone alerted to our activities."

"Yes sir, you can count on me, Professor!" Fessel stood up excitedly, nearly knocking over a framed photograph sitting on Dustimaine's desk. "Sorry sir, I promise I'll be careful." Fessel clumsily re-positioned the photo, smiling nervously.

"See that you are."

CHAPTER

38

♀

The Party

The Egyptian Antiquities' Council was holding their annual gala for the Egyptologists and their excavation teams. The black-tie affair was intended to let everyone discuss the status of the various excavations and findings in a more social setting near the end of the dig season as well as mix and mingle with the wealthy sponsors of the various teams. It was expected that everyone attend, even those of a more reluctant nature.

"I'm not going!" Alex was storming around her room the afternoon of the party. "We have too much work to do and we've been falling even further behind. Going to this party is a complete waste of our time."

Mitch and Alex had spent the past several days deciphering the scrolls, looking for clues to the secret chamber underneath the Sphinx, but found nothing.

"We'd be in a lot more trouble if we didn't go," Mitch pointed out. "Remember what Dustimaine said? He'd have our heads if we didn't attend."

She just shook her head.

"Alex, you know this is the annual show-and-tell and we are expected to make an appearance. We have to sing for our supper, make friends so that the funds keep coming in. Besides, we could use a break. We've been doing double duty, with Dustimaine's work, and spending hours deciphering the scrolls at night."

Mitch watched Alex fuss and fiddle with clothes and papers, not really accomplishing anything. He had been expecting this minor battle with his partner. He knew how she felt about formal events.

"I'm sure they won't miss us," she replied. "Nobody ever pays attention to us at these things anyway, Dustimaine sees to that. Listening to him hob-knobbing at these parties, you'd think we either didn't exist or could be easily replaced with mindless robots." She smirked, "You know like Fessel."

They both broke out in laughter, which eased the tension somewhat.

Alex paused and sat down, putting aside her busywork. "Mitch, you know he's never acknowledged our efforts or given us any credit for the work we do."

Mitch nodded his agreement, "Maybe this year we can step out from under his shadow a bit, you know be a little more brave and go talk to some of the money people and council members ourselves. Every year we sit silently listening to Dr. Dust Bucket talk like he's personally doing all the excavating himself."

Alex thought about that for a moment. "I don't think he'd appreciate us stealing any of his spotlight."

"So then we do our best to avoid him. It would be totally under-standable considering how he's been chewing us out lately." Mitch watched her for a moment then smiled, "So, how 'bout it partner? Shall we put our game faces on?"

Alex couldn't help but laugh, "Oh all right, you win. Looks like we're playing dress-up tonight. But I am not going to have any fun."

"Of course not," Mitch said.

That evening, after spending nearly an hour getting ready, Alex went out to join the boys in Mitch's room. She was dreading facing them dressed like this. She much preferred her khakis and ponytail and just being one of the boys.

The moment she walked in the room, mock catcalls and whistles besieged her. She promptly turned a bright shade of red.

"My, my, my, don't we clean up well?" Bob teased.

"I could say the same for you boys," she said, sitting down in a chair. "I see you shaved today Bob, I hardly recognized you."

Mitch laughed, as Bob grumbled.

Alex was already getting a headache from her up-do. She also worried about getting one of her heels caught in the hem of her dress and falling flat on her face in front of all the society types who would be at the party.

Jack had been sitting silently on the bed. His jaw had nearly dropped when Alex walked in, he had turned beet red, then looked away and began staring at his shoes.

Bob noticed Jack's reaction to Alex, along with his uncharacteristic silence. He smiled to himself, shaking his head.

"Why is it that you men don't have to put up with pantyhose that twists around your legs cutting off all circulation and large metal objects hanging from your ears? Or, how about the joy of teetering on unspeakably painful high-heeled shoes? Could someone explain this to me please?" Alex was having trouble sitting in a comfortable position in the form-fitting dress. She kept squirming in her chair.

Jack had still not spoken a word. He had a very funny look on his face.

Mitch answered first, "Don't for a moment think we've got it all that good. Do you have any idea how hot these tuxedos are? And how would you like fabric nooses tied tightly around your throat for an entire evening? Our shoes may not have spikes attached to the heels, but they are stiff as hell."

Bob piped in, "Yeah, not to mention try wearing this many layers of non-breathable fabric when one has an extra pound or two and a healthy coating of body hair!"

"That's really too much information Bob," Mitch said with a mock frown.

Alex, feeling eyes on her, looked to Jack who quickly looked away, blushing furiously once again. "Jack, are you all right? You haven't said a word. Don't tell me your tie has already begun to asphyxiate you," she laughed.

Jack laughed a nervous, self-conscious laugh in response. "I think I am a little light-headed. Perhaps a good stiff drink will set me straight. Got any booze in here?"

Mitch looked at his watch, "Jack, I don't think we've got time, we should get going. We'll make a beeline for the bar as soon as we get there."

With that the foursome left and headed for the Imperial Ballroom.

Mitch, Alex, Jack and Bob headed first to the bar for cocktails and then to the appetizer buffet. It was still an hour until dinner and all they had eaten all day was their usual diet of several pots of coffee, pop, orange juice, and a smattering of junk food.

"Whose stomach is that I hear growling?" Mitch asked. "It sounds like a pack of hungry lions!"

"I'm working on the problem right now," Bob answered, filling his plate with all manner of fancy finger foods.

"Don't look now," Alex whispered, "but Old Dusty's over there, holding court with some council members. Let's find a quiet, dark corner and hide there."

"I'm with you!" Jack replied.

"Too late, I think he's spotted us," Mitch said. "I wonder where Fessel is? It's unusual to see the Professor without his trusty sidekick."

"I'm sure he'll show up soon enough," Alex said.

"Oh no," Mitch whispered, "he's waving us over, guess there's no way out of this one. Hey guys, we'll be right back, don't have too much fun without us," he said looking sympathetically at the fallen faces of Jack and Bob. He knew how uncomfortable they were at social gatherings.

Mitch and Alex walked over to join Professor Dustimaine.

"Mitch, Alex, there's someone here who wants to meet you. This is Dr. Khadesh, he's the Director of Egyptian Antiquities and has been an avid supporter of my field research over the last three years."

The Professor had emphasized the word 'my', which was not lost on either Mitch or Alex.

"How do you do?" Dr. Khadesh said as he smiled and shook their hands enthusiastically. "I have heard much about you. It is a pleasure to finally meet you both."

Professor Dustimaine could barely mask his displeasure at how graciously they were being greeted by Dr. Khadesh.

"We're honored to meet you, sir," Mitch replied.

"Yes, this is an honor," Alex agreed. "It's so nice to finally have the opportunity to meet you in person."

"Unfortunately, my duties often interfere with the more pleasant social activities. My aides often benefit from the many opportunities I miss," Dr. Khadesh smiled warmly at them.

"Yes, Dr. Khadesh is a very busy man," Dustimaine added, not liking how the three of them seemed to be hitting it off.

"Miss Logan, I knew your father, Devlan. He was a fine man and a gifted Egyptologist. He would be very proud of the work you and Mr. Carver are doing."

"Thank-you sir, it means a great deal to us to hear you say that," Alex beamed.

Mitch noticed how Professor Dustimaine bristled at the mention of Alex's father, so he mischievously added, "Dr. Logan was the most talented archaeologist I ever knew."

The Professor looked like he wanted to throttle him.

Mitch kept a straight face, but was laughing on the inside.

"Indeed," Dr. Khadesh replied. "I have been very interested in the work you two have done here in Egypt. I also understand you were both first in your class in university, and are well on your way to completing your doctoral program. Very impressive."

Mitch and Alex positively glowed.

"We are very happy you have taken an interest in our work, Dr. Khadesh," Alex replied. "We have often wondered if anyone took notice of us."

Dustimaine silently fumed at her audacity.

"Oh believe me, Miss Logan, I am always aware of the goings-on here. Though I may not make many appearances, I am kept well informed of all activities, I assure you."

Dr. Khadesh looked towards the door and nodded his head. "I must apologize, I will have to excuse myself. Please enjoy the evening, I will see you all at dinner."

Professor Dustimaine looked ill at ease with the prospect of being left alone with the very two people he had been chastising recently, so he quickly excused himself as well.

"Wow, that was more than a little unexpected," Alex whispered to Mitch.

"Yeah," Mitch agreed, "maybe Dustimaine hasn't been so successful in stunting our reputations, after all." He looked around the room and spotted Jack and Bob standing next to a tall potted palm tree. "Let's go re-join our friends over there, they look like they could use some company."

Shortly before six pm, Mitch, Alex, Jack and Bob headed towards the dining hall. Just as they were leaving, a waiter approached them.

"Mr. Carver? Miss Logan?" the young man inquired.

"Yes, that's us," Mitch replied.

"I was asked to deliver this to you." He handed Mitch an unmarked envelope.

"What is it?" Mitch asked. "Who is it from?"

"I am sorry, I do not know. A man asked me to relay it to you at once, then he left immediately."

"Thank-you," Alex replied. The waiter hurried away leaving them with the mysterious envelope.

"Were you expecting anything?" Alex asked Mitch as he was turning the envelope over.

Jack and Bob were peering over his shoulder to get a look at it.

"No, but we may as well open it. If it was delivered here, it might be time-sensitive," Mitch proceeded to tear one end of the envelope open.

He pulled out three pieces of paper. Two of them appeared to be official documents, the other a handwritten note.

"Who's it from?" Alex asked.

"I don't know, there's no name," Mitch said as he led them over to a corner of the room, away from prying ears and eyes. He quietly read what was on the single piece of paper:

Seek out the words of the one who stands guard,
Under one's heart does the gateway rest,
Only they who know the secret shall be allowed to pass,
But be warned of the power that lies below

Jack spoke up, excitement filling his voice, "Whoa, cool! A riddle!"

"Really Sherlock? Boy, it sure is lucky for us you're here. We never would have figured that out," Bob replied to his skinny friend.

Alex leaned in, "Sshhh, guys keep it down, we don't want to attract attention. What are the other two papers?"

Mitch looked at the documents. He was bewildered. "They are permits for excavation in Egypt."

"What?" Alex, Bob and Jack exclaimed in unison, forgetting to stay quiet and not attract attention.

"Take a look for yourself," Mitch said. "These look like official permits. They have Alex's and my names on them. This an official government seal, I've seen it on the permits that allow archaeologists to excavate in this country. This doesn't look like a forgery."

"Who authorized them?" Alex asked in disbelief.

"I can't make out the signatures," Mitch replied.

"It looks like you two got your wish," Bob whispered.

"Someone is definitely trying to help us," Alex said. "I can't believe this! We'd better keep this to ourselves until we figure out what we're going to do."

"You're right," Mitch agreed, "any number of people would love to usurp our efforts and get a hold of something like this."

"Yes, god forbid they were usurped, sounds quite unpleasant," Jack whispered to Bob.

Bob responded by smacking the back of his head.

"Ow!" Jack exclaimed.

"Children, behave yourselves, this is a formal event," Alex admonished them.

Mitch shook his head, "Ok, look we've got to get in there for dinner. We can't be late. We can figure this out afterwards." Mitch put the note and permits back in the envelope, and tucked it inside his jacket pocket.

Unraveling the Riddle

Mitch and Alex were relieved to have finally been able to leave the function. It was now quite late. Jack and Bob had managed to duck out early, much to Mitch and Alex's chagrin. The evening had seemed to drag on endlessly. All they wanted to do was get back to their rooms and discuss the new development in private, away from anyone who may be listening.

"Man, I can't wait to get out of this dress and these shoes are killing me!" Alex said as they reached their rooms. "Who the hell thought that walking around on skinny spikes was a good idea?"

They went into Mitch's room to discuss the note and permits.

Alex nearly teetered over trying to unhook the fiendishly small buckles on the offending footwear. "Honestly, I could have killed myself walking down those stairs from the grand ballroom. Not to mention this dress, I haven't been able to take a deep breath all night! That will teach me not to bother buying a new dress, I thought this one would still fit."

She looked over at Mitch who was smirking. "Not a word out of you Carver. I'm sure the drycleaner shrunk it."

"Of course, I wasn't thinking anything else," he said feigning innocence.

"Right," she replied, as she began to pull down her up-do, which had been giving her a headache all night. "I swear that's the last formal function I attend."

Mitch had been grinning the entire time.

Alex stopped in her tracks and looked at Mitch, "You're laughing at me," she said with her hands on her hips. "You're quite enjoying my misery, aren't you?"

"I can't help it, Alex, you're hilarious. Every single time, we go through this. You know it's the price we have to pay to remain barely inside the outskirts of the in-crowd."

"Could someone please explain to me what fancy dresses, excruciatingly painful shoes and fruit plates have to do with archaeology?"

Mitch was no longer paying attention to her little diatribe, but seemed fixated on his desk.

"Are you listening to me?"

Mitch still didn't answer. Slowly he walked over to the desk and picked up his notebook turning it over, then looked again at the desk.

"What is it?" Alex asked.

"I'm not sure. Did you come back to either of our rooms at any time during the party?" he turned to look at her.

"Sadly no," she replied wistfully. "Why do you ask?"

"I could have sworn I left this in the desk drawer," Mitch said hesitantly. "The door was locked when we came in, wasn't it?"

"Yeah, I unlocked it when we got here. I remember because our keys were about the only things that would fit in this useless excuse for purse." She tossed the tiny, sequined evening bag on the sofa. "Do you think you just forgot and left it out? We were in a bit of a rush to get there."

"I don't think so," he said. "Just the same, let's have a look around and see if anything else looks out of place. I might be getting a little paranoid with all the excitement lately, but I think I'd sleep better if we checked things out a bit."

"Sure. I'll go have a look around my room, too," Alex said, heading next door.

Mitch started examining every item in his cluttered room. After a few minutes, he heard Alex in the adjacent room.

"What the…" her voice trailed off. "Mitch! Come here, quickly!"

He raced over. "What is it? Did you find something?" He looked into her room and saw her kneeling down next to her bedside table. She was holding a small, white figurine.

"What is that?" Mitch asked.

Alex's hands were trembling slightly. "It's my porcelain angel. It was a gift from my father when I was ten. I carry it with me everywhere. I've never slept a night without it since my tenth birthday." She stood up, still cradling the precious object in her hands. "Look here, its wingtip – a small piece has been chipped off. I have carted this around for years, everywhere I've gone and never broken it. I know this wasn't damaged before." Alex looked at him, a small tear in her eye. "Someone's been in here."

"Did you find anything missing?" Mitch asked.

"No, just this," she said looking at her broken angel.

"Me neither."

She looked back up at Mitch, "Guess that means this wasn't just a burglary?"

"Nope, not a burglary," he said, frowning. "This is serious, Alex. Someone may be suspicious of our off-hours activities. We're going to have to watch our backs."

"Do you still have the note and the permits?" she asked.

Mitch nodded, patting his jacket pocket.

"Why don't we go see Jack and Bob right now, tell them what's happened," Alex said as she put on her dusty old work shoes.

"Nice combination, Logan," Mitch snickered.

"Thanks! Personally, I think it's an improvement. C'mon, let's hurry."

Mitch and Alex ran over to Jack and Bob's rooms. Alex knocked furiously on Bob's door while Mitch banged on Jack's door.

Jack was the first to answer, holding a can of Coke, "Hey, what's up?"

"Jack, sorry to bother you so late, but it's important, we need to talk to you guys right away," Mitch said.

Alex was still knocking on Bob's door. She could hear him snoring inside.

Jack stepped out to see Alex banging away on Bob's door. He chuckled, "No problemo. This is still early for me. But Bob there, good luck waking him. He'd sleep through Armageddon. Wait a second. I've got a key to his room. I'll let you in."

"Does he know you've got a key?" Mitch asked.

"I thought it was a good idea," Jack winked. "One never knows when it will come in handy, like right now," Jack smiled devilishly. "Hold my Coke."

Mitch took the Coke, and looked at Alex. She just shrugged her shoulders.

Jack quietly opened the door. There was Bob, still snoring away. Jack turned the room lights on, walked over to Bob and shook him hard.

Bob awoke with a start and yelled out.

"Sshhh, you big oaf, we're being sneaky." Jack grinned.

"What the hell are you doing in my room? How did you get in here?" Bob then saw Mitch and Alex out of the corner of his eye and jumped again. "What's going on? Why are you all in here?"

"Bob, we're really sorry for doing this," Alex said, "but I was knocking and knocking on your door. You're a hard guy to wake."

"That still doesn't answer how you all got in here." Bob looked over at Jack, who began to examine the wallpaper. "I see. Jack, I think you and I need to have a little chat."

"I don't know what you're talking about," Jack replied.

Mitch stepped forward, "Bob, Jack, the reason we couldn't wait until morning to talk to you guys, is that when Alex and I returned to our rooms, we noticed some things out of place. We think someone was in there while we were at the party."

"Really?" Bob asked. He was fully awake now.

"Did you observe anything or anyone unusual either at the party or on your way back here tonight?" Alex asked. "You guys left a good hour before we did."

Jack was staring at Alex's shoes, smiling to himself when he realized she was asking a question of him too. He started blushing and proceeded to swig some Coke to cover his red cheeks.

Bob shook his head.

"No, I didn't see anything out of the ordinary," Jack responded, nearly choking on his Coke.

"Me neither, other than…" Bob's voice trailed off. "Where was Old Dusty's shadow tonight?"

"I asked about that," Mitch replied. "Apparently Fessel was sick. Dust Bucket said he had come down with something and wouldn't be attending the dinner." Mitch looked at Alex. "You don't think…"

"Interesting," she nodded. "If it was Fessel, it's highly doubtful he acted on his own. Professor Dusti-mean's been none-too-pleased with us lately. I wouldn't put it past him to get that little weasel Fessel to spy on us." Alex stopped, thinking. "Well, we can't prove anything right now, but what about the note and permits we were given? It appears someone is trying to help us. Any ideas who?"

The room was silent.

"Me neither," Alex said. "Ok then, let's take another look at the note." Mitch pulled the envelope out of his pocket. He read the note aloud:

Seek out the words of the one who stands guard,
Under one's heart does the gateway rest,
Only they who know the secret shall be allowed to pass,
But be warned of the power that lies below

"It has to be referring to the Sphinx," Mitch said. "Otherwise why would we have been given the permits? It's close to where we've been working. Maybe whoever gave this to us is aware of our interest in the Sphinx."

Alex nodded. "The power that lies below…it's exactly what we've been seeing in the scrolls. There is something down there, in the subterranean chambers."

"So does '*Under one's heart does the gateway rest,*' point to the Sphinx's chest? Under where its heart would be?" Mitch asked.

"That would mean the entrance is between the Sphinx's paws, below the head," Alex said.

"What about this line," Jack pointed, "'*Only they who know the secret shall be allowed to pass?*' What does that mean?"

"We probably need a special technique to gain entrance," Alex replied. "It's likely very well hidden."

"Hey, it might be booby-trapped!" Bob exclaimed.

"It may well be," Mitch said.

Bob's expression abruptly changed when he realized Mitch wasn't joking.

"We're never going to know until we find it," Alex said, "but we have another mystery to solve before we get there."

"You're right. Someone would either have to know what we're up to, what we've found, or…" Mitch paused for a moment. "…or they know a lot more than we do and have kept quiet. Until now."

"Whoa, this is heavy man," Jack said, gripping his Coke.

"This would have to be someone with a lot of clout, who knows what's going on and wants you guys involved," Bob said.

"You mean, us guys, don't you Bob? You two are very much involved in this now," Alex added.

"We're here for you, you know that," Bob replied.

She smiled, shaking her head. "What I mean is that the stakes are getting higher, day by day. You two are going to have to watch yourselves, too. We don't know exactly what – or who – we're dealing with here."

Jack, mid-swallow, nearly choked on his Coke.

Bob was agape.

"She's right," Mitch agreed. "Our rooms have been broken into, whoever it was that slipped us the note and the permits likely knows the four of us have been working together. We've got to be pretty careful from here on in." Mitch put the note back in the envelope and placed it back in his pocket. "We've all got to get an early start tomorrow morning and it's very late now. Let's act as if nothing is out the ordinary and go about our day – keeping our eyes and ears open."

A Princess' Treachery

Circa 10,000 B.C.

Zazmaria paced the room in the little red house, nervously. Meeting in this clandestine fashion always made her edgy and she was uncertain as to how this conversation would go.

She jumped when she heard a knock on the door. She stepped to the window to peer out. "It is him," she whispered, her heart pounding in her chest. She opened the door and in strode Zhek.

Smiling widely, he embraced her and kissed her passionately, his strong arms holding her tight against him. "Mmmm, how I have missed you, Zazmaria," he said as he stroked her luxurious long, black hair.

"I have missed you too," she replied, growing increasingly nervous. She was unsure how to begin.

"Come, my love, let us lie down. I wish to hold you close. I felt terrible the way things left off the last time I saw you. I was not sure when you would return to me," Zhek said as he held her hand to lead her over to the bed.

She hesitated. She stayed standing where she was.

"What is wrong? Are you not well?" Zhek asked as he stood before her, his deep sapphire blue eyes searching her face.

Still, no answer came. Her heart was pounding in her chest.

Zhek, concerned, held her face in his hands. She could not look up to meet his gaze. "Zazmaria, what is it?"

"I-I have something to tell you Zhek. Something important. Please, just sit down," she said as she motioned him over to the chairs, and away from the bed.

He obliged, waiting for her to continue.

Zazmaria took a deep breath, "I do not know how to say this, so I am just going to say it directly." She was visibly shaking now. "Zhek…I am pregnant."

Silence. Zhek stared at her, his expression unreadable.

"Zhek? Please say something."

"I am sorry, Zazmaria, I am just stunned by your news." He suddenly jumped up, pulling her up with him, a wide grin spreading across his face. "But I am overjoyed, my love! We are going to have a baby!"

"Zhek, wait…you do not understand," Zazmaria said as she pulled away, feeling the knot in her stomach grow.

"I know, I know, this is complicated, I am not that naive. We will not be able to reveal that I am the father until circumstances change, but still this is wonderful news, a child, Zazmaria!" Zhek was beaming with pride. "I could not be happier!" He tried to pull her to him again, but she resisted.

"It is not yours." Her words were cold and harsh, crushing all the emotion and tenderness in the room; then giving rise to new emotions. The silence that ensued was almost unbearable for her. She watched the color drain from Zhek's face and braced herself for his reaction.

"What did you say?" Zhek whispered hoarsely.

"The baby, it is my husband's, you are not the father," Zazmaria stated as she met his gaze head on. It took every ounce of courage in her to say those words. She could see the rage beginning to boil within him and she took a step back. "I am sorry, Zhek. I must be going." She turned to leave.

"You are not going anywhere," Zhek's tone had now turned menacing.

"I cannot stay, I must get back to the Palace," she insisted, again turning away from him.

Zhek reached over and grabbed her arm. No gentleness remained in his touch.

"You are hurting me Zhek, let me go," Zazmaria pleaded as she struggled within his grip.

"Would you mind explaining to me, your Highness," he nearly spat the words at her now, "how it is that I have been sharing your bed for the past two months and yet, somehow I am not the father?" He did not loosen his hold on her arm.

"Zhek, please you are hurting me," she cried, her voice rising. Tears began to stream down her face as both his words and his grip assailed her.

"Fine," he shot back and with a push he nearly threw her across the room. "But you will answer my question."

Zazmaria, shocked and humiliated at being treated so roughly, regained her balance. Trembling, she straightened her gown and tried to regain her composure. "You know I am another man's wife Zhek, must I spell it out for you?" She looked at him defiantly through her tears.

Zhek took a step towards her. "Do you take me for a fool? Do you honestly think your lies and deceit will work with me? Your husband may be so easily manipulated, but I am another matter altogether or have you forgotten to whom you are talking?"

He waited, but she did not respond.

"I am just as clever as you are, Princess," Zhek glared at her. "I see right through you."

Zazmaria said nothing in defense of his accusations. Her mind raced, dreading his next move.

He moved to within mere inches of her. His hostility was palpable. "You think I do not know how much easier the situation would be for you if it were Alaj's child? Your lover can simply be tossed aside with no ties remaining, and then you and your Royal Prince can claim how greatly your family has been blessed by this event."

Zazmaria wrapped her arms around herself to try and stop her shaking.

Zhek continued, "But…if this were your lover's child, you would have to lie to your husband, to the entire Royal Family, to the people – to everyone. Ever living in fear that your dirty little secret may come to light."

Her emotions welled up uncontrollably within her. "You delude yourself, Zhek," Zazmaria fought back, " just as you have all along about this little love affair. Did you really believe that you and I had a future together? It is just not possible. It would be scandalous! We would be outcasts, left with nothing, shunned by our families and our society. It was just a fantasy, Zhek!"

She took a deep breath, letting her words sink in as much for herself as for Zhek. "I am a Princess, a member of the Royal Family. That will not change!"

"You are the one who is deluding yourself that this little deception will work!" he yelled at her. "Your marriage to Alaj is crumbling. How long have you two been married and produced no heirs? This child is mine and you know it!" Zhek was enraged. He had never felt so betrayed in his life.

"I know nothing of the sort!" she shouted back at him. "Your arrogance is astounding, even for you!"

"You filthy harlot, you will not get away with this!"

Zazmaria slapped him hard across his face, leaving a bright red handprint on his scarred cheek. "You bastard! How dare you say these things to me!" she screamed, shaking in anger.

Zhek stood still for a moment, stunned at the stinging blow she just delivered, both with her words and with her hand. His deep blue eyes narrowed and he stepped even closer to her, an act of defiance to the violence she had just delivered.

His tone was now measured, "We shall see Zazmaria. Time will tell. Your little plan has a fatal flaw, you see, you will not be able to mask the likeness of this child, which will only become more pronounced with time. Alaj may be fooled for the time being, but even he will see through your lies once this child grows. Mark my words woman, I will claim my child in due time."

Then in a move that startled her even further, Zhek roughly took her head in his hands and kissed her hard. He then looked deep into her topaz eyes, "Do not forget, I know something of the secrets you carry within you. You think you can control everything and everyone around you at will, at any cost? What will you do when you find out you cannot control me or that I no longer fit into your selfish plans? Try to kill me, too?"

"I...I have no idea what you mean, Zhek." Her voice was hoarse, her throat constricted. She felt like she was trying to dodge blows without knowing where they were coming from.

He laughed bitterly, "Of course not." Then, releasing her, he tossed her aside, pushing past her and out the door. Before he left, he turned to look back at her.

Zazmaria stared at him in stunned disbelief.

"Farewell, Princess, until we meet again..."

And with that, the man who had swept into her life so suddenly – was gone.

41

The Heir

"Grandfather, may I speak with you?" Zhek asked.

"Of course, my boy, come in." Lord Draxen dismissed the soldiers he had been conferring with.

They nodded to Zhek as they left.

"What is it?" Lord Draxen asked.

Zhek hated the fact that every time he faced his grandfather he felt as though he was that small boy again, about to be disciplined by the man who had once towered over him. "I have some important news to share, though the exact nature of the news is not certain at this time."

"Sit down, Zhek, and let us talk. What are you trying to say?" Lord Draxen motioned to Zhek to take a seat at his desk.

"It is about Princess Zazmaria." Zhek's nerves were wound tight.

"Yes, I assumed as much. Continue." Lord Draxen leaned forward on the desk, his hands clasped in front of him.

"She came to talk to me today, she had something to tell me." Zhek was having difficulty getting the words out. "She, uh, well she…"

"She what, Zhek?" Lord Draxen asked, becoming impatient.

"She is with child," Zhek spoke quickly.

Lord Draxen showed no expression for a moment, processing what he had just heard. Slowly an evil grin crossed his lined face. "With child," he repeated slowly.

"But that is not all," Zhek added.

"Oh?" Lord Draxen asked, raising an eyebrow.

"She claims the child is not mine," Zhek admitted, unable to look his grandfather in the eye.

Lord Draxen said nothing for a moment. He stood up slowly, walked around the desk and stood, facing his grandson. "Zhek?" he asked.

"Yes?" Zhek answered.

"Look at me boy!" he ordered sternly.

Zhek looked up uncertainly.

"Do you believe the child is yours?"

"Yes, I know it is, but she denies…"

"I do not care what she denies, Zhek!" Lord Draxen shouted at him. "I will not allow that wretch to make a mockery of this family. Either you deal with this, and straighten her out…or I will. Do I make myself clear?"

"Yes, Grandfather," Zhek replied quickly.

"Good, now we have that out of the way…" Lord Draxen walked back around and sat down at his desk. "She has also never admitted to you that she is responsible for the deaths of Queen Axiana and Princess Anjia?"

"No, though I have let on my beliefs in that matter. She still will not speak of it."

"Then this situation is no different. Princess Zazmaria does what she feels she needs to do, when she wants to do it, no matter the consequences. You are going to have to take that into consideration when dealing with her. She is dangerous and unpredictable, but fortunately more-so to her own family and that is a distinct advantage to us."

"She could help us further crush the Royal Family," Zhek added, "from the inside out."

"Precisely," Lord Draxen smiled. "We could not ask for a better ally, really, and we will decide how to best leverage that position in the days to come. We have something very powerful to hold over her now and we are going to use that to our strongest advantage." Lord Draxen reveled in this most fortuitous turn of events. "You are under her skin in the most powerful and undeniable of ways now. She is going to be afraid of her infidelity being revealed and you are going to keep reminding her of that fear. You could ruin her and she knows it. But remember, she is treacherous."

"I will, Grandfather."

42

Zazmaria Faces Alaj

Zazmaria steeled herself to give her husband the news of her pregnancy. Over the last few months, they had spent very little time together, seldom sharing a bed. She worried her husband might wonder why she was with child at this time, after so many years, and especially after they had been apart so much.

Alaj walked into their bedroom, "Zazmaria, you called for me?"

Zazmaria took a deep breath and walked over to him, "Yes, I have wonderful news I wish to share with you." She desperately hoped her smile had a semblance of sincerity in it. "Please, come sit down next to me."

"What is it?" Alaj asked, as she took him by the hand.

"Something that we have wished for, for years, has finally happened. Alaj, you are going to be a father. I am with child!" she tried to keep her voice steady and her tone happy. She scanned Alaj's face for any hint of mistrust or misgivings.

He hesitated. "A child…" he whispered. "You are pregnant?" He looked down at her belly, trying to absorb the unexpected news.

"Yes, my husband. We are going to have a baby! After all these long years of hoping, it has finally happened." Zazmaria tried to sound warm and enthusiastic. She feared what could be going through Alaj's mind.

He did not respond.

"Alaj? Is something wrong?" she asked hesitantly.

He paused then shook his head. "No. No, I am happy. It is just this news is…unexpected. Things have not been well between us for some time now." He looked into her topaz eyes searchingly, eyes he felt he hardly knew any more.

"But this is wonderful, is it not?" she asked him, her heart pounding.

"Yes," Alaj replied, trying to manage a smile. "Wonderful." This was something he had yearned to hear for so long, but now that it was real he found himself feeling strangely uneasy.

43

A Celebration

An official parade had been arranged to celebrate the expectant Royal couple. It was a day Zazmaria was both excited by and yet dreaded. She felt transparent, that people would somehow see the truth about her. Her feelings of trepidation were growing day by day.

The Royal couple was carried by members of the Royal guard inside a draped carriage. The people cheered and threw flower petals as they passed by. Zazmaria looked resplendent in her deep emerald silk gown, with an empire-waist, festooned with a gold sash. Her hair was pulled off her face, and braided with gold ribbon, showcasing her high cheek-bones.

Alaj was also dressed in emerald green, which matched his eyes. He looked proud and handsome, but inside he felt unsettled. However, he attributed his sense of unease to all the excitement and attention that was being bestowed on him and his wife, something he was quite unaccustomed to.

Through the city they wound their way, accepting the shouts of well-wishers, as they smiled brightly and waved to the adoring crowd.

Zazmaria was thrilled with the attention and love she was feeling from the people, trying to make eye contact with as many as she could. Out of the corner of her eye she caught sight of a tall man, standing towards the back of the crowd. She sensed a presence, a penetrating gaze, and quickly inhaled with a sudden sense of shock. She nearly fainted, her face turning pale, and sweat beading on her brow.

"Zazmaria, are you all right?" Alaj asked as he noticed his wife teeter backwards, visibly shaken. He grabbed her and looked out towards the crowd, but the man had vanished, unseen by Alaj.

"I-I am fine, it was just a fainting spell. I think I may be overwhelmed by all the activity, and it is a very hot day. I am sure it will pass." Zazmaria sat back up, placing a hand on her forehead. "I just need some water."

Alaj reached down for the flask of water they had brought with them and gave it to his wife. He also took a fan and began trying to cool her. "We should return to the Palace at once. I do not want to take any chances with your health." Concern was clearly etched across his face.

"No, I will be all right. We are almost to the end of the parade route. I am feeling better now with the water and the breeze," she said, managing a faint smile, as her husband continued to fan her.

'Zhek, was that you?' she thought to herself, closing her eyes. It had been nearly three weeks since she had last spoken with him. Having been swept up in all the excitement surrounding her pregnancy, she had managed to separate herself from the events of the past three months, distancing herself emotionally from Zhek.

But now, believing she had seen him, her defenses fell. Her heart raced, her feelings became jumbled, as her memories surfaced and threatened to overwhelm her once again.

She opened her eyes and tried to forget the man she saw, or thought she saw and turn her attentions back to the throngs of happy subjects, here to honor her and her unborn child.

Suddenly a voice yelled out over the din of the crowd, "Hail Princess! A new child is coming to heal our sorrows!"

Then another voice cried out above all the others, "Queen Axiana and Princess Anjia would have been so happy for you!" The crowd began to cheer ever more loudly.

Zazmaria, terribly shaken at hearing those words, turned to see who had spoken them, but the sea of faces became a blur. The images became frightening, menacing and she suddenly felt as though she was burning up, beads of sweat forming all over her. The remainder of the journey back to the Palace was an agonizing one.

That night, Zazmaria slept fitfully. As she tried to go to sleep, the thought that she may have seen Zhek in the crowd and hearing the disturbing words spoken by the townspeople, replayed in her mind over and over again tormenting her. Finally asleep, her mind descended into a nightmare world of disjointed images and faces.

She was back in the parade, the crowd pressing in around her. The din was deafening, the heat unbearable. Then, dark, menacing storm clouds rushed in. The winds howled and blew all around her. The people, who just moments before had been proclaiming their happiness, began screaming in panic.

The carriage Zazmaria rode in bounced dangerously down the road, carried by unseen hands. She looked around her, but she was now alone. Alaj had vanished. Terrified, she searched the crowd. She tried calling for help, but she could make no sound.

All around her faces contorted, becoming disfigured, hideous. Voices, now only distortions, were filled with hate and anguish, malevolence, but she could make out no words.

Then she saw Assan in the crowd, a still figure amidst swirling chaos. He glared at her with utter contempt. "Your treachery will be exposed!" his voice boomed through the fierce winds. Rain began to fall in sheets, battering the carriage. Zazmaria screamed and turned away in fear.

Suddenly Zhek was sitting in the carriage beside her. For a brief moment, she felt safe. He reached for her belly, but she noticed his hand was maimed and blackened, the fingers only stumps, as though his hand had been partially consumed in a fire. He looked at her menacingly. "I will take what is mine," he said as he continued to reach towards her with his mangled hand. Then his face began to blister and burn before her very eyes. Zhek howled in agony, falling towards her.

Zazmaria screamed again and jumped from the carriage. She felt herself falling, but instead of hitting the ground, she fell through it, becoming submerged in icy, black water, her heart pounding fiercely from the shock. Desperately she struggled, trying to get to the surface, but just as she reached it, a strong hand grabbed her shoulder. Zazmaria, gasping for breath wheeled around and saw Anjia, standing over the water, again as a young woman, a white light surrounding her form. She stood motionless looking down at Zazmaria. The water did not touch her. Zazmaria felt Anjia's gaze piercing her soul.

The expression on Anjia's face spoke of unspeakable pain, anger and vengeance. She spoke in a voice low and strong, "It had to be." At that moment, Zazmaria felt a cold hand grip her leg, violently dragging her back under the water's surface. As she struggled in the dark, cold water, she turned and to her horror, a face slowly became illuminated in its depths. Axiana stared at back her, but her once beautiful face was now a mask of death, her skin preternaturally pale, her eyes cold and dead.

Zazmaria awoke, screaming in terror.

44

Events Begin to Unfold

Zazmaria continued to have nightmares on occasion. Though Alaj had tried to speak to her about it, she would not say what it was that was tormenting her in her sleep. She grew distant and cold to him again. However, with the birth of their first child nearing, he had tried to shake his fears and doubts and focus on the new responsibilities he would have as a father. But now, there was something else troubling him.

"I was not expecting to see you so soon. Is something wrong? " Zazmaria asked. Her husband had been working long hours again, so that once the baby came, he could scale back on some of his responsibilities.

He walked into their chambers and sat down in a chair, putting his head in his hands, obviously agitated.

She looked at him for a moment, assessing his demeanor. "Alaj? What is it?"

He inhaled deeply. "I just found out today, quite by accident, that Traeus has been purposely downplaying…no, more like outright lying to me about that chamber underneath the Amsara site."

"I knew it!" she said. "I knew there had to be more to it than what he told you."

Alaj gave her a look. He did not need to be reminded of that. "I overheard Traeus talking to Assan in his study today. I had come by to talk to Traeus on another matter, but I stopped outside the partially open door when I heard Assan say, 'There have been some energy fluctuations. The chamber seems to be containing it, but Victarius is looking into the matter as a precaution.' Traeus asked him if it was serious, if it would affect its operation. Assan said that it seemed to be operating fine, but that Victarius would give them a report as soon as he had completed his inspection. I did not hear any more because Assan went to leave, so I quickly left before they could see me."

She frowned. "What exactly is it that is having energy fluctuations?"

"I have no idea," Alaj said angrily, "but whatever it is, is in that chamber below the monument. Traeus has been lying to me all along, and hiding this, this…device or whatever it is!" He huffed as he paced about the room. "I despise him for this! Can you imagine how he would react if I went behind his back on something of this magnitude?"

"No, I cannot Alaj, and do you know why?" she asked.

Alaj looked at her, bracing himself for what she would say next.

"Because he assumes you never would, which means you are going to have to find out yourself what that device is."

"I doubt he would tell me the truth even if I do ask."

"Then you are going to have to find out another way."

"And just how would you propose I do that?" he asked heatedly.

She met his tone. "Whatever way you have to. You have an heir to think about now. I warn you, you had better start looking out for our child's future…or I will."

Zhek and Zazmaria

Zazmaria had been a nervous wreck in the weeks following her son, Setar's birth. No one suspected anything, but she could not shake the looming sense of dread which hung over her since the day so many months ago she met with Zhek to tell him she was pregnant; to lie to him and deny his right to claim this child as his own. She wondered what he would do.

One day, feeling especially trapped by her life, Zazmaria decided to go out walking alone, against the strong protests of Medetha. It was a warm, sunny day, soft breezes blowing. She needed to clear her head, to get away from everyone, even her son. Though she had tried, she could not stop thinking about Zhek and the feelings he stirred in her. She once again felt things closing in around her, strangling her. She was restless, filled with emotions she tried in vain to suppress. She walked and walked in no particular direction, when suddenly she heard a voice.

"Zazmaria."

She whirled around, startled.

"I have waited a long time to find a moment where you were alone."

"Zhek," she said, her voice barely audible. He stepped out from the trees where he had been hidden. She was outside the Palace grounds now, far out of earshot of any guards or staff. She had not met with him since the day she told him she was pregnant. So much had happened since then, so much time had passed and yet here he was standing before her once again.

He wore a hood, which he now pulled back. His thick black hair was looser than he usually wore it, with strands falling about his face. "It has been quite a long time, Zazmaria. You are looking well. Motherhood must agree with you."

His voice was as deep and sensual as she had remembered it. "What are you doing here?" she asked, frozen where she stood, her heart racing, the blood rushing to her face. She could not read his expression, and was nervous as to his intent.

"As I said, I have waited for a moment to catch you alone." He too was uncertain as to how she would react to him. "You looked so radiant the day of the parade, I had to see you again," he said as a sadness now tinged his handsome features.

"That was you…" Zazmaria said, her mind racing. A part of her wanted to run to him, while part of her wanted to run away.

Zhek stepped closer, but kept a respectful distance. "Yes, I knew you saw me, but I thought it best to keep a low profile." He looked deep into her eyes.

"That was wise," was all she could think to say.

Her words came off cold and unfeeling. "Is it really so easy for you, Zazmaria, to be apart like this? To have the father of your child estranged from you, from Setar?" He could not hide the emotion in his voice.

"Of course it has not been easy, Zhek."

"Indeed, Princess? Your actions belie your words," he said angrily.

"What do you mean by that?"

"How do you think this has been for me, being separated from you all this long, empty time, never seeing Setar, knowing you are living your life without me as another man's wife? I have not even been able to hold my own son!" he shouted, now stepping only inches from her.

"Zhek, please, what do you want from me? Do you have any idea how difficult things have been for me? I am Alaj's wife, a member of the Royal Family. I was that before you and I met. Be realistic, we got ourselves into something that had no future, you knew that." Zazmaria's resolve was breaking down and her self-control began to crumble.

"No future?" he yelled at her, incensed. "We have a child together, Zazmaria. There is no greater future than that!"

She burst into tears. All at once she understood how painful this must all be for him, the man she loved, her son's true father.

Zhek reached out and pulled her to him. He held her close for a moment then kissed her softly on the lips. "I am not your enemy, Zazmaria. I only want to be a part of your life, of my son's life. I am not a man who gives up when circumstances become difficult."

Zazmaria pulled away, "Zhek, someone might see us."

"Tell me something," he pressed, "are you happy? Truly happy living this lie?"

No response.

"Then tell me something else, does Setar have the birthmark?"

Zazmaria was too shocked by the question to answer.

"He does," Zhek said, reading her expression, and feeling emboldened by it. "Then you know there is no doubt. Do you think of me every time you see it?"

Her cheeks flushed. She looked away.

"I will take that as a yes." He paused, letting the knowledge sink in, emboldening him. "I think of you constantly, Zazmaria, and of my son. It tears me up inside to not be a part of your lives, to not be able to see him. Could you even begin to imagine what that has been like for me?"

Tears swept down her cheeks.

"I know deep down you are not happy with your life. I have a way to resolve all of this. My family is strong Zazmaria – you know that. We want things to change. We will see that they do change. At that time, you must decide what you want."

"What do you mean by that, Zhek?" she asked nervously.

"Perhaps one day," he said reaching for her hand, "Setar could ascend to the throne."

His words thrilled her.

He looked at her, his expression serious, "In the days to come, you will have to choose your path very carefully. I love you, Zazmaria. When the time is upon us, should you choose to be with me, I will protect you and honor you and our son, no matter what we are to face."

Zazmaria listened intently, taking in every word. "Zhek, are you saying…"

"Yes, and I mean every word of it," he said as he kissed her forehead.

She melted into him. "Zhek, I have thought of you so many times, I wanted to talk to you, to see you, but…"

He cut her off with a long, lingering kiss, then held her close.

Her feelings now came pouring out of her, "I love you, Zhek. I do. I think of you constantly. I can barely look at Alaj. I see Setar and it breaks my heart that he is not with his true father. I feel that I am letting him down, robbing him of that important connection. I worry that once he is older, he will never forgive me for taking that from him, time we can never get back."

"Then we must make changes, Zazmaria, soon. I cannot bear this much longer."

"Nor can I," she said, pressing her face into his strong chest. She felt safe once again, protected, loved, passionate…alive, and she was grateful for it. She made her decision. "Zhek, there is something I need to tell you."

"What is it?" he asked, looking deep into her luminous topaz eyes.

"It is about the Amsara site."

He looked surprised. "Go on," he encouraged her.

"Alaj overheard Traeus and Assan talking about it. They were saying something about the chamber below it. There is an energy source there, but it was fluctuating. Victarius was attending to it. I believe the chamber was designed to contain whatever this energy is."

Zhek took in the valuable information. For so long he and his family had tried to find out the truth of what was actually going on at the site, but their spies had always come back empty-handed. "Did they say anything else about it?"

"No, nothing, and Alaj refuses to confront Traeus on it."

Zhek kissed her again. "Thank-you for sharing this with me Zazmaria. It took a great deal of courage for you to tell me."

"What are you going to do now?" she asked.

"I am not sure yet, but I think we have a right to know what they are doing down there, would you agree?"

"I said as much to Alaj. It infuriates me to think how Traeus lies to us, hides things and then has the audacity to expect us to tolerate it."

"Precisely. His actions could be putting us all in grave danger." Zhek paused for a moment, considering the matter. "Zazmaria, I should go now, but I will contact you again soon, I promise. Remember everything I have said here. My words are sincere. I will take care of you and our son, if you will let me…"

Zazmaria looked up at him with tears in her eyes, "I will."

A Deadly Crime

L ate one night, Traeus was summoned to Assan's private study in the main temple. The messenger said it was extremely urgent and that the King must come at once. The King was accompanied by two of his personal guards. He bid them stay outside the room while he went in to speak with Assan. Victarius was also waiting inside.

"Your Majesty," Assan bowed.

Victarius bowed, but did not speak. His face was blanched. He was visibly shaken.

The King looked to Assan. "You summoned me?"

"Your Highness, we are sorry to send for you at such an hour, but we have some troubling news. There was a break-in in one of the engineering rooms."

Traeus quickly glanced over at Victarius who was clearly very upset.

"There has been a murder," the Head Priest stated gravely.

"What?" Traeus asked, shocked. "What happened?"

"Someone broke into the room where the plans for the chamber and Pharom are kept. It appears they did not know at first which room to search as another room also shows signs of forcible entry."

Victarius now had his face buried in his hands.

Assan decided to continue, "Fortunately, whoever broke in was unable to take anything, but he managed to find the plans to the chamber's locking mechanism and the Pharom, even though the room was secured and the plans were kept in a locked cabinet. One of Victarius' engineers, Rhodan, was working late in a nearby room and came across the intruder. Whoever it was, broke Rhodan's neck."

Traeus was taken aback, "I cannot believe this!" Then realizing how close Victarius was to his engineers, he turned to him, "I am so sorry, Victarius." The King walked over and placed his hand on the older man's shoulder.

Victarius struggled to maintain composure, but through his tears he spoke, "Rhodan…he was always trying to prove himself. He was my hardest working engineer…I do not know how I am going to tell his family, but I must. I-I should go now…"

"Victarius, I know this is difficult for you, but I must ask you to do one thing," Traeus said. "You must not let the family, or anyone else for that matter, know anything about what the intruder was after. Tell them that we do not know why it happened, but that it is being investigated."

"I understand," Victarius replied. He paused before leaving. "Your Majesty, I cannot stress enough, how dangerous it would be if someone tried to steal the Pharom. It must be protected at all costs."

"It will be, Victarius."

Victarius nodded and left to carry out his grim task.

Traeus turned to Assan, "Do we have any idea how much the intruders may know?"

"We must assume they know enough to be a threat."

"Could information about the Pharom have been leaked?"

"Perhaps, or it may be just someone who was dangerously curious about the site," Assan countered. "We cannot know for certain either way at this point."

The King was deeply troubled. "What must we do?"

"Your Majesty, we must consider permanently sealing the chamber. It may be too dangerous to leave any kind of access to it, even by members of the priesthood. Our enemies would not know the consequences of tampering with it, or why it is housed in that chamber. The results would be disastrous…"

"I understand what you are saying, Assan," Traeus conceded. "Someone out there is willing to take enormous risks to learn what it is. However, I do not want to seal the chamber yet if I can avoid it. We still need access to it. I will have Commander Koronius increase security and watch for anything suspicious, but I want to keep things quiet. I do not wish to arouse suspicion or let on how valuable the Pharom is. The intruder could not have learned its true purpose from those plans."

"With all due respect, your Majesty, is this not too great a risk?"

"It is one I am willing to take…for now," Traeus stated. "Do you think the Draxens could be responsible?"

"It is possible, but we must have proof of their involvement."

"And none has been found?"

"Not yet, Your Majesty."

"I must tell Alaj about this, but I will not mention the Pharom. I will tell him thieves broke in, looking for we know not what, and that Rhodan was killed when he confronted the intruder."

"Will he not ask what was so important that someone was willing to kill for it?"

"Perhaps. I will try to convince him it was simply a burglary gone terribly wrong. The bigger questions are who did it, why they were looking for information and what they plan to do next. I will go see Commander Koronius first then I will speak with my brother."

CHAPTER

47

Evil Takes Hold

"Jace, come in, we have been expecting you," Lord Draxen said. Getting up from behind his huge desk, he motioned the young man to have a seat. Lord Draxen had been awaiting his return. Two of Lord Draxen's guards, large burly men, stood on either side of Jace watching him closely. Their steely gazes made him uneasy. Zhek was sitting nearby. Jace appeared disheveled and nervous.

"Do share with us the results of your mission, Jace," Lord Draxen urged.

"I managed to find the room where they kept their constructions plans. I only had a short time before someone found out I was there," he stopped, hesitating to go on.

"Continue," Lord Draxen said.

"Well, I found the plans of a double-chamber underneath the Amsara site and of some kind device stored within it. It is definitely what Princess Zazmaria told Zhek about. I have to say, whatever they have created, it looks highly advanced."

"And can you tell us what it is?" Lord Draxen asked.

All eyes were on Jace.

"Not exactly, there is a complicated locking mechanism to gain entry into both chambers, but I think I could figure out how to defeat them from the plans I saw."

"And…?" Lord Draxen asked, growing impatient.

"All I saw was that it is in the shape of an obelisk, but is a sophisticated design. It appears that Princess Zazmaria was right – it needs to be connected to that chamber, placed on some kind of platform to operate. I would guess the obelisk itself is the energy source the Princess referred to. The device and the chamber were probably designed to work together somehow, but I could not tell how from the plans I saw. There are likely other blueprints that I did not find. However, I would guess that the chamber might amplify its energy somehow…"

"Do you think it could be a weapon?" Zhek asked.

"If it is, it is the most unusual design for a weapon I have ever seen. I would speculate that is has some other kind of purpose though, but unfortunately, I do not know what its true function is."

"And you can tell us nothing else of this device?" Lord Draxen questioned him, his irritation showing. This had been their best chance to get answers. He was not at all satisfied with the scant information Jace was providing.

"If I only had had more time I might have been able to find out more about it, but something happened…"

Lord Draxen looked at him sharply.

"What is it Jace?" Zhek asked. "You had better tell us everything."

Jace took a deep breath, "Someone else was there. He must have been in a far room down the hall from where I was. I did not expect anyone to be there at such an hour, everything seemed quiet and dark at first."

"Go on," Lord Draxen prodded him.

"I suddenly heard footsteps outside the door. There was no time to hide or do anything, I had no choice…" Jace started to reply.

"No choice in what, Jace?" Zhek asked.

"I had to kill him. There was nothing else I could do. It was too late, he saw me. I do not know who it was, but he was young though. I lunged at him…I broke his neck. Afterwards, I left in a hurry in case anyone else came looking for him. In my rush to get out of there, I did not stop to take anything with me, I am sorry…I-I panicked."

The men were speechless as they processed what he told them.

Finally Lord Draxen spoke, "What is done, is done. We will have to decide where to go from here. Jace, you are dismissed, for now."

"Yes sir," he replied and walked out the door.

Lord Draxen turned to his grandson, "Zhek?"

"Yes Grandfather?"

"The stakes are now much higher, we have little time for indecision. I want you to pay another visit to Zazmaria. Find out if there is anything else she knows or can find out for us about that device. It is also time we set some other plans in motion. Get her to strongly encourage Alaj to start taking matters into his own hands. We need him to start making Traeus' life a lot more difficult, to actively challenge his authority, if you get my meaning. If we can get the King and eldest Prince to look at one another as the enemy, they will be too busy to see us coming."

"You are clever Grandfather," Zhek replied. "I will do what I can."

"And Zhek, I would prefer to avoid any more unplanned 'incidents'. They could prove dangerous to us. If we did not still need Jace's expertise, well..."

Zhek nodded, he knew what his grandfather was saying.

"Be cautious, be vigilant, keep tight control of things," Lord Draxen warned.

The Lovers' Plan

Zazmaria could not stop thinking of Zhek. Traeus had informed the family of the break-in and murder, but, as usual, did not provide details. She knew it had to be the Draxens.

She felt a sense of urgency. She had to see Zhek. She knew she should not go to the little red house at this time, in light of what had happened to the young engineer, but she no longer cared. She would risk everything to be with him.

She did not have to wait long.

Zhek came in through the back door. She raced to him and into his strong arms.

"Zazmaria, my love, I have missed you." He held her tight.

"I feel the same, I cannot bear to be apart from you any longer."

"Then you shall not," he said as he kissed her passionately. He felt his body respond to her presence. He picked her up and carried her to the bedroom. He was a bit rough with her, he had been aching for her and could scarcely control himself, but she did not mind. They made love, their desire for one another ravenous, primal.

Afterwards, they caught their breath and allowed their heartbeats to slow to normal. However, they could not linger.

Zhek raised himself on one elbow, and looked down at the face of the woman he loved. He wished he could stay longer. "We do not have much time I am afraid. I love you and I need you Zazmaria, more than I can possibly say." He kissed her forehead. His expression turned serious. "I need you to listen to me very carefully."

She nodded for him to continue.

"You know about the break-in?" he asked.

"Yes. It was your family, was it not? Were you directly involved?"

"It was my family, but no, I had nothing to do with what happened. We had not meant for things to turn out the way they did…the man that died. We thought no one would be there at that time."

"I see," she said, waiting for him to continue.

"Have you been able to learn anything more of the device you spoke of? It would help us avoid any more unpleasant occurrences," he said, looking at her intently.

"No, Alaj and I barely speak these days."

Zhek took a deep breath. "All right then. My family will figure out where to go from here." He took her hand in his, "Zazmaria, I need to ask you to do something, something very important."

"What is it?" she asked anxiously.

"We need your husband to actively work against Traeus and begin to undermine his efforts and authority. I know Alaj tends towards inaction and passivity, but if you could strongly encourage him somehow to weaken and challenge Traeus' position, it would enable us to put our plans in motion much quicker."

She hesitated. "What would happen to Alaj if he succeeded in this?"

"That would be entirely up to him," Zhek stated.

"I see," she replied.

Zhek held her by her shoulders, his grip firm. "Zazmaria, things are falling into place for you and I. Everything we have talked about will be ours for the taking. When this is over, and we are successful, you could be my Queen. Together we could rule, and make way for Setar to take his rightful place as well. One day, he could be King. But I need your help to make it happen."

She nodded, her mind filled with dreams she would finally see realized. "I will do whatever I can, Zhek."

"You are an amazing woman Zazmaria. You will be a strong and powerful Queen one day." He kissed her again. "I have to go, but I will see you again soon, my love. You always know where to find me."

His words meant everything to her. Her heart pounded with anticipation of the days to come.

49

Zazmaria Makes Her Play

Energized and re-affirmed by her encounter with Zhek, Zazmaria exuded a new confidence. An undeniable change had taken place within her. She felt strong, bold…fearless. She could taste the power she and Zhek would soon share. She could hardly wait to see him again, she thought of him every moment of every day.

She could no longer disguise her contempt for her husband. Zhek was coming for her – that was all that mattered to her now. All the things that her husband could not, or would not do, Zhek would. Zazmaria would finally get what was due her.

She decided to confront her husband, and to put events into play. "Alaj, have you learned anything else from Traeus about this mysterious chamber of his?"

"No, I am afraid not," he replied, dreading where this conversation was going.

"Why not? Does he refuse to speak to you now?"

"I have not broached the subject with him again."

She narrowed her eyes, "What are you waiting for Alaj?"

Alaj sighed, "Zazmaria, you know I am in a difficult situation. I am waiting for the right time. Traeus is my brother, we are still family."

Zazmaria looked at him with a challenging gaze, "So family is important to you then?" Not waiting for a response, she continued, "How about your son, Alaj? What future are you establishing for Setar? What example are you going to set for him?"

Alaj did not answer.

She continued unabated, "I will answer that for you, Alaj. It will be the kind of future where Traeus and his miserable son lead our people and your child becomes a mere figurehead, powerless…just like his father." She was now slowly walking around Alaj.

Her words angered him. "Zazmaria, just what would have me do?"

"You do not deserve the title of Prince," she sneered. "What have you done for your family? Nothing! You let that insolent brother of yours walk all over you, you allow him to make all the important decisions. You think that is the kind of man I am proud to call my husband? To call the father of my child?" she was yelling at him now. "Well, it is not! I am ashamed of you, Alaj. I am tired of listening to you whine, but do nothing. Action is what is needed, but that would take strength and the courage of your convictions. You have shown me nothing of that. I can hardly stand the sight of you any longer."

"How dare you speak to me this way!" Alaj shouted back at her.

But she was not deterred. "Tell me then, how long do we wait, while Traeus keeps his dangerous secrets? A man was killed for what your brother hides. Have you ever thought that the reason he keeps you out of these matters is because he has no intention of including you in his vision of the future?" She looked at him with utter contempt, laughing scornfully. "You are such a fool, so blind. You play right into his hands. He will take everything from you…from us!"

"That is not true!" Alaj was becoming very upset. "He would not…"

"Oh no?" she replied, continuing the attack. "You delude yourself. I will tell you what you should do, what you must do. Strike first! He would never expect it."

Alaj was taken aback. "What are you suggesting?"

"You know exactly what I am suggesting."

Alaj was too shocked to answer.

Zazmaria continued, "Whatever that thing is he has been hiding, you can be certain that it is not for our benefit. Why do you think he keeps the priesthood so close and you so far away? It is only the beginning. How do we know that whatever he has created is not incredibly dangerous? It could be some kind of weapon! He told you nothing of the reasons for the break-in. He knows exactly why it happened and yet still he lies to you! If I were you, I would not stand for it. I would do something about it, before it is too late!"

She left the room without another word, slamming the door hard behind her. Her words had cut him as no words ever had. But perhaps she was right about this. He had let his brother push him around, lie to him, hide things, diminish him in the eyes of the people, and take advantage of him. He had been a fool, a pawn, and now he was losing his wife, losing everything…because of Traeus.

A Terrible Realization

"**P**rince Amoni, what are you doing here at this late hour?" asked one of the King's servants, eyeing the young Royal with a measure of alarm.

"I am here to speak with Traeus. It is most urgent, please wake him at once."

With a nod and a bow, the servant backed away, "As you wish, Prince, I will rouse the King."

Amoni paced the hallway nervously. The news he had to pass on to his brother was grim indeed. Surely Traeus would know what to do, know how to interpret what Amoni was about to tell him.

Amoni was waiting outside as the King stepped from his bedchamber, a look of grave concern on his tired face, "What is it Amoni? What is wrong?"

"Traeus, I am sorry to wake you, but I had no choice."

"Let us go to my private study, we can talk there."

Amoni took a deep breath and the story came pouring forth, "A villager came to me just a little while ago, with the most unsettling of news. He had been quietly working on his land late this evening when he saw a craft moored at the river's edge, not far from his property. He went to check it out and overheard the two men arguing about their load, the one insisting it was too heavy, while the other stating angrily that they had no choice, that the goods must be delivered before sun-up or the Prince would have them both executed."

Amoni paced the room. "The villager said he ducked down behind some bushes as he feared being seen. The men continued arguing and then one said something that caused him to run all the way to the Palace. He overheard them say that the Prince could not wait any longer, that his army of two thousand soldiers must move tomorrow night. They then sailed off into the night." Amoni was watching his brother's reaction intently. "What do you think this means? Surely they cannot be talking of Alaj."

Traeus looked down, saddened and angered at the news he had just been told. He squeezed his eyes closed and clenched his fists.

Amoni watched his brother, dumbfounded. "Traeus, it cannot be…"

Traeus knew that the time had come. He now had his answers. It had been six months since Assan and his priests had investigated the break-in and the murder of Rhodan. They felt that, in spite of the absence of evidence, the Draxens had to be involved, but they had no proof that they could act on. Never in his wildest dreams, did Traeus ever consider that his own brother, Alaj, would be involved, yet now even worse, willing to attack his own family, but there could be no other explanation.

He felt Alaj must have had help in raising this army and the Draxens were just the kind of people who had that kind of expertise. But Traeus could not accept this. Alaj must have done this some other way. He knew Alaj had as much disdain for that family as he did. Though Traeus now realized why he had not seen Alaj much over the past months. He had a feeling Alaj had been up to something, but it never occurred to him that his own brother could be raising an army to overthrow him.

Pain and regret would have to wait, right now he had much to protect and precious little time. Traeus slowly walked over to the window. He gazed out at the night sky, the stars shone brighter tonight than he had ever seen.

Amoni had been watching his brother anxiously. He was in total disbelief. "Traeus, what are you thinking? Talk to me! What does this mean?"

Traeus turned to his youngest brother and thought to himself how much he looked like their mother. He was no longer a child, but a young man. *'What a pity he has to live to witness this treachery,'* he thought.

"It means Amoni, that a time I have long dreaded and hoped would never happen, has come." He hesitated, but it was time for the truth. "Do you remember the break-in and murder six months ago?"

Amoni nodded, "Yes."

"Well there was much I did not tell you about it. Someone was likely after some very specific information – plans on the tunnel and chambers below the Amsara site."

"But why? You said it was just a special place for the priests to worship."

"What I told you about the tunnel and chambers is only partly true, it is much more than that."

"What do you mean? What is down there?" Amoni asked.

"There is something very powerful down there, something that was created for the benefit of our people, but if it were to fall into the wrong hands…it could have devastating consequences. I am sorry I did not tell you of this before, but I had my reasons. You have to trust me on this. I do not have time to explain it all right now."

"What does this have to do with Alaj? Did he find out about this secret of yours? Is that why he is doing this?" Amoni asked, trying to make sense of what he was hearing.

"We never found out who was behind the break-in and murder, or what they were planning to do with the information they uncovered, until now," Traeus replied. "Alaj has been angry with me all along about keeping information about the Amsara monument and the chamber from him. We have fought many times about it. He must have found out what was down there, or at least that there is much more to it than he was told. He has deluded himself into thinking he can wrest power from me, take control of everything."

"But surely he would never be involved in a murder, Traeus. This is our brother we are talking about. You seem to forget that!" Amoni was upset. He was feeling as though he did not really know either of his brothers any more. They had both been living their lies, keeping so much from him and from each other.

"I do not think I know anything for sure right now," Traeus replied.

"There has to be more to this," Amoni insisted. "Why would he take such extreme measures on his own? This does not sound like our brother at all. He would not destroy his own family over this!"

"I do not want this to be true any more than you do, but you heard the news yourself. Who else would they call Prince? They certainly were not talking about you," Traeus' voice was rising. "It can be no one else!"

Amoni was stunned at what was unfolding.

"Amoni, we must act quickly, there is very little time."

51

Defenses Are Prepared

The King had sent for Commander Koronius and Assan to meet him and Amoni immediately in his private study in the Palace. "Gentlemen, we have some terrible news to share with you. Prince Amoni came to me tonight with information regarding those who were likely responsible for the break-in and the murder of Rhodan."

Assan and Commander Koronius were listening intently. Traeus continued, "I regret to inform you that the person who may have masterminded it is now planning an attack against us tomorrow evening. It is Prince Alaj."

Commander Koronius frowned. "What?"

Assan could not hide his disbelief either, "Prince Alaj? Attack us? It cannot be…"

"There is no mistake," Traeus stated gravely. "I wish there was, but we have very little time, we must mobilize the army at once. Fortunately, I had Commander Koronius begin provisions for just such an event almost six months ago. I regarded the security breach and murder as a very serious threat. We are not as unprepared as those who oppose us would believe."

Amoni was shocked. "I do not believe what I am hearing! Is there anything else you have neglected to tell me?"

"Amoni, this is not the time for this discussion," he said sharply.

Amoni's face turned crimson with anger.

Traeus turned to Koronius, "Commander, we have to move quickly now. Set up a command post at the front of the Palace. I believe they will try to attack the Palace first so I want your men positioned accordingly, but they must remain hidden. I do not want Alaj to realize we are ready for him."

Amoni looked at Traeus, who seemed a stranger to him now. He now felt a deep sense of resentment and mistrust towards the brother he had always admired, even idolized. He felt completely betrayed by both of his brothers.

Commander Koronius nodded in agreement, "Do we have any idea how large a force they have?"

"We have heard that Alaj has a force of two thousand soldiers," Traeus replied.

"Two thousand?" Commander Koronius repeated, stunned at the number. "Where and how did he get that many soldiers to stand against you?"

"Good question," Traeus said. "I was not aware I was that unpopular."

"Something is very wrong here. I have a feeling there is more to this," Assan said.

Traeus paced the room, "Our information is very sketchy, but at least we know the timeframe and who is behind this. Alaj had access to the weapons, knowledge of our defenses and vulnerabilities and a great deal of time to plan his strategy. We must assume his army will be heavily armed and well trained."

"So the Draxens are not involved?" Commander Koronius asked.

"Right now we have no evidence to support that," Traeus replied, "but let me say this, Alaj has never liked nor trusted that family. I would have a very hard time believing he was working with them. Besides, it is no secret that Alaj and I have long been at odds."

"That is true," the Commander agreed, "but never would I have believed he would be capable of something like this."

"Perhaps it was only a matter of time before he turned his discontent into action." Traeus turned to the business of war at hand. "Commander, how many troops do you have ready right now?" the King asked.

"We have fourteen hundred highly trained soldiers which can be mobilized immediately, your Highness. I will do what I can to ready more troops."

Traeus was disappointed at the numbers. "Please do, Commander. We will have to proceed carefully. We are outnumbered and must devise strategies to ensure that is not our undoing. Gentlemen, remember, we do not have much time and we do not know if they have spies watching the Palace."

"Understood," Commander Koronius said.

"Your Majesty," Assan said, "before the Commander takes his leave may I make a suggestion?"

"Of course, what is it?"

"What about Princess Zazmaria? We must assume she is also involved and as such cannot be trusted. If we find her, should we have her confined?"

Commander Koronius nodded. "Your Highness, in light of these circumstances, I agree it would be prudent."

Traeus took a deep breath. This was most unfortunate, but he shared their misgivings. "I authorize her detention if she can be located."

"Very good, your Majesty," Assan said. "I will also inform the priesthood of what we have learned. I will assign many of them to the Palace to tend to the injured if things go badly. We will provide assistance in whatever way we can."

"Thank-you Assan," Traeus replied. "I do appreciate your candor with me. You are both dismissed to begin preparations. Report back to me as soon as possible."

Both Assan and Commander Koronius left.

Traeus turned to Amoni, who seemed lost in his own thoughts. "Amoni, once the fighting has started, I want you to stay away from it. Stay at the back of the Palace, you will be safe there."

Amoni just glared at him.

"Inform Mindara of what is happening at once and ask her to stay with the children. I want you to keep on eye on things and ensure they are safe.

I do not want anyone wandering the corridors from here on in. The Palace is the most heavily fortified building we have, so you will be safe if you stay inside. Our soldiers will set up out front to try and keep the fighting away from the Palace but I cannot guarantee it will not end up here."

"What if they sneak around back? Alaj knows the Palace layout as well as anyone. What makes you think we will be safe anywhere in here?" Amoni snapped.

"Alaj knows that the best strategy to attack the Palace grounds is to hit it head on from the front. It would be a tactical nightmare to send that many soldiers through the dense woods behind the Palace. The terrain is treacherous and wild animals abound. Besides, I have a feeling Alaj is not looking for bloodshed. It is not in his nature. We are still brothers. He likely hopes I will simply back down at his show of force. I doubt he wants it to go further than that, or that he has planned beyond it."

"I do not believe this is happening."

Traeus placed his hand on Amoni's shoulder, "Amoni, Alaj is not a military man, he is not easily given over to fighting and he has a natural distaste for it. I am certain he wants this to end peaceably with him claiming the throne, nothing more. However, we have one advantage, he does not know we are ready for him."

Amoni shook Traeus' hand off his shoulder, saying nothing.

"Amoni, I understand you must be angry with me right now, and I am sorry for all of this. I will send word to you if you need to leave. If that happens, get the women and children and go where I tell you. Do you understand?"

"I do not want to stay out of the fighting! I am a man now. I should help to defend the Palace. It is my home, too!"

"Amoni, listen to me, if anything happens to Alaj and I, you would become King. Do you understand the gravity of this situation? Our line cannot end this way. We have to keep you safe!"

"Why should I listen to you or trust you ever again?" Amoni yelled back at him.

"Amoni, I will not debate this with you any further right now," Traeus said. "You must stay out of the battle. I will not pit you against your brother. His argument has always and only been with me."

"Not any longer. He is the one who is coming here, to our home with an army. He has betrayed us all!"

"No, not you! Whatever he has done, whatever he has planned – it has nothing to do with you. Now please, go to Mindara, tell her everything and stay away from here!"

Fighting back tears and hating the way his world had turned upside down, Amoni left.

52

Devious Plans

Lord Draxen had grown increasingly ill over the last few months after contracting a dangerous lung disease, a particularly virulent strain of bacteria. Though his healer had been treating him, his illness had steadily worsened and his strength was failing. He often coughed up blood, but no one other than his healer had been permitted to know exactly what was wrong with him. However, people had noticed the constant wheezing and sweating along with his dramatic weight loss. Whispers abounded about his condition. He had taken to spending most of his time in bed, too weak to go outside.

"Zhek, what news do you bring?" Lord Draxen demanded, coughing hard.

"Alaj's band of mercenaries and soldiers are gathering," Zhek informed him. "You were very effective in secretly enlisting men to fight in his army. I think he was likely surprised at how many made their services available to him. The resources we have funneled through Zazmaria ensured Alaj's soldiers were easily bought. They all think they are doing this for the Prince. Zazmaria told Alaj the funds they used to draw the army came from friends of hers who are sympathetic to him.

He has no idea where they actually came from. The army is secretly mobilizing to attack the Royal Palace tomorrow night."

Lord Draxen smiled. "He probably thinks they are there just because of him. Such a fool!" Lord Draxen turned serious again, "How is our man, Diette, doing?"

They had ensured that Diette, who had always held secret loyalties to the Draxen family, had been put in a position of authority. Zhek had Zazmaria introduce him to her husband.

"Alaj promoted him to second in command, he is now Commander Diette. He knows he must ensure Alaj's army does not back down, to light the match so to speak. He has managed to gain the Prince's trust and will be at his side during the battle."

"And if things do not go according to plan?" Lord Draxen asked.

"Diette knows full well what he has to do," Zhek replied.

"Splendid!" Lord Draxen exclaimed. "You know, it is all about choosing the right man for the right job. Have you told Zazmaria about that particular part of the plan?"

"No. I thought it was better to leave it out."

"Very good," Lord Draxen replied, satisfied that the plans were going ahead as he had envisioned. "I assume Diette is with Alaj now?"

"He is."

"Excellent, everything is falling into place perfectly. The Prince is even more foolish than we thought," Lord Draxen mused. "I will enjoy watching Alaj weaken his own family's power by dethroning his brother. Did you make sure that the villager 'informed' the Royal Family about the imminent attack?"

"Yes, Grandfather," Zhek answered, "The King knows full well about Alaj's treacherous acts. Our spies tell us Traeus is mobilizing his forces as we speak. However, they seem to be much more prepared than we would have thought."

"Traeus must have suspected something," Lord Draxen said.

"I am afraid Prince Alaj will have a great surprise when he realizes that the Palace is solidly defended and quite prepared for his arrival."

"The young fool will not realize what hit him, but this actually works to our advantage," Lord Draxen smiled. "His and Traeus' armies will annihilate each other." The old man coughed violently again. He reached for his handkerchief. Blood was evident on it, but Zhek said nothing. Instead, he poured his grandfather a glass of water and handed it to him.

Lord Draxen took a big drink. "By the way, have you dealt with Zazmaria? Does she know what to do when this all begins?"

"She does. I told her to sneak away from the Palace once the fighting is about to begin and wait for me at our usual meeting place. No one will look for her there. She will be safe and out of harm's way."

"And the boy?"

"She said she would not be able to escape with Setar. His caregiver, Medetha, is unaware of our plans and Setar will be with her. Zazmaria felt, and I agree, that it would be too risky to be seen sneaking off with a child. She can disguise herself well enough, but to carry a child who will likely be crying would make it impossible to get away without someone noticing. I told her that we will go back for him as soon as the Palace was taken."

"Excellent," Lord Draxen said. "When the fighting starts, make sure none of our people within the Stronghold get involved. We will keep a low profile until the proper moment comes for us to strike hard at the Royal Palace. Lock the gates and put our army on high alert. Let no one in, under any circumstances."

"I will see to it that the military personnel are informed and prepared."

"Good, Zhek. Now, we will not move against the Palace until the attack has almost ended."

"Why wait to seize the Palace?" Zhek objected. "Why not move in right in the heat of the battle while they are occupied with one another? Under the cover of darkness, our army can quietly move into position and deal with any survivors. We could have control of the Palace before daybreak."

"It is the fool who rushes into things without thinking things over first," Lord Draxen admonished him. "The value of patience and choosing one's time carefully should not be underestimated. I have dealt with Traeus' family before and they are a cunning people. They have not held onto power for this long by being imprudent. Our family has waited this to long, we can wait a little bit longer."

Since Lord Draxen became so ill, he had become desperate to see his family seize the throne. He refused to die with his enemies in power.

"Very well then, Grandfather," Zhek acquiesced, "We shall wait."

"Zhek, I have another mission for you. It is extremely important."

"What is it, Grandfather?"

"Regarding the device inside the chamber, I want you to retrieve it and bring it here. Do this once the battle is underway. Take Jace and gather a small team of our best soldiers. Jace has the most expertise to deal with it. He should be able to defeat the locking mechanism once he gets a good look at it."

"What about the reports that the chamber is specially designed to house it?" Zhek asked. "We have no idea what exactly what we are dealing with, or how dangerous it could be to remove it. Besides, I doubt that it would be left unguarded."

"Traeus will have his hands full dealing with Alaj's assault, he will need all available forces at the Palace. He will not expect another assault from a second source. If there are guards posted there, you and your men will have to deal with them, do I make myself clear?" Lord Draxen ordered.

Zhek was about to protest, but he knew it was no use. "Perfectly," he replied.

As Zhek set out to do his Grandfather's bidding, he was troubled. His arrangement with Zazmaria was to meet her once the fighting was underway and escort her to the Draxen Stronghold where she would remain until everything had settled down. His relationship with her was a secret to everyone but his grandfather. She would have to be accompanied by Zhek to be allowed inside. However, now he was unsure as to how quickly he could get back to meet her. He would have to hope she would be patient and wait for him.

Lord Draxen watched Zhek go. He was deceiving him, but it was the only way. He had perceived Zhek's feelings for the Princess though Zhek had claimed he was only manipulating her. As far as Lord Draxen was concerned, Zazmaria had served her purpose. She was no longer needed. He knew Zhek expected to bring the Princess into the Draxen family, and be granted a place of power when the takeover was complete. But Lord Draxen would never tolerate a member of the Royal family, even a traitor, into his Stronghold. He was using her to help destroy the Royal Family and enable him to take possession of Setar. He smiled to himself. In one fell swoop he could sever their relationship, remove an unwanted presence and then have the power to do as he pleased.

53

Secrets Unleashed

Present-Day Egypt

Mitch and Alex had decided to put the break-in of their rooms in the back of their minds and focus on deciding where and how to excavate for the ancient entrance to the tunnel and chambers they believed were hidden deep beneath the Sphinx. They wanted to cause as little upheaval as possible to the site and so intended to layout very precise parameters for their excavation. From what they could determine from the mysterious note they had been given at the party, it appeared that the entrance was between the Sphinx's paws, underneath its chest.

They had also found another diagram in the scrolls that showed people, a king and some priests, perhaps, that were standing between its paws. At first Mitch and Alex had thought it to be just a ceremonial picture, capturing the creation with its creators, but when they considered the note they became convinced that not only was it ceremonial, it was a specific ceremony, the one which marked the completion of the chamber and its hidden entrance beneath the monument they had come to know as 'Amsara'.

Mitch reread the note:

Seek out the words of the one who stands guard,
Under one's heart does the gateway rest,
Only they who know the secret shall be allowed to pass,
But be warned of the power that lies below

"You know Mitch, there was also a passage in the scrolls that said, '*Let Amsara welcome you, who rightfully have the secret knowledge, into his heart, into places of power.*' That makes twice the monument's heart has been mentioned. This is no coincidence."

Mitch nodded, "I remember it."

From what they could determine from the note and the scrolls, the entrance had to be where Tuthmosis' granite Dream Stela was. During the period of 1427-1401 BC, Tuthmosis had placed the Dream Stela in front of the Sphinx's breast and on it recorded the events of his dream, in which the Sphinx came to life and asked him to remove the sand away from the Sphinx as it was choking him.

In that time, all that was above the surface of the sands of Egypt was the Sphinx's head, the body remained engulfed in the desert. In return, the Sphinx promised Tuthmosis that he would become the next Pharaoh. Both kept up their ends of the bargain.

Mitch and Alex presupposed that Tuthmosis had no idea of what he was inadvertently covering up by placing the stela where it was. That also led them to the conclusion that whatever entrance may be behind the granite stela, it must have been incredibly well disguised, even in ancient times.

Mitch and Alex knew no one in modern times had ever tried, or even thought of trying to move the stela, for it had never been postulated that there was anything more behind it other than the limestone body of the Sphinx.

Undaunted they had set about planning to have the Dream Stela moved. This was no small task as it was huge and heavy and must be handled with the utmost care. The idea they came up with was to somehow try to shift one side of the stela away from the Sphinx, like opening a door, just wide enough for Mitch and Alex to squeeze through and search for signs of an entrance.

They had chosen the first day of the excavation to be their day off from their regular duties. This way they wouldn't fall even further behind on Professor Dustimaine's work…and more importantly, he wouldn't be around to see what they were doing. Some mysterious, yet powerful person sanctioned this dream excavation of theirs – Dustimaine would hit the roof. They knew he'd be incredibly offended that he had been sidestepped and accuse them of backstabbing him.

"I can't believe we're doing this Alex," Mitch said. "I guess part of me thought those permits would turn out to be fakes, some kind of hoax and we'd be hauled away in cuffs if we even tried to set up here." Mitch gazed up in awe at the majestic Sphinx. He knew that to be allowed to excavate right below one of the most important monuments ever created was a staggering honor.

"I know. It feels like a dream. I keep thinking someone's going to come along and wake us up and tell us we were delusional to think the likes of us would ever be allowed to work near the Sphinx." Alex felt like a little girl again, lost in her fantasies only this time, it was absolutely real. "Hello, Amsara," she spoke softly.

Mitch smiled and looked up at the familiar face of the Sphinx, imagining what it must have looked like with the head of a lion, decorated and newly created.

Mitch and Alex put together their own team for the excavation. They had approached Khamir first and he readily agreed to participate as the leader of the team. Much to their surprise, he did not seem surprised at their request. Instead, he just replied that he was honored they asked him to participate. They had grown to depend on him. He was reliable, good with the Egyptian workers, respectful and a hard worker himself. He was very knowledgeable, yet respected Mitch and Alex's authority.

Obviously the workers would see a lot of what was going on, so all that Mitch and Alex had told them was that they were looking for artifacts that may be hidden behind the stela. They didn't go into much detail, but they did tell Khamir privately that they were actually looking for the entrance to a tunnel and a double-chamber beyond. Khamir knew that there had long been rumors of a tunnel and chambers below the Sphinx and they trusted him with the sensitive knowledge of their mission.

It took the workers a great deal of effort and time to carefully and safely shift and secure the tremendously heavy granite stela far enough for two people to get behind it. It had not been easy to budge from its long resting place. Finally, the stela was braced and supported. Only when Mitch and Alex were completely satisfied that it had not been damaged and was securely placed, did they proceed with the next phase of their plan. They asked Khamir to stay nearby, but to have the workers take a break away from the area.

Mitch and Alex brought flashlights and a complement of tools to begin the search for something they knew must have remained hidden for nearly 12,000 years. They stepped behind the stela to examine the area. All they could see was the body of the Sphinx, there were no obvious doors or entranceways, much as they had suspected.

"Well, I don't see anything that jumps out at me. Any thoughts on what that 'secret' or 'secret knowledge' might be?" Alex asked.

"There has to be something we've come across in the scrolls that is the clue, or within the note itself," Mitch replied. "Whoever gave it to us had to assume we'd be able to figure it out, so that gives me confidence."

They ran their flashlights over every square millimeter of limestone. Even though it was daylight, the small, cramped space they were working in was cast in shadow. "There are no obvious markings here, but…" Alex stopped.

"But what?" Mitch asked.

"Well, in our limited knowledge of these people, the one time we found them hiding something was in the chest – the false bottom. So that is a technique they have experience with."

"Good point," Mitch said, "and we have to remember that no one has had reason to look for anything like that before now, so that should give us an advantage." They kept looking and feeling around for anything out of the ordinary.

Alex began tapping the stone on the ground near where the stela had been, gently, to see if she could detect any differences in its composition. She did. "Mitch! Listen." She repeated the tapping motion. "It definitely sounds different right here, a little more hollow."

As they searched for an outline of some sort, Mitch noticed something,

"Hey Alex, look here, this strata of limestone at the base of the Sphinx, the color is slightly off from the surrounding stone."

"That could just be because it's been hidden behind the stela for several thousand years."

"Maybe, but I'm going to check it out." Mitch pulled out a couple of tools and a brush and began to examine the area of rock more closely. He set his flashlight down to illuminate the area as he worked. "I don't think this is part of the original Sphinx's body, it feels slightly loose."

Alex heard the stone shift slightly under the pressure Mitch was applying. The segment of rock was several inches thick and was solid limestone. "Mitch, let's see if we can try and pull it out." Slowly, carefully the two of them worked the stone free. They managed to ease it towards them. "Incredible, it's a good size chunk of limestone."

"Did you feel that?" Mitch asked as they gently laid the stone down on the ground.

"I did – a slight rush of air, this has to be it!" Alex exclaimed hopefully.

They shone their flashlights into the roughly rectangular hole that had been revealed. "Now what? I can't really see anything," Mitch said as he looked around. The surrounding rock of the Sphinx felt quite solid and there were no other discolorations in the limestone. There weren't any other loose slabs of stone as far as they could tell. "Well, care to stick your hand in there?" he asked Alex, grinning.

"Oh gee, thanks, so some nasty poisonous thing can bite me?"

"Alex, do you really think anything once alive would still be alive after having been trapped inside there for thousands of years?"

"No, but something very small could have snuck in and then grown into a nasty poisonous thing, with big fangs," Alex protested.

Mitch just rolled his eyes.

"All right, fine. But I'm tired of having my smaller bone structure taken advantage of," she pouted as she reached inside.

"Feel anything?" Mitch asked.

"Fear."

Mitch laughed.

She felt around gingerly. "Wait a minute," she said as her fingers traced something unusual. "I think I found something." She furrowed her brow as her fingers kept tracing and retracing the same spot. "It is! It's the Kierani symbol for power, engraved in the stone on the bottom of this opening."

As she continued to explore the engraving blindly, her hand slid, accidentally putting extra pressure on the rock. "Crap! My hand slipped…"

"No, wait Alex, I heard something creak."

Spooked, Alex quickly pulled her hand out of the opening.

Mitch peered inside. "That has to be it! The secret that keeps being referenced, a person would have to recognize the symbol for power. The secret that lies below is the Pharom is associated with the word power. You know, Alex, you being accident-prone has come in very handy for us, I must say."

Just as she was about to reply, she jumped, as a slight fissure suddenly creaked opened in the rock directly below where they had removed the chunk of limestone. "Geez, that scared me," she said checking her heart.

"Yeah, caught me off guard too," Mitch said, laughing nervously.

"The pressure on the symbol inside the opening must move this segment of rock out of the way. I'll try again," Alex said as beads of sweat formed on her forehead. She applied pressure to the carven symbol for power inside the body of the Sphinx and once again, after a brief delay, the fissure widened. What they initially thought was ordinary bedrock revealed an opening in the ground. The rock Alex was pressing on was also sliding further inside.

The opening inside the Sphinx was wider than they originally assumed. There was a hollow area behind where the stone slab had been. Finally the stone stopped. By now Alex's arm had all but disappeared inside.

"Well, I think we found the entrance, but how do we get in there?" she asked, pulling her arm out, and brushing the dust off.

"Can't you squish yourself down to a mere, what eight or nine inches?"

"How 'bout I squish you?" Alex challenged back.

"Um, no, but I have another thought," Mitch replied. "Where the Dream Stela stood, that's probably not original rock. It may have been built up."

"Good thinking," Alex said. "We can chip away at it, but we'd better be careful so we don't accidentally damage anything that may be underneath."

"Agreed."

Together they began to carefully chip away at the stone. After some painstakingly slow work, another fissure was revealed in the bedrock. They cleared away the rest of the base that the stela had once rested on.

"We'll have to put something here to support the Dream Stela when we replace it," Mitch added.

Alex nodded.

They examined the section of stone that had been uncovered and they found what seemed to be the edges of it. Alex started to push on the rock to see if it would move. Mitch pitched in to help and together they began to ease it forward. Remarkably it slid without too much force, they had not realized that there was a hollow space in front of where it lay.

Finally it came to a stop, but they had been able to push it a couple of feet forward, widening the opening. They had found their secret entrance. They shone their flashlights inside the narrow entrance and saw there were a few stairs and beyond, a long dark tunnel.

"We did it!" Alex said excitedly, biting her lip. She looked at Mitch, "Well, this is what we came for. Shall we?"

"Why not?" Mitch said nervously.

With Alex in the lead, eager to find the chambers beyond, they squeezed through the narrow opening, and went down the set of stairs that had been hewn into the rock. They shone their flashlights down the tunnel. They could see it ended about thirty feet down the passageway.

They made their way down the long, dark, narrow, sloping tunnel and came to a set of carved, metallic doors, bronze in color, which were inscribed with the Kierani symbols they had come to recognize.

"Metal doors? I've never seen anything like this!" Mitch marveled. "All this time, this has been down here and no one knew."

"Incredible," Alex said, admiring them.

The two of them examined the intricately carved doors. It appeared to be the same technology that had engraved the metal cylinders.

"Look, here, these three symbols – heaven or sky, travel or move, and beginning. And here – the symbol for power again," Alex said as she pointed out them out amongst the numerous symbols present.

"Alex, look at this. I've seen this before!" Mitch said, pointing to a round apparatus in the center of the two doors, where a doorknob would be. It was about five inches in diameter and had another round piece inset in the center of it, three inches in diameter. Surrounding the main circular feature were a series of Kierani symbols.

"You're right," Alex recalled, "in the scrolls."

"I just never knew what it was until now," Mitch said. "Let's be careful how we proceed."

"Right," Alex said, not taking her eyes off the strange, metallic doors. "I'm beginning to understand what Howard Carter must have felt when he discovered King Tut's tomb."

Mitch nodded and smiled as he took a closer look at the circular apparatus inset in the doors. Other than the engravings of the symbols, the doors were smooth. "I don't see anything else, this must be the way to open them."

"Should we give it a try?" Alex asked.

"Seems like the reasonable thing to do," Mitch said as he took a deep breath and proceeded. He had a firm grip on the centerpiece, pulling it hard, but the doors did not budge. He then tried pushing. Still nothing. "It's not working. I don't want to try to force it any further, we could damage something." He bent down to look at it again. He took hold of the inset part and tried turning it. "Alex, it rotates!"

"I'll bet it's some kind of combination lock. That could be what all these symbols represent," she replied. "But the question is, how do we know which symbols and in what order?"

"Let's see what we have to choose from," Mitch suggested.

The two archaeologists examined the various ancient symbols surrounding the apparatus. They focused on the ones they recognized and discussed various combinations of them.

"Think back," he said. "We need to remember what we read in the scrolls. The passages relating to this might have been giving us the code to open these doors."

"I remember something," Alex said. "Wasn't there a mention of the children? A Prince and Princess? I didn't think of it before because it seemed out of context. But, what would the children have to do with the entrance to a secret chamber?" At that moment a couple of symbols caught her eye. "Mitch, here and here," she pointed. "Look at these two, do you recognize them?"

"I think so," he said. "This one means carrier, and this, warrior."

"Right, and this is the symbol for light. Do you remember when we found what we thought must be names of members of the Royal Family, the names of the Prince and Princess: their names meant *'Warrior of Light'* and *'Carrier of Light'.*

"And since the Amsara monument and the chambers below were commissioned by the King, he probably got to choose the codes," Mitch followed. "But he wouldn't have made it too obvious, like using their actual names. He might have used the meanings of their names – but which one? And what happens if we don't get it right the first time?"

They both looked around for possible hidden traps.

"I think I've watched Raiders of the Lost Ark too many times," Alex said, "because I'm almost feeling the spears piercing into me if we get it wrong."

"Why don't you stand back and I'll have a go at it," Mitch offered.

"You know, maybe I will," Alex said as she backed up a few feet from the doors.

Mitch secretly hoped there weren't actually any poison darts waiting for him to slip up. He tried the combination, *'Carrier of Light'*. Nothing happened. He first pushed then pulled on the centerpiece but it didn't budge. His heart was beating faster now. He tried the second combination, *'Warrior of Light'*. Immediately he heard a snapping sound. He instinctively ducked, expecting something to come flying out at him.

"Are you all right?" Alex asked nervously, still at a distance.

Mitch was gripping his chest, "I think my heart stopped. That scared the crap out of me!" He looked at the doors. "Alex, come here! It looks like two handles on either side of the apparatus. They popped up from the door when I hit the combination 'Warrior of Light'.

Alex cautiously stepped forward and looked over Mitch's shoulder.

"You big chicken!" he said. "I think if anything was going to happen it would have happened already. I hope you appreciate how I just risked my life."

"I do. So now are you going to try and open the doors?"

"I guess I will," Mitch replied, mumbling something about yellow feathers under his breath. He pulled on the metal handles, which before had been invisible to the naked eye. No effect. He pushed and instantly the doors opened up into the darkness beyond. They felt a rush of air.

"It worked!" Alex exclaimed. "Look how thick these doors are! I can't even begin to explain how these people had technology like this thousands of years ago. They look like ancient bank vault doors!"

"Unbelievable…we are probably the first people to set foot inside this place for almost 12,000 years. This is a very humbling experience," Mitch said, his heart racing a mile a minute. He noticed the ancient combination lock was built into the door on the right.

They looked at one another and each nodded. Together, they cautiously stepped through the thick, heavy doors into a chamber. They shone their flashlights around inside. They were stunned by what they saw.

Four large limestone columns extended nearly ten feet to the vaulted ceiling above them. Beyond the columns, in the center of the room, stood an exquisite obelisk carved of limestone and covered with the same strange hieroglyphs. The obelisk was roughly five feet tall with a small opening, which had been carved near its top that resembled an upside down diamond.

"That looks just like the obelisk we saw in the scrolls!" Alex said, stepping towards it. "So, it is an opening and not just some kind of marking."

"This is incredible," Mitch said as he shone his flashlight around the chamber.

The walls were painted with scenes of royal processions. The figures appeared to be the same king or pharaoh and queen from the outdoor ceremony papyrus. The flashlights gave the scenes an eerie illumination, as though the figures moved, breathed with the movement of the light. Ghosts from the distant past seemed to now come to life once again.

The royal couple was depicted seated on thrones, with circlets of gold atop their heads. Dozens of figures dressed and painted beautifully, stood around them. They all had long, jet-black hair, golden skin and golden jewelry inlaid with many gemstones. Their clothing was elegant, and evidence of great wealth was everywhere around them – paintings of tapestries, linens, chests, sculptures, vases.

"This was obviously a sophisticated and wealthy culture," Alex remarked.

Mitch had started walking around the room. "Yet there are no artifacts in here. I was hoping there would be something."

They continued to walk through the chamber, flashlights glowing. They gazed upon the beautifully painted walls that time had not damaged.

"Mitch, look, past the obelisk," she pointed. "See how the room narrows. It looks like another door, that must be the second chamber…perhaps where the mysterious Pharom lies."

This time it was a single door, also of the same bronze-colored metal, and had a similarly designed locking mechanism with symbols around it.

"Same idea?" he asked.

"Why not?"

"I'll try the Princess' name this time: *'Carrier of Light',*" Mitch said. "Here are the symbols." He tried the combination. It worked. This time he was prepared for the hidden door handle to spring out, though Alex jumped a little. Mitch pushed the door open.

"Wow, same thickness," Alex said. As they peered inside, they realized the chamber was empty except for a platform in the middle of the room.

"Look! That's the platform we saw in the scrolls!" she exclaimed. "But where is the Pharom?"

They both looked around the room.

"I don't see anything," Mitch said.

"Damn it!" she said, gripping her flashlight tighter.

Disappointed, they walked over to the platform. Alex stooped down in front of it and shone the flashlight. The room was dark, however the flashlight revealed an interesting discovery.

"Mitch! Look at this. There's writing here!"

Mitch knelt down beside her. They examined the inscription carved into the front of the ancient platform. "I can't read all of this. I'll have to copy it down in my notebook and we can decipher it when we're back outside. I brought all of our notes along."

After he finished copying it down, he glanced around the room. "There's nothing else here. I can't believe this…this chamber hadn't been opened in 12,000 years. The scrolls indicated this is where the Pharom would be. What could have happened to it?"

"It has to be here! We were given the note and permits for a reason," Alex said anxiously.

"Maybe whoever gave them to us didn't know this chamber was empty," Mitch ventured.

"Possibly…but whoever's been feeding us information is extremely knowledgeable about this area. They seem to know things that aren't part of any known written records. This can't have escaped their attention. We need to keep looking."

"This chamber has been sealed for 12,000 years. Whatever happened to the Pharom had to have happened that long ago as well." Mitch walked slowly around the room, shining his flashlight, searching for any kind of clues.

"According to the scrolls, the Pharom or obelisk was left here. There is no other mention of it," Alex said, twisting her ponytail the way she always did when she was trying hard to figure something out.

"I think we need to conduct a detailed examination of this chamber," Mitch replied. "Something's missing here."

CHAPTER

54

The Secret Chamber

Alex continued to scan every inch of the chamber walls, running her fingers along the smooth stone. After looking around and finding nothing, they were getting frustrated.

"I give up, Alex," Mitch said. Just then, he noticed something on the ground. He looked down to see what it was. He was disappointed. "There's absolutely nothing in this room except for dirt and this rock." He went to toss it, but then paused for a moment, as he realized it was the only object in the room. He picked it up and examined it. Dried dirt, which had been caked on, broke off.

Alex bent down to look at it as well. "Mitch, it's shiny," she said as she held the flashlight to it.

"This is no rock," Mitch stated as he continued to chip away at the caked on dirt. "Look it's some sort of crystal."

Alex thought of something, "Mitch, do you remember our dream of the Sphinx? There was a crystal…I had forgotten about it before."

"You're right! The obelisk in the first chamber, the opening is the same size and shape of this crystal." He looked to his partner. She nodded that she was thinking the same thing.

Quickly they went to the obelisk in the adjacent room. Mitch gently placed the crystal into the opening. It fit perfectly. Alex turned her flashlight on the crystal. The light from the flashlight shone through the crystal and projected the same image of the lion's head they had seen in the scrolls, onto the back wall of the adjacent room they were previously in.

Mitch and Alex watched in awe of the three-foot by three-foot image on the wall. Alex continued to shine the flashlight on the crystal while Mitch walked to the image in the other room and inspected the wall.

"The rock where the image is projected looks kind of different. It almost sparkles," he remarked. "How come we didn't notice this before? Alex, take your flashlight off the crystal."

When she did, the image disappeared. Mitch shone his own flashlight on the wall. The area where the image had been, once again looked indistinguishable from the rest of the wall. "Now it all looks the same," he frowned.

"I think your eyes are going," Alex remarked.

"I'll prove it," he said. "Let's switch places. Keep watching that exact location on the wall as I remove the light." Mitch shone the flashlight on the crystal for a moment and then directed the light onto the ground.

She searched for the sparkling effect, but it was gone. "You're right. I guess I owe you an apology." She thought for a moment, "You know, maybe this is an optical illusion. Try taking the crystal out of the obelisk and shine the light on it, but aim it towards a different section of the wall."

Mitch took out the crystal and shone the flashlight on it, aiming the light far to his left.

"Does it have the same effect on the wall?" Mitch asked.

"Nope, there's no lion image and the rock isn't sparkling like it did before."

Mitch tried holding the crystal in front of the obelisk and shining his flashlight on it, aiming the light towards the same section of wall where the image of the lion's head had appeared. "Do you see it now?"

"No," she shook her head, "there's nothing."

Mitch put the crystal back in the obelisk and shone the light on it. The image immediately re-appeared.

"Do you think there could be something behind the rocks where the image is?" Alex asked.

"Could be," he replied. "Maybe that's also where the Pharom is."

"The scrolls didn't indicate anything like this," Alex mused.

"I don't think they were meant to. Either this was purposely hidden or it was added later on." Mitch started walking towards the back wall where Alex was still standing.

"There's got to be an outline or something," Alex said.

"Alex, why don't you go back and shine the light through the crystal again. I'll use some tape to mark the outline of the image."

"Good idea," she agreed and ran back to the obelisk.

"Perfect, hold it there while I trace the head," Mitch said as he traced the image with tape.

Once he finished, Alex joined him. She ran her fingers over the outline. "Wait, I think I feel something. It's just a hairline groove, but it's definitely there. Do you have something super thin we can try to slide in?"

"Try this," he said as he pulled a small, thin, knife-like object out, normally used to work with very small, fragile artifacts.

While Mitch held a flashlight on the area, Alex took the tool and traced around the groove. Thousands of years of dust had settled in, but she was able to remove some of the buildup, making the groove slightly bigger. "The dust and dirt is coming loose!" Slowly, she continued to work around the tape Mitch had placed. "Done! Now what?"

Mitch was deep in thought, looking at the outline of the lion's head, now clearly visible on the wall. "Let's try to pry it out." They both attached their flashlights to their forearms with tight Velcro holders, which held them snugly in place, freeing their hands.

Alex nodded, "Ok, on the count of three, just gently try to wiggle it out."

Mitch started counting, "One, two, and three." They started to pull the rock towards them.

"I think I felt it give a little, "Alex said as sweat started to roll down her face.

Suddenly they felt it shift. "I think this slab is fairly thick. I'm going to try and find the end of it." Mitch aimed his flashlight through the groove. "I think it ends about six inches back."

"How much do you think this thing weighs?"

"I think it's going to be fairly heavy. We'll have to be careful to keep control of it."

They kept prying. Slowly inch-by-inch, the slab moved forward.

Mitch took a look with the flashlight again. "I see the end! It's only a couple more inches. Hang on to the front of the slab, its weight is going to shift here right away."

As they continued to pull it forward slowly, they felt its weight shift forward.

"Geez this is heavy!" Alex complained.

"You've done your push-ups haven't you, Miss Logan? I seem to re-member a certain arm-wrestling competition you cleaned up at one night over a few pints of ale," he laughed.

"Well yes, that was one of my finer moments. I just don't want to drop this."

"Just brace yourself. Get a good firm grip on the bottom of the slab, let it fall into your shoulder."

They pulled again and the slab finally came free. The momentum quickly pushed them down, and it fell the last few inches with a huge thud. They both fell back on the ground, staring at the slab. Fingers and toes still intact, they looked at each other, nervousness and anticipation written all over their faces. Then they looked back up at the opening in the wall.

Mitch stood up to peer through it. "It's a tunnel. I can't see the end of it, but it's not much wider than the opening. We're going to have to crawl through on our bellies. You're not claustrophobic are you?" he grinned.

"No comment. After you, Mister Carver."

"You would ask me to go first." He shook his head. "Fine, I'll be the brave one. Again. Ready?"

"Ready as I'll ever be."

Once Mitch moved far enough inside, Alex pulled herself up into the tunnel. She inhaled a big cloud of dust he kicked up and started cough-ing. "Watch it, will you!"

"Sorry!" He continued on a little more carefully.

After crawling for quite awhile, Alex asked, "How far do you think we've gone? It feels like we must have left the borders of Egypt by now."

"I'd say nearly forty feet. Wait…I think I see the end! Hang on just a little longer."

"I'm not sure how much more of this I can take," Alex moaned. Her eyes were beginning to burn from all the surrounding dust and dirt in the crudely hewn tunnel. It was getting difficult to breathe.

"Just a few more feet, Alex. I think I can make out a small chamber ahead." Mitch continued on. "We're here! It's a small room, but I think we can both fit inside."

He dropped down into the chamber and held out his hands to pull Alex through. The cramped room was approximately seven feet by eight feet and was as crudely carved as the tunnel they just passed through. In the center of the room was a box, intricately carved with two figures on its lid. The figures were kneeling, each holding what appeared to be a scepter, pointed straight out, resting on the other's shoulder.

"It's beautiful, Mitch. It has similar markings as the first chest we found. Should we open it?"

"Oh yeah, I didn't crawl what felt like miles through a tiny, dirty tunnel to stop now."

"That's what I was hoping you'd say," she smiled.

They each took hold of one end of the lid, gently lifting it off. Inside was an obelisk.

"We found it! This must be the Pharom," Alex exclaimed. "And look – it's metal! This is incredible…"

"And how…" Mitch said, his eyes wide.

They examined it as best they could with it resting in the container.

"It's too dark and cramped in here to make a thorough examination," Alex said finally. "We need better light."

"Ok, but let's be careful," Mitch said. "Remember the warning in the note, '*Be warned of the power that lies below*'. We don't know what we're dealing with here."

"It seems to be safe enough," Alex said. "Besides, we're trained in dealing with fragile artifacts."

"I know, but we haven't dealt with anything quite like this before."

"Good point. But remember the drawing in the scrolls? This is supposed to go on the platform in the chamber. I think if we're careful, we should put it back where it belongs. We'll keep the chamber secure and make sure no one goes in."

"Ok, Miss Logan, but I hope we don't regret this," he said as he put the lid back on.

Alex entered the tunnel first and slowly crawled backwards through the narrow space, very glad to be leaving the cramped passageway.

Mitch followed behind. They carefully inched the box with the precious item through. Once they reached the end, they gently lowered it to the floor.

They sat for a moment, catching their breath.

Eager to see their prize, Alex removed the lid. She reached inside to lift the metallic obelisk out. It was deceptively weighty.

Mitch helped stand it up inside its box then told hold of his flashlight to examine it more closely. "Look at this, it has a reflective surface…and it looks almost fluidic." He frowned, "At first I thought it was the way the light was hitting it, but it seems to be inside the metal itself. I can see my reflection, but it's like the metal is in a state of quantum flux or something."

"I can almost see colors and wave patterns within it," she said.

"Jack and Bob are going to be blown away by this. Remember how in awe they were of the metal cylinders we found? This has to be far more advanced."

Alex nodded. "Let's place it on the platform," she said anxiously.

Together they carefully lifted it out of the container.

"Wow this thing is heavy," Mitch said as they carried it over to the platform, then positioned it and lowered it down onto the platform. It suddenly latched into place. "Whoa, it was definitely meant to sit there!"

They both heard a low hum. They looked at one another nervously.

Alex wavered slightly, "I'm feeling a little nauseous and a bit light-headed. I think I need to sit down."

"Me too," Mitch said as he steadied himself. "Can you feel that? It's like the faintest vibration. What the heck is this thing?"

"Good question. This wasn't at all what I expected, though I'm not exactly sure what I was expecting." Alex wiped her forehead. She was very hot. "Whoa, I'm really not felling well. It's getting worse. Crap, I've got to get outside for some fresh air before I get sick."

"I'm with you," Mitch said, wasting no time following his partner outside.

CHAPTER

55

A Deadly Mistake

Mitch and Alex sat down for a few minutes waiting for the feeling of nausea to pass. Alex had been very close to throwing up. She poured some water over her head to cool her. They both took deep, slow breaths.

"Mitch, where are our notes?" she finally asked. Her head began to clear.

"They're in the duffel bag, I'll go grab them."

Mitch ran off to retrieve the bag. Hurriedly he returned and sat back down. "I have a funny feeling about this."

"Other than the nausea?"

"Yes, smarty pants," he replied. "The inscription on the front of the platform – what if it's some kind of warning? Maybe we should have translated it first, before plowing ahead. I think we'd better figure out what it says and quickly."

Rifling through their papers, they found their crib notes. Slowly, they managed to piece together the following:

The power of thought is like no other
Only for this may the light shine forth

For those who would wield it for ill purpose,
May they be turned to ashes and cast asunder
Beneath its rays of power

For those who would wield it for good,
May they ever be wise in their ways,
And to them, the ultimate power made known

They looked at each, wide-eyed.

"The energy surge…" Mitch started to say.

Alex gasped, "What have we done?"

"We've got to get back in there and take that thing off the platform. We have no idea how dangerous it could be!"

The two stood up and ran back towards the tunnel entrance, when suddenly an incredibly bright flash of blue light blazed out from it. They stopped in their tracks as a low rumble shook the very ground. A piercing scream echoed from deep inside the tunnel.

"Oh no!" Alex cried as they looked at each other, horrified. In spite of the danger, they raced to the tunnel entrance. The workers were in a state of panic, everyone looking around to see what had happened.

One of the workers rushed forward, "I think someone snuck down there!"

Khamir came running over. "Take the workers back to town at once," he ordered the man. "I will deal with this."

"Yes sir," the worker replied.

"We need to go down there and find out what happened," Mitch said.

Khamir nodded his agreement and followed Mitch and Alex into the tunnel and then into the chambers beyond. The smell hit them first. It was acrid, overpowering. Alex put her hand over her mouth and nose to keep from getting sick.

They continued on down the shaft. A horrific sight met them. A body lay there, charred beyond recognition. Smoke still billowed from it. Not far from the body, lay the melted remains of what appeared to have been a screwdriver.

"Oh my God!" Alex shrieked.

Mitch turned white as a ghost.

"I will contact the authorities and have the body removed," Khamir stated firmly. "I will let them know it was an accident. I will be back shortly to deal with the authorities. You both must be gone by then."

They were too shocked to notice the way Khamir was suddenly and decisively taking control.

"But what about that?" Alex asked, pointing to the Pharom. Her hand was shaking. "It looks like he tried to pry it off the platform…it killed him…"

"Leave it where it is," Khamir ordered.

Mitch looked at the melted screwdriver, then back to the Pharom and nodded. "That's probably a good idea. We can't risk it. We'll have to leave it there until we can figure out how to take it off safely. There's got to be something in the scrolls that can help us."

Alex looked at the smoldering body. Her stomach turned, tears welled up. She was terrified. "I can't believe it killed him. How are we ever going to explain this?"

"You will not," Khamir stated. "I will."

Questions to Answer

By the time Mitch and Alex were called upon to give statements about the incident that resulted in the death of a worker, Khamir had already spoken to the authorities and blamed it on a generator accident. Khamir had informed Mitch and Alex of what he would say and instructed them as to what their responses should be. The circumstances were so frightening, so surreal, they agreed willingly and without question.

All Mitch and Alex told the authorities was that they weren't there when the accident occurred and weren't sure what happened, which in a basic sense, was true. There was no way they were going to volunteer any more information if they didn't have to.

They had no idea how Khamir managed to divert attention away from the Pharom, but somehow he had. No one had even brought up the strange metallic obelisk that had unfortunately been left in plain view of anyone who went down there.

When they returned to their rooms, exhausted and confused, Jack and Bob were outside, anxiously waiting for them.

"What happened?" Jack asked worriedly. "We've been waiting forever for you two. What's going on?"

"Let's go inside," Mitch said wearily. "We can talk there."

Once the door was closed, Bob couldn't stand it any longer. "Guys! What's going on? We've been worried sick! We've been hearing rumors that someone died on one of the excavations!"

Mitch dropped down into a chair. "We found the secret chambers. There was an accident inside one of them."

Alex sat down quietly.

"A worker was killed," Mitch said shakily.

"How?" Jack asked.

"Well, that seems to depend on who you talk to," Alex replied, staring straight ahead.

"What the heck does that mean?" Jack asked.

"Well," Mitch said, "the official story is that there was a generator accident and one of the workers was electrocuted."

"What do you mean, 'the official story'?" Bob asked.

"It's our fault…" Alex whispered, fighting back tears.

"Alex, we didn't know," Mitch said, but deep down he felt just as guilty and responsible.

"What didn't you know?" Bob asked.

"We found the Pharom," Mitch answered, "the obelisk we were telling you about that was associated with the word 'power'. It was hidden deep within the chamber, through another well-concealed tunnel. We brought it out and placed it on the platform like the drawing had shown."

"Which now we know was a very bad idea," Alex added.

"Yeah," Mitch agreed. "As soon as it locked into place, we started feeling sick, very sick. We went outside to get some fresh air before we threw up all over the place. We were only outside for a few minutes when…when we saw a flash of light, followed by a low rumble. Then we heard someone scream."

"Someone snuck into the chamber behind our backs," Alex said. "When we got there, we saw him…he was burned beyond recognition."

"What?" Jack yelled.

"Oh my God…" Bob said.

"My words exactly," Alex said. "It looks like he tried to pry the Pharom off the platform. Apparently once it's latched into place, it's a helluva thing to get off. He was likely killed in the attempt."

"And someone is covering this up?" Bob asked incredulously.

"We don't know what's going on," Mitch answered. "Khamir told us we had to leave and that he would deal with the authorities. When we next spoke to him, he said he questioned the other workers and found out that the man who died was trying to steal equipment and artifacts. From what we've learned, this guy had been making quite a career out of that."

"Guess he was overdue for a career change," Jack piped in.

"Jack…" Alex said crossly.

"Sorry."

"Anyways," she continued, "all we've been told is that the site has temporarily been closed off while they ensure this type of 'generator malfunction' doesn't happen again. Mitch and I have said as little as possible. Khamir told us right after it happened that he would let the authorities know it was an accident and that's apparently exactly what he did."

"From what Khamir has said, he expects the site to be closed only for a short time. He told us to stay ready to go back in when we get the word."

"No way!" Bob said. "After all that, they'll let you back in?"

"I guess so," Mitch said.

"Where's the Pharom now?" Jack asked.

"On the platform," Mitch replied, "where we left it."

"You guys just left that thing there after it killed someone?" Jack asked.

"We didn't have a choice," Alex snapped. "We could have been killed as well trying to remove it."

"Right," Jack said sheepishly, realizing his mistake.

"We were told to leave," Mitch said in their defense. "Someone had just been killed. We had no idea what to do and we didn't have a lot of options."

"So what happens now?" Bob asked.

"We wait," Mitch replied. "In the meantime we try to figure out what the hell happened and what we are dealing with."

57

♀

Clash

"Dr. Khadesh, I realize this is a bad time. Thank you for seeing me."

"Professor, please take a seat."

Professor Dustimaine sat down in one of the plump leather chairs seated in front of Khadesh's antique cherry wood desk. The office was very well appointed with numerous degrees, awards of recognition and framed photographs of various dignitaries.

"Dr. Khadesh, I wish to speak with you regarding the tragic accident involving the local worker."

"I assumed as much," he said, though his face bore no expression.

"The reason I'm here is to offer my support regarding the expulsion of Mr. Carver and Miss Logan from Egypt."

"They are not going to be expelled from Egypt."

"What?"

"There has been an investigation and they have been cleared of any wrongdoing involving the death of the worker."

"But what about the fact they were digging illegally by the Sphinx? They did this without my knowledge or permission."

"They were not digging illegally, Professor. Mr. Carver and Miss Logan were granted official permits allowing them to excavate there."

"Excuse me?" Dustimaine exclaimed, stunned. "Who gave them permission to dig by the Sphinx? And why wasn't I informed? Aren't you the person who issues these permits?"

"I have many people working for me. I trust my people to make sound decisions and issue the proper permits accordingly. As for why you were not informed, that could have been an oversight."

"An oversight!" Dustimaine shouted. "I'm the head archaeologist in that area. They report to me! I should have been informed even before they were."

"Calm down, Professor. I will personally look into this."

"Well, I still want them out of here! They were involved, even if indirectly, in the death of an Egyptian worker!"

"It was a terrible accident, nothing more. Mr. Carver and Miss Logan should not be held responsible for a worker trying to steal from an excavation. Some of the other workers have come forth, informing us that the man who was killed had snuck into the dig site and was planning to steal artifacts, equipment, anything he could get his hands on. He apparently had a reputation of doing this. He tampered with a generator that powered the lights, and was unfortunately electrocuted while everybody else was outside."

"But that doesn't absolve Mitch and Alex entirely," Dustimaine protested. "They should have kept a better watch over things and ensured the area was safe."

"Professor, they cannot be held responsible for another's criminal acts. The police agree this was an accident, but our safety inspector will investigate this more as a matter of official procedure. I have cordoned off the site for now. However I expect the matter to be closed shortly. Now if you will excuse me, I have some other matters to attend to. Good day, Professor Dustimaine."

Red-faced and furious, Dustimaine grudgingly took his leave.

☥

Dustimaine's Wrath

Mitch and Alex were back in their lab with Jack and Bob, trying to concentrate on their regular duties, which had now fallen seriously behind.

Without warning, the door to the lab flung wide open. "I want to talk to you two. Now!" It was Professor Dustimaine and he was fuming.

"Professor, we were just…" Mitch started to reply.

"Jack, Bob, get out. I want a word alone with Mitch and Alex."

Jack and Bob just stared at him in stunned disbelief.

The Professor was nearly purple with rage. "OUT! NOW!"

Jack and Bob looked at one another and then quickly left the room, making faces behind the Professor's back as they left.

Mitch and Alex were frozen in their seats.

"I seem to be having a hard time getting answers about the accident," the Professor said as he stalked around them. "For starters, would one of you mind filling me in on what exactly you were doing over there? How in the hell did you get permission to excavate at the Sphinx? And why was I not notified of any of this?" Dustimaine was boiling over with anger and indignation.

"Professor Dustimaine," Alex said, trying to calm him down, "we didn't go behind your back. We were just given the permits. We assumed you were involved in getting them for us. We were grateful for the opportunity to…"

"I did no such thing!" Dustimaine shouted, cutting her off. The veins in his neck were nearly popping out.

"What?" Mitch replied, feigning shock. "You had nothing to do with it?"

Dustimaine glared at Mitch and Alex. "You two think you're pretty clever, don't you? You must also think I'm incredibly stupid!"

"Professor Dustimaine, we had no idea you didn't know about it," Alex lied. "We even made sure we began the work on our day off, so as not to fall behind on your work."

"Oh shut up!" he yelled at her. "Do not patronize me any further! I don't believe either one of you for a single minute. You did it on your day off to make sure I wouldn't be around to see anything." He looked hard at both of them, realizing that he wasn't going to get any further with this line of questioning.

"I have been told that it was an accident, a malfunction in the generator used for lighting. I have never heard of such a thing killing a person!" The Professor continued to seethe. "I don't know how you two have gotten off the hook so easily. This whole situation looks extremely suspicious to me."

"It was a very unfortunate incident," Alex said. "A terrible accident, we're deeply sorry it happened."

"I'm sure the equipment has been thoroughly examined," Mitch added.

"Are you telling me you're sticking to that ridiculous story? Just how stupid do you think I am? I want to know what really happened and you two are going to tell me!"

"Sir, Mitch told you all we know. We didn't see anything. We weren't even near the equipment when it happened."

"I know you weren't 'near the equipment' when it happened, you imbecile, or likely you wouldn't be here talking to me now."

Alex turned beet red.

"I want to know what was going at that site. What were you two up to? I want some goddamn answers!"

Neither Mitch nor Alex responded. They had no idea what to say at this point that could possibly help their situation.

"Listen you two troublemakers, I tried to go over there to have a look at the site to see for myself, but you know what? I couldn't get anywhere near it. To say that is surprising is a giant understatement. And no one is talking, except in vague generalities concocted to give people the brush-off."

There was still no response from either Mitch or Alex.

"I see. So this is how it's going to be, is it? Well, you're not going to get away with this. As far as I'm concerned you're both lying through your teeth and hiding something and you are going to pay for that! Mark my words, I am going to find out what it is, and when I do, you two will be finished in the field of archaeology!" He turned and left, slamming the door behind him.

59

The Battle Begins

Circa 10,000 B.C.

Alaj was a nervous wreck. When he did sleep he had nightmares. He would be running screaming, away from huge flames. He would wake up in a sweat, breathing hard. Alaj had never been an aggressive, overly ambitious person, so what he was doing now caused him great anxiety.

Over the last few months he had begun to develop serious doubts about the plans that were unfolding, the aim to wrest the throne from his brother. But he did not expect any real fighting, so to him the consequences, and the risks, were mitigated. Alaj's intent was that the army and weapons he had amassed were only meant to intimidate. To prove to Traeus he was serious and wanted change.

Alaj could not bear the thought of losing Zazmaria over his own inaction. He loved her. He regretted the many times when he had neglected her, either out of spite or because he was too cowardly to face her growing disapproval of him. Zazmaria was right. Traeus brought this on himself. He deserved exactly what was coming to him.

It was nighttime now, the city was dark and most people were in their homes in bed. Alaj and his army had assembled several leagues outside of the city and were preparing to depart. Alaj paced nervously.

"Commander Diette, have you seen my wife?" he asked, feeling the panic inside him beginning to grow. Zazmaria had extolled the man's virtues, claiming him to be a brilliant, trustworthy and skilled strategist. Alaj had been adamant with him that no one would fire unless Alaj gave the command.

"No, your Highness, I have not," Diette calmly replied.

"We cannot go until I find her. She should be here. I told her to remain close by." Alaj paused for a moment, greatly troubled by this turn of events. "Send someone to locate her," he ordered.

"We do not have much time," Diette protested.

"I do not care!" Alaj shouted. "We cannot go into this confrontation not knowing if she is safe!"

"I will have someone search for her, but…"

"But what?" Alaj snapped.

"With all due respect your Highness, we cannot wait long. The men and equipment are ready. It would be too risky to remain gathered here for long. If we were detected, we will lose the element of surprise. We must move out as planned." Commander Diette was now taking on a surprising tone of authority.

Exasperated nearly beyond reason, Alaj paced back and forth, weighing his options.

"Your Highness, I am sure once the Princess sees we are leaving, she will come. She knows what is happening."

Alaj felt uneasy, but he did not see what choice he had. "Fine, Commander. Give the order."

"At once, sir," he said as he left the room.

This was all starting to feel wrong for Alaj.

Prince Alaj and Commander Diette led the troops through the dark streets. The mercenaries marched in unison with the heavily armored phalanx taking up the front, the cannoneers behind them, and the siege engines taking up the rear.

Alaj knew the element of surprise would be to key to achieving a swift victory. His army came within one hundred yards of the Palace gates.

"Charge!" Commander Diette ordered.

Alaj, caught off-guard by the Commander's sudden directive, given without his permission, shouted to stop him. But it was too late.

As the army charged towards the gates, hundreds of Royal troops armed with bullet cannons sprung from behind their concealment on top of the massive fortified walls and battlements affixed to the gates. Their weapons were drawn and ready to fire. Beyond the gates, siege weapons rolled out, coming into full view of the advancing army.

Alaj's army stopped in their tracks at the sudden and unexpected show of force. Alaj and his army looked around and saw that the rooftops and windows of the surrounding buildings were manned by Royal troops. Their weapons aimed directly at them.

Alaj spun around as hundreds of Royal Phalanx Pikemen came out of their hiding places, blocking Alaj's retreat. His army was completely surrounded.

"Halt! Hold your fire!" someone shouted from above the fortified wall. It was King Traeus.

"Hold your fire!" Alaj shouted to his own army in response. He could not believe this. He realized, to his dismay, that Traeus must have learned of the plan somehow and prepared for it. Alaj's fears had proven true. Things were going terribly wrong.

The Prince's troops, still shocked at being ambushed, went into a defensive stance. They nervously trained their weapons on the Royal troops surrounding them, outlined in the moonlight. Each side aimed their weapons at each other, waiting for the other side to make a move.

Traeus broke the tense silence, "Treacherous brother! How could do you do this?"

Alaj decided he had no choice but to try and stand his ground and do what he came to do. He could not back down now, for if he did, his life would be ruined.

"I am tired of your secrets and lies!" Alaj yelled back. "You manipulate everyone around you! You think you are the only one who knows what is best for our people? Well, you are not. It is time someone else stepped in to lead our people!"

"And you think that someone is you?" Traeus shot back at him.

"Yes!" Alaj retorted defiantly. "You have kept me on the sidelines long enough while you plan your projects to keep yourself flush with power and control. How long did you think I would tolerate that? I am tired of it, I have tried time and again to talk to you, but you have always dismissed me. Well, no longer. You cannot dismiss my army so easily. You will have to deal with me now!"

"Watch him, your Highness, he sounds like a desperate man," Assan whispered to Traeus. "I doubt he fully understands what he is about to do."

Traeus nodded, but he was having a hard time controlling his own temper. "You fool!" Traeus shouted. "Everything I did was for the benefit and future of our society! It was for you, for me, for our family – for all of us. I told you that you would know everything in time, but you could not wait! And now your impatience has carried a high price, brother. I never would have expected this from you, Alaj. You have betrayed your own family."

The two Royal brothers faced each other in silence, their eyes full of fire and determination. Their armies waited nervously for the command to break the standoff.

"I do not want any blood spilt!" Traeus yelled. "You can see that I am not unprepared, brother. The terms of this conflict have now changed. Now, order your army to back down and call off this attack before lives are lost!"

"No!" Alaj shouted. "For too long have I listened to you, taken a back seat to you, but not this time. You can no longer order me around. Now you are going to have to listen to me and do what I say for a change!"

"I see," said Traeus. "Then it has truly come to this."

"It does not have to come to this," Amoni shouted suddenly, as he made his way past the cannoneers on top of the wall.

"I told you to stay inside the Palace!" Traeus yelled at him.

"I could not stand by and let both of you destroy each other like this. We are brothers! This is wrong! You have both lived lies and kept your own secrets. And now look at what it has done to us!"

"Amoni!" Alaj called out. "Join with me! I have no grudge with you. Together we can lead our people. You and I can reign together. We do not have to live in anyone's shadow any longer!"

"I am sorry, Alaj," Amoni replied, "but I cannot join with you. I was the one who found out about your surprise attack and told Traeus."

Alaj was shocked. *'How could Amoni have known this?'* he thought. Confused, but still defiant, Alaj refused to back down.

60

Chaos and Death

"**A**ttack!" Commander Diette hollered all of a sudden. He fired his bullet cannon, hitting a Royal soldier squarely in the forehead, killing him instantly.

With this sudden act of violence, the opposing forces responded. Royal Cannoneers avenged the loss of one of their own by firing their weapons. Alaj's army, responding to the command to attack and the volleys of bullets fired at them, returned fire and charged the gates. The silence was suddenly filled with loud bangs, clanking of metal, and screams of men in embroiled in combat, fighting to the death. The firepower lit up the dark night.

Alaj dove for cover as events spiraled out of his control into utter madness and chaos. He knew, in that moment, how wrong this had been for him. He was not a man of war, of fighting. He was a fool for ever believing he could keep control of such a serious situation.

"Hold your fire!" the King shouted desperately. "Hold your fire, damn it!" he yelled again, but his voice was lost in the sound of the horrific battle ensuing. All around him, Royal troops fell to the ground, hit by fiery stone bullets. Some ran around frantically, screaming for help as they caught on fire. The second row of Royal Cannoneers quickly moved to replace the first row of troops who fell.

Traeus could hear the loud bangs from the bullet cannons as the Royal troops fired them. Behind the gates, catapults launched their flaming missiles at the attacking forces. The dark night blazed.

In front of the gates, Alaj's army was being decimated. They were surrounded. The army was showered with flaming bullets and missiles from the front and side. The Phalanx Pikemen blocking Alaj's army from behind prevented Alaj and his troops from retreating.

In the midst of the onslaught, Alaj pulled himself together and tried to order his army to hold their fire. A bullet hit him on the shoulder. He cried out and dropped to his knees, grimacing in pain.

Traeus was still screaming at his men to cease firing. A Royal guard roughly pushed the King down behind the defensive walls to protect him.

"Cease fighting!" Alaj yelled loudly at his men, his shoulder bleeding badly. Suffering heavy casualties and facing total annihilation, men from Alaj's army began to surrender on his command. As the fighting slowly abated, soldiers from both sides could now hear Traeus and Alaj frantically ordering them to stop the fighting.

The dead and dying littered the ground in a macabre scene.

"Your Majesty!" a soldier shouted to his King. "Prince Amoni is in-jured!"

Traeus ran to his youngest brother, who lay bleeding.

Alaj heard the soldier as well. He gasped audibly. He had to get to Amoni. In a total panic, caring not for his own safety, he quickly pushed his way past his own soldiers. As he faced the Royal troops guarding the Palace gates he shouted, "Let me through! I must see Prince Amoni!" Clearly unarmed and wounded, he struggled to get through the Royal troops, who reluctantly let him pass.

Alaj no longer noticed the pain in his shoulder. He managed to make his way to where Amoni was lying. The sight that was before him was too much. He collapsed to his knees with an agonized cry.

Traeus was hunched over Amoni, desperately trying to stop the blood gushing forth from a large wound in his abdomen. Amoni's eyes were wide with shock. His hands shook uncontrollably. One look and Alaj knew that there would be no sunrise for his beloved younger brother.

Amoni, with blood seeping from the corner of his mouth, tried to speak. His voice was weak, shaky, "Traeus…I-I…disobeyed you…"

Traeus held his brother's hand tightly to his heart, crying. "No Amoni, do not worry about that. Save your strength. Do not try to talk."

Alaj edged closer to his brothers, trying to muffle his own sobs.

Amoni's eyes squeezed closed as he winced in pain. His breathing was now only short gasps. His eyes fluttered open for a moment. He saw both his brothers by his side. "We are brothers…it should never…have come to…" His eyes glazed over as he exhaled one final breath. His body went limp.

"No, Amoni!' Traeus cried as he saw his brother's life slip away forever. "Please do not leave us!" he begged. But he knew it was too late. He grabbed him and held him close, rocking, his tears falling into Amoni's dark hair.

"I have caused this. I have killed my own brother," Alaj wept. "I will never forgive myself." In that moment, he wished, prayed, he could take Amoni's place, to give his life instead. "I never thought it would come to this. I never meant for the fighting to start. Oh no…what have I done…."

Traeus, with Amoni's blood smeared all over him, looked up at Alaj with eyes reddened, full of tears. "I told him to stay in the Palace, to stay away from the fighting. He did not listen…" Traeus again broke down.

Commander Koronius walked over. Alaj looked up, making eye contact with him. The two men nodded at one another, acknowledging the tentative truce.

Commander Koronius leaned down to whisper to Traeus, "Your Highness, please, my men will take care of him." He gently released Amoni from Traeus' arms and four of his soldiers quickly stepped up and with great care, carried the Prince's lifeless body away. The Commander then lifted his King to his feet.

The Commander then noticed Alaj's injury. "You are injured, I will have someone come to tend your wound."

Alaj shook his head, "It is only a flesh wound. I just need a dressing for now."

"As you wish," Commander Koronius replied and ordered a healer to come at once to wrap the Prince's shoulder.

Once his wound was cleaned and a dressing applied, the three men went inside the Palace.

Head Priest Assan joined the men, eyeing Alaj with deep mistrust. He also felt the pain of Prince Amoni's loss. Now here in their midst was Alaj…the traitor.

Alaj collapsed in a chair. Traeus stared blankly ahead.

"Prince Alaj, your men, now that they have surrendered, can they be trusted not to try and fight again?" Commander Koronius asked.

"Yes, I have ordered them to stop fighting," Alaj replied hoarsely. "Even they can see a hopeless situation."

"You would not mind if I have my men ensure that is the case?" he asked.

Alaj nodded for him to proceed.

"Then I will have one of my captains oversee their surrender and take them to a holding area until we decide what is to be done with them."

61

A Traitor Is Revealed

The explosions rocked the Palace walls. Mindara and Medetha, though frightened, tried their best to keep Tramen and Setar comforted and safe as they heard the commotion from the battle. The boys were nearly hysterical as they covered their ears against the terrifying din. Though the battle did not last long, it was harrowing.

"Is it over?" Medetha whispered.

"I do not know," Mindara answered nervously.

Together they waited in silence for what seemed like an eternity. They had managed to calm the boys down, but Mindara could not stand not knowing any longer. *'Where is Amoni?'* she thought to herself. *'Why has he not come back to let us know what is going on?'*

Finally, she turned to Medetha, "I am going to look outside in the hallway, see if I can find anyone who might be able to tell us something."

"It is worth a try," Medetha agreed. "We cannot sit here like this indefinitely."

Mindara peered outside, she called Amoni's name, but there was no answer and no one was in sight. She knew it could be dangerous to leave, but she had to do something.

"Medetha, I cannot see anyone. I am going to try and find out what is going on."

"No Mindara," Medetha protested, "if it was safe to leave, someone would have told us."

"We cannot stay here. I will not be long. If I am unable to find anyone fairly close by, I will come right back and we will wait."

"All right, but do come back quickly."

Mindara nodded and she left. She walked cautiously down the hallway, listening for any signs that the fighting was resuming. The hallways were eerily empty. She could smell smoke, but it seemed to be coming from somewhere outside the Palace…at least for now.

As Mindara slowly walked the hallways she thought she heard someone. She carefully looked around the corner. She inhaled quickly, ducking back. It was Zazmaria.

Zazmaria had lain in wait for the sounds of the battle to begin. She knew she had to be careful. Now that people realized Alaj was spearheading a takeover, she feared she would be taken into custody if anyone spotted her.

Zhek had told her to remain inside the Palace until the fighting started, then sneak out her usual way. She would be able to get away unseen in the blackness of the night. Alaj would not know where to find her. He would never expect her to still be in the Palace knowing his army was coming to confront it.

'I must tell someone she is here,' Mindara thought, panicking. As she turned to leave, she heard Zazmaria's footsteps creeping towards her. She hid herself, her mind racing. Medetha would be frantic if she did not return right away.

She held her breath as Zazmaria passed within feet of her. 'I cannot let her get away, we need to know what she is up to.' She took a deep breath and crept along the path she heard Zazmaria take. She followed the Princess to a seldom-used back entrance of the Palace.

Zazmaria seemed lost in her own thoughts. She left the Palace grounds with Mindara trailing not far behind.

'What am I doing?' Mindara thought. 'I am going to get myself killed out here following her.' Still she pressed on through the dark night, knowing how important this information could be for the King.

In the distance, she saw signs of the battle that had been waged and heard soldiers yelling not far off. The battle had occurred near the front of the Palace.

Mindara followed Zazmaria to a small red house near the edge of the city. It appeared empty. She could see the Princess pacing in the window. She seemed to be waiting for someone. Not knowing what else to do, Mindara waited and watched, hidden from view.

After a long while, Zazmaria grew impatient and left the house. Mindara once again followed her. Little by little, Mindara realized that Zazmaria was heading straight for the Draxen Stronghold. *'Is she mad? She is going right into the enemy's lair.'* Mindara's stomach was in her throat. This was an extremely dangerous situation.

She crept to the side of a nearby house and from the shadows she watched Zazmaria approach the Draxen guards. They eyed the Princess cautiously, taking a defensive stance.

"Princess Zazmaria," one of the guards acknowledged her tersely. "What are you doing here?"

Mindara stepped a bit closer to hear what was being said. She hid herself behind some thick bushes. Her heart was pounding. She could feel the sweat dripping down her back.

"I want to see Zhek," Zazmaria demanded.

"That is out of the question. You are going to have to leave," another guard replied harshly, as he took a step toward her.

"How dare you speak to me in that manner?" the Princess shot back. She stood her ground. "I must speak with Zhek immediately. Is he here?"

"With all due respect, Princess, Lord Zhek's whereabouts are none of your concern," he replied, the warning in his voice clear.

Zazmaria remained defiant, undaunted. "I am tired of dealing with you! If you are not going to give me an answer, I will find it myself. Let me by!"

The first guard held his hand out to keep her back, his weapon now positioned menacingly. "This is a time of battle. We will not let anyone past us."

"You will let me pass!" she yelled at him.

"We will not!" he shouted back at her. "Now leave at once!"

Zazmaria slapped the man hard across the face and tried to push her way past. The guards struggled with her, but she began kicking and yelling for Zhek. She tried to fight them off, but they would not release her. Desperate and frustrated as her world fell apart before her very eyes, she knew she had nothing left to lose. She could not go back.

"Zhek! Zhek, come out here!" she screamed. She was beyond all reason now. "I waited for you! Why are you doing this to me? You promised me I would be your Queen!"

The guards thought she had gone mad. They kept their hold on the overwrought Princess.

Now crying uncontrollably, Zazmaria fought with all her strength, but the guards held on. "Zhek!" she screamed again.

Inside the Stronghold, though weakened by his condition, Lord Draxen stood watching her through a window in his private chambers. His weathered and sunken face betrayed no emotion.

One of his guards approached him, "Sir, Princess Zazmaria, she is adamant, she is looking for Zhek. What should we do?"

Lord Draxen, his breathing raspy, kept watching her before answering. He had waited for this moment, to see her disgraced, defeated. He looked on as she went nearly out of her mind with rage. However, he had received reports regarding the situation at the Palace and knew that the fighting had ended in a cease-fire. *'This is not going as planned,'* he thought, *'and she is a liability.'*

He turned to the guard, "Remove her immediately."

"As you wish sir," the man replied, bowing as he left.

Outside, the order came to have her removed from the property. Zazmaria struggled fiercely, but the guards easily overpowered her. They grabbed her and threw her down the lane. She hit the ground hard. She knew she had lost everything and there was nothing she could do. For the first time in her life, she was powerless.

Slowly, in a daze, she picked herself up. Stumbling and bruised, she started to walk away from the Stronghold into the cold, dark, friendless night, not knowing where she would go. Her dreams of walking into the Draxen Stronghold, revered as their future Queen, died inside her.

Heartbroken and humiliated, she had never felt so alone, so hopeless. Zhek had forsaken her, used and ultimately betrayed her.

Mindara caught her breath and realized the magnitude of what she had just heard. She tried to sneak away. She ran as quietly as she could down a dark road leading away from the Draxen Stronghold.

Out of nowhere, Zazmaria appeared in front of her. Her cold, steely face streaked with tears, her expression one of pure hatred. "Going somewhere?" Zazmaria asked as her hand reached down into the folds of her dress.

Mindara did not answer. She took a step back.

Zazmaria stepped towards her. "Heard everything, did you?" She did not bother to wait for an answer. "I can tell by the look on your face."

Mindara backed away further.

"You had no business following me," Zazmaria said angrily.

"You are a traitor!" Mindara shot back defiantly, but inside she was terrified.

"It was time for things to change," she said, continuing to step towards Mindara.

"You betrayed your own family? To those people?"

Zazmaria let out a hollow laugh. "My family? They have never valued me. They deserve whatever is coming to them." In a flash, she lunged towards Mindara, drawing a jeweled dagger.

Mindara shrieked and stepped back, raising her arm to protect herself. Zazmaria brought the dagger down with great force, cutting her deeply on her arm.

Mindara cried out in anguish. Holding her arm, which was bleeding badly, she stumbled backwards and cried, "Do you not realize that everything you tried to do has been for nothing! It is over for you. Your treacherous friends want nothing to do with you!"

She saw the expression on Zazmaria's face change as she became enraged at the bold statements. Zazmaria lunged at her again brandishing the dagger, which dripped with Mindara's blood.

Mindara managed to grip Zazmaria's wrist before she could cut her again. They wrestled violently. As they fought, Mindara stumbled backwards to avoid another slash and fell to the ground.

Zazmaria leapt on top of her, brandishing the dagger close to her face. "I have always hated you," Zazmaria hissed as she managed to inflict a small cut across Mindara's cheek.

Mindara cried out in pain.

Zazmaria pulled her arm back, ready to strike a lethal thrust. Suddenly she stopped, a look of shock registered on her face. She heard a voice in her head, *'I cannot allow this.'* At that moment Zazmaria saw in her mind the face of the young Princess she thought dead. She began to shake. "Anjia? No! I killed you!" Zazmaria screamed. "You drowned with your mother!"

Mindara used Zazmaria's hesitation and hysteria to grab the Princess' wrist. Mindara then lunged upwards toppling Zazmaria backwards, in the same motion she thrust the dagger into the Princess' belly.

Zazmaria gasped and looked down at the jeweled dagger protruding from her stomach, at once recalling the vision she had so long ago where Anjia had been the one to thrust the dagger. "No..." she cried.

Mindara quickly got up and stood staring over Zazmaria, who was lying at her feet. The Princess was breathing in short gasps as blood began to seep through her clothing. Mindara was shocked. Never before had she imagined she could be capable of such violence. She made the decision to abandon the dying Princess, she ran as fast as she could through the night, back to the Palace. She had to tell the King what happened and what she had learned.

Mindara reached one of the side doors of the Palace. She ran down the hall, but she was dizzy and growing faint. She stumbled into the Palace kitchen. "Is anyone here?" she called out, collapsing to the floor.

A servant, who had been hiding in a pantry since the fighting started, heard her. He came running to her side. "Mindara! What happened to you?' he asked as he saw the blood that covered her arm and face.

"I must get to the King, I have urgent news. Please help me."

"Of course," he said as he helped her up. "But first I must tend to your wounds. You are bleeding badly!"

"No, there is no time! You have to help me get to King Traeus."

"All right, we will go. Here, put your other arm around me for support." Together they ran to the front of the Palace in search of the King.

One of the guards saw Mindara and the servant coming. Mindara called to him, telling him she must speak with the King immediately. He nodded. "Yes, Mindara."

Once summoned, the King ran out to meet them. Traeus' face went pale seeing her bloodied. "Mindara!" he cried, as he took her from the servant and gently lowered her to the ground.

"I will be fine," she answered, then noticed Traeus covered in blood, "but you are hurt!"

"No, it is not my blood…I wish it was," Traeus said sadly looking down at the blood of his youngest brother. "Amoni…he was caught in the fighting…I could not save him." He shook the tears away. "But how did this happen to you? I told Amoni to instruct you to stay in the rooms at the back of the Palace."

"He did. Oh your Majesty, I am so sorry about Prince Amoni," Mindara whispered. Once again feeling her consciousness slipping away, she knew she did not have much time before she passed out.

Traeus gently took hold of her. "I have to get you to a healer. You are losing a lot of blood."

"No wait, there is something I have to tell you first. I followed Zazmaria. She went to the Draxen Stronghold looking for Zhek. They would not let her in and when she could not see Zhek, she became hysterical. Then she spotted me. She tried to kill me."

"What? What are you saying?" Traeus asked. "I do not understand…"

"Please, just listen," she interrupted, "she killed Axiana and Anjia and she betrayed the Royal Family to the Draxens. She has been working against you all along."

Traeus gasped, "Zazmaria? This was all her doing?"

Alaj had walked in just in time to hear the gut-wrenching news. "My wife? No…it cannot be true…" He slumped down against the wall.

"My wife, my daughter…she killed them?" Traeus was trying to process what he had just heard. His heart was pounding and his head began to swim.

"Yes, your Majesty. I am so sorry," Mindara cried, but realized she had to continue. "After she attacked me with a dagger, I fell. Then she became crazed. She screamed Anjia's name as though she had just seen her." Mindara's voice became quiet, "She said she killed Anjia and Axiana." Mindara told Traeus about how she, acting on Zazmaria's momentary hesitation, defended herself, stabbing Zazmaria.

"What?" Alaj asked hoarsely, gathering himself. "Is she dead?"

"I do not know…she was alive when I left her."

"I have to go…I must get to her!" Alaj said, regaining his feet. "Where is she?"

Mindara told them where she had left the Princess.

"Alaj! You cannot go alone. I will come with you," Traeus stated. He wanted, needed his own answers.

"I do not deserve your help, Traeus. I deserve nothing again in this life." Alaj felt ill as the terrible news sunk in. "Zazmaria disappeared shortly before we moved against the Palace. I did not know what happened to her…" Alaj said with a hollow voice.

"I am coming with you."

"Traeus, I did not know…about Axiana and Anjia. You have to believe me. I would never have…" Alaj hung his head in shame, he wept. "I do not know what I can possibly say…"

"We will talk later. But right now, we must hurry before it is too late…"

63

☥

Good and Evil

Traeus and Alaj raced through the still dark night to where Mindara had told them the Princess was. They found Zazmaria lying in a crumpled heap. The extent of her injury was immediately obvious. There was a large pool of dark red blood beneath her. She was barely alive. What life was left was rapidly ebbing from her.

Alaj knelt down beside her. Crying, he gently stroked his wife's hair, "Zazmaria, my love…"

Her eyes flickered open and a faint look of surprise washed across her now pale face. She tried to speak, her voice barely audible, "Alaj, how…."

"Mindara told us everything," he replied, the tears streaming down his face.

"I had no choice." She started coughing and choking on the blood, which ran down her throat.

"Why betray your own family? Why betray me?" Alaj wept. "To the Draxens!" He knew this was the last time he would ever speak to his wife. "You have lied to me for so long, manipulated me into this war. Killed Axiana and Anjia! I do not understand, Zazmaria. What drove you to all of this?"

Traeus stood in the background out of her sight, listening. He was trying to contain his hatred of the woman who had taken his beloved wife and daughter from him, and who was in part, responsible for Amoni's death. However, he knew that she was paying the price for her treachery. Whatever seeds she had sown in life, she would now reap in death.

Zazmaria's eyes flickered, but she managed to look up at her husband. "I did what you could not…"

"But how? Why did they have to die? They never harmed you!" he cried.

"Anjia…she was dangerous to me, I saw it in my dreams. She would have destroyed me…I had to stop her. I knew the storm was coming. I overheard them planning their trip. I made it look like an accident. My family…" she gasped for breath, "my family has been able to read the skies for generations, we possess great knowledge of…"

"What?" he asked incredulously. "You never told me anything about this. Was our whole life together a lie?"

She gasped for another breath, "Setar…" It was too late. Her eyes closed, her pain was evident. She shuddered, tensed and finally her body relaxed. She was gone.

"No!" Alaj cried out in unbearable grief. He still had so many questions that now would never be answered.

Traeus walked over to him after a few moments and whispered, "We have to get out of here, Alaj. It is not safe."

"But we cannot just leave her here, like this. Whatever she has done, she was my wife."

"We will take her with us back to the Palace. Come, together we can carry her."

64

Revenge

Carrying Zazmaria's lifeless body, Traeus and Alaj returned to the Palace. Neither had spoken a word. The brothers placed Zazmaria's body in a room, covering her with a sheet. Traeus searched out Assan and informed him of what they had learned and asked him to standby and wait for instructions.

"Traeus," Alaj said, "I am so sorry…about everything. She betrayed me as well. For months she pushed me to go against you, threatening my future with her, with my son, if I did nothing…"

"But you raised an army against your own family!"

"I never meant it to go that far, you must believe me. I-I thought you would back down once you saw I was serious…wait, Diette," Alaj recalled what had happened in the nightmare battle. "Where is Commander Diette?" Alaj asked a nearby soldier.

"He is over there with the rest of the wounded," the soldier replied, pointing to an area that had been set up for triage. "He is badly injured. I am told he will not last long."

Alaj stormed over to the bed where Diette lay dying. The blood was seeping through the bandages. Diette was pale and barely conscious.

"Diette!" Alaj hollered as he grabbed the mortally wounded man by the neck. He cared nothing for the man's injuries. Diette had betrayed him and he had to know why. "I told you to wait for my orders! Why did you order my army to attack?"

"Let him go, Alaj! He cannot talk if he is dead!" Traeus shouted, trying to restrain him.

Alaj released him.

Traeus looked the man straight in the eye, "Commander Diette, you might as well tell us what you know." Traeus waited for a response from Diette, but none came. "We know about Zazmaria, we know all about her ties to the Draxens. Tell us what your part was in this."

Diette knew his own life was slipping away, "Your family's time in power is ending. My life may be over, but your time will come soon enough, King."

"Was my wife going to participate in the murder of us all, Diette? Is that what you are saying?"

Diette only smiled, the malevolence on his face unmistakable.

"You tell me what you know!" Alaj hit him hard across the face.

Diette spat out blood then laughed, "You are such a fool, so blind! No wonder she was able to manipulate you so easily."

Rage completely took hold of Alaj. Adrenalin coursed through him and numbed the pain he had in his injured shoulder. Alaj knew this man would tell them nothing else, he only mocked them, caring nothing for the damage he had done or the pain he had caused.

Alaj wrapped his hands around Diette's throat. He could hear Traeus yelling for him to stop, but it sounded far away. With fury in his eyes, Alaj poured all of his anger and hate into this moment. Every lie, every deceit, Amoni's death…it all swirled in his mind like a lethal poison.

"Alaj, he is dead! Stop!" Traeus was trying to pull his brother off the man. "Let him go now!"

As if awoken from a trance, Alaj looked down at the glassy, unseeing eyes staring back at him. He stepped back from the man whose death he had just hastened.

Traeus looked at his brother for a long moment, letting the horror pass. Alaj slumped down against the wall. Weeping, he put his hands over his face.

"Alaj, it is about time we took care of the Draxens. Diette, Zazmaria – the Draxens used them to get to us, to destroy us." Traeus helped his brother to his feet. "We must find Commander Koronius."

Alaj silently nodded his agreement.

Shortly, they tracked him down. "Commander, have one of your captains summon your men," the King ordered. "I will be leading them in an attack on the Draxen Stronghold. The Draxens were behind everything."

"But, your Majesty," Commander Koronius protested, "should I not lead them? I should be by your side..."

"I know you are going to object to this Commander," Traeus interrupted him, "but I need you to secure the Amsara site. Take Victarius and assemble a band of men and head straight there. This is extremely important. I believe it is in imminent danger from the Draxens. I am entrusting you to do this."

The Commander knew the Pharom had to be protected. "Very well, your Majesty. We will go at once."

"My soldiers will also help against the Draxens," Alaj said determinedly. "I will gather all who can fight."

"Do you think we can trust those mercenaries?" Traeus asked.

"They did not know it was the Draxens who bought them to betray their King. Zazmaria funneled the funds through me," Alaj replied with shame. "If they have any loyalty and honor left in them, they will fight for their King."

"Then we attack immediately."

65

☥

Retribution

After asking Assan to oversee matters at the Palace, Traeus and Alaj gathered every able soldier in their armies and led them through the still dark city, towards the Draxen Stronghold. Many who joined them now bore injuries.

Traeus and Alaj had spoken to the soldiers jointly and explained the treachery of the Draxens. When the men found out, it incensed them. They vowed to avenge the Royal Family. Traeus and Alaj led their now joint army to attack the Draxen Stronghold.

Finally, they reached the Draxen gate. There would be no negotiations. The Draxen soldiers had been put on alert. Draxen scouts, stationed on the balconies high on the building, spotted the advancing army and shouted the alarm. Lord Draxen had prepared for the possibility that King Traeus might attack the Stronghold, but he had not expected an attack from such a large force. Unknown to him at this point, it was a combined force. His plans had crumbled.

"Damn you, Diette, you failed me," he said to himself. "Commander, attack the oncoming army!" Lord Draxen ordered. "Defend the Stronghold to the last man!"

"Take cover!" Traeus shouted as several flaming missiles were launched from behind the Draxen walls, headed towards them, lighting up the night sky.

The soldiers scurried to find cover. The flaming missiles crashed down all around them. Wood-made machineries were instantly obliterated. Splinters of wood and rock flew in every direction.

"Siege engines, fire!" Alaj ordered.

The King's army returned fire. Multiple clanking sounds echoed throughout the city as dozens of catapults launched their fiery rain of destruction in a shower of angry red and orange flames. Loud explosions filled the air as the missiles smashed into the gate and walls. The catapults hurled huge boulders into the Stronghold. The front gate protecting the Stronghold began to crack, but did not break. As Traeus' catapults fired on the walls, new waves of flaming missiles rained down on the band of catapults.

"Phalanx, rush the gate, use the battering ram!" Traeus called out. "Target their siege engines with our catapults. Cannoneers, give the phalanx cover. Their catapults cannot fire at such close range."

Cannoneers fired their hand held cannons at the Draxen troops in the towers, which were interconnected with the walls and gate. The phalanx group quickly rushed to the gate carrying a large ram as flaming missiles from their own cannoneers flew over them, onto the walls and towers of the Stronghold.

Draxen troops, on top of the fortified walls and in the towers, had a high ground strategic advantage and easily picked off the invading troops. The heavily fortified walls and towers provided the Draxen soldiers with cover from the onslaught of missiles and bullets. They now aimed their weapons at the phalanx group that was rushing towards the front gate.

The Royal Phalanx Pikemen, equipped with armor that could withstand limited attacks from the cannoneers, were showered with hundreds of flaming bullets. Scores of Royal soldiers fell to the ground, wounded or dying.

"We have to bash that gate down!" Alaj shouted. "They are slaughtering our men!"

"Captain, give them more cover!" ordered Traeus.

"Yes, your Majesty!" the Captain replied.

"Our cannoneers are useless against their fortified positions!" Alaj yelled.

"We should pull back and let our catapults weaken their fortifications before we charge again with our troops," Traeus suggested.

"That could take hours," Alaj shook his head then making a sudden decision, he raced forward.

"Alaj! No!" Traeus called after him as he saw his brother rush towards the main gate. '*Damn it! He is going to get himself killed.*' "Give him some cover!" Traeus shouted as he ran after his brother.

Alaj rushed towards the main gate, ignoring his injured arm. Flaming bullets raced by his head, narrowly missing him. He ran towards the ram and grabbed hold of the top strap and started to ram the gate.

Traeus and some of his guards joined him and grabbed onto the other parts of the ram to help him break down the gate. Other troops fired their weapons at the Draxen soldiers on top of the wall, drawing fire away from the others.

The Draxen soldiers returned fire, killing or wounding numerous Royal soldiers. The cries of the injured and dying were everywhere. At last, the gate started to buckle with the constant pounding. With a loud bang, it tore off its hinges and it crashed down on the ground. Troops and mercenaries poured into the Stronghold with Alaj leading the charge. He fought like a man possessed.

"Alaj, wait!" Traeus called after him, as he drew his sword and fought his way to Alaj's side. Traeus' troops overwhelmed the Draxen force. Alaj and Traeus fought their way into the main building of the Stronghold.

Alaj grabbed a Draxen servant who was hiding underneath a table. "Where is Lord Draxen?" he demanded, holding a long sword to the cowering man's throat. When the man hesitated to answer, Alaj pressed the blade harder against his skin.

"He…he is upstairs on the fourth floor," the servant stammered.

"Wait, Alaj! You do not know what is up there," Traeus called after him, as the angry and determined Prince headed for the stairs. "You could walk right into a trap!"

"He is mine," Alaj said fiercely, ignoring the warning.

Traeus saw that he could not stop his brother. He decided to go with him, to protect him if he could. "Captain!" the King shouted. "Take care of things down here. Make sure there are no pockets of resistance. Take anyone you find as prisoners. Do not allow anyone to follow us upstairs."

The man nodded his acknowledgement. Traeus ran up the stairs after his brother.

Alaj ran into several Draxen guards on top of the stairs on the fourth level. He drew his short sword, his long sword still in his other hand. As the stairway was only wide enough to accommodate two adults, all of the Draxen guards could not attack him at once. Alaj parried and deflected swings from the ferocious attacks. He thrust his long sword into a guard. At the same time he used his short sword to defend against the attack from a guard to his left.

The guard brought down a swing to Alaj's head that would have been fatal had it not been blocked by Traeus' sword. Alaj used the opportunity to plunge his short sword into the guard. Fighting side by side, the Royal brothers were able to repel the attack by the guards. The narrow stairway worked to Alaj and Traeus' advantage. In fierce fighting, the Draxen guards were eventually slain one by one.

Down at the end of the hall, they burst through Lord Draxen's chamber door. Alaj charged towards him. With vengeance in his heart, he intended to kill the man who had manipulated his wife and was ultimately responsible for the deaths of so many people, including his beloved younger brother.

Lord Draxen, now lying in his bed as the result of a particularly brutal coughing fit, had bloodstains on his chin and down the front of his shirt from the disease. He knew he was at death's door. He did not need a healer to state what was so brutally obvious. In agony, his lungs burning from the pain of his illness, he waited for the King and Prince to advance on him.

"I am here to kill you, you treacherous old man!" Alaj shouted as he grabbed Lord Draxen by his soiled shirt collars and yanked him up.

"No! Wait, Alaj!" Traeus said trying to restrain him. "He must stand trial and face punishment from the Royal Court."

"This filthy, evil man turned Zazmaria against our family. He is the one who is truly responsible for Amoni's death!" Alaj pulled out his sword with one hand while gripping Lord Draxen's thin, wrinkled neck with the other hand.

"Are you going to kill a defenseless old man, ravaged by a fatal illness?" Lord Draxen asked with a sneering smile on his weathered, drawn face.

Alaj looked upon Lord Draxen's face with hatred and contempt. He could see how frail he was, but Alaj did not care, he had already dispatched one enemy this day, he could execute another.

He pulled back his sword to deliver a killing thrust to Lord Draxen's throat. "The bloodstains on your face and shirt are but the start of what you are about to endure." Alaj gripped the sword he held so tightly that his knuckles turned white. He stared into Lord Draxen's face.

But then, Alaj relented, releasing his hold on Lord Draxen. "No, my brother is right. It would be too easy. I want you to suffer like this." Alaj sheathed his sword. He stood over him, "You will bear the shame you have brought on your family as the charges of murder and treason are laid upon you and all your evil relations," Alaj spoke with great fierceness, his hands clenched tightly. "People will speak your family name with contempt."

The old man laughed a dry, rasping laugh. "After the trial, the people will realize that my family had nothing to do with the takeover you orchestrated, Prince. After all, it was you who raised a mercenary army to overthrow your own brother."

"You had my own wife manipulate me into it!"

"Idiot!" Lord Draxen stated with contempt. "Zazmaria was never forced, manipulated or talked into doing anything she did not want to do. She wanted this just as much as we did, but for her own reasons. We simply benefited from her wanton ambitions."

"Liar!" Alaj yelled.

"If you do not believe me, you can ask her yourself. Tell her what I have told you and see how she responds. Oh, and you might be wondering how I know so much about it. You see, my grandson, Zhek, has had what you could call a very 'close' relationship with your wife."

"Liar! You are a filthy liar!" Alaj screamed as he lunged at Lord Draxen and struck him across the face.

"Stop it, Alaj!" Traeus shouted, trying to restrain him.

Lord Draxen spat out more blood, laughing hideously. "When she first became involved with Zhek, she probably wanted to manipulate and toy with his affections to further her own dark ambitions. She believed, mistakenly of course, that she could use us to help her gain power and standing. We gladly helped her of course. I had never seen my grandson happier than when he was spending time with your wife. She just kept coming back for more."

"I will kill you!" Alaj screamed.

Traeus fought hard to hold him back. "Alaj, no!" he shouted. "Can you not see what he is doing? He is just trying to torment you. This all he has left, he knows this is his end."

Lord Draxen continued, "Tell me, the child, Setar, does he have a mark on his chest that looks like this?" Lord Draxen opened his shirt and pointed to the large, star-shaped birthmark on his bony chest, over his heart. It was unmistakable. He smiled when he saw Alaj's stunned reaction to the sight of the birthmark, identical to that of his son's. "My grandson Zhek has one just like it too. It is a Draxen family trait amongst the men." He saw the shock register on Alaj's face. "That is right, you gullible fool, Setar is not your son. You are so pathetic. You could not even recognize the child was fathered by another man!" He spat out more blood. "It took a man like my grandson to give your woman a child."

"No!" Alaj screamed and lunged at Lord Draxen, trying to strangle him. The horror of his wife's full betrayal hit him hard.

Traeus pried his brother's hands from Lord Draxen's neck, "Alaj! Enough! She is gone now, we will find out the truth for ourselves. We do not have to listen to the insane ramblings of a dying, evil old man."

Alaj fell back on the floor. "It cannot be true," he cried, covering his face with his hands.

"So, she is dead, is she?" Lord Draxen repeated. "What a shame, Zhek will miss her," he said, enjoying Alaj's pain. "But, so much the better."

Alaj screamed unintelligibly and tried once more to lunge at the despicable man lying before him.

It took all of Traeus' strength to hold him back this time. "Alaj! Stop! We will make them pay for what they have done, I promise you that."

Alaj shook with grief and rage.

"We will find Zhek. If he wants his life spared, he will talk and we will have all the evidence we need to convict and punish his family once and for all."

"Traeus! Look out!" Alaj yelled as Lord Draxen hoisted himself up on his elbow and took aim with a small cannoneer pistol. Neither brother had thought to check the frail old man for weapons.

Alaj pushed Traeus out of the way of a fiery bullet, ducking as he did. The bullet barely missed Traeus' head. Alaj threw his sword full force at Lord Draxen. The old man clutched the sword, slumping over dead.

"Alaj! Are you all right?"

"Yes," he answered staring at the hilt of the sword protruding from Lord Draxen's chest. It had pierced his heart. The star-shaped birthmark that was there a moment ago was now punctured by cold steel, dripping with blood.

"You saved my life! You could have been hit by that bullet!"

"That would have been a small price to pay for my transgressions, brother."

"Come, Alaj. Let us get out of here."

✝

Fates Unfold

Prior to the battles, Zhek, under the cover of darkness, had led his small band of heavily armed soldiers, along with Jace, towards the Amsara site to complete the mission his grandfather sent him on.

Zhek sent a scout on ahead to check for guards. The rest of the group waited quietly for the man to return. Zhek and Jace had carefully gone over the plans for the chambers and device that Jace had written down from memory, prior to leaving for the site.

The soldiers they brought with them were the men most trusted by Lord Draxen himself. They possessed absolute obedience to the Draxen family and had no qualms about whatever they may be asked to do. They were skilled soldiers, fierce and fearless.

The scout returned. "Sir, there are four Royal soldiers guarding the entrance to the chamber. They are not dressed like guards though, more like workers, but I believe it is just a disguise."

The group devised a plan of attack to eliminate them. With stealth, four of Zhek's men crept up on the soldiers, dispatching them with brutal efficiency. They signaled for the rest of the group to join them.

Zhek then sent two soldiers to scout the surrounding area. He did not want any surprises.

The entrance was well hidden. If not for Jace's earlier mission when he saw the plans, along with the fact the guards were standing near it, they would have had a very difficult time detecting it.

"Cleverly disguised," Zhek commented. He had two of his soldiers pry the entrance open, though it was not easy to do. It opened to a long, dark passageway. They found a torch on the wall and lit it. The men crept down the tunnel until they reached a set of metallic doors, which were locked shut.

"This is the lock I saw in the plans," Jace said, examining it closely.

Zhek held the torch to provide light for Jace to work. "Can you open it?"

"I think so," Jace replied and went to work on the lock.

After a few minutes, Zhek could see he was struggling. Sweat was pouring down Jace's face and his lips were pursed. Zhek decided to just let him work. Jace was their only hope of gaining access to the chamber beyond.

Finally, much to his relief, Zhek heard a clicking sound. Jace exhaled heavily. Zhek left two of his soldiers to stand guard at the entrance to watch for anyone who might show up. The rest of the group passed through the entrance into the secret chamber. Zhek and Jace immediately walked up to an obelisk.

"Is this it?" Zhek asked.

"No, this is only the first chamber," he replied as they looked around the elaborately designed room. "I think it is meant to throw anyone off who does not belong here. As far as I can tell, it is probably just a ceremonial room. There is a second chamber, the entrance should be back there," he pointed.

They walked to the back of the room. Jace sighed with frustration as he saw the second lock. Zhek again held the torch while Jace worked on the lock. Finally he managed to get it open. Jace pushed the door open and before them stood the smaller metallic obelisk situated on a platform.

"That is it," Jace said, "the device I saw in the plans."

Zhek ordered the rest of his men to remain in the first chamber. Both he and Jace began to feel queasy, but neither one said anything. They both heard the faint hum. Zhek looked at Jace.

"All I can say is that it is some kind of energy device. From here on in, I have no idea how we should proceed," Jace admitted.

Zhek nodded and walked over to the metallic obelisk. He gently ran a finger across the smooth metal and felt a shiver go up his spine, like some sort of unknown powerful force passed through him. His family had to have this. He noticed on the platform a message was inscribed, and he read it aloud:

> *The power of thought is like no other*
> *Only for this may the light shine forth*
>
> *For those who would wield it for ill purpose,*
> *May they be turned to ashes and cast asunder*
> *Beneath its rays of power*
>
> *For those who would wield it for good,*
> *May they ever be wise in their ways,*
> *And to them, the ultimate power made known*

Realizing they had no time to waste, Zhek turned to Jace who had been standing back from the device. "Jace, we had better get going. We need to get this thing to my grandfather. Do you think we can just take it off the platform?"

"I do not believe we have a choice," Jace said as he inspected the base. "It seems to be just sitting here, there do not appear to be any locks or switches." He wondered about the implied warning in the inscription, but dismissed it as Royal pretentiousness.

"Well then, we should not waste any time. Help me with it," Zhek ordered.

In the distance, they could hear the explosions, clanking of metal, and the screams of people fighting in the city. The tremors from the blasts could be felt in the chamber.

"It sounds like the battle has started. Good, the longer they are kept busy, the better our chances are of getting out of here unseen," Zhek said as he looked at Jace who had grown visibly pale. "Are you all right?"

"I-I think so, I just seem to be a bit dizzy," Jace replied.

"I feel it too. Do you think this device is causing it?"

"It must be," Jace said worriedly.

"We need to hurry," Zhek urged. He and Jace each took hold of one side of the base of the device and tried to lift it. It would not budge. They tried again, exerting great effort, so much so that they both nearly fell backwards when their grips slipped off the device. "What is it held on with? I cannot see anything," Zhek said.

"I do not know," Jace replied. "I did not see anything in the plans about how it was attached." He furrowed his brow as he knelt down, examining the deceptively simple-looking base.

"We cannot wait any longer. We must get this thing back to my grandfather. We will just have to force it off," Zhek decided.

"Lord Zhek!" one of the soldiers standing guard called. "One of the scouts has found something you will want to see."

Zhek turned back to Jace, "I have to go see what this is about. Get that device no matter what you have to do, understood?"

"Yes sir."

Zhek ran out and up the tunnel.

"Lord Zhek," the soldier said anxiously, "the scout caught this priest sneaking around trying to hide this book of scrolls in their temple. He knocked him unconscious and brought him here." The soldier gave the book of scrolls to Zhek.

Zhek looked through the book, scanning the scrolls torchlight. His eyes went wide as he read through some of the pages. "'The Book of the Old and New World'... – these scrolls detail everything that has happened since we came here," Zhek said in amazement. "Everything is documented in great detail; our history in this land, our journey here, everything. The first book is written in the old language. That would mean this record has been kept, in secret, for generations. It mentions all the great Houses, House Selaren, House Zaracon, House Draxen and even House Ele..."

Zhek quickly broke off his reading, knowing that there were some descendants of House Eleshia in the band of soldiers with him, including Jace. He did not want them to read what really happened to House Eleshia. That it was really House Draxen who destroyed House Eleshia, not the Royal Family. He closed the book.

"Wake him up," Zhek ordered.

The soldier slapped the young priest, but there was no response. He slapped him again and finally the priest, groggy at first, awoke.

"Who wrote these scrolls?" Zhek demanded. "We already know you were trying to hide them in the temple. They must be pretty important if you were sneaking around during a battle with them!" Zhek grabbed the priest by his throat.

"I-I do not know who wrote them. I was just putting them back for someone else..." Essen stammered, obviously terrified.

"You lie!" Zhek's grip tightened, choking him.

"Please, I do not know anything," Essen gasped.

Zhek released the priest and drew his knife. "I find that a blade is often a more effective way to get the truth."

A second soldier grabbed the priest. As the two of them held him, Zhek slowly moved the knife to the young priest's face.

Just then, Essen noticed the open entrance to the tunnel. His eyes grew wide with fear.

Zhek looked at him closely. "You know what is down there," he said menacingly. "You are going to tell us what you know."

"I-I do not know anything," Essen faltered.

Zhek pressed the knife to his throat, "I think you do."

Suddenly, several dark figures sprang out of the darkness, hitting the soldiers across the backs of their heads with heavy staffs. Zhek was struck in the face. Essen was released.

"Get the book! Run!"

Having staggered up after the crashing blow to his face, Zhek was livid. He could taste the blood that flowed from his nose and cut lip.

Jace and the other soldiers emerged from the tunnel after hearing the commotion. Off in the distance, they could see several fleeing forms, but then noticed the Draxen soldiers lying on the ground. Zhek was trying to steady himself.

"Zhek! Are you all right?" Jace ran over. "What happened?"

"We were attacked, I suspect by the priests. We found one of them trying to hide something in the temple. We were caught by surprise." Zhek looked around and yelled at his men to get up.

"Jace, we are going after them. You must finish your task, get that thing to my grandfather at once!" Zhek ordered. Blood seeped into his mouth. He spat it out.

The soldiers had regained their feet and headed out with Zhek in pursuit of their attackers. Jace and two of the soldiers raced back into the tunnel to finish their work.

"I am so sorry, Odai," Essen said in tears as they raced away from his Draxen captors. He was badly shaken. "I was trying to put The Book back. I had just taken it out two days ago. I know I should have asked permission first, but I was so curious. I had only wanted to read some more about our history, I meant no harm. Then the battle started, I heard explosions, I got scared so I ran to put it back where it would be safe, in case something happened."

"What is done is done," Odai replied breathlessly as he and the three other priests who rescued Essen, ran as fast as they could back to the temple. Odai now carried the scrolls.

"I was going to return The Book when I finished reading about House Eleshia. Forgive me," Essen pleaded as tears flowed down his face.

"Essen," Odai said, sounding stern, "I can forgive you for leaving the protective walls of the Palace and disobeying Assan's orders. I can even forgive you for taking The Book without permission and reading it before you were meant to, but I will not forgive you if you do not run faster!"

Off in the distance, they could hear the sounds of their pursuers.

The priests made their way to their temple and scrambled inside. Two of them barred the doors with wooden poles. The rest ran to the back of the temple to the inner sanctuary. Odai moved some benches aside and worked frantically to uncover a well-concealed trap door in the ground underneath the wooden altar.

"There is no way out from here, we must do something!" Essen whispered.

"We have no chance to escape, but I must hide the book in the chest below. It must be protected!" Odai replied. "You have to keep them out long enough!"

Finally managing to open the trap door, Odai held the book of scrolls tight. He knew they had to place them back in the protective cylinders inside the chest – the scrolls were priceless.

"I will be right back!" Odai said as he scrambled down the earthen stairs. He found the stone chest lying at the bottom. Opening it, he took out one of the two protective metal cylinders kept inside, which were inlaid with jewels. He replaced the book of scrolls within the cylinder and sealed it. Then he closed the lid of the chest. He ran his fingers reverently over the ankh engraved on its lid, tracing its elegant form, praying the secret and powerful knowledge contained within would be safe.

He suddenly heard the heavy door slam closed above him, trapping him inside.

Zhek and several of his soldiers followed them to the main temple, but the entryway had already been barred. "They are not going to get away with this! Bash that door down!" Zhek shouted to his soldiers. He had to get that book back. The damage it could do to his family would be irreparable. He feared what else may contain regarding their dark past.

Two of the priests ambushed the first Draxen soldiers who came through the doors. One soldier was hit over the back of the head with a staff, while the other was struck in the face with a torch. The third soldier had a fine powder thrown into his face, choking him immediately. He fell to the ground, dead.

Zhek charged in with the other soldiers, surrounding the two priests who were at the door, savagely impaling them on their swords. Essen, horrified, screamed and rushed forward to avenge their murder. Without thinking, he grabbed the sword from one of the soldiers who had been slain, lunging at Zhek, slicing his hand. Zhek cried out in pain and struck back at him, viciously thrusting his sword through the young priest's chest. Essen gasped and fell to his knees.

Just then, Zhek saw a blinding bluish light rapidly streaming through the open temple door, flooding the building and overcoming all darkness in the temple.

A Price Is Paid

Jace and his men decided to forego other, more time-consuming methods, which were failing one after another and use brute force to remove the device they were ordered to steal. After several arduous attempts, there was a loud snap and the heavy metallic obelisk fell with a loud thud on the ground. Jace lifted the weighty object, examining it for damage.

"It seems to be intact." But just as Jace spoke, he felt a surge of energy emanating from it that made his skin crawl. Startled and afraid of the mysterious device, he quickly put it into the wooden crate they had brought along to transport it.

"Help me take this outside," he ordered the soldiers.

With utmost haste, Jace and his men carried the crate out of the tunnel. The two soldiers grew nervous as they felt the crate begin to vibrate.

"Sir, Royal soldiers!" a scout shouted, pointing at the figures, still a ways off, heading towards them.

"We must hurry," Jace said. The vibrations intensified as Jace and the Draxen soldiers tried to move faster.

"Sir, something must be wrong with it!"

Jace nodded. He quickly decided the risk of what they were carrying was at least momentarily greater than those who were chasing them. "Put it down for a moment. Gently! See if the vibrations stop." He had no idea how it was supposed to work, but his instincts were telling him something was very, very wrong.

They carefully placed the crate on the ground and backed away from it. The crate shook violently then stopped. Jace held his breath. It seemed to stabilize. But then a low hum began emanating from the crate. The hum grew louder.

In a split second, a brilliant blue light, like a giant flame erupted, instantly reducing the wooden crate to ashes. The light grew in ferocious intensity.

Jace and his soldiers felt the ambient air being rapidly drawn into the intense flame-like light. One by one, they dropped to the ground as the air in their lungs was also forcibly sucked into the hot blue flame.

An intense heat grew. As the three men lay dying from lack of oxygen, they felt their skin burning as though the very air itself was on fire. The fierce blue light continued to grow in both size and intensity, expanding out an incredible distance, completely surrounding the Amsara monument on its deadly path.

Jace, lying on his back gasping for breath that would not come, and feeling the heat that burned him alive, realized his fatal mistake. The inscription on the platform had been a warning.

A low rumble manifested into massive, violent explosions, tearing out from the source. The deafening blast blew the head off the colossal Amsara monument in a spectacular concussive force. A latent power melted away its protective coating leaving only exposed, charred rock. The force of the blast streaked away from the epicenter in powerful shockwaves, blasting through structure after structure. It tore past the Amsara site and through the city with an insatiable energy turning night into day with an eerie bluish light, incinerating nearly everything in its path.

CHAPTER

68

Dangerous Paths

Present-Day Egypt

Later in the evening, after a full day's work on Dustimaine's excavation, Mitch and Alex met up with Jack and Bob, who had also put in a long day. The site at the Sphinx could open up at any time and they knew they had to have their answers before then. They could not risk it being opened and a second accident occurring.

There had to be something on the Pharom that they missed when they first examined it, perhaps some kind of hidden mechanism, which would release it and disengage its power source.

They went back to deciphering the scrolls. After several hours of searching, Mitch exclaimed, "Hey, I might have found something!"

"Really? What is it?" Alex asked.

Jack and Bob quit what they were doing, and peered over Mitch's shoulder.

"I think something happened to this ancient civilization. This section of the scrolls appears to be different somehow, perhaps a little more hastily written. There is also this line I've translated which reads, *'Our civilization was nearly destroyed by the power we have created. The power of the Pharom was meant to save us, not destroy us.'"*

Alex gasped, thinking back to the accident and the worker that was killed tampering with the Pharom, "Mitch, that thing could be some kind of weapon. We may have just opened the door to our own doom!"

Mitch nodded, grasping the seriousness of the situation, which just seemed to be getting worse and worse. The more they learned, the more the fear grew. A fear of something they did not understand and had little hope of controlling.

"We have got to find a way to deactivate that thing and take it off the platform," Mitch said as he continued to read the scrolls. "Look, it says here, *'The Pharom was taken by evil hands, which did not know what they held.'* It must have been an accident! Someone mishandled it, probably when they tried to steal it…just as the worker did this time. Only in the past, the consequences were far worse."

"Maybe that's why we've found no other evidence of these people, their homes, the palace, temples. It might have been all destroyed," Alex said. "And the head of the Sphinx…"

Mitch nodded, "It's interesting, even today many Egyptians are still afraid of the Sphinx. Maybe this is part of the reason. Some nameless fear that has been passed down through the ages."

"Yet they have no idea what the true and original source of that fear is."

"But one thing troubles me," Mitch said, "if it is some kind of weapon, then these people obviously went to great lengths to hide it. Why not just destroy it?"

"Good question," she said.

Jack and Bob were rapt listening to this conversation.

"Maybe we'll find the answer to that," Alex continued, "but for now, we have a potentially major disaster to avoid. I don't suppose that passage tells us exactly what went wrong? How we can avoid blowing ourselves and everyone else around here to smithereens?"

They scanned the scroll for answers. "Mitch," she said excitedly, "here's a passage that may shed some light, *'Pay heed to the warning, for within it lies the power to unlock the Pharom.'*

"But we've read the warning inscribed on the platform. I didn't see anything there that could help us, did you?"

"I'm not sure now. Maybe we weren't looking closely enough." She sat back, mulling the passage she had just read over and over in her mind. "'...*the power to unlock the Pharom*'. What if that means to physically unlock it, you know, rather than unlock the mystery of it?"

"You may be on to something, Alex," Mitch said as he grabbed for his notebook and read out loud the warning he had copied down:

> *The power of thought is like no other*
> *Only for this may the light shine forth*
>
> *For those who would wield it for ill purpose,*
> *May they be turned to ashes and cast asunder*
> *Beneath its rays of power*
>
> *For those who would wield it for good,*
> *May they ever be wise in their ways,*
> *And to them, the ultimate power made known*

The foursome stared at the passage, but nothing was coming to them. The night was wearing on, and exhaustion and frustration were now their enemies.

"I don't see anything," Bob said. "Maybe we're looking in the wrong place."

"In the wrong place..." Alex whispered.

"What is it?" Mitch asked.

"The worker," she answered, "he tried to pry the Pharom off with a screwdriver, but was killed in the attempt. In the past, someone tried to steal it and somehow set it off. When we placed it on the platform, we felt it latch firmly into place. I didn't see any visible mechanisms, buttons, anything on the surface of it to indicate how to release it."

"Right..." Mitch said.

"So maybe, it can't be disengaged that way. We've been thinking that there must be something on the Pharom itself. But what if there isn't? That's it! That must be the key! The Kierani wouldn't have wanted it to be something that could be easily removed, or stolen. It's too powerful, too valuable. They wouldn't have made it obvious how to remove it."

"The platform…" Mitch suddenly realized.

"Exactly!" Alex said. "It has to be there."

Khamir came to give Mitch and Alex word that the site had been re-opened and that they could return to it. When they asked him how this was all taken care of so quickly, he would only say that the Egyptian authorities were satisfied that it was an unfortunate accident.

Mitch and Alex had wanted to ask Khamir about the cause of the accident, but they didn't know what to say without bringing up a subject they did not want to discuss. However this was playing out, it seemed for the moment to be in their favor and they had no time to waste or second-guess things.

When Mitch and Alex arrived back at the entrance to the tunnel, they were afraid of what they might find once they went inside. They had wanted to go in alone after dark, but Jack and Bob had insisted on joining them.

Down the long tunnel the four of them went, flashlights in hand. They had been hearing rumors regarding the accident. Even though it had been inexplicably explained away as a generator accident, it seemed that the workers were very superstitious and now quite afraid of the site.

On the one hand, this helped Mitch and Alex, because the likelihood of someone else trying to sneak down into the chambers and steal the Pharom was greatly reduced. But on the other hand, it might be hard to find people willing to work on their team again, should they need them.

Flashlights ready, they took a deep breath as they entered the chamber where they had left the Pharom. It was still sitting there, on its platform, looking beautiful, mysterious yet now menacing, all at the same time. The low hum, though barely audible was still present.

"It's still here," Mitch whispered, scarcely believing his eyes. They moved closer to examine it. "It doesn't look as though it's been touched."

"Holy! I've never seen anything like this," Bob exclaimed. "The metal, you guys were right, it doesn't look quite solid…it looks almost liquid somehow."

"I'm sure we don't need to remind either of you not to touch it," Alex added.

"Yeah, pretty sure we got that with all the death and destruction we've been talking about Alex, but thanks just the same," Jack retorted.

"The colors, they're beautiful," Bob marveled as he took a closer look. "It's the most extraordinary thing I've ever seen." He took a deep breath, then frowned. "I don't feel so good. Maybe it was that third bag of chips I ate after dinner."

"No Bob, it's the same thing that happened to Mitch and I when we first placed it on that platform. It has something to do with the energy it puts out. We can't stay here long. I'm starting to feel it too. Who knows how this thing is affecting us."

"Great! Our kids will end up with three heads or something," Jack quipped.

"Oh, there are just so many jokes I could make about that," Bob grinned.

"Very funny."

"I thought so," Bob smiled, pleased with himself.

"Alex is right, we've got to hurry," Mitch said. "Look for anything that might help us remove it."

They all looked around the platform to see anything that might be a mechanism of some sort, but there was nothing.

"Let's examine the inscription again," Alex suggested.

The four of them knelt down. Mitch and Alex kept reading the inscription over and over again.

Jack and Bob, however, were much less familiar with the specific symbols, so their studying of the writing on the platform was more aesthetic in nature.

They could all feel the effects of the Pharom begin to intensify. Beads of perspiration dripped down their foreheads and necks.

Alex steadied herself by sitting down in front of the platform and occasionally putting her head between her knees.

"Think. It has to be here! The answer must be in these words," Mitch said, sounding desperate.

Jack had stood up. He was squinting and looking at the Pharom closely. He looked at it, then back at the inscription. He looked perplexed. "How come you guys didn't mention these symbols?"

"What symbols?" Alex asked.

"The ones on the Pharom," he said still squinting and moving his flashlight around the front of the metallic object.

Mitch and Alex looked at one another and then they both stood up.

Bob was not doing so well, his head drooped, and he held his stomach.

"Where?" Mitch asked.

"Here, here, and there," he pointed. "Three times, the same symbol. It also occurs three times in the inscription."

Mitch and Alex still couldn't see it.

"You have to shine the light a certain way," Jack said. "The pattern is almost lost in the waves in the metal, but it's definitely there. Look," he said as he shone his light directly on the top corner of the obelisk. "Can you see it now? It's in all three corners on the front of the Pharom."

"I don't believe it! How could we have missed this?" Alex exclaimed. "Jack, you are amazing!"

"Yes I am!"

Bob was now moaning on the floor and sweating profusely. As much as he wanted to get up to see what they were talking about, he couldn't. His head was starting to spin.

"He's right! Jack, way to go, man!" Mitch said. "The design, it's, it's…"

"Out of this world?" Jack offered.

Mitch looked at him and smiled. "Alex, it's the symbol for power and he's right. It shows up three times in the inscription…and three times on the front of the Pharom." He checked the rest of the Pharom's surface carefully, but no more symbols were visible.

Alex read the inscription out loud, emphasizing each occurrence of the word power:

> *The **power** of thought is like no other*
> *Only for this may the light shine forth*
>
> *For those who would wield it for ill purpose,*
> *May they be turned to ashes and cast asunder*
> *Beneath its rays of **power***

For those who would wield it for good,
May they ever be wise in their ways,
*And to them, the ultimate **power** made known*

"And what did that passage from the scrolls say about unlocking the Pharom?" Jack asked.

"*'Pay heed to the warning, for within it lies the power to unlock the Pharom,'*" Mitch repeated.

"The symbol for power, that has to be it!" Alex leaned in to have a closer look at the symbols on the Pharom and in the inscription. She shone her light directly on each of the symbols on the platform. "Mitch, take a look at this!"

He bent down to see what she was pointing out.

"It's very faint," she said, squinting, "but when I shine the light directly on these symbols, it's like something sparkles ever so slightly. Guys, can all of you turn your flashlights off? We'll just use mine for a minute. They did as she asked, "Look!"

"I see what you're saying," Mitch said. "They sparkle and change color slightly under the direct light. So now what do we do?"

"It's kind of the same design as what led us to find the hidden entrance to where the Pharom was. It's a clever technology, if that's what this is indicating," Alex mused. Without thinking she reached out and brushed her fingers against the three symbols. She felt a tingling sensation in her fingertips and pulled them away quickly, rubbing them.

"What is it Alex, did you feel something?" Mitch asked.

"Yeah, kind of like an electrical buzz, but it's ok. Be quiet for a moment." She listened to the silence and then repeated the action. She felt the tingling again, but there was something else, "Did you hear that?"

"What?" Mitch asked.

"Listen," she said as she touched each of the symbols again, this time more directly and more firmly. There was a sound, faint, but unmistakable. "Pressing the symbol for power again, I should have known…" she whispered.

They looked up at the Pharom. The colors in the metal became fainter. The low hum they had grown used to hearing, ceased. They all held their breath, except Bob, who was now lying in the fetal position on the ground, trying not to get sick.

No one moved for another minute or two. They heard a faint clicking sound, as though something had been unlatched. They all stood up.

Alex shone her flashlight on the base of the Pharom examining every inch at close range. "Mitch, I think that did it…I think it's free," she said. "Look, there's a sliver of space showing at the base of it."

"I see it," he said. "Well Alex, do we dare?"

Their hearts were beating fast. They knew the next moments were crucial.

Bob sat up, feeling his head clear a bit. "I think the nausea is beginning to pass."

"I'm not feeling so sick and dizzy any more either," Alex said. They were all starting to feel better. "It has to be turned off now. We've got to try."

Mitch nodded. Together they reached for the Pharom. Jack backed away every so slightly.

They all said a silent prayer, except Bob who was saying his out loud, "Please don't kill us, please don't kill us…"

Alex concentrated and as she touched the Pharom, she squeezed her eyes closed, cringed and paused for a moment, half expecting to be electrocuted. No strange sensations, no instant death. Relieved, she opened her eyes, still touching the Pharom and looked over at Mitch. "Well, so far so good." She took a deep breath, counted to three. Gently, but firmly she and Mitch lifted it off the platform.

Jack and Bob stood close to one another, wide-eyed as Mitch and Alex lowered the heavy metallic obelisk to the ground.

"Where did we leave the box it was in?" Alex asked, looking around.

"Over there," Mitch pointed to the wall. "Jack, bring it here."

Jack immediately complied and Mitch and Alex cautiously placed the Pharom back in its box.

"Now what?" Alex asked. "We can't just leave it sitting here."

"No, we can't and we can't risk taking it out of this chamber for someone to find either. He looked around the chamber. "I think it would be safest to put it back where we found it."

Alex groaned at the thought of having to crawl back down the long, cramped tunnel. But she knew he was right.

"You're not going to study it further?" Jack asked. "I mean it's disabled now, right? It should be safe."

"Oh really, and I suppose you know that for a fact?" Bob interjected. "Being an expert on alien technology and weapons and all."

Jack didn't reply. Bob had a point.

"Come on Alex, let's get moving," Mitch urged. "Unless Jack and Bob want to do this for us."

"Yeah right," Jack said.

Bob went pale.

Mitch laughed, "Just kidding! We can still come back in here as long as our permits are valid. In the meantime, we'll keep studying the scrolls to see what we can learn. Who knows, maybe we'll find an instruction manual in there."

They all laughed nervously.

Mitch and Alex returned the box with the Pharom inside to its resting place. Alex had also taken the crystal that revealed the location of the hidden entrance, wrapped it in a cloth, and placed it with the box containing the Pharom. No one would be able to find the entrance the way they had. They carefully re-sealed all the entrances.

CHAPTER

69

Desperate Measures

T he Professor stormed around in search of Fessel. He found him in the lunchroom. "Fessel! I need to speak with you in my office. Now!"

"Yes sir!" Fessel replied as he chomped down the last bite of sandwich and gathered the rest of his lunch up and took it with him.

Fessel scrambled behind Professor Dustimaine dropping things along the way.

"Close the door behind you," Dustimaine ordered as they reached his office.

Fessel obliged, nearly dropping everything he had left in the process.

"Pick up after yourself, will you! I've never seen anyone as messy and clumsy as you," the Professor snapped as he sat down behind his desk.

Fessel organized himself and sat down in front of the desk, keeping the remains of his lunch on his lap. Somehow he had managed to spill pop in his lap. He squirmed uncomfortably and tried dab it with his one remaining dirty napkin.

The Professor watched him with a measure of disgust. "I assume you heard about the accident?"

"Uh, yes, but not much, everyone seems to be keeping a pretty tight lid on it. The Egyptian workers are pretty spooked, though I don't know why," Fessel answered. "I thought it was just a generator overload or something. What exactly happened?"

"That's what I would like to know. No one will give any specifics. All I keep hearing is 'we're satisfied as to the cause of death, it was an unfortunate accident'. If I didn't know better, I'd say there is a huge cover-up. But what I don't understand is how Mitch and Alex figure into this. I'm certain they know more than they're saying. For crying out loud, someone on their team died! I'm fed up with those two and now I am sure they are outright lying to me."

"Would you like me to 'look into it' sir?"

"Yes, Fessel. Something big is going on here, and I'll be damned if I'm going to be left out in the cold by the likes of those two. They think they can get away with this? I'll see to it they regret crossing me!" He shook his head. He was fuming. "How they ever got permits to excavate such an important site is beyond my comprehension. I'm not sure how far their involvement goes, but this time I want not only their personal rooms searched, but the lab they use, and check into the rooms of their two useless sidekicks, too."

"Jack and Bob?" Fessel asked.

"Yes, I have a sneaking suspicion they're also involved in this."

"Gladly, I've never liked them."

"No one does, except Mitch and Alex. Find out what they're up to. They must be hiding something and it might relate to the diagrams you saw in Mitch's journal."

Fessel eagerly listened to the details of the plan.

"I will see to it that all four of them are kept busy for the next two days. I'll move them to one of the smaller labs. There is one that is rarely used. It is far enough away so they shouldn't see anything. I will tell them that the main lab is going to be tied up with other work. I have already sent all the artifacts they will be working on to the small lab. The items are all in rough shape and there are a lot of them. They'll be so busy they won't have time to think of anything else, let alone tend to the other excavation."

Professor Dustimaine was already envisioning them being kicked out of the country in disgrace. He turned back to Fessel, "Take anything that looks like it doesn't belong."

"Yes sir! I'll let you know as soon as I find anything," Fessel said as he jumped up, pop stains evident on the front of his pants.

"And Fessel, I mean it, be careful this time. I don't want them suspecting anything."

The Professor informed Mitch, Alex, Jack and Bob that night that they would need to step up their efforts over the next couple of days until they were caught up and that they were also being moved to the small lab. He told them he would check on their work and that he expected it all to be completed within two days. No excuses. If that meant they had to postpone their work near the Sphinx, so be it, he told them, they didn't deserve it anyways.

"What a spiteful jerk!" Jack said after the Professor left. "I hope locusts get him in his sleep!"

"I have half a mind to punch his lights out," Bob seethed.

"Is he crazy? We'll be up all night for the next two days," Alex lamented.

"I think he's getting even with us for not cooperating with his questioning earlier. He's trying to make us pay for not telling him anything and for having those permits," Mitch replied.

"I'm going to require a lot of Diet Coke for this," Bob quipped.

"Do you really think that drinking diet pop is going to help? You drink eighty of them a day!" Jack needled him.

"Well I'm sorry if we don't all have your freakish metabolism, you skinny mutant!"

"Guys, enough," Alex said. "Look, I don't see what choice we have. We'll just have to put everything else on hold for the next two days. The Pharom is safe for now. I'm just choked he's assigned that crappy lab for us to use. The lighting is terrible, the air conditioner barely works and there's not much space, particularly for four us to be working in there."

"Yeah, this is going to be fun," Mitch scoffed. "You'd think if this was so important and he needs all four of us to work non-stop for the next two days, he would have let us keep using the main lab. Especially with the amount of items we have to go through. He must be taking great delight in making us suffer like this."

"Maybe we shouldn't be all that surprised. I'm just amazed it took him this long to find a way to punish us," Alex said.

Mitch nodded, "Let's make sure that everything is locked up tight. We don't want anyone snooping around while Dust Bucket has us cooped up in his prison…I mean lab."

They laughed mournfully then decided to retire for the night.

70

☥

Salvation

Circa 10,000 B.C.

The blinding blue light and subsequent powerful shocks from the blast, which had spread out from the Amsara site, reverberated throughout the city, and had broken through the Palace walls. Dust and debris were flying everywhere. The air was choked with smoke and the cries of the injured could be heard around the Palace.

Mindara, having been knocked out from the medicine the healer gave her, woke up with a start. She was disoriented and groggy from the effects of the drug. She was unsure how long she had been unconscious, but the blast woke her out of her deep sleep.

She looked around and saw that many items had been knocked to the ground. She could smell smoke. She quickly got off the bed, but the pain from her arm nearly caused her to faint. She had briefly forgotten her injuries and had used the wounded arm to lift herself off the bed. She looked down at it. It was heavily bandaged but her sudden movement had caused it to bleed again.

She took a moment to steady her spinning head. She felt nauseous. The cut on her face had been stitched up and had stopped bleeding, but was still throbbing with pain. Around her she could hear screams coming from various directions within the Palace. The healer was nowhere to be seen.

Mindara needed to find out what was going on. She took a few shaky steps to the door and collapsed. She protected her injured arm, falling on her good arm. She grimaced with pain for a moment, but pulled herself up. The effects of the medicine were still upon her. She tried to steady herself.

With a deep breath, she made for the door. She was just in time. With a loud creak the ceiling of the room collapsed behind her. She shrieked, panic propelling her forward. Weak with pain and dazed from the drugs, she made her way down the smoky hallways as quickly as she could, keeping her hand on the wall for balance.

Mindara headed back to where she had left Medetha and the boys before she had followed Zazmaria out. Her pace quickened as she stumbled on through the smoke. She tripped over something large and soft. She screamed. It was one of the servants. He was not moving and made no sound. Blood poured from a wound to his head where a piece of the ceiling had hit him, splitting his scalp wide open. She felt for a pulse. He was dead.

Terror gripped her, but she kept moving. She could barely see a few feet in front of her. The smoke thickened the further on she went. She had to get back to the children and help Medetha. She prayed they were safe.

She struggled along, feeling her way down the passageways she knew so well. She could hear shouts and cries of anguish coming from places near her. A wall collapsed, crashing behind her, taking part of the ceiling with it. The large statues of King Mesah and Queen Elenia, which had stood proudly in the hallway, fell to her side, smashing into pieces. Everything around her was becoming a potentially deadly weapon. She knew she must keep moving.

At last she reached the room where she had left Medetha and the boys. The door was closed. Her breath caught in her chest, she listened for any sound, but she heard none. The smoke was getting thicker, something was burning, but she could not tell from where. Slowly she opened the door. One of the windows had a massive hole blown through it, leaving the room covered in dust and debris.

Mindara called out in a panic, "Medetha! Tramen!" but no answer came. Fearing the worst, she searched the room. She saw Medetha's hair sticking out from under a fallen portion of wall. "Medetha!" she shouted, picking her way through the toys and broken furniture that littered the floor.

The woman did not move. Mindara thought she could hear some tiny whimpers. She reached out to touch Medetha's hair, still no movement. She heard a small voice coming from under the debris.

She found a fallen beam and used it to pry the wood and stone of the wall off Medetha, then braced it on her back. Her face and arm throbbed with pain and she knew she was bleeding badly again, but it did not matter to her right now.

As the wall lifted, she heard a distinct cry. It was coming from underneath Medetha. Mindara knew she could not keep the weight balanced on her back long, so she carefully stepped over Medetha, bracing the heavy wall with her good arm and moved it far enough away from the woman, leaned over and let it crash to the floor. She stepped back over to Medetha and turned her over. She was dead. Her face was covered in blood. Her neck had been broken, but still cradled in her badly battered arm was Setar.

The little boy began to cough and cry, but he was alive. In tears, Mindara removed him from the protective, final embrace of Medetha. She gently picked the child up and then softly placed Medetha's arm back down.

"You gave your life to protect him. I will never let anyone forget what you have done here today," Mindara whispered, cradling the frightened child. Setar had no obvious injuries on him. Medetha's body had cushioned the impact of the falling debris.

She now had to find Tramen. "Tramen!" she called out frantically. "Tramen, please answer!" Carrying Setar, she searched the room looking for him. It was in complete disarray, but she noticed a small sandal in the corner of the room. Quickly stepping through the rubble, she picked it up and looked around. She spotted a small foot sticking out from behind an overturned dresser. "Tramen!"

She raced over. Still holding Setar with her bleeding arm, she lifted the dresser and set it upright. Mercifully, it had been positioned close to the wall, breaking the dresser's fall. Crumpled in the corner, Tramen was unconscious, but breathing. He had a few scratches, but otherwise did not appear too badly hurt.

Mindara bent down to try and rouse him, she knew she would have difficulty trying to carry two children in her present state. "Tramen! Tramen!" she cried. "Please wake up! It is Mindara, please wake up!" She gently shook the little boy, but he did not respond.

Growing increasingly afraid, she shook him again. Finally he coughed and whimpered. "Tramen, we have to leave! You must get up."

"My head hurts," he moaned. He looked around at the room, which was now in ruins. "What happened? Where is Medetha?" He struggled to lift himself up.

"Tramen, listen to me, we must hurry. We need to get out of here, but I need you to walk. Can you do that?" she asked.

"I think so," he coughed again and winced. He was sore everywhere. Mindara helped lift him to his feet. Still wearing his one sandal, Mindara helped him on with the other one.

"Come, we must hurry," she urged him. With Setar in one arm, she took Tramen's hand to lead him out of the room to find the nearest safe exit out of the Palace.

As they made their way out of the room, Tramen saw the body of Medetha lying on the floor, "Medetha!" When she did not answer, he tried to go over to her, but Mindara held him back.

"Tramen, we must leave now!" Mindara insisted, pulling him away. She wished he had not seen her.

"We have to help her!" he pleaded.

"Tramen, it is too late," Mindara said as she bent down to look him in the eyes. "She is dead. She died saving Setar. There is nothing we can do for her. Please come, we have to hurry!"

Tramen began to cry.

At that moment another loud crash was heard followed by screams.

Mindara was frantic, "We have to get out of here! Now!" With Setar crying in her arm, and Tramen tightly holding her hand, they ran as quickly as possible.

As they ran down a hallway, Mindara saw the strange sight of colorful, fresh-picked flowers strewn about in the grey dust and debris. She looked up, the painting of Princess Anjia still hung on the wall, miraculously undamaged.

"Anjia's picture! We must take it with us!" Tramen cried out.

"Tramen, there is no time!" She pulled the crying boy along, racing through the smoke.

Finally they neared an exit, their eyes stinging and red, their lungs dangerously filling with smoke. A loud creaking noise was followed by another huge crash. The Palace had become a deathtrap. Mindara, keeping a firm grip on Tramen's hand and with Setar's face pressed into her neck, raced out into the night as fast as Tramen's little legs would allow.

71

☥

Redemption

Alaj and Traeus made their way back down to the main level of the Draxen Stronghold, when Traeus looked up and saw a brilliant blue light streaming into the Stronghold from somewhere outside, followed by a terrible explosion.

The Royal soldiers who had been waiting for them, yelled in horror as the Draxen Stronghold shook violently under the power of the blast. Walls and ceilings were ripped apart. Many of the soldiers and their Draxen prisoners were killed instantly. The walls that were still intact were on fire.

The blast threw Traeus and Alaj across the room. Alaj cried out in pain as he landed hard against his injured shoulder. Momentarily stunned, he tried to catch his breath. He shook the dust from his hair and face. He spotted Traeus lying under a pile of rubble. "Traeus, are you all right?"

"I think so." He winced as he pushed the debris off of him. "Captain!" he shouted. There was no reply. "Captain!" Still nothing.

"This way!" Alaj shouted. "We have to get out of here!" Alaj helped Traeus to his feet. He could see that his brother was injured.

Traeus looked around, he saw injured men on the ground. "Soldiers, we must get out of here at once! Take any wounded with you that you can manage."

"There is an open door over there," Alaj pointed to the opening of light in a room full of smoke and fire. Holding Traeus up with one arm around his waist, and followed by the few men who had survived, Alaj navigated their way past debris, intense fire and thickening smoke. The structure was extremely unstable. "Hold on, we are almost there!" Alaj coughed.

A few feet from the door, Alaj saw a large beam fall down to his right and looked up to see that the ceiling was about to collapse on top of them. He grabbed Traeus around the waist with both arms and dropping down to use his weight for momentum, threw Traeus out the door. Traeus landed hard on the ground outside as the building crashed down behind him.

Winded, he picked himself up off the ground. The others were no longer behind him. "Alaj!" he shouted, causing himself to cough violently. He could taste the smoke and dust that burned his lungs. He limped back to the devastated structure, which was little more than a smoldering pile of rubble now. Desperately he dug through the ruins looking for his brother, calling his name out again and again.

No answer.

As he scanned the wreckage in search of Alaj, his eyes could not help but take in the total devastation all around him. The sight was unbelievable. What he at first thought may be the result of a renewed battle with the Draxens, was actually much, much more. As far as his eyes could see, there were buildings burning, huge flames blazing against the backdrop of the night sky. A terrifying thought crept into his mind of what could have caused such widespread destruction. There was only one thing he knew of that would be capable of this.

Agonized, he shook his head. He had to focus on the moment. "Alaj! Answer me! Where are you?"

Nothing.

With furious resolve Traeus ripped off part of his tunic and wrapped it around a long wooden pole. The cloth provided him with a grip and insulation from the heat. With a strong push downward on the pole, Traeus was able to pry apart the beams stuck in the rubble. He pulled the beams out, throwing them aside. In a desperate frenzy, he dug through the rubble with his bare hands. His knuckles bled as he searched.

"Alaj!" Traeus screamed after finding his brother lying tangled in a mess of wood and stone. Alaj moaned. He was barely conscious. Blood and dirt covered his face. Ignoring the pain he was in himself, Traeus worked with pure desperation to free his brother. He cleared the rubble off Alaj's head, chest and arms, but his lower body was pinned too tightly under the rubble of ceilings, walls and beams. Traeus tried hard, but he could not lift the larger sections.

"Traeus, it is too late for me," Alaj whispered hoarsely.

"No! It is not too late. I have already lost one brother this night, I will be damned if I am going to lose you, too!" Traeus fiercely kept digging through the rubble, trying to find a way to lift the heavy debris off his brother's legs.

"Traeus," Alaj said weakly as his bloodied and battered hand touched Traeus' arm, "forgive me."

Traeus stopped what he was doing. "You were tricked by evil people. It was not your fault, Alaj."

"I am responsible for Amoni's death. It was my fault, everything…" the tears were now freely flowing down Alaj's face, mixing with the dirt and blood, as though they were trying to wash away the damage done to his body.

"No!" Traeus cried, softly caressing his brother's face. Alaj's eyes showed such depths of pain and sorrow…regret. For a fleeting moment, Traeus saw in them the innocent boy his brother had once been, before treachery and lies came into his life. His heart could not accept what his head was telling him. He was losing Alaj.

"I was a fool," Alaj confessed, his voice weakening, becoming raspy. "The Draxens used me. They used my wife. I know you can never forgive Zazmaria for what she did, but do not hate Setar. He is only a child, innocent…"

Traeus shook his head, "I could never hate him, Alaj. Whatever else has happened, he is a part of this family and will always be so. I give you my word."

Alaj gripped Traeus' hand, his emerald eyes tinged red, brimming with tears. "Please take care of Setar for me. Let him know I loved him…"

"I will, I promise," Traeus whispered, his own tears falling. "As long as there is life in me, he will be loved and protected."

A faint smile of relief passed Alaj's bloodied lips. He inhaled sharply, gasping for breath. He died in his brother's arms.

Traeus looked down at his long-estranged brother, at the now lifeless emerald eyes. With a soft pass of his hand, he closed them forever. He bent down and kissed him on the forehead. "I forgive you my brother. Go now…be at peace. I love you."

Reluctantly he let go of his brother's hand and got up, tears still streaming down his face. He had to go find help, find out what had happened. He managed to walk a few steps, before collapsing to the ground unconscious. Exhaustion and pain from his injuries finally overcame him.

CHAPTER

72

☥

Sacrifice

O dai crept up the stairs to the trap door and listened. He had heard no further sounds after the explosions. The fact that no one had come back for him filled his heart with fear.

He had heard the screams above which were followed by an even more terrifying silence. He could feel the heat from above. The explosions had shaken the cellar he was in. He had managed to safely conceal the chest in the ground.

Odai pushed on the trap door. It was loose, but still jammed shut and hot from the explosions. He went down a few stairs and took a run at it, hitting the door with his shoulder. The wood splintered, having been damaged and burned. He emerged from the cellar, his shoulder throbbing.

The smell of burnt wood and flesh was overwhelming as the smoke rose from the smoldering ruins. He held part of his robe over his mouth to help him breath. There was almost nothing left of the temple.

Tears filled his eyes as he looked around for his fellow priests who had so bravely stood their ground to fight the Draxen soldiers. He saw remnants of the battle: swords, which had been blackened, a sandal, and a pendant. He reached for the pendant. It was one of the ankhs the priests wore. He turned it over. The name engraved on the back was Essen.

Odai bent his head down and wept. He knew in his heart they had all died here. "Be at peace, my brothers," he whispered holding the ankh to his heart, tears streaming down his face. He left the temple in search of survivors. After a time, heard a familiar voice.

"Odai!" Senarra shouted as she, Assan and several priests spotted him. She ran to Odai and embraced him. "I thought… I thought I lost you," she said with tears in her eyes.

"You will never lose me, not if I can help it," he said, holding her close.

Assan and the others joined them. "Odai, what happened here? We suspect it was…" Assan started to ask.

"The Pharom, yes, it did this. The Draxens, they were at the Amsara site. They must have accidentally set it off in an attempt to steal it. They were interrogating Essen when several priests and I reached the site."

"Why were they interrogating Essen?" Assan asked.

Odai told Assan and the other priests what Essen had done. "Essen had been acting strange all day. He was being very secretive. I noticed he was not where he was ordered to be. I asked some of the priests to help me search for him." Odai then told them of confrontation at the temple. "Essen saved my life."

"He will be remembered for his bravery," Assan affirmed. "Our main goal now must be to retrieve whatever is left of the Pharom and secure it. We will help with recovery efforts once that is taken care of."

Odai, Assan, Senarra and the other priests headed to the Amsara site, to the last place the Pharom was known to be. Nearing the site, they could see that the once majestic head had been utterly destroyed. The sight was unbelievable, surreal. There was nothing left of it to even try to put back together and the outer covering had been stripped away, exposing bare rock.

They were all humbled at the power responsible for such large-scale destruction. "We must find the Pharom," Assan said, drawing their attention back to the matter at hand. "Fan out and begin the search."

The priests all worked silently trying to absorb what had happened. The ground around the site had been blackened from the heat of the blast. It looked as though a raging fire had scorched the area.

After an hour of digging and searching one of the priests yelled out, "I found it! It is buried deep!"

Assan ordered the others to help him dig it up. "The Pharom must have been thrown by the force of the blast and embedded deep in the ground."

As they continued to dig they saw something astonishing. The Pharom itself was still intact.

"How could it have survived when there was so much devastation around it?" Odai asked, bewildered.

It was cool to the touch, undamaged...still. No vibrations. Nothing at all to indicate what it had done.

Hope Is Not Lost

The day was dawning, the sun starting to come up over the horizon. Traeus realized he must have been unconscious for hours. His mind began to clear as he struggled to regain his memory. He moaned with sorrow as his last memory came flooding back, Alaj's face as he died in his arms. A tear slipped down his face.

Traeus lay there for a few more moments, but as he fully recalled the terrible events, he realized the danger might not be over. He pushed himself up, grimacing. Not only were several of his ribs broken, his shoulder was dislocated and he had a gash on the top of his head, caked with dried blood.

As he stood up, he swooned, nearly fainting. He managed to steady himself. He held his head for a moment until the dizziness passed. He did not dare allow himself to fall, with his injuries he may not be able to get back up. He found some wood and using strips of his clothing he tied together a crude crutch. His lips cracked from dryness and began to bleed. Wiping the blood from them, he knew he desperately needed water and shelter.

Traeus looked back at the ruins of the Draxen Stronghold, knowing his brother's body lay beneath the smoldering rubble. He hesitated. He wanted to go back and retrieve Alaj's body, but he knew he was in no condition to do so. Every step caused him excruciating pain.

He had to find help and determine the circumstances the terrible disaster had left his people in. Then, the thought of finding his son propelled him forward with a sense of urgency in spite of his pain.

The ragged and wounded King walked and walked, but the area was eerily quiet. The Draxen Stronghold was near the edge of the city. Traeus continued on, leaning on the crutch for stability. As he walked, his eyes were met with more desolation. He saw bodies, some burned, others with their arms and legs sticking out from beneath the ruins of homes and shops. He kept checking for signs of life, but found none. His heart broke further with each step.

As the King carried on amongst the ruins, he stopped to pick up a small shining object. He dusted the dirt and ashes from its glistening surface. It was a pendant, an ankh. He fell to his knees as tears streamed down his face. It was Axiana's pendant. The one he had given his son after the accident, which claimed the lives of his mother and sister.

Carved on the back of the gold ankh, the words still visible, 'May this symbol of life protect you, all of your days'. He gripped it and pressed it to his heart, the anguish of his loss written in the stains the tears marked down his ash-covered face. "Tramen, my son, I have failed you," he agonized.

He then remembered Mindara, had he lost her too? His heart broke at the possibility. He cared for her so much, much more than he had ever admitted to himself.

Traeus thought at that moment, it might be possible for him to simply curl up and die from his grief, that if he could surrender himself to it, life would cease to course through him. Dehydrated and his will to live fading, he collapsed. Lying there, his grief washing over him in wave after unbearable wave. He became delirious. Slowly a vision came to him…

He was sitting alone in the shadow of the Amsara monument. He looked up and saw a figure clothed in white robes standing in front of him. The

figure looked down at him with a deep expression of compassion in his eyes. His eyes were the color of pure gold, flecked throughout with amber. His skin a flawless, pale golden color with a luminous opalescent quality to it. His long jet-black hair gleamed in thick waves over his shoulders. Around his neck was a pendant, made of pure platinum and in-laid with a perfect ruby at the top – it was an ankh.

The figure knelt down and touched Traeus' face, and then reached to touch the pendant Traeus still clutched to his heart. "Do you know what this means?"

Stunned and confused, Traeus asked, "Who are you?"

The figure asked again, "Do you know what this means?"

Traeus looked at the pendant around the man's neck and then to the one he had given to his son. "It is the symbol of life, of immortality."

The figure smiled faintly, "Yes. So then, why do you invite death?"

Traeus felt his tears begin to fall. "I have lost everything, my family, everything I tried to create, to build, is gone and it is my fault. In my arrogance, I believed I could achieve anything. And now, I sit in the ruins of this place, amongst the dead, those that perished because of a foolish dream. I have failed my people, I deserve to die."

The man lifted Traeus' face. Traeus gazed at the ethereal beauty of the mysterious figure. "But you did not fail, you followed your heart... your destiny. What you see before you now are but the ashes of a time in history that has now passed. This is not the end. It is a beginning. Look over the horizon, as the forest springs new growth from the burnt remains of its former self, so too does the Phoenix rise from the ashes. Traeus, you are that Phoenix. Do not lament the circumstances of which you know not their purpose. Only follow the voice inside – it is calling you to life. Now rise!"

With those words, a swirl of dust and ashes clouded Traeus' vision. Once it cleared, he realized that he was still curled up on the ground, he had not actually moved. He looked up to see the form of a majestic bird soaring over him, towards the mountains in the west. His son's ankh was still in his hand, and the rays from the rising sun glinted off its surface, making it appear radiant, as though nothing, no war or destruction, could ever dim its beauty.

He picked up the makeshift crutch and began to walk again. He found a well, and drank thirstily from it.

Stepping amongst the still smoldering remains of the once great city, he vowed that he would not squander the gift of his life. For some reason he could not yet comprehend, he had been spared.

Finally Traeus came across two men, carrying another who was badly injured and unconscious. They were happy and relieved to see their King, their spirits buoyed a little. They were carrying the man to a nearby temple, which had been converted to a makeshift camp. Traeus walked with them, thankful to have found other survivors.

They reached the temple. Bedding had been laid out on the floor and a few people were sleeping or resting around the edges of the room. One area near the back had been set up to treat the wounded. The injured man was attended to immediately.

Traeus set his wooden crutch aside, feeling he could now manage without it. Just then he thought he heard something familiar. He stopped and listened for a moment. As he walked slowly towards the familiar voice, no one took much notice of him in his unrecognizable state. His ears picked up the sound more clearly, it was a children's song.

As he scanned the people scattered about, his eyes fell on a woman holding two small children, rocking them gently and kissing the tops of their heads. Her back was to Traeus, but he recognized the long, dark braid, which though in slight disarray, fell down her back.

"Mindara!"

She turned around suddenly, her eyes registering shock, disbelief and exhilaration all in the same moment. "Your Majesty!"

Tramen, who had been resting against her, recognized the voice that called out.

"Daddy!" he squealed as he ran to his father, practically leaping through the air.

Traeus wrapped his arms around his son, grimacing at the pain in his ribs and shoulder.

Mindara took notice, but said nothing.

"Tramen, my son, I am so happy you are all right!" he said as he kissed his face and held him.

"I knew I would see you again, I knew it!" Tramen exclaimed, taking his father's hand. "Mindara told me to be patient and wait, that you would come for me."

Traeus looked with great emotion and gratitude at Mindara who now stood close by, holding Setar.

"It was a matter of faith," she said. "I just felt it."

He felt his heart stir at her words. He gazed into her eyes for a long moment as he held his son's hand. Then, he reached into his pocket. "Tramen, I found something of yours," he said as he took out the ankh pendant his son had lost in the frantic race away from the Palace.

"You found it!" he exclaimed.

Traeus placed the ankh in his son's hand, "Keep it safe." Tramen looked at the precious gift that had been returned to him. Traeus took Mindara, Setar and his son into his arms and held them tight, realizing how close he had come to losing them.

74

The Path Home

Traeus had not wanted to remain at the temple long. His injuries were treated, he had rested and had some small meals. He spoke privately with Mindara, informing her of all that had happened. The other people there allowed their King some privacy with the children, and time to heal a bit. Soon after, he announced that he would be heading back to the Palace to try and make contact with other survivors. Anyone who wished, was welcome to join them. For those that stayed, he would send back help.

As they made their way through the devastated city, Traeus, Mindara and the boys along with numerous people who had decided to accompany them, were shocked at what they saw. Entire buildings had been razed, trees incinerated and the ground scorched.

Without thinking, Traeus reached for Mindara's hand and held it tight. Walking beside Traeus, Mindara was lost in her own thoughts. Her skin tingled at the touch of Traeus' hand holding hers. She tried to ignore the sensation. She told herself he was just being comforting, nothing more. Still, her heart leapt whenever he looked at her.

In the short time they had spent at the temple with the boys sleeping between them on the floor, she had pretended to fall asleep, then she would open her eyes and just look at Traeus for a while. Seeing him sleeping beside the two little forms nestled between them filled her heart with such…love. The word shocked her, though she had always loved the Royal Family. Her loyalty to Axiana was still strong. Mindara felt ashamed at the feelings and sparks of emotion, which were beginning to grow within her.

At last, they made it to the edge of the Palace grounds. Traeus looked at what was left of his home. It would have to be demolished. A few sections were still standing, but much of it had collapsed. Large sections of the roof were missing and many of the walls had been badly damaged. The smell of burnt wood was still thick in the air.

Two people he recognized came racing towards them. It was Assan and Odai. "Your Highness, how wonderful it is to see you!" Assan exclaimed in an uncharacteristically exuberant fashion. Without thinking, he embraced his King.

"It is good to see you both, too," Traeus replied, happy and grateful.

"You cannot imagine how worried we have been," Assan said. "We thought you might be…well it is wonderful to see you. And Mindara, Tramen, Setar, all of you! We have been searching the ruins of the Palace, looking for survivors who might have been trapped underneath. We did not know Mindara had escaped with the children. We are so relieved!"

"Your Majesty," Odai said, "I would like to show you something that we were able to salvage from inside the Palace." He went around a corner, then came back holding a painting. "It is a miracle that it survived," he said as he handed it to his King.

Traeus' eyes welled up with tears as he took it. It was the painting of Anjia that had hung in the hallway.

Mindara could not believe it had been spared. She remembered running past it as they escaped, never thinking she would see it again.

"The picture of Anjia!" Tramen exclaimed.

"Thank-you for bringing this to me. I cannot express what this means to me…" Traeus' voice broke as he gazed upon the cherished painting of his daughter.

Odai politely bowed his head.

"Your Majesty, may we speak in private for a moment?" Assan asked.

Traeus nodded and followed Assan out of earshot of the others. Assan told the King of what they had learned of the Draxen attempt to steal the Pharom, inadvertently causing the explosions and subsequent devastation.

"I knew in my heart that the Pharom was responsible for this horror, I just did not know how it had happened," Traeus said, looking down, once again feeling defeated.

"Your Highness, there is something else."

Traeus looked up at him, searching his expression. "Go on," he replied hesitantly.

"Once you and Prince Alaj left, Commander Koronius took Victarius with him to the Amsara site as you ordered. After the explosions, some of us went out looking for them. We knew what must have caused it. When we found them, Victarius was already dead and Commander Koronius was severely injured. They had not yet reached the Amsara site. We brought the Commander back here." Assan paused. "I am sorry to tell you this, your Highness, but he is not expected to survive long. The healers have done the best they could, but his injuries are just too extensive."

Traeus was devastated. Not his two dear old friends, too…he could not believe how many people he had cared about had been lost. "I wish to see him."

Assan looked at his King sadly, "Of course, your Majesty, but I must warn you, he is in pretty bad shape. He lost a leg and his one arm is badly mangled. His face… his face is also quite marred. His mind is still sharp and he asks about you every day. I am sorry, but you needed to know before we go in."

Traeus tried absorbed the terrible news. He took a deep breath and steadied himself. "Let us go see our friend Koronius."

When Traeus saw the Commander he did the best he could to keep his reactions to himself and his emotions in check, but seeing the once strong and proud man that way absolutely crushed him.

Traeus filled him in on events as though he was still Commander in charge of the military and general protection of the Royal Family.

Commander Koronius also did his best to put on a brave face, in spite of the incredible pain he was in. He knew the healers did what they could to ease his suffering, but his injuries were simply too much for them.

The Commander died that night. Traeus felt that somehow the Commander had held on just long enough to see his King one last time, as though he now accepted his work was done and he could leave this world safe with the knowledge he had not outlived his charge.

75

A Decision Is Made

The next priority Traeus had to focus on was what to do with the Pharom. Odai had rejoined the King and Head Priest.

"What should we do with it? I do not wish to destroy it," Traeus said, "but we can never allow something like this to happen again. We thought we took enough precautions, but..."

Odai jumped in, "Your Majesty, with all due respect, so much has already been lost, so many lives wiped out. The Draxen Stronghold was completely destroyed. The threat that was there before is gone. Perhaps we do not need to change that much after all."

"Odai, before the King responds to your comments, I would like to add something," Assan said. "We did not know before how serious a threat the Draxens posed to us all or in how much jeopardy the Pharom actually was. It would be highly irresponsible of us now to allow ourselves to remain blind to such possibilities in the future. It is true that a major threat has been eliminated, and perhaps we are safe. But it is often the case that evil lurks in the shadows, through which our eyes cannot, or somehow, do not, see. Once the danger is perceived, it may be too late."

"Wise words indeed, Assan," the King said, "and I do not think we can be completely certain that the Draxens have been eliminated, can we?"

Assan shook his head. "Our searches were able to identify many of the bodies from the Draxen family, but all have not been accounted for…namely Zhek, as well as a few others. Besides, if anyone in that family survived, I doubt very much they would willingly choose to come forth."

"I agree," Traeus replied. "Odai, I too would prefer not to take on the view of suspicion, waiting for evil deeds that may befall us. But befall us they have once before, and that one time could have destroyed us all. I will never forget that and neither should any of us. Mercifully, many of us lived to see the sun rise again, but many more did not. As leaders, we must carry the awful weight of truth within us, that we are not ever truly safe. Vigilance must be our constant companion the rest of our days and one day, we will have to pass that heavy burden on to those that come after us."

The three men sat in silence for a few moments as they each thought about how their lives had now changed.

Assan was the first to break the silence. "Our first decision then must be whether or not to keep it operational once any damage has been assessed and repaired."

Traeus nodded. "I would deeply regret it if all of our efforts and hopes were cast to dust because of what that evil family did."

"I agree, that would be a terrible loss," Assan replied. "But it may best to focus on rebuilding our society for now. We have so much to do."

"You are right, Assan, of course," the King said. "Much work lies ahead for all of us." Traeus sat thinking for a moment sad that he had to let his dream be put on hold indefinitely, but he knew it was the right decision for his people. "It is decided then. The Pharom will be stored indefinitely. I want this just between us. No one else is to be told of what is said here unless expressly permitted by me. So how and where could we keep it so that it will be safe until we choose to retrieve it?"

"I may have an idea," Odai offered.

76

A Powerful Truth

Present-Day Egypt

After the foursome's first day cooped up in the tiny lab Professor Dustimaine had relegated them to, they all left exhausted. Mitch, Alex, Jack and Bob had started work at five am and kept working straight through until nine when they just couldn't work any longer. Their eyes were red and blurry from the painstaking work and they were all stuffed up from the minimal air circulation in the old, cramped building. Their backs ached from being hunched over all day and from the worn out, wobbly chairs they had to use.

The only thing that made the day at all bearable for Mitch and Alex was listening to the relentless banter between Jack and Bob, who had found all sorts of colorful ways to express their displeasure with the unfortunate situation.

Mitch and Alex, on the other hand had barely spoken all day. They took one look at the work ahead of them and they knew they were in trouble. It was going to be next to impossible to finish on schedule. Dustimaine had really done them in this time.

After having a quick, late dinner with Jack and Bob, Mitch and Alex had briefly discussed just the two of them going back to the lab and working for a couple more hours. They knew they needed the extra time, but they were just too tired, they could barely keep their eyes open.

Finally, with weary bones and weary brains, they returned to their respective rooms. It did not take either one long to fall asleep. However, their rest was punctuated by wild dreams.

Mitch and Alex were walking together near the Sphinx. It was late at night, all was quiet and there was no one else around. The stars were out in full force. As they stood there silently gazing at them, they saw what at first appeared to be a shooting star. Suddenly, the light came closer and grew in intensity. Its incredible brightness surrounded them.

Then, the light faded and they found themselves sitting in the sand beside the Sphinx, but now it once again had the head of a lion.

A figure, glowing, came walking up to them.

"Who are you?" Alex asked, looking up at the strange figure dressed in flowing white robes with long black hair and golden eyes.

There was an aura about the figure, as though his being was made from light. As he came closer, he came more into focus. The figure possessed an ethereal, timeless beauty.

The figure looked at them, studying them for a moment, then a faint hint of a smile crossed his lips. "You have many questions."

Mitch spoke up, "We do."

"But do you not also have many answers?" the figure asked of them, his kind eyes looking from one to the other, eyes that seemed filled with mystery, sparkling with untold depths.

"There is still much that we do not know," Alex replied.

"That is the way of things," he said. "Truth is revealed in its perfect time."

"Then what are you revealing to us now?" Mitch asked.

The figure smiled warmly at them, giving them a knowing look. "Open your minds. Try to understand who we are."

"You are one of the Kierani," Mitch replied. "You are not from this world."

The figure nodded slowly, "Do you sense something else about us?"

"I do not understand," Alex replied, feeling her breath slow and deep.

"What answers do you seek?" the figure asked.

"To know our history, so we may understand ourselves better," Mitch replied.

"So then again, I ask you, do you understand who we are?" As he asked this, the figure knelt down and touched each of their faces. An ankh of exquisite beauty hung around his neck with a glittering ruby embedded in the silvery metal. He looked at them with such benevolence and caring.

Neither one replied to the mysterious figure's question. Their eyes were filling with tears.

He smiled kindly at them and looked deeply into their eyes, "You sense the truth, but are afraid of it."

"The Pharom, what is it?" Alex almost whispered.

"Do you not know… even now?" the figure asked, his eyes seeming to peer into their very souls, as though now only pure truth between them was possible.

"It is powerful, but we do not know its true purpose," she replied.

"The answer to that lies within your name, Alexandra."

Both Mitch and Alex found words now difficult…they continued to stare at the beautiful figure before them. They felt such warmth and peace in his presence.

Alex's gaze dropped to the ankh around his neck. As she reached out to touch it, the figure vanished.

When their alarms went off at four-thirty the next morning, both Mitch and Alex felt oddly full of energy and completely awake, in spite of the long day they had the day before. They met Jack and Bob again at five am at the lab as planned, but they could tell by the looks on one another's faces that they needed to talk. Alone.

They excused themselves to go outside. They checked around, making sure no one was nearby.

Alex looked at her partner curiously for a moment, her eyes searching his. She knew and she knew he knew. "Had a strange dream?" she asked.

Mitch nodded, unsettled, "Uh huh." He paused. "You first."

"Well, I'm sure you know this already," she said, "but the dream was of the Sphinx, or rather…the lion version of it, and of a rather unusual person talking to us." At that point, the cat, proverbial and otherwise, was out of the bag and they shared every detail of the dreams they had. Once again, they were eerily identical in every aspect.

"I can't believe this," Alex said. "It has to have something to do with the Pharom."

Mitch nodded, "I can't think of any other reason this would happening to us." He rubbed his eyes in frustration and confusion. "This is just the most bizarre experience…if anyone overheard this conversation they'd lock us up for sure."

Just then they heard something fall over in the lab. They went running back inside.

Jack and Bob were trying to act nonchalant as they righted a stool that was beside the high window near where Mitch and Alex had been standing outside.

"Uh, hi guys, we were just…grabbing this stool here to use over there for…" Jack was trying to save face but it was no use.

Bob couldn't even make eye contact with them. He just stared at his feet.

Mitch and Alex looked at the two of them for a long moment, their arms crossed, with stern expressions of disapproval on their faces.

"Well boys, now we've become spies, have we?" Alex asked.

"We've always been spies," Jack countered. "Did we forget to mention that? I know we may not look like James Bond-types, but…"

"Shut up Jack," Bob said as he smacked the back of Jack's head.

"Ouch, you have to stop hitting me!" Jack whined as he rubbed the back of his head.

"You have to stop deserving it!" Bob shot back.

"So, I guess we should assume you both overheard everything?" Mitch challenged.

No response.

"I thought so," Mitch said. "Well, what are we going to do about this, Alex?"

"Good question," she replied, eyeing the two culprits. "I suppose we could lock them up somewhere until it's time to leave Egypt."

"You know Bob," Jack started, regaining his courage and bravado, "I do believe they were afraid of being locked up themselves if anyone knew of their 'dreams'. They do look a little crazy to me, what do you think? Maybe we should alert someone," he said looking Mitch and Alex up and down through narrowed eyes.

"Jack, I swear…" Bob said through clenched teeth. "Look, guys, we're sorry, it was wrong of us to eavesdrop. We let our curiosity get the best of us. We just wanted to know what you guys were up to, we're really sorry." He looked at Jack with a raised eyebrow. When Jack didn't say anything, Bob gave him an elbow in the ribs to prompt him.

"Ow! Yes, yes, we're really very sorry," he said, holding his ribs.

"Well, we can't change the fact that they did overhear our conversation as wrong as it was," Alex said.

"No, I don't suppose we can," Mitch reluctantly agreed.

"So!" Jack exclaimed excitedly. "Now that's out of the way, tell us more! You're having the same dreams? How is that possible? How long has this been going on? Do you think you've lost your minds? Tell us, we really must know!"

Bob looked like he was about to strangle him.

"Jack, we don't have time for twenty questions," Mitch said, "and we don't actually know what's going on."

"It's got to have something to do with the Pharom, Mitch," Alex said. "Think about it, the energy it produces, how much time we've spent around it, the reference to it in our dreams. Something has to be causing this…aside from us losing our minds, of course." Alex looked at Jack and mock-glared at him.

"But it's no longer active!" Bob said, slightly panicked. "You guys said we'd be safe with it hidden."

"It wasn't active the first time either, Bob," Mitch said. "We hadn't even found it yet when Alex had the first dream…" his voice trailed off as he realized too late that he had promised not to say anything about that.

She gave him a look.

"Sorry, Alex," he said sheepishly.

"First dream?" Bob asked.

"Oh, this is most interesting," Jack remarked. "Hey Bob, I do believe these two have been keeping some sneaky little secrets from us." He mock-glared back at Alex, "Most evil and underhanded."

Alex shook her head, "Well, I guess there's no point in keeping them any further." She paused, "Remember when we first found the chest?"

"Yeah," Bob answered.

"Well, we didn't tell you everything about how we found it," she said.

"Please do go on, Miss Logan," Jack said.

She took a deep breath. "Well, it was true that I tripped in the spot where we found it…."

"But…?" Jack asked.

Alex hesitated.

Mitch decided to finish the story for her. "Alex had sat down and ended up catnapping. It was pretty hot that day and we think she might have gotten a bit of sunstroke."

"She is pretty pale," Bob said.

"I was working not far from her," Mitch continued, "and a short while after she sat down to rest, she got up in a panic and took off running."

"Why?" Bob asked.

"I had a rather disturbing dream," she said. She filled them in on the rest.

"That is quite the story," Jack said, "I guess I can understand why you might have chosen to keep it to yourself."

"Thanks, Jack," Alex said.

"You know, especially since it does make you look rather bonkers," he smirked. "Both of you, in fact."

"So, what does this mean?" Bob asked.

"That we should probably have them locked up," Jack jumped in.

Bob smacked him.

Jack giggled.

"Ok, enough out of the 'peanut gallery'!" Mitch held up his hand.

"Even though we hadn't yet found the chest, we were working relatively close to the Sphinx and the chest was very near by, when my first dream occurred," Alex said. "We never would have found it if it hadn't been for that."

Mitch nodded, "And our first shared dream started off the same way..."

"With us walking near the Sphinx," Alex said.

"Which then turned into the form of 'Amsara," Mitch added.

"Right," she said.

"Hey, how come Jack and I haven't had any weird dreams? We were all in the same room with this freaky Pharom thing while it was on," Bob protested. He didn't know if he felt good or bad about that. "Jack, you haven't had any strange dreams, have you?"

"None that I care to share with you guys," Jack grinned mischievously.

Bob shook his head at his friend.

"Mitch and I have had more exposure to it, you guys weren't working in the field with us before," Alex said. "Besides, maybe it doesn't affect everyone the same way."

"In the first dream we both had," Mitch recalled, "the Sphinx, or rather Amsara, also glowed, like an energy was surging through it and it did feel like it was somehow trying to communicate with us."

"That's right, and in the one last night," Alex said, "the figure was glowing, I had the unmistakable feeling that although we were 'talking' to him, our minds were being probed even further in a way – a deeper communication." She looked to Mitch, "I can't think of any other explanation, can you?"

Mitch shook his head, "Nope."

Jack cleared his throat, "If I may...I read somewhere about people who study dreams. Many scientists believe the subconscious mind is a powerful tool and we have yet to tap our full potential, that dreams are much more than the mind working out problems and issues, or trying to show us what we really feel and believe."

"What?" Bob asked incredulously.

"Just bear with me, my friend," Jack smiled. "There are also those who believe the dream world is as important as the waking one; that the mind is actively working on levels we haven't begun to understand or unlock. Some philosophers even claim that the dream world is as real or even more real than the waking world."

Jack started to pace the room, caught up in his emerging theory. "What if these people, the Kierani, were able to construct a tool to tap into that part of the mind? Maybe it could be used to facilitate communication through dreams. The communication would be much more pure, more direct and truthful, and possibly infinitely faster. Essentially nothing could be hidden."

"You have some hobbies I never knew anything about," Bob remarked.

Jack winked at him. "I am a man of mystery and intrigue, you know. I do a little reading from time to time on certain areas of science and philosophy."

He turned back to Mitch and Alex. "You know what I'm talking about…conscious intent, the focusing of thoughts on a specific idea or object. As you said Alex, you and Mitch have had more exposure to this Pharom-thing. Maybe that's also part of the reason why you guys are being affected this way. Maybe it honed in on you, on your thoughts…" Jack said making scary faces.

Bob was turning more and more pale.

Mitch and Alex were rapt, their minds racing with these possibilities.

"Oh yeah and ironically," Jack continued, "that is also part of one of the theories of quantum mechanics, that an observer can affect the way certain particles act, just by observing them. But in this case, perhaps it's also the way a person thinks or what they think of."

"He's right," Mitch said. "I think he's hit the nail on the head."

Jack smiled and bowed dramatically.

"Holy crap…" Bob said, growing increasingly unnerved by what he was hearing.

Alex nodded in agreement, "I hate to admit you're right on something like this Jack, but I have to agree with Mitch. That's brilliant!"

"All in a day's work, my dear Miss Logan."

Alex laughed. She then turned to Mitch. "Maybe the Pharom sort of amplifies what's already in a person's mind, like a person's thoughts, dreams or fears." She paused, recalling something. "You know, that's exactly what I felt in the dream, that the figure was seeing directly into the core of my being. That it was completely open, effortless communication."

"I felt the same," Mitch agreed. "Actually, it would make sense in a way, considering the papyrus we identified as relating to dreams. And I didn't get a bad vibe from the figure in the dream. You know, maybe the Pharom isn't a weapon at all, or at least wasn't originally intended for that purpose."

"Well, for something that isn't a weapon, it seems to be excellent at achieving what weapons are generally used for," Bob commented worriedly.

"That's true of many technological advances that weren't originally designed for evil intent," Alex reminded him. "Let's assume for the moment, that it wasn't designed as a weapon, specifically. We can't deny that it's dangerous and extremely powerful, whatever it is. Having said that, it also has to be more than a communication tool that amplifies or affects dreams."

"Why do you say that?" Bob asked anxiously.

"Because of the context of the dream," Mitch explained, following her line of thought. "Alex, in the dream you specifically asked about the Pharom and the figure replied that the answer lies in your name."

"And he called me by my full name, Alexandra. Almost no one calls me that." She thought for a moment, "You know, my dad named me after Alexander the Great, who eventually had an ancient city in Egypt named after him, Alexandria."

"Was there something of significance in Alexandria that could relate to this?" Bob asked.

Mitch pondered the question. "There was a lighthouse there over two thousand years ago. It was one of the Seven Wonders of the Ancient World…and it was called the 'Pharos of Alexandria.'"

Alex instantly realized the possible connection, "Of course…"

"That sounds familiar, go on," Jack said, leaning in to hear more.

Mitch continued, "I remember from one of our university classes that the lighthouse was built by Ptolemy Soter, Alexander the Great's commander, at around…290 BC, I believe. The lighthouse was completely destroyed by earthquakes around 1300 AD. And, the lighthouse or Pharos was often referred to as the 'Beacon of Alexandria.'"

"Beacon…" Alex repeated then looked at Mitch. "Could the name Pharos be a derivative of the earlier word Pharom? Pharos is the Greek word for lighthouse."

"It has to be, it's too close. It couldn't be a coincidence," he agreed.

Alex nodded, wide-eyed, "If the name Pharom is some kind of form of the word, Pharos, and I would agree with you Mitch, that it would be too much of a coincidence for it not to be, then it does means lighthouse, or something along those lines."

She was getting excited now. "Think about it, we've seen time and time again in all kinds of languages, words that are adapted for more modern use, but retain their roots, so to speak. If that's so, the device's effects on our brains, regarding dream imagery and strange messages may only be part of what it does or some kind of bizarre side effect…" Alex paused, looking at each of the guys, "of its true purpose."

"What?" Bob asked. "What is she saying? Mitch?"

"I think what she's saying is that the Pharom may indeed be some kind of beacon. And beacons are used to warn or guide travelers…to or from a certain place."

"You can't be serious…" Bob said. He felt as if he was going to faint.

Jack sat listening.

"Bob, think about it," Mitch said, "you analyzed the metal of the cylinders yourself. Remember, you're the one who told us that 'the elements were not part of the periodic table.' We know the Pharom wasn't created here, unless you've seen metal in a state of quantum flux before."

"Well, no, I know, that's true…but, how can you…I mean, what…?" he couldn't even get his sentence out.

Jack turned to Bob, "I think what they're saying, my panicky friend, is that the people who created those cylinders, likely have many other highly advanced skills. They came from somewhere else. That 'somewhere else' didn't go away just because a few of them were here. Some kind of communication would likely have been set up eventually between places, you know, a form of long distance calling?"

"Well put, Jack," Alex smiled at him.

"Thanks!" Just then another thought occurred to him. "Guys, this may be a stupid question, but if these people were from 'someplace else'…" Jack started, then, grinning he leaned over and whispered in Bob's ear, "got to use this kind of cryptic language in case spy satellites are listening, you know."

Bob went even paler.

Jack turned back to Mitch and Alex, "Then, tell me this, why would their technology work on our brains? Wouldn't we be, you know, wired differently, being from different places and all?"

Mitch wanted to answer him, but then realized he had no idea.

"Mitch…" Alex said as another thought occurred to her.

"What? What is it?" he asked, getting worried.

"What if that thing sent off some kind of signal when we inadvertently activated it? The people who monitor radio transmissions and other such things: governments, space agencies, other organizations, could have picked it up. We have no way of knowing who else may be aware of this."

"But they would have no idea what they are looking for," Mitch replied frowning. He was becoming more and more unsure of himself, of what he thought he knew, of anything.

"It doesn't matter, couldn't they triangulate the signal somehow?" she asked.

"Then why hasn't anyone come around?" Bob replied, dearly hoping that would mean no one would.

"We don't know that they haven't," Alex argued, shaking her head. "I don't think those are the kinds of people who announce themselves, you know? Besides, someone who is already here must know of this: the note at the party, the permits, not to mention the cover-up of the accident. Someone is pulling our strings and we don't know why."

"If that's true, then the people here could be analyzing the information you've provided by doing this work for them, work they couldn't be caught doing themselves. Others, either related or unrelated parties, may be on their way here," Jack added.

"But…all it would take is asking a few questions before the incident in the chamber came up. That would point them directly at…us," Bob said, clearly freaked out now.

"Aside from our own safety being in jeopardy, which is obviously a concern I'd say, what if this 'device' fell into the wrong hands?" Mitch asked nervously. "We are in way over our heads here…this goes so far beyond archaeology. That beacon, or whatever the hell it is, could change the entire future depending on what it's capable of, who found out about it, and…worse yet, wanted to try and use it."

He ran his fingers through his hair. "Can you imagine the consequences? Something so advanced, that could be adapted as a powerful and deadly weapon, with potentially some kind of mind control applications, communication with…who knows who, and to what end? We already know it caused a major disaster in the past, and it killed someone moments after being turned back on after thousands of years!"

"Mitch is right," Alex said wringing her hands. "We can't think of ourselves any more, hoping for archaeological glory. We've just found a very dangerous Pandora's box and I don't think we are ready or able to cope with something of this magnitude. There's way too much at stake and too much we still don't know about it. The responsibility this kind of knowledge requires…" she said as she put her head in her hands, she couldn't even finish the sentence, her head was swimming.

"We have to decide what to do next and we have to decide fast," Mitch stated.

☥

Intruder

It was late the second night and the four edgy and very nervous prisoners were still slaving away, working on all the artifacts Dustimaine had assigned to them. They had made their decision a few hours earlier about what to do with the Pharom. Now they just had to wait and hope for the best.

They knew they couldn't drop Dustimaine's work. Regardless of whoever had been secretly helping them, he was still their boss and he had made it very clear that failing to do this assignment would not be tolerated. They were skating on thin ice with him, so they decided to focus on the task at hand, then take the actions they needed to.

Everyone else had long since quit for the day. Mitch, Alex, Jack and Bob still had a long ways to go, and the coffee, pop and orange juice, and snack food supplies were getting perilously low.

"I can't take this anymore, this is my last Coke. I will not survive without more!" Jack's eyes had now become burning red orbs.

"Quit your whining, Jack. We're almost there, maybe another two, three hours. Just keep working. We'll get done faster that way."

"I'll die, I swear! I will not last," Jack had now dramatically thrown himself over the table face down.

"Here, drink this," Bob handed him a Diet Coke from the cooler.

"Are you mad? I'd gag on that swill. I want…no I need, the full effect!"

"Jack, have a cup of coffee, there's still some left in the pot," Alex offered.

"Alex, my dear darling Alex, as I mentioned before, I take my caffeine from a can and besides, I couldn't possibly deprive you of your last cup or two of coffee. I've heard the rumors that you 'took care' of someone who drank the last cup of coffee once," Jack said, feigning a fearful look.

"I thought I got rid of all the witnesses, hmmm…" Alex said, playing along.

Jack put his hand to his mouth in mock terror. "Anyways…I'm just going to run back to our regular lab. I know I left a Coke there. It's not cold, but desperate times call for desperate measures."

"You keep a stash?" Bob asked.

"Of course! It's a survival thing," Jack replied. "Don't tell me you don't do the same thing."

Mitch interrupted them, "Bob, why don't you go with him, just to make sure he makes it back here in a timely fashion. We wouldn't want you to get lost and end up in your bed, asleep," he grinned at him.

"Me? I take great offense…" Jack was doing his best 'look shocked' expression.

Bob got up and grabbed Jack's arm, "Yeah, yeah, yeah. Well I take great offense to listening to you bellyache. Let's go!" he said as he dragged Jack out with him. "We'll be right back, I promise."

Jack and Bob headed off to the main lab, continuing to banter back and forth about their mutual irritation with one another. As they finally reached the lab, Jack fumbled in his pockets, "Crap! I forgot my key. Do you have yours?"

"What? I'm gonna throttle you! No I don't have my key. It's back in the other lab with Mitch and Alex. I wasn't the one who wanted to get in here, you dolt!"

Jack kept searching his pockets, realizing they were empty. He looked longingly at the darkened lab. Just then something caught his eye, "Did you see that?" he whispered.

"See what?" Bob replied.

"I thought I saw a flash of light. Look! There it is again!"

"I saw it that time," Bob whispered. "Quick, let's get out of sight." He motioned for Jack to follow him. They sidled up close to the building.

"What should we do? Should we go get Mitch and Alex?" Jack asked, huddling behind Bob.

"Sshhh, I think I heard something. It sounded like something being pried open," Bob said as he tried to listen.

"Let's go call for help," Jack whispered as he started to creep away.

Bob yanked him back by his collar. Now he was being the courageous one. "We don't have time. Whoever's in there might be breaking into the cabinet. We can't let them find the chest with the cylinders."

Jack was clearly scared now. "What are you going to do? You could get killed!"

"We have to stop them, that's what *we're* going to do," Bob said. "Look, get up on my shoulders and peek through the window. See if you can see anyone. Quickly!"

Jack scrambled up on Bob's shoulders, then crouched, "What if I get shot?"

"You're too skinny to get shot, there's not enough of you to hit. Now shut up and tell me what you see!"

Jack peered through the small window. "I see a flashlight. Whoever it is, is right by the cabinet where the chest is. I only see the shadow of one person. I think he's alone."

"Can you tell who it is? How big is he?" Bob urged.

"No, I think he's wearing a face mask. He doesn't seem too big. Whoa!" Jack suddenly ducked.

"What? What is it?"

"He turned suddenly. He may have seen me!"

"All right, get down." Bob helped Jack down. "We've got to get in there and stop him. There's no other choice. If he's in there, the door is probably unlocked. We can't let that chest fall into the wrong hands.

There's only one door in or out. So we either wait for whoever it is to come out…or we go in after him." Bob carefully and quietly tested the door handle. It was indeed unlocked.

"With only one door we won't be able to sneak up on him," Jack said.

"No, but if we rush the door, we'll catch him off guard. If we wait until he exits, there's a greater chance he'll get away. We can flip on the lights, blind him momentarily and take him down."

"What if he's got a weapon? Skinny as I am, I'm sure there's enough of me to stab!"

"Jack, we're out of options. Besides there's two of us and we have the element of surprise. Don't worry, I'm here, and he's not getting through me!"

"Oh man, I don't know, this is crazy!"

Bob grabbed his sleeve, "C'mon, let's go before he gets that cabinet open!"

The two pals ran over to the door, "On the count of three, you follow behind me." Bob counted, "One, two, three!" He swung the door open, flicked on the light, yelled and charged the startled figure.

Bob crashed over the table, knocking it over, and grabbed the struggling man. They wrestled, the man desperately trying to get away.

Jack snuck up on the other side of the table, grabbed an artifact and clubbed the burglar over the head with it. He slumped to the ground. Jack stood there grinning, still holding the artifact, which thankfully, remained intact.

Bob stood up, "Way to go, man. A victory for Rogue Squadron!" They high-fived. They looked back down at the unconscious figure lying at their feet.

"Well, let's see who this is," Bob said as he pulled the mask off the intruder's face. "Well, well, well, what a surprise. If it isn't the little weasel himself."

"Fessel!" Jack exclaimed. He picked up a bag that Fessel had been carrying. "Well, looky here. I don't think these things belong to you."

"Let's go get Mitch and Alex. They can decide what to do next," Bob said as he flung Fessel's limp form over his shoulder.

While Jack and Bob went in search of Jack's precious beverage, Mitch and Alex continued to discuss the decision they had tentatively arrived at. Neither felt completely happy with it, but they were pretty sure that there was nothing that would put them at ease right now.

"Mitch, I've been thinking about something Jack said and it's bothering me."

"What is it?"

"Remember him asking about the beacon or Pharom, and why it would affect us if we are different from the Kierani?"

"Yeah, I gave that some thought, too. Why couldn't it affect both us, and them? Just because we're different, doesn't mean we're immune," Mitch stated. "Maybe it affects us in a different way than it did them."

"I realize that's a possibility, but thinking about what we saw in the dream papyrus, what we've learned and experienced in our own dreams, I'm not so sure it is affecting us differently. I mean, I know there's no way to prove it, but still…did you get the feeling from your experience that it was acting strangely?"

"I really can't answer that, Alex. We've got nothing to compare it to. Besides, we've had a lot of strange experiences lately. I don't know what's normal and what's strange anymore."

"I know, but…well, maybe it's just instinct, I just have the feeling that it's working exactly as it was designed to. Something about the way the dreams felt…"

"You're thinking maybe it's a 'universal' design, like a universal remote – works with all TVs, DVRs, and DVD players?"

"Maybe…" she said.

"Alex, I get the distinct impression you're going somewhere with this…"

She smiled and looked up at him, her blue eyes sparkling. "You know me pretty well." She paused for a moment, framing her thoughts. "Well, what if we're not so different?"

"Go on," Mitch encouraged her.

"We don't know what happened to these people, right?"

Mitch nodded for her to continue.

"For all we know, the survivors never left."

"You mean you think they all died off?"

"That's one possibility, yes, but that doesn't explain how we've come to find all these records."

"Someone else knows all about them, and somehow that knowledge has been preserved, passed down and guarded for thousands of years," Mitch finished the thought. "So what's the other possibility Alex? You think they still live here somewhere, but no one knows about them, other than our mysterious secret-keepers who they've been passing information to? Or do you think that maybe they are our secret record-keepers?"

She looked at him, "As I said, maybe we're not so different. What if..." she hesitated biting her lip, but decided to get it out. "What if, they 'blended in' with us, you know, really well?"

"Alexandra Logan, do you know what you're saying?"

At that moment, they heard a bang at the door. They both jumped.

"Open up guys! We have something you should see!" It was Jack and Bob.

Confessions

M itch and Alex were shocked when Jack and Bob brought Fessel in. They set him down, still unconscious, on a chair and filled their friends in on what they found him doing. It brought their work to a screeching halt.

"So this was all a set up! To keep us out of our own lab," Alex said, fuming.

"I'd say so," Jack added, as he tied Fessel's hands behind his back. "Dustimaine put his little evil minion of the devil to work spying on us."

"What do we do now?" Bob asked. "Want me to dump him out in the desert somewhere?"

They all laughed.

"As tempting as that is," Alex said, "I think we should see if we can get a few answers out of him first."

"Then let's take him to Dr. Khadesh," Mitch added. "I don't know who else we could turn to. He'll know how best to deal with this situation."

They waited for a time for Fessel to come to. After a while, Jack got a little impatient, so he splashed some cold water in Fessel's face.

Fessel woke up.

"What the…" he said, then noticed the four people he was sent to spy on staring at him. He tried to jump up, but he realized his hands were tied. Then his head started to spin. "Someone hit me," he complained.

"That's what you get for skulking around places you don't belong," Jack stated.

"Yeah," Bob agreed, "it's not like we were expecting you. All we knew is that someone was breaking into our lab."

Fessel went quiet.

"So, Fessel," Mitch started, "I think you have some explaining to do."

When Fessel didn't answer, Bob gave him a little nudge to the ribs to encourage him to talk.

"Ouch!" he whined.

"I'd suggest you start talking," Jack said. "Bob is itching to take you way out into the desert and dump your body."

Fessel's eyes went wide.

"Talk," Bob said in his most serious voice.

Knowing he was in no position to argue, he gave in. "Dustimaine."

"No kidding," Jack smirked.

"Go on," Alex said.

Fessel filled them in on everything.

Mitch and Alex listened intently.

"So, can I go now?" Fessel asked.

Mitch and Alex were quiet for a moment. Then he whispered something in her ear. She nodded.

"Before you go anywhere, Alex and I are going to make a stop by the lab you were rifling through. Jack, Bob, would you guys mind babysitting for us for a few minutes?"

"Not at all," Bob sneered, glaring at Fessel.

They went to leave.

"Wait, you can't leave me here with these two!" Fessel cried out.

"Oh, don't worry, you're in good hands," Alex smiled.

Dustimaine's Fate

Professor Dustimaine was summoned to an urgent meeting in Dr. Khadesh's office. He was accompanied by two of Dr. Khadesh's assistants.

"Abner," he said, "please take a seat."

Professor Dustimaine was annoyed at the use of his first name, for he was customarily addressed as 'Professor'. "May I ask what this is about? I don't appreciate being hauled over here so abruptly. Your assistants were quite rude, I must say and I have important work to…"

Dr. Khadesh raised his hand to cut him off. He nodded to the men he had sent to bring Dustimaine in. They promptly left the room to wait outside.

Dr. Khadesh turned his attention back to Dustimaine. "Your work here is finished, Abner."

"Excuse me?" Professor Dustimaine replied, offended. "My work is far from done, I still have…"

"No, I am afraid it is over."

"What do you mean over?" the Professor asked haughtily. "I think you are highly misinformed…"

Dr. Khadesh cut him off, "I have just had a most illuminating conversation with Fessel." He looked directly at the Professor with a challenging gaze.

Dustimaine's mind raced, his heartbeat quickened, and beads of perspiration began to show on his brow. He replied, his voice quaking, "May I ask the topic of this conversation?"

Khadesh, smiling faintly, replied, "I think you know full well what the topic was. In fact, I think it is high time I was direct with you."

Dustimaine squirmed uncomfortably in his seat, but said nothing.

"I must admit Abner," Dr. Khadesh continued, "I have never really trusted you. You always seemed to be a little shifty, a little defensive and paranoid. I once thought it was an overriding inferiority complex you had and felt sorry for you. Actually, it is quite likely that is precisely where your problems began."

Dustimaine listened with a growing sense of dread.

"You set out to undermine and ultimately destroy if you could, the efforts and findings of others, taking credit for work that was not yours."

The Professor, feeling his temperature rise, took out a handkerchief and wiped his brow.

Khadesh leaned back in his high-back leather chair. "Tell me something. Did you ever take the time to really examine the work Mitch and Alex were doing? Did you ever consider helping them, encouraging them?"

Dustimaine was sweating now, his thin dress shirt sticking to his back and underarms. He nervously cleared his throat.

"No, I do not suppose you did. Instead, you had Fessel sneak around like a thief, breaking into places he had no business being…and report back to you."

"I was only trying to check on their progress, they were falling behind and I…"

Khadesh did not need to hear his explanation. "Abner, when you put your faith and trust in someone whose moral fiber and personal judgment is severely underdeveloped, they cannot be counted on to back you up when the chips are down."

"What do you mean?" he asked nervously.

"Fessel was quite eager to point the proverbial finger squarely at you. Rather afraid for his own skin, I would say, and for good reason."

Dustimaine again wiped his brow, and swallowed hard.

Dr. Khadesh leaned forward, looking him straight in the eyes. "You never took the time or had the nerve to realize how talented, bright and courageous Mitch and Alex are. That is why they were granted those permits Abner. They deserved them. They are hardworking, driven, resourceful and passionate. Those are exactly the qualities that make someone great, someone outstanding in their field. That is what Alex's father was like, and yes, I am fully aware of the rivalry you had with him. I assume that is why you treat Mitch and Alex so poorly. Devlan Logan was a great man, and a good friend."

Dustimaine bristled at the mention of Devlan Logan.

Khadesh read Abner's expression. He shook his head in disgust. "Abner, what drives excellence and achievement is not simply following established guidelines, or someone else's directions or ideas. Nor is it professional jealousy. Those who bravely forge new paths will move forward, they will move us all forward. And, I am afraid those who stand in their way get run over. Which, ironically, brings us back to you."

"Dr. Khadesh, I-I would like to say something in my own defense..."

"It is too late for that, Abner. I brought you here to inform you that your permit to work in Egypt has been permanently revoked. I have spoken with your superiors. Your tenure with the University will be terminated immediately. You will be on the next flight out of Cairo. A police escort will accompany you to ensure you leave the country without incident."

Dustimaine gasped as the men who had brought him were summoned back in.

"That is right, they are policemen, so I would advise you to be cooperative."

Before Dustimaine left, he turned back, "Those two are trouble. I was doing all of us a favor."

Dr. Khadesh shook his head, "You have done no one any favors." With that, he motioned for the police officers to take him away.

CHAPTER

80

The Renewal of Life

Circa 10,000 B.C.

Three years had now passed since the catastrophic destruction occurred. In that time, Traeus had made the decision, with the support of Assan and Mindara, to keep Setar's true parentage a secret and raise him as his own son, and Tramen's brother. There had been no signs that any of the Draxens had survived, but if any of them had somehow managed to remain in hiding, or anyone was still secretly sympathetic to that family, Traeus feared they might come after Setar.

He also worried about those who might wrongly harbor ill will towards him simply because of his bloodline. Traeus felt very strongly that he wanted to protect Alaj's memory and dignity and secure the future of Setar. Therefore, it had also been decided to permanently keep the secret from Setar himself. Traeus fervently hoped that the day would never come when Setar would learn the terrible truth.

In addition, Traeus told his people that the Draxen family had been responsible for the catastrophic destruction, that they had used a terrible weapon against the Royal Family in their hopes of eliminating them and seizing power. He said that the weapon had been dealt with and would not harm them again. The truth of the Pharom would remain a secret for now.

Though he greatly disliked not telling his people exactly what had occurred, he felt it was what he must do for many reasons. He also stood fast in his decision to protect Alaj's memory and so did not speak of Zazmaria.

Through all the difficult times, Mindara stood steadfastly by the King's side, helping in any way she could. She supported him in each and every painful decision. He could no longer imagine his life without her and the children especially loved and depended on her. Day by day, Traeus and Mindara had grown to depend on one another in a myriad of ways. He fell in love with her and asked her to be his Queen. She happily accepted.

The King chose this particular day, exactly three years to the day that their lives had been torn apart, for the Royal wedding. It was his way of showing his people that they had overcome their past and also to replace the dark reminder this day brought, so it would not only be remembered as a black day, but would now be associated with joy and the reaffirming of life, love and family.

Assan and Odai were walking back to their residences after the Royal wedding's evening festivities. "Odai, it has been a very happy day for us all. But tell me, why do you look so troubled?"

"Your Grace, even though there is great joy in seeing the Royal Family resurrect itself and build a new life, I can still see a glint of sadness in their eyes. Can we not return Princess Anjia back to her true family now? Why must we continue to allow them to believe that she is dead? Surely she has no more enemies."

"Odai, there is nothing more I would want than to reunite Princess Anjia with her family. Our King has suffered so much. But we cannot bring her back, not yet. We do not know for certain if any members of the Draxen family survived. Remember, Zhek's body as well as a few others, were never recovered. There have been rumors some of the Draxens survived, though nothing substantiated."

"People are given over easily to fearful imaginings," Odai said. "After all this time, would we not have heard something, seen something, if any of them had lived?"

"To return would mean to be put to death. If Zhek or any other member of that family lived, they would remain in hiding, until such time…" Assan stopped.

"Such time as what?"

"Such time as they again decided to strike first against us," Assan said gravely. "Do not forget, we were also fooled by Princess Zazmaria. A member of Princess Anjia's own family tried to kill her, then conspired with her family's enemies to destroy what was left of the Royal line! Who is to say that such a threat does not still exist within the Royal household? Even Prince Alaj was deceived into betraying his own family. Think about it Odai, our people were betrayed more than once, on multiple fronts! How we could have been so blind…"

"But, your Grace, the threat must be gone now, after all the time that has passed, how our society and all of our lives have changed."

"Odai, we lost a Queen to such veiled evil once before. We cannot be certain there is no further threat waiting in the shadows to strike at us once again. Would you be willing to risk the Princess' life? Would you be willing to risk robbing our people of the child of the prophecy?"

Odai did not answer. He now felt unsure.

"If she was lost, everything would be lost. Everything our people have hoped and lived for." Assan shook his head. "She must remain where she is for now."

Assan and Odai walked in silence for a while.

Odai considered Assan's words. Odai knew not everyone believed in the prophecy and there were those who were threatened by it. He could only imagine how those people would react to the Princess, whom they thought dead, if she were suddenly brought back to take her place as the chosen one.

"There are those who would fear her," Odai said finally.

"Yes there are," Assan replied. "So you see why we cannot put her in such danger, until we are certain she can be protected?"

"Yes, your Grace."

Assan looked at Odai. He saw the depth of sadness in his young face. "This pains me deeply as well. Each day, each year, that passes is time that can never be recovered. I know the cost, but understand she is also still too young to take her place as the chosen one. Her powers are somehow linked to the Pharom and the Amsara monument, as we have seen in the incident several years ago. Those powers must be allowed to grow. We do not know what she may be capable of in the future."

"I think I understand. Anjia would also be more capable of defending herself when she is older and not depend on us as much as she would right now."

"Precisely. Keeping her hidden is the only way we can protect her until she is ready to take her rightful place. She is safe and well cared for where she is. In time, Odai, she will be reunited with her family. Just pray that they understand and forgive us for this when that time comes."

Odai nodded. "Perhaps they will realize that had it not been for her being hidden away, she could have been killed when the fighting and destruction occurred. What we did may have saved her life."

"It may have..."

As they continued to walk, a question came to Odai's mind. "How do you think she came to possess such unusual abilities? I know the prophecy speaks of such a person, but was there anything you know of that caused this?"

"There was an unusual chemical in Queen Axiana's system when she was trying to conceive. Senarra and I were unable to identify it. Senarra created a potion to counteract it, in case it was harmful, and shortly thereafter, the Queen was pregnant with the twins. The unusual chemical could only be traced to a tea that Zazmaria prepared for her, which she claimed would help in conception and was passed down by her family. Knowing what we know now, I suspect the chemical may have been harmful, but fortunately we counteracted it in time."

"Are you saying that in a way, Zazmaria could have inadvertently been responsible for creating that which she feared most? Someone who would be powerful enough to see through her?"

"Perhaps, but it is quite likely that the combination of elements was the catalyst, though Princess Anjia would have still had to have some latent abilities for that to occur. We never know what the outcome of our actions may truly be. Zazmaria may have been meant to play the role she did. Without her, who knows, the chosen one may not be with us today."

"That is an incredible thought," he mused. "But how could such pure good come from such evil beginnings?"

"These things are beyond our understanding, Odai. The powers of this universe work in ways we may never be able to fully comprehend. We must trust that good will prevail, as long as we stay vigilant to see it so."

"Is that why we are hiding The Book of the Old and New World?"

Assan nodded, "That is correct. The Book contains powerful knowledge. There are those who might use it for ill purpose. The Book must never fall into the wrong hands. It will be safe where you hid it. We can take it out to add to it when needed."

"There will be much more to include in its pages."

"Yes, in time. Now Odai, onto more personal matters, you have your own new bride to look after. Speaking of which, I understand congratulations are in order."

"For what?" Odai asked, surprised at the question.

"For what, indeed. I think you are going to make a great father."

"Pardon me?" Odai asked incredulously.

"Oh no, I thought she would have told you by now," Assan turned red, embarrassed at his inadvertent slipup.

Odai's eyes went wide, and his jaw dropped. "Senarra said she wanted to talk to me right after the celebrations." Slowly the news sank in. "I am going to be a father! Would you mind…?"

"Go find your wife," Assan said smiling as Odai ran off excitedly.

81

Protecting the Future

It had been decided that since the Draxen Stronghold had been almost completely destroyed by the blast, and no survivors, if there were any, had come forth, the grounds were to be taken over by the Royal Family and donated to the people. Plans had been made to re-landscape the grounds and turn them into a park where all Kierani could come and enjoy its natural beauty.

The home had been situated on a particularly beautiful piece of property with a view of the surrounding area, the Amsara site and the city. Now the property was being turned into lush grasslands with ponds and flowering trees and bushes. A small temple would be built on the site along with a memorial commemorating that dark day in their history when so much had been lost.

After looking over the site for a while, Traeus went over to speak with Assan, who was standing with some other priests overseeing the building of their new temple. "Assan, may I have a word with you?"

"Of course, your Majesty," Assan said as he excused himself from the group. "I am surprised your wife would let you out of her sight so quickly," he remarked with a sly smile and a twinkle in his eye.

Traeus laughed, he enjoyed the more relaxed nature his relationship with the Head Priest had taken on in the last three years. "Queen Mindara is very understanding of the responsibilities of the Royal Family. Would you walk with me?"

"Certainly, your Majesty." Assan followed him out of sight from the others.

"Assan, do you think the Pharom is safe enough in its new hiding place?" Traeus asked, keeping his voice low.

"Yes, I do, your Majesty. We have taken every precaution. The design Odai came up with is truly ingenious. It will be safe for a very long time, I assure you. No one else knows of its location."

"That is actually what I want to talk to you about, Assan." Traeus looked very serious. "I have given this a great deal of thought, and I have not arrived at this decision easily. I have spent many sleepless nights in silent debate, going over other possibilities, but I have arrived at the only solution my conscience will allow."

Assan listened intently.

"I have considered the possibility that we may choose not to fully reactivate the Pharom during my reign. I know I am not yet that old, but experience has taught me that we can never count on having many more days in front of us. Each new day is a gift, it is not promised."

"Indeed," Assan replied, nodding.

Traeus took a deep breath. "Should I die before the Pharom has been revealed to our people, I am placing the priesthood solely in charge of protecting and guarding it from evil hands for as long as it takes until the Pharom no longer poses a threat to our society. No one, not even the Royal Family itself, is to be told about the Pharom and its resting place until that time. As we have witnessed, there are too many ways for secrets to escape the Royal Family. I will leave it up to your order to decide if and when to inform the future King and Queen of the existence of the Pharom. At that time, should they choose to destroy it after hearing all the facts, they must be allowed to do so."

The King paused for a moment to emphasize his request, "Assan, do you understand and accept the responsibility I am placing on you as Head Priest?"

Assan could scarcely believe what he was being asked to do. He had not considered the long-term implications of the Pharom.

"Of course, it is my duty and privilege to serve your Majesty," he bowed. "But may I ask why should all future kings and queens not be informed of the Pharom and its purpose?"

"I understand your reservations, Assan. I realize what I am asking you is unprecedented, but I do not think it is right to burden them with this responsibility. It was my decision and mine alone to create such a powerful device. I do not want our people to fight over the Pharom or risk misusing it. It is too dangerous. In time, our people may have the wisdom to handle such knowledge, but until that time comes, this secret must be kept within your order."

"Your Majesty, you should have faith in your people. They will understand what the Pharom can do and what it is capable of if misused. They will respect its power."

Traeus shook his head. His mind was made up, "With good or bad intentions, people will fight over something that holds such power. My decision is final Assan. That is why I am entrusting the priesthood as its guardians. Your order has not been tainted by politics or greed or the lust for power, and has always remained loyal."

Assan knew there was no use in debating the matter further. He had a duty to uphold the wishes of his King. "Your Majesty, the priesthood is honored by your faith in us. We will pass this secret and responsibility from one generation to the next, if need be, until the time comes when such knowledge can be safely returned to our people."

The Keeping of Secrets

Present-Day Egypt

Mitch and Alex had a hard time with the decision they had arrived at. They knew it was the only prudent option. Still as people trained and devoted to discovering the past and gaining knowledge, this was a staggering disappointment.

They had decided to hide the chest, cylinders and scrolls where they had left the Pharom in its original resting place along with the crystal, essentially leaving behind everything they had learned, everything they had discovered.

The 'crib notes' had also been placed back in their original hiding place in the false bottom of the chest. Without the crib notes, the documentation Mitch and Alex had compiled and the scrolls, it would be very difficult for anyone to follow in their footsteps.

However, if anyone were to find the hidden chamber, they would have everything, the writings and the Pharom. But without the crystal to shine on the back wall of the second chamber, and Mitch and Alex's own notes, it would be next to impossible for anyone to find the entrance to the small cramped tunnel, let alone even suspect what was hidden in the chamber beyond. It was an imperfect solution, but the best they could come up with.

The permits they were mysteriously given to excavate in Egypt were still valid. No one had restricted their movements at all in light of what happened to Dustimaine and Fessel. Still, to ensure complete secrecy, the local workers, at least the ones they could find who weren't so superstitious that they couldn't bear to work near the Sphinx, were sent home earlier in the evening after dismantling the site. Mitch and Alex went in under the cover of darkness, taking only Jack and Bob with them.

They had also spent the past few hours destroying all their documentation about the discovery. They knew they couldn't risk having it fall into the wrong hands. Alex had nearly been in tears as they destroyed their own work. Even Jack and Bob were unusually somber. The jokes and insults were few and far between.

Finally, they only had the last step to take. Mitch and Alex ensured the precious items were placed back in the furthest reaches of the hidden chamber and that the entrance to it was carefully resealed. They examined every inch of it to see that it was properly back in place, and they took every precaution to seal the main entrance to the double-chamber as well.

The four of them struggled to place the Dream Stela back in its original position, along with the limestone and rock slabs that had been moved to reveal the chambers below. As they were still the current permit holders, they hoped they would be asked back, should the decision be made to excavate the site further, but they had no guarantee of that.

As they prepared to leave the site, the full realization of what they were about to do hit them. Hidden beneath the ground, lay the answers to so many questions.

Even though Mitch and Alex fully realized how potentially beneficial the knowledge from this discovery could be, they also knew that many people would be unable to accept the implications and would be outraged and hotly challenge their conclusions. There was also incredible risk inherent in the technology. The risk was simply too great. There was too much they still had to learn about the Pharom and the people who created it. That technology had once nearly destroyed its creators.

Until modern society was ready to accept what it likely represented and act responsibly, and in an enlightened manner, they feared history could repeat itself, but the next time it could be on a potentially much larger scale.

There was a great sadness in their hearts. As young and unproven archaeologists, this had been the discovery of a lifetime for them. Their funds were running low and it would be difficult to acquire additional funding unless they made a big find. Now, ironically, they had to hide the fact that they had done just that. There would be no history books written containing their names and what they had found. At least not now.

Once they returned to their rooms that night, the four of them sat around with long faces and heavy hearts. However, one question remained.

"Guys, I know this is hard. It's a terrible letdown, but there is one thing we've forgotten," Jack offered hopefully. "Someone out there was helping you two, someone with a lot of knowledge and a lot of power. For once, the good news is that they're on your side."

"We don't know whose side they're on," Mitch said sullenly. "For all we know, they were just using us and as soon as we're gone, they're going to swoop in, steal the Pharom and make a weapon of mass destruction out of it. We may all be dead by next week."

"That's not very encouraging," Bob said.

"Mitch is right," Alex said. "We don't know who they are or what their motivations or aims really are. It would be nice to think they truly believe in us and trust us with this and want us to continue our work, but that's probably naïve and overly optimistic. It's a scary and dangerous world we live in. People often don't have the best interests of others at heart you know."

"Well, if no one objects," Jack piped in, "I am going to think that they were helping you guys and had the best of intentions and would only use this knowledge, this technological marvel, for the good of society. Otherwise, I don't think I could sleep at night."

"I may never be able to sleep at night again with all that's happened," Bob admitted.

Jack smiled sympathetically at him.

"Well, what's done is done," Alex said. "We don't know what the future will hold for us."

"Dr. Khadesh has been very helpful to us. Maybe he can help us again one day," Mitch suggested.

"Maybe," she answered, then thought for a moment. "You know Mitch, we just voluntarily gave up probably the biggest discovery in the history of archaeology, perhaps in the world. We never did get to decipher the older parts of that book, to find out about their earlier history. Do you know how much we could have learned from it? What an unbelievably priceless opportunity! And we just buried it," she moaned. "What are we ever going to discover now that could possibly match this?"

"Well, there are rumors about a map that leads to the Lost Ark… " Mitch replied, grinning.

Alex laughed, "Ok, but this time you fall on your face to find it."

They all laughed, but the laughter was mixed with sadness and loss and uncertainty about the future. All they could do is hope that one day, the path would be laid out before them, back to that secret chamber, to study and learn from what they had discovered. But they had no idea how that would ever happen.

The Watchers

Unknown and unseen to the foursome working fast and furiously to hide the priceless objects, were two dark figures watching from the inky blackness of the Egyptian night. These two figures had been observing them from the moment they set foot on the mysterious sands of Egypt. They had known of Mitch and Alex, their work, their theories, long before they landed in Cairo.

"Father, are you certain we are doing the right thing, allowing all that has just been found, to be hidden away from the world once again, for who knows how long?"

"Khamir, my son, we must be patient," Khadesh replied. "It may be hidden from the world for now, but the knowledge has been revealed, if only slightly. Mitch and Alex found the chest on their own. It had been lost for so long and now we have it back. I do not believe in coincidence, only providence. It was a sign that they were meant to be involved with us, with what we know."

Khamir sighed.

He gave an encouraging smile to his son. "Remember always Khamir, we must look at the greater picture. Mitch and Alex will not simply go about their work as though this had never happened. What they have learned is now an inextricable part of them, of their lives. The hunger for more knowledge, the thirst for understanding will grow inside them, day upon day, until one day, nothing else will matter and then they will know what they must do, what they must sacrifice. They will return and we will be here, waiting, to help them once again."

"But father, how long must we wait? I dearly wish this to happen in our lifetime. So many countless generations have come and gone, this knowledge passed from one to the next, and our people have always remained silent."

Khadesh placed his hand reassuringly on his son's shoulder, "We will wait for the proper time, Khamir. Do not forget, we are the keepers of this ancient secret and the responsibility has been entrusted to us to be ever mindful of the world around us."

He pointed to the foursome now emerging from the chamber, "That is why Mitch and Alex are doing what they are doing now. They also know that it is yet too dangerous to bring this knowledge into the light. But take comfort, my son, the seeds that have been planted will grow. We will see Mitch and Alex again. Until then it will be up to you and I to watch over these things once more and keep them safe. I will ensure that the chamber remains sealed and its contents protected. I will keep Mitch and Alex's permits to excavate this site open and valid. The chamber will not be unsealed until they return."

"They are good people, father…I will miss them," Khamir said sadly, as he watched the four finish their task.

Khadesh nodded, "As will I."

The end…

*Look back over the past, with its changing empires that rose and fell,
and you can foresee the future, too.*
~Marcus Aurelius

DESTINY
OF THE
SANDS

Some secrets cannot remain hidden...and some cannot be forgiven...

"A triumphant epic sequel
to the best-selling novel,
Secret Of The Sands!"
Gary Val Tenuta, author of
Ash: Return Of The Beast

RAI AREN
& TAVIUS E.

COMPLETE THE EPIC JOURNEY WITH...

REVELATION
OF THE
SANDS

From the Shadows Surfaces...

A new enemy, and an even greater challenge to face a truth that is about to reveal itself...

Vengeance is Sworn for the Pain of the Past...

Choices were made and destinies forged. The past propels the future of those left scarred, toward an uncertain and precarious fate...

A Difficult Journey Begins and Ends...

In the sands of Egypt, to uncover deeper truths and startling realities that will be both frightening and awe-inspiring...

A Revelation of Life Itself...

Will break free of the earthly and otherworldly confines that have held it in secret for so long. Faith and trust will be severely tested, and a journey to the past and future all at once will be undertaken...

From the Great Sphinx to Petra to the Great Pyramid, join this final adventure in the Secret of the Sands trilogy...

RAI AREN

A stunning revelation of secrets and destiny
that will change everything...

REVELATION
OF THE
SANDS

About the Authors

Photo by Dave Anton
Tavius E. (left) and Rai Aren (right)

RAI AREN and **TAVIUS E.** have been friends since college. Their common interests in ancient Egypt and archaeology, as well as fantasy and adventure stories, led them to pursue their passion in storytelling. Secret of the Sands was their first novel.

You can visit them at: www.secretofthesands.com or send them an e-mail at: rai-tavius@secretofthesands.com.

For news on upcoming releases and exclusive bonuses, sign up for Rai's newsletter: raiaren.com/Subscribe

Additional Work by Rai Aren

Lost City of Gold

A dangerous adventure beckons deep in the Amazon jungle...

Reckless treasure-hunter Rick Braeden sets out into the uncharted reaches of the Amazon jungle in a dangerous search of the fabled Lost City of Gold. It's a quest for an ancient city shrouded in mystery that he believes will place him in the history books and bring him all of the riches and redemption that have eluded him. He also hopes to succeed where more than one hundred others, who were either lost or died in the attempt, have failed. As he embarks on his journey something or someone deep in the jungle waits and watches...

You can get this book absolutely FREE by signing up to my mailing list: raiaren.com/Subscribe.

Printed in Great Britain
by Amazon